REQUIEM
FOR THE
DEAD

VICTOR M. ALVAREZ

Black Rose Writing | Texas

ISBN: 978-1-68433-437-7
PUBLISHED BY BLACK ROSE WRITING
www.blackrosewriting.com

Printed in the United States of America
Suggested Retail Price (SRP) $21.95

Requiem For the Dead is printed in Sabon

*As a planet-friendly publisher, Black Rose Writing does its best to eliminate
unnecessary waste to reduce paper usage and energy costs, while never
compromising the reading experience. As a result, the final word count vs. page count
may not meet common expectations.

Dedicated to the courageous men and women that make up the
US Army Criminal Investigation Command CID
And for all they do.

Author's Note

A brief history of the
United States Army Criminal Investigation Command

The CID Motto:
"Do What Has To Be Done!"

During World War 1, General John J. Pershing ordered the creation of a separate organization within the Military Police Corps to prevent and detect crime in the American Expeditionary Force in France.

The newly created Criminal Investigation Division (CID) was born.

In 1971, the United States Army Criminal Investigation Command was formed with command-and-control authority over all Army Wide CID assets.

With well over nine-hundred agents and five separate CID commands, these agents, like their civilian counterparts investigate a wide range of crime, and just like their counter-parts, have arrest authorization under the Uniform Code of Military Justice.

These agents are highly trained, highly decorated men and women, who make up the United States Army Criminal Investigation Division, CID.

The stories of these brave men and women are the basis for the fictionalized character of Special Agent Jacqueline Belle Sinclair.

New Smyrna Beach, FL
March 11, 2019

Acknowledgment

Before I even attempt to write a manuscript, I can spend upwards of several hours per day in research, delving into history, current events, gathering facts and the back-story. Here, it was of Americans being held in captivity in North Korea. I also required a fair amount of military history along with weapons profiles; what is in use today as opposed to what I've experienced in my twenty-one-years in the military. At that point, I build the characters: who will be the protagonist and so forth. Here, I decided on a very tough female, her worthy sidekick, a male. Next, is the building up all contributing characters that make up the story plot.

It just doesn't happen without help!

I have to start by thanking my beautiful and awesome wife, Pamela-Jean. Reading early drafts, she contributed so much invaluable advice and aid.

Writing a fiction book is harder than writing my semi-autobiography of my experiences in and out of law enforcement. Having an idea and turning it into a book is as hard as it sounds. I dare say that none of this would have been possible without my best friend, Dan Russell. Dan, the second to whom I shouldered my manuscript read chapter after chapter. He was steadfast, there during all my struggles and all my successes. He is the picture of true friendship.

I'm also indebted to Mike Valentino for his editorial help, insight, and continued support in bringing my story into what you have in her hands. I would be remiss if I did not mention Jim Flautt, who took time off from his music career to read through and offer his invaluable advice and recommendation to the manuscript.

A very special thanks to Mr. Reagan Rothe in reading my manuscript, and the very talented staff at Black Rose Writing for their contributions to the book's existence. Without it, this book may not have seen the light of day.

REQUIEM

FOR THE

DEAD

REQUIEM

FOR THE

DEAD

Prologue

Blood Spilled

The North Central Highlands, North Korea,
Two years ago

Jason Randolph Scott woke; something startled him.

He was alone and in total darkness.

Slowly, he realized where he was, although he couldn't see two feet ahead of him. He'd lost track of time, not caring anymore. He felt forgotten, alone. The perceived sensation of abandonment swept over him as it did day after day.

It was three years ago when he'd thought they'd discovered his identity - that of a spy working for the CIA while acting as a reporter for the New York Times newspaper.

Coming for him in his sleep, they dragged him away, beating him senseless. The Koreans struck, kicked, and threatened his live-in girlfriend, a fellow reporter, Jenny Addams, when she tried to intervene on his behalf. He'd seen her curled up in a fetal position on the floor, bleeding and crying as they dragged him away.

With the air cool and moist, it was as if being in a cave down in some deep hole in the middle of nowhere and no one hearing your screams. Every day they came, twice a day, sometimes more, as they'd tied his hands and feet and stretched him on the cold floor, naked. Placing a plastic tube down his mouth, they filled it with water until he was near drowning. They'd wait a few seconds and start in again; always asking the same questions over and over:

"Who do you work for?"

"What is your connection to the CIA?"

"What is your name?"

"Admit you're a spy and we'll let you go."

Jason knew that last question was a barefaced lie!

They'd continued beating him senseless until he could only open an eye. Clipping electrical leads to his hands and feet, an electrical current would flow through his body, always with the same effect—total blackout—which he always welcomed like a long-lost brother.

The dungeon he had called home for the last three years was almost unbreathable. They'd beaten him over and over, compelled to confess time and time again to whatever they wanted.

Jason Randolph Scott was thirty-six when he died at the hands of his captors, never seeing the light of day.

In July, marking the three years of his captivity, they turned his body over to the Americans during a prisoner exchange between the two countries.

His father, Lieutenant General Thomas Randolph Scott, Deputy Commander, USEUCOM, received his son's body at the DMZ and had it transported to their home in Texas, there vowing that someone would pay for his son's death.

US Military in Germany and the White House, along with the CIA, did nothing to secure his release. General Scott had knowledge of who they were, although *they* knew the North Korean Government held his son as a spy against their state.

—Chapter One—

Present day – Wednesday, August 7
Patch Barracks, U.S. Military Installation, Stuttgart, Germany

The sixteen-year-old, blue-eyed, blond-haired teenager walked toward a waiting brown Volkswagen Bug parked outside her father's on-post government quarters. She clutched her handbag close to her small bosom as if someone could come along and relieve her of it. Her restless eyes scanned the front of the two-story quarters behind her, hoping against hope her father would not catch her leaving at such a late hour.

Temperatures hovered in the low 60s, and it was a cool evening in mid-August, with a gentle prevailing wind, as the dying sun threw darkened shadows over the sweeping lawn to the US military headquarters in Patch Barracks, Germany. It was the home of the US European Command (EUCOM) where Chief-of-Staff Brigadier General Carl C. Chapman lived with his only child Helen Chapman. It was a picture post-card scene, as the blood-orange sky gave in to the night with a full moon appearing over the horizon.

With the nascent moonbeams lighting her way, her throat was dry and tight, and her heart beat faster as she approached the car. "Billy!" she yelled. "Start the car."

She glanced behind her and caught a glimpse of the living room curtains being pulled back. However, she wasn't sure. As she reached the car, her boyfriend, Billy Ackers, fired up the engine. He had the passenger door already opened for her. Now, oblivious to everything else around her, Helen came around to the passenger side. And there, for a slight second, she stood—a youthful figure, dressed in skinny jeans, a dark blazer underneath a black top with a white scarf and ankle boots, her blond hair blowing in the wind as she once again stared at her home.

With a deep breath, she arched an eyebrow, as if to say something but shook her head.

"Get in, babe," Ackers said in a low voice. "We're wasting time."

As she took her seat, she had second thoughts about going away for the few days and not telling her father what she'd planned. She knew full well he'd disapprove of it. It was giving her food for thought—but just for a second or two. This wasn't her first time, and it always seemed to end with her father setting up boundaries with which she didn't comply. But somehow it was different now. She couldn't pinpoint or explain what that was. Yet here she was, doing it all over once again.

She slipped a hand into her boyfriend's outreached hand. He leaned toward her, and her apprehensions erased as she met Billy's lips with her own in a quick kiss. As they parted, she glanced at him, noticing his intense blue eyes held her own as a slow smile curled her lips.

She blushed as she looked at him. He was only a year older but much more intelligent than her. He reached over once again and caught her hand. "Helen, are you okay, babe?" he asked in his slow Southern drawl.

Helen Chapman paused, frowning.

"Do you believe we'll be okay?" she asked, as a sense of foreboding hung on her mind. "Nothing bad will happen, right?"

"Honey," Billy replied. "What can go wrong? The night and the weekend are ours to have fun with."

In the semi-darkness of the car, Helen Chapman inclined her head.

"I guess you're right."

Billy Ackers nudged the selector on the gearshift, turned on the headlights, and eased away from the curb. He did not notice the twin set of headlights that flared on behind them.

* * *

With the night pitched black and only moonbeams playing across the road, the late-model Lincoln Navigator flipped on its headlights. With the vehicle's plate lights out, it left all details unreadable. The SUV moved at a leisurely pace down the street, gaining slightly on their intended target—the VW Bug and its two occupants.

They were in no hurry, knowing full well their destination and the route they would take. She and her boyfriend had been under surveillance for the last month—following their every move. With their cell phones monitored, they knew what their plans were. Now, with the go-ahead order, it would be up to them to bring the mission to a close.

The route they would take would lead them six miles through a wooded, unpopulated, unlit country road. And that's where they would make their move.

The driver of the first Navigator pulled back and slowed the pace, as did the second vehicle. As the VW reached the main gate to the military installation, he watched as the military police gate guard waved them through.

Slowly the two Navigators inched their way forward, turned into the gate and waited to be waved through. Turning, they drove under the arch sign and through the brown and white sign of *Patch Barracks, US Military Installation Main Gate:* The only gate operational during off-duty hours.

Once stopped at the intersection, they turned east on MontanaStrasse and caught sight of the VW's taillights.

* * *

Billy Ackers turned to his girlfriend. "You seem quiet. Usually I can't stop you from talking."

Helen sighed. With eyes half-closed, her mind wandered toward her father—what would happen to her once he found out she'd gone yet again? With her mother passing away only last year, she wasn't ready to deal with her father. She blamed him for her mother's death—not being there for her, at the crucial time when she needed him to be, instead of traveling. Helen had been with her mom when the poor woman took her last breath. All alone, she didn't know what to do, whom to call; it was too much for a sixteen-year-old to go through all alone. For several months afterwards, she'd been undergoing considerable emotional stress.

But now she was here with Billy. He was the first and only person she'd called that night. It was Billy that made all the phone calls. Breathing deep, she sank deep into her seat, her mind revolving around *that* day. God, I hope I'm doing the right thing, she thought.

Exhaling, Helen cleared her throat. "Um, thinking of all the fun we'll soon be having."

"Yeah, aha," he said with a smile. "Sure, you were."

She laughed. "I'm fine. I'm—"

He cut her off by blowing her a kiss. "It's okay, Helen."

The leader of the strike unit in the first Lincoln Navigator reached for his cell phone and dialed a predetermined number, waited for his boss to answer it, and said, "Made contact. We're following our target as we speak, Mr. Alpha." They used no regular names during the operation.

Alpha said, *"Do you expect any problems with the boyfriend?"*

"There's nothing for us to worry about."

"I hope not, for your sake."

"Yes, sir."

"Check back as soon as you complete the operation."

"Roger that, sir."

* * *

They were traveling through a thick forest on a two-lane road when Billy spied a set of headlights approaching from behind on the left lane wanting to pass but not in any hurry to do so. He could see what appeared to be a black SUV pull up abreast of his VW and speed up. It passed and pulled out in front. He couldn't make out the inside of the SUV because of the dark tinted windows. Nor could he make out the license plate—American or German, he couldn't tell.

With one vehicle in the front and the other toward the rear, the front Lincoln Navigator slowed at first, braking once or twice and letting the VW get close to its bumper, while the second SUV slowed, tapping the VW's bumper.

It was at that moment that Billy knew something was wrong, and he was getting scared!

He tried to swerve away to his left to pass the SUV in front, but he did not have a chance, as the rear SUV bumped his VW hard.

Helen screamed.

Billy yelled, "Son-of-a-bitch!"

Billy Ackers, holding hard to the steering wheel with both hands had no alternative but to brake to a stop.

Seconds later, Helen gasped as she looked behind her, and two black-clad men, holding what appeared to be machine guns, stepped out of the SUV and stopped, staring at the back of the VW, weapons at the ready.

"Oh my God, what's happening, Billy?" Helen said, almost yelling.

Turning in his seat, Billy gazed out past the back of the VW. For a moment he froze. "Helen, get down in the seat and don't come out for anyone."

"Billy!" she yelled.

He looked at her. Shock and disbelief were written all over her beautiful young face. So, he smiled at her.

"Please, Helen, for once, do as I said."

That gave her pause, as with eyes wide open, shaking her head, she stared straight back at him.

Once out of his car, Billy Ackers walked forward scared out of his wits and said a little prayer, hoping against hope it was nothing more than a big mistake. Coming to a stop as his VW's headlights illuminated him in the beams, he made out four black-clad men wearing balaclavas stepping out of the SUV, holding what appeared to be assault weapons.

Helen didn't do as Billy had instructed. Instead, she sat straight up in her seat and watched as Billy walked forward and stared at the four men standing behind the SUV holding machine guns. She gazed at the two closest to Billy when they pointed their weapons, and she heard the loud gunfire. She stared, agape, when Billy was driven back by the impact of the bullets striking his body, his arms flaring, as a bullet pushed through Billy's head. She yelled as blood and brain matter splashed onto the VW's windshield, and she kept yelling as she watched Billy's limp body slide to the ground.

She stopped yelling when the killers came for her.

Helen gasped, too stunned to realize what had happened. However, she noticed that the shooting had stopped—and they weren't shooting at *her*. Two of the killers walked toward the VW's passenger side door. The one who seemed to be the leader, opened the door, grasped her by her arm, and tried to pull her out. Screaming and yelling, she tried kicking at the killer to no avail. Grabbed by her hair, they dragged her to the ground and forced her to her feet. Someone came up behind her, pinned her arms to her chest, and placed a rag to her mouth. She smelled a sweet pungent scent. Moments later, she went limp in the arms of the killer. Her eyes rolled to one side as the chloroform took effect, and she blacked out, losing consciousness.

The leader of the group threw Helen across his shoulders, carried her to a Navigator, and tossed her in the back seat. He slammed and closed the right-side door, opened the front passenger door, pulled out a manila folder from the center console, extracted a folded sheet of paper, and slammed closed the door. Heading over to the VW Bug, he placed the sheet of paper on the passenger-side seat, returned to the Navigator, got in on the driver's side, and pulled away from the scene as the second Navigator followed.

He stared at his watch. It had taken them only eight minutes to secure the woman. *Eight*—two minutes shy of the time allotted.

He arched an eyebrow and nodded. "Not bad."

As he reached for his cell phone, he dialed the same number and said, "Target in the bag, sir."

Alpha said, "*And the boyfriend?*"

"He's neutralized."

"*Good work. You know what has to be done next, sergeant.*"

"Yes, sir."

The team had another to bag, their last *one*!

* * *

Six hours later

The white and green Mercedes-Benz four-door sedan, with its blue light-bar and siren atop the roof and displaying police markings on the hood, sides, and back of the car, made its way on the lonely unlit country road. It was the end of his shift, and it included this part in his patrol area, though he rarely patrolled it, because few vehicles ventured out at this time of the night.

The two-lane road, with several large potholes, was in dire need of repairs. Large trucks were the only vehicles that traveled on it, and teenagers looking for a place to sit, drink, and make out. He remembered having to run off two or three cars loaded with them, in the past.

Officer Karl Schultz, a three-year veteran, rolled down his window and listened for any sounds that would indicate the presence of teenagers in the area when his headlights caught sight of a car stopped on the side of the road about three or four hundred yards ahead.

Turning on his blue emergency lights, he drove a little faster and what he observed as he approached the scene made his blood run cold. For there, lying on the ground and trapped under the intense glare of his high beams, was a human body.

He came to a stop, turned off the engine, and stepped out of the patrol car.

"Heilige scheisse!" he said as he approached the body. "Holy *shit*!" It was his first dead body he'd ever come across.

With the rumbling of his stomach, he heaved.

Seconds later he wiped his mouth, and, once back in control, he called it in to his dispatcher. Approaching the body, he kneeled down and turned it over on its side, and once again heaved, as he observed that animals may have eaten off parts of the corpse.

Standing, he pulled out his flashlight and looked inside the VW Bug. But it was empty except for a letter or a note lying on the passenger seat. Not touching it, he returned to his vehicle, and waited for the Bundespolzei, German Federal Police, to arrive, along with the US Army Military Police—the VW had American license plates—and Crime Scene personnel.

* * *

Helen Chapman woke with a lurch, opened her eyes, and was met with total darkness as she gasped for air, coughing and making gagging noises.

Was she alone or was someone with her? the thought crossed her mind. There were no sounds to show so. She called out, but no one answered.

She didn't know how long she'd been unconscious—her watch was missing, as was her cell phone and purse.

Helen sensed a cool breeze blowing on her face. She had a terrible headache, and the wall against her back was cold.

With harrowing eyes, Helen tried to remember what had happened to her. But it was no use, her mind was still groggy.

Billy, she thought.

"My God," Helen whispered, her voice breaking. "Shot . . . dead."

She gasped and lifted her arms. But they'd bound her with rope.

Her mind was still a blur, slow, and her legs stretched out in front of her felt like lead.

Yet, all she knew was that she was alive and, she reasoned, they wanted her for something else besides being dead.

What could be worse than death, Helen...? Oh—my—God!

—Chapter Two—

10:45, Thursday morning, August 8th

The 5th MP Battalion Criminal Investigation Detachment (CID), under the control of 3rd MP Group, was the central command for the Stuttgart (CID) Field Office, at Patch Barracks, Stuttgart, Germany.

With four male agents and one female agent assigned, they were charged with investigating terrorist crimes and major crimes involving the US military and US civilian government personnel in their sector of responsibilities. The field office conducted overt and covert surveillance services and investigations.

The agent in charge or AIC Chief Warrant Officer Four Phillip Randall Jones, a 15-year veteran agent, was the top dog, responsible for directing and planning investigations. Today, he was instead taken aback when word came through channels assigning his top agent Jacqueline Sinclair to a time sensitive assignment, and they told him to have her report to the Provost Marshal's Office within the hour.

Someone had just undermined his authority, and that pissed him off.

"God damn it!" he yelled through his open office door aimed at his secretary. "Get someone over to the courthouse and get me Agent Sinclair."

CID Special Agent Jacqueline 'Belle' Sinclair's nine o'clock general courts-martial case on the 3rd floor of the Staff Judge Advocates (JAG) building in Patch Barracks ended early. As soon as the two judges left the chamber, she checked her watch. She had enough time to get back to her room, shower, and get dressed for her late lunch date with Captain Jeffrey Cory.

This would make it her third date, and she was looking forward to more. She looked out of the six large windows and saw the afternoon sun streaming in. It will be a very nice afternoon, she thought.

She looked forward to a quiet conversation that didn't include her explaining away her case or her testimony. Her Captain didn't care; all he wanted was to talk about her, and she adored him for it.

As she turned to leave, the sun through a window on her right side caught her eyes. The heat overpowered the German made air-conditioning as she noticed a small bead of sweat rolling down from her forehead. Brushing off the wetness from about her eyes, she walked toward the double doors leading out of the courtroom.

U.S. Army criminal investigator Chief Warrant Officer Belle, as friends knew her by, was just short of thirty, attractive, and self-assured. Her uniform was tight-fitting and spotless, which showed off her hourglass figure. She was of medium height, with short brown hair, cut to military regulation.

Belle was a confident woman, well in control of herself. Her Silver Star and Purple Heart, positioned for all to see on her uniform, gave credence of her dedication to her country.

Before she could leave though, the prosecuting attorney strode up to her. Ignoring the attorney, Sinclair just kept walking past her. From across the room, two male civilian-dressed CID agents snickered and cleared their throats. They both knew there was no love lost between those two. They stared at each other and smiled. Sinclair noticed them and smiled too.

Pulling out her cell phone from her handbag clutched under her right arm, she checked her text messages, looking for one in particular. And there it was, from Captain Cory. She read:

Let me know when you're finished, honey.

Smiling, her fingers typed across the keyboard and pressed the send button. Not dating long and he's calling me honey already, she thought. How sweet. She wrote:

Just did. I'll be ready in 30 minutes. Pick me up then.

His reply was quick as she heard the pinging of the phone's return text. She read:

Roger that.

Agent Sinclair walked out through the double doors and caught sight of her father as he strolled over to her. She was a little annoyed at seeing him there, but relieved that her sound testimony, as she thought, led to a conviction. But she wondered what her father was doing here.

As he approached, she noticed a small smile played across his face. Apparently, he knew of the court's outcome, or he wouldn't have been present, unless there was more to his being there. And that made her feel a little suspicious of his presence.

Her father, Colonel Richard Longstreet Sinclair, dressed in his Class A uniform, a tall man with a six-foot-three frame and broad-shouldered, was the area Provost Marshal. He was a West Point graduate and a veteran of over thirty-five years' service to his country. He had a rugged body for his age and was lean and fit. And like his daughter Jacqueline, and his family before him, a military family, all in the service of the Army, going back to the Spanish-American War.

Jacqueline, or Belle—his nickname for her—waited until he stopped in front of her before acknowledging him. She often marveled at his resemblance to an older Brad Pitt's strong facial features, and so did other women.

Stopping in front of his beautiful young daughter, the Colonel removed a pair of sunglasses, and placed them in his trouser pocket. Shaking his head ever so, he muttered, "Sounds like you had a successful conclusion to your proceedings, agent."

She replied, "Hi there, Dad."

"Not when we're in uniform."

"Sorry, sir."

Smiling, he said, "I need you to—"

Then her phone rang.

Taking a step or two back from her father, she pulled out the cell phone, and made a disapproving face.

"One moment, sir," she told her father, "while I answer this."

"Agent Sinclair," she answered.

"*Jones here,*" came the response. "*I've been trying to reach you. If you're finished at the courthouse, get yourself over here now. Don't take any short cuts. This is very important.*"

"But sir, I have—"

"*The only thing you have to do is get over here. Sinclair. I'm warning you. Don't piss me off any more than I already am.*"

His statement annoyed and irritated the agent. She was at a court martial proceeding on her day off, of all things. "But why, sir?"

"*You'll know once you get here,*" was the curt reply.

Considering his terse answer, she stared at her father—who just kept looking at her—then she replied, "Yes, sir."

Pocketing her cell phone, she walked back to her father.

"I'm sorry, sir, you were saying?"

"Your AIC wants you back in his office, I gather."

She stared at him rather suspiciously. "How did you know?"

"I'll explain soon," the Colonel said. "But like I was saying, I need you to start an investigation, a sensitive investigation. And only you are qualified to undertake it."

"Can you tell me what the circumstances are?"

"I'm unable to at this point. But we'll be seeing each other soon."

"We will?"

"Yes."

"Hell, there goes my lunch date and my day off," she muttered.

Twenty-five minutes later, Agent Jacqueline Sinclair walked into her AIC's office.

The man behind the desk was wearing a long-sleeve white shirt and red tie over a black vest. He wore steel eyeglasses and had a very serious air about him. He didn't look at her, not yet. His gray hair was cut short and balding at the top.

Jones was a desk-bound agent now, but, once upon a time, he served as a protective service agent to some long-forgotten VIP for over three years until they promoted him to his current assignment two years ago. He was now the agent in charge of the field office.

Agent Sinclair said, "Sorry I'm late, Chief. I was meeting with my father over at JAG."

Her AIC didn't look up nor acknowledge her as he paged through a folder in front of him.

Seconds went by, and she was still standing in front of his desk.

Then, Phillip Randall Jones said, "Sit down, Agent Sinclair."

Jacqueline Sinclair sat down in the visitor chair next to his desk. She waited to be spoken to, instead of the other way around. Military protocol called for a strict adherence to command presence. He was her senior, and she had to respect his position of authority—military courtesy and respect were invoked, not asked, just inferred.

Jones stared at her a few seconds and said, "You spoke to the Provost Marshal, your father? What did he say to you?"

She knew something very important was about to be discussed; now he was curious as to the conversation she may or may not have had with the Provost Marshal (PM). And she surmised either Jones didn't know why she was here or was fishing for information.

Playing along for now, she crossed one leg over the other.

She said, "He mentioned something about a sensitive investigation, which only I could do."

"Son of a bitch," he said. "That's why you were chosen. The PM wants just you on this case."

She asked, "What's this about, Chief?"

Chief Jones leaned forward, pushing away the folder, and placed his hands on his desk. "I don't know. I thought you knew."

"Me?"

"You. Didn't you finish talking to the PM?"

She took in a deep breath. The questions were getting under her skin. "First I heard about it was from the PM a little while ago."

"Agent Sinclair," Jones said. "You're to report to his office after you leave here. And I expect full reports on whatever your assignment entails."

Sinclair's expression didn't change. "Yes sir," she said. "Is that all?"

"Go on now, get out of here."

Jacqueline Sinclair rose, stood and, nodding to her chief as she opened the office door, exited without saying a word, closing the door behind her.

"The asshole could've just told me over the phone," she muttered, a little annoyed.

* * *

It was later that afternoon when Chief Jones reasoned what Agent Sinclair's investigation would entail. After reading through the military police Serious Incident Report (SIR) on the daily desk sergeant's blotter, she would have her hands full when push came to shove. And he also knew why she'd been handpicked by the PM—she was the only one who could pull it off.

Leaning back in his chair he said, "Good luck, Agent Sinclair. You're going to need it."

* * *

The temperatures in Southern Germany during the month of August average between fifty to seventy-five degrees and with about fifteen to seventeen rainy days in the month, today would be a pleasant day, as temperatures would reach about seventy-five.

With no rain in sight, Belle walked the two miles to the PM's building. All the time thinking, what the hell this was all about, and what *shit* was she getting herself into this time?

If she only knew what lay in front of her and the dangers she would encounter in the next few weeks. And it would all start the moment she leaves the Provost Marshal's office; the EUCOM Provost Marshal holds the same responsibilities as that of a large city Chief of Police.

A few minutes later, Agent Sinclair walked through a three-story office complex, through a set of double doors, and up a long flight of winding stone stairs. She'd been up these same stairs hundreds of times.

Sinclair could've used the elevator, but what the hell; she wasn't in any mood to converse with anyone at that moment. And as it was, she was in a grumpy mood missing out on her date. She met no one on the stairs, but there was a bevy of activity throughout the complex as usual.

At the top of the stairs, she made a right turn and, knowing where she needed to go, walked down the long hallway as she passed military and civilian personnel on either side of her.

As she reached the end of the hallway, at the door on her left side she saw two MPs standing on either end of the doors, guarding the Provost Marshal. The MPs changed every two hours and were detailed to stop anyone from entering without proper clearances or identification.

She stopped in front of the closest MP, a dark guy she assumed was in his mid-thirties, presented her ID and said, "I have a scheduled meeting with the PM."

Both of the military policemen looked well over six feet and somewhere around two hundred pounds. Both were wearing the new US Army Combat Uniform, were armed with 9mm semi handguns, and wore the MP silver badge under their right-side pocket. They were both wearing Velcro-attached Staff Sergeant Insignias positioned just center-chest.

Taking her ID, the MP checked it and said, "Yes, ma'am. Please wait one."

The MP left his post, walked into the office and, seconds later, returned handing back the ID, and said, "Please go on ahead, ma'am."

Agent Sinclair walked into the small lobby and stopped in front of the PM's secretary's front desk. Mary Elders had been the PM's Secretary for the last three years. An attractive, fortyish woman, with blond, shoulder-length hair, a German born of German and American parents, she was busy typing on her computer.

Sinclair had known Mary off and on ever since being interviewed and selected for the position by her father three years ago. She was a divorcee and living with her daughter. And although Sinclair's father was a widower, their relationship was professional and all business.

She said, "Hi, Mary. Here to see my father."

"Oh my," the woman said.

Mary Elders looked up, paused, stood, came around her desk, and hugged Belle Sinclair.

"You're looking wonderful as ever, Belle. I'm glad to see you again. It's been too long."

"Thank you. Yes, over a month now."

"Oh my God, that long, we—"

Then from inside the inner office of the PM, they heard his voice, as he asked, "Is that my daughter, Mary?"

"Yes, sir."

"Please send her in."

They stared at each other and shrugged.

Sinclair moved toward her right, took several steps, and stopped at the all wood door that was slightly ajar.

Agent Sinclair knocked.

She heard her father's low voice sounding as if he was far away. Enter, was what she may have heard but wasn't too sure. So, taking a little breath, she opened the door, walked through, and closed the door behind her.

Looking around the office, she noticed nothing had changed since the last time she was there over a month ago. A glass chandelier hung over the center of the office. The walls were still adorned with his certificates, citations, awards, and an old Cavalry sword presented to him by his men, when he served with the First Cavalry Division—the old horse soldiers of yesteryear.

Remembering the event as if it was yesterday, while stationed in Fort Hood, Texas, her father had served as the assistant operations officer for the division. Happy times she'd spent with her mom and her father. She was only twelve, and on that day, she knew what she wanted her life to become—a military officer. Belle graduated from the University of Maryland, earning her Bachelor's degree in criminal justice, and aspired to be a police officer in the Army.

Agent Sinclair strolled up to her father's desk; coming to attention, and saluting, she said, "Sir, Warrant Officer Sinclair, reporting as ordered."

"Stand at ease, Belle. Take a seat."

Taking a seat in one of two visitor's leather armchairs on the other side of the office window, it was the same chair she sat in whenever she came to visit. And it was at that point, she'd realized he'd used the nickname he'd given her years ago, Belle. She surmised this would be a father and daughter meeting.

The Colonel said, "What did your AIC ask of you, Belle?"

The question brought a slight smile to her lips. She said, "The same cryptic message you spoke about at JAG, a sensitive investigation."

"Did he add anything else?"

"Well, he mentioned something about being held in the loop to any ongoing investigation."

After a short pause, the Colonel frowned, but said nothing to that.

She shook her head, leaning slightly forward in her seat. "What's going on, Dad?"

The Colonel stared at her and said, "What I'm about to say will stay in this office. In the last few days, someone has kidnapped two American dependent children. They left notes behind warning of any police involvement or the children would suffer with their lives. And that further information would follow. How or when wasn't said."

The Colonel waited for her to speak. All she did was nod. So, he continued.

He said, "They discovered two bodies. The first was Billy Ackers, identified through his military dependent ID found in his wallet. He was found at the scene where Helen Chapman had disappeared from. Dennis Jackson, also a military dependent, also identified by his ID, when his body was discovered at the kidnapping scene of Lisa Shaffer.

"Both young men were dating the two kidnapped subjects. Leaving of the bodies at the scene suggests whoever is responsible is serious. The German police crime scene investigation revealed little." He paused. "No witnesses, no one hearing anything. Considering that they conducted the abductions and murders in secluded areas, suggests prior planning and or surveillance. We speculate the children were the prime target. Why them becomes quite simple. All the parents are high-ranking military members in the command."

Colonel Sinclair went on. "Like I mentioned, the German police conducted the crime scene investigation, and although both bodies discovered were riddled with bullets, they retrieved no casings. This would show a high level of professionalism and coordination. The bullet holes on the bodies seem to be of small-bore ammo, not yet identified. It would seem the German police are slow in providing us that information. I'll have their report sent over to your office in an hour."

He continued. "The EUCOM commander has tasked me through the CID command at Quantico, to use local professional agents to handle the investigation going forward. Besides you, I had two other agents considered. I gave the Commander all personnel folders, and he recommended you, with my final approval."

She leaned back in her seat, took a deep breath, and closed her eyes. This was big, she thought, and could get involved.

"What convinced Command," he said, "were your qualifications. You received the Silver Star and Purple Heart for actions in Afghanistan, black belt in Japanese karate since the age of fourteen, close quarters combat expert, counter surveillance training, proficient in covert communications, jump qualified, expert in unarmed combat, expert in small arms and automatic weapons. I could go on and on, Belle, but as your father I know you better than most, so I won't. And, as much as I hate doing this, I have to place my daughter in harm's way."

Her expression remained almost blank, with just the hint of an arched brow. "Will I be able to choose a partner?"

'No."

"Why?"

"We have already chosen one for you."

She took in a deep breath. "Damn, Dad."

"I considered it prudent," he said, "to have an outsider join up with you."

Sinclair shrugged. "It's your party, Dad, so far."

Just then, a knock came from the door, and Mary peeked her head in. "Sir, the second person is here," she said. "Should I send him in?"

"Please do."

She watched as the man walked forward and stopped in front of her father's desk.

The man was a lean individual with a tanned face, wearing a black two-piece business suit with a white shirt, no tie. He appeared to be well muscled, as suggested by the bulging outline of his suit jacket; a very stocky chest, she thought. He had long blond hair tapered at the back, about her age, and tall, not as tall as her father, but not by much.

"Sir," he said. "I'm Agent Tom Price, reporting."

She noticed as he spoke, he had a Mid-western accent, maybe, she guessed, from Minnesota somewhere. And the Agent bit wasn't lost on her either.

The PM said, "Agent, please pull up a chair."

Agent Price slumped in the vacant chair as he inclined his head toward Sinclair, like he was just maybe noticing her for the first time.

Sinclair shrugged and averted her eyes from him. She already thought he was an asshole—first impressions and all.

"Agent Belle," the PM said. "Meet Agent Price from military intelligence. He has already been briefed by his command. He will join you in your investigation. Price is a twelve-year deep cover agent and knows his way around the intelligence side of things." He paused. "Tom Price will help in case your investigation turns up any suspicion of terrorist's action or information to suspect the act of terrorists. We don't think it will, but we plan for the worst and hope for the best."

Price rose and walked over to Sinclair offering his hand, which she took. He smiled. She didn't. She glanced back at her father and saw a faint smile play across his face.

Now she felt a little annoyance that was aimed at her father.

Her father asked, "Well, ah, now will you proceed?"

Agent Price said, "Well, sir—"

"I was speaking to my daughter, Agent Price. Not you."

"Yes sir, oh . . . your daughter, sir. Geeze, I didn't—"

"Relax, agent."

Agent Sinclair was smiling as her father turned his gaze on her.

"Yes, sir," she said. "Well you mentioned the fact that the perpetrators acted professionally. Well, as you know, Father, professional hits or snatch jobs are the hardest to investigate and to close, because of the anonymous nature of the murders. The usual rules like motive and relations to victim don't apply. So, I would like to visit the crimes scenes and get a feel of the areas, see what I can dig up first. Then I'd like to interview the parents and take it from there."

"Good. You two get going then," the Colonel said. "And I'm the only one you report to. All chain of command starts and ends with me. That goes with you too, Agent Price. No one, I repeat no one, is to know we are investigating. And no outside agencies are to be contacted for any reason, unless it comes through me. Is that clear?"

Sinclair stood. "Yes, sir."

Agent Tom Price also stood and, snapping the fingers on his left hand, said, "Um, what about my—?"

The Colonel turned to face him and stared into his soul, "No one, Agent Price!"

And the Colonel added, "The German authorities have given us full rein on this investigation. They have offered their help if we have need of it."

"One more thing, Agent Sinclair," the PM said, staring at his daughter. "Do what has to be done."

Agent Jacqueline Belle Sinclair nodded.

The man in military uniform glanced at the door that led to the Provost Marshal's office just down the hallway.

He watched as he saw two people, a man and a woman, whom he identified as the Provost Marshal's daughter, CID Agent Jacqueline Belle Sinclair, and the other he suspected of being Agent Tom Price from MI step out of the office. Then, he palmed his cell phone, surreptitiously pointed the camera at the pair, and snapped their photo.

Then, dialing a predetermined number on his cell phone, he waited, let it ring three times, hung up, and dialed once again and waited for it to be picked up at the other end.

"*Alpha here, report please.*"

He said, "Made contact with both agents coming out of the PM's office. They have placed both of them on the case. The bug in the PM's office came in loud and clear."

Alpha said, "*Good. We knew they would put someone on the case. Get your men to shadow them and have them report to me.*"

"Roger that, sir."

—Chapter Three—

A s they walked side by side down the hallway after their meeting with the PM, Agent Price was trying to recall something he'd read and heard about a certain investigation. He'd read several files that came across his desk, a few that were terrorist related and a few that weren't. But there was one that he remembered in particular. Glancing her way, his eyes narrowed almost to the point of squinting as some information held in the back of his mind seemed to push forward into his consciousness, and then he realized who this woman by his side was.

"Christ," he said, as he gently tugged on her arm, begging her to stop.

Agent Sinclair showed no signs of slowing as she brushed away his hold on her.

"Hey, come on now, wait a second," Price said.

"What?"

"Ain't you that cop that brought down an army Major three months ago in a high-level investigation?"

"Yeah, and?"

"Whatever became of it?"

She came to a stop, faced him and said nothing.

"Come on now, the word is that was some piece of investigative work. And word got around that a couple of army dudes tried to muscle you into quitting the investigation."

"You hear a lot," she said.

"I'm intelligence operative, you know."

"Yeah," she said shrugging. "Well the Major was convicted, and his sentencing is set for next month."

"And the dudes that came after you?" Price asked.

She looked around the hallway before answering, her violet eyes taking in all around them. "Ah, in the hospital nursing broken bones," she stated in a bored voice. "Both will be in wheelchairs for a while. They'll see the inside a courtroom soon enough."

Price smiled.

"How interesting," he said, "and what was the Major charged with?"

Another shrug.

"I'll tell you about it as we walk," she said.

For a second he said nothing and followed her down the hallway.

"In answer to your question, Agent Price," Sinclair began, "he kidnapped a fifteen-year-old German girl who'd been reported missing for over two months. He kept her locked up in a barn and raped her repeatedly, then stabbed her and dumped her body into a water spillway. An asshole like that should be put to death."

He noticed her voice had gone low gloomy, almost melancholy.

He paused as his eyes fell back on her. "How did you track him down?" he asked.

For a moment, Sinclair didn't reply. "It was unremarkable. It was the girl that led me to him. Stupid *shit* left behind trace evidence. Our lab was able to compare DNA samples left behind on her body, submitted by German authorities on the off chance it could have been one of ours. According to German police, the samples matched none known profiles on their data bases. When we got a hit on our data base, it was just a simple matter of identification, surveillance, and tracking."

"So, I shouldn't get you mad at me then?"

"As long as you behave, you have no worries."

"Aha, and please call me Tom."

"Certainly, Agent Price."

"We're going to get along famously, I see."

She shrugged again.

After a moment of silence and just before reaching the elevators, he asked, "So . . . you have a boyfriend or something?"

She veered over to an elevator and stopped. "That's my business and none of yours," she replied shaking her head, not allowing him to upset her.

She thought, as she extended a hand and used a finger to press the down-button to the elevator, the guy is already getting on my nerves.

Just before the elevator door opened, she spied a uniformed soldier. She couldn't tell his rank from so far away, about medium height, dark tan, skinny, standing just by the water cooler down the hall from the banks of elevators.

The guy looked harmless enough, but something about him didn't sit right with her. It was her cop senses coming awake. He was the same guy she'd noticed before, as she and Price exited the PM's office—too much of a coincidence, she thought. He had the same watchful look he was giving her right now. As she stared him down, the guy averted any further eye contact and walked away in the opposite direction.

Yeah, awfully fishy, she reasoned.

Could be nothing, then again . . . but what could happen in the most secure building in Germany? Nothing that couldn't be handled, she thought.

What she did next caught Tom Price by surprise.

Not sure if it was anything, Sinclair started walking in the direction of the soldier, trying to catch him—she had questions. The guy quickened his pace on seeing her following.

"Hey, you—!"

But the guy didn't stop or slow down.

"Agent Sinclair, what the hell—?" Price asked as he set off after her, struggling to keep up.

Agent Sinclair doubled her speed and, pulling out her phone, she dialed the MP Station Desk Sergeant.

"Sergeant Brooks, how can I help you?" came the reply.

"Agent Sinclair, CID," she said almost breathless. "Chasing a male suspect, request MP backup in front of the PM building, ASAP!

"Roger that, dispatching two patrol cars as we speak. Can you describe the —?"

But just then, she cut him off and pocketed the phone.

Suddenly, she saw the guy pushing open the stairwell door on his right and flying through it. Just as she burst through the door, she saw him open a door at the bottom of the landing and disappear.

She took off after him, flying down the stone steps two at a time.

Price was now pursuing at a dead run as he rushed through the door. Pausing for a second, he quickly glanced down and spied his partner at the bottom of the landing. Taking them two a time, he flew down the stone stairs.

He was halfway down the last few steps when he saw her disappearing through the same door her prey had gone through a moment ago. Taking a leap and jumping down the last steps, he fell, rolled on his left side and quickly scrambled to his feet running. He pushed open the door and stepped out into bright daylight.

Coming to a stop just at the curb, and shielding his eyes from the sun, Price saw Agent Sinclair standing in the middle of the street, hands on her hips, trying to catch her breath, as traffic came to a screeching halt on both sides of the street. He glanced quickly around but could not see any sign of the guy.

Without a word, he waited for her to get back on the curb.

A moment later, she was standing by his side, as traffic flowed once again.

Agent Price, slightly annoyed with her, shook his head. "Hey, what the hell was that all about?"

She said, "If you got to ask, then you're useless to me."

"Ah, come on."

"If you have to know, I saw the guy twice, both times staring at us from two different places. A suspicious affair, considering the case we just inherited. Don't you think?"

After a moment, Price nodded. "*Shit*, at least you could've called out to me."

"Why? You're a big boy."

With a hint of a smile, he said, "Oh, you're hilarious."

"Not really," she said in a straight face, shaking her head. "No, I'm not."

Then they heard sirens.

* * *

Sitting in the Post Exchange cafeteria across the street, Sergeant Richard Stevens, late of the US Army Special Forces Green Beret, now working for some heavy hitters, stared out through the glass panes at the street and noticed Agent Sinclair and Agent Price looking around dumbfounded, searching for him.

He pulled out his cell phone.

Stevens dialed Alpha's number and said, "I think the agents have made me, sir."

Alpha said. *"Did they see your face?"*

"Don't think so, no... not sure."

"Stay with them until Bravo relieves you."

"Yes, sir."

Hearing sirens, Sergeant Stevens glanced at his watch, half-past three. Then he heaved himself up with a slight grunt, pushed back his chair, and walked out of the cafeteria, as two MP patrol cars screeched to a stop at the intersection. He stood back, watching.

* * *

Once the MPs arrived on the scene, Sinclair flashed her badge and credentials and gave them a general description of the man that had gotten away from her.

Admittedly, she thought, the case was turning against them. Someone was already on to them, shadowing them. How or why? These were questions better left for another day; right now, they had plans to put together. But it was slightly disconcerting and a little worrisome.

She would have to keep a watchful eye all around them at all times. This was something she'd done in the past and was part of her training and conditioning.

Agent Price stepped toward her.

He wanted to get back to his office and pick up a few things. Agent Sinclair told him to meet up with her at her office in an hour. They had things to discuss and do.

She arrived at her office twenty minutes later after picking up something to eat along with a tall mocha coffee. She'd already called Captain Jeffrey Cory, her date, and explained they gave her another case, an important case, and asked for a rain check on the date for tonight after nine. He sounded cheerful and understanding, and nine was fine by him.

The offices of the CID were located in a two-story, stone and brick building next to the military police station at Kelley Barracks, an old Nazi office complex used during WW2. Refurbished in 2010, it was brightly lit, packed with closed off offices, various machines, desks, telephones, and the main reception area just situated at the entrance to the building. A narrow hallway leading toward the back of the building led to a wood and stone staircase to the second floor—the offices of the operations chief, her AIC, and conference room.

When she arrived, she found the building almost deserted.

The only person visible was the secretary, and she just looked up from her typing, smiled, and returned to her computer. The woman was an American dependent wife.

She said, "The chief's not around. He's taken a late lunch."

"So much the better," Agent Sinclair said.

Agent Sinclair proceeded on through, her office being the last one down the hall on the left. A moment later, she arrived at the solid metal door painted green, with glass on top. Below the glass was a name plate: *Agent Jacqueline Sinclair*. She reached into her pocket and pulled out a set of keys, inserted one into the lock, turned the handle, and walked in.

Flipping on the light switch on the wall to her right, she walked toward her double pedestal desk, undid the four buttons on her jacket, pulled off her black tie, and laid it on her desk.

Her office was devoid of any hanging photos, certificates, or anything else that would resemble a cop's office. With just a desktop computer and a laptop, a telephone, and a four-drawer metal filing cabinet, the office was bare; not even a flowerpot was visible. She reasoned, if anyone visited her office, which many had, the only thing they would concentrate on was her. And she liked it that way.

It gave her an edge.

Pulling up her high-backed chair, she sat, exhausted. Then she opened her ham and cheese quiche, devoured half, and washed it down with her mocha, as she waited for Agent Price to arrive. It was the first meal she'd had all day.

Agent Sinclair was just about to close her eyes, hoping to get a little nap, when she saw a large brown envelope sitting in her Inbox. Curious, she reached over, picked it up, opened it, and read. It was the English translation of the preliminary German police crime scene report conducted the night of the kidnapping that her father had promised to have on her desk. She read through it, but nothing it said gave her any further information about the crime that she hadn't already known. But the last line of the report convinced her of the outcome—professional through and through.

No doubt about it.

Her conclusion, and that of the German police, lay in the unusual nature of the crimes, and what was left at the scene, or for that matter, what was not left at the scene.

There were aspects to the murders that, well, she found baffling. According to the crime unit at the scene, there were no bullet casings found. Now she asked herself why that would be.

So that they could mask their weapons?

She sighed and muttered, "Maybe."

Plus, the method of attack had been planned and executed flawlessly; hence, no witnesses.

"Lot of trouble for two girls," she said.

The ringing of her cell phone broke her chain of thought. Picking it up, the screen registered an unknown number. She pushed the talk button.

"*Agent Sinclair?*" the voice on the other end asked.

"Yes. Who's this?"

"*It's me, Price. I'll be along soon.*"

"How the hell did you get this number? Wait; don't tell me, I don't want to know."

A dry little chuckle. *"You have your methods, I have mine."*

"How soon until you get to my office?"

"About thirty minutes, maybe less."

"Hurry it up then," she said, ending the connection.

Then her desk phone rang. "What now?" she thought.

Removing the receiver, she said, "Agent Sinclair. CID. How can I help you?"

"Belle?"

"Yes, Dad," she said, recognizing her father's voice on the opposite end.

"We got conflicting reports that two more children may have gone missing, or kidnapped."

"Holy *shit!*" she said in a whisper.

She leaned back in her chair and glanced at the ceiling. "Someone is making a statement, Dad."

He said, *"I'll have a full report on your desk within the hour."*

She cradled the phone and paused.

One question burned through her mind: What the hell was going on?

—Chapter Four—

Later that afternoon

A gent Tom Price stood to one side of the front door leading into Agent Sinclair's office, where the secretary had directed him. A black Puma bag packed with files and other accessories he deemed appropriate for the coming days was slung across his left shoulder. And he was late. With a small breath, he stepped up to the door and knocked. Seconds later, the door opened, and he shuffled into a semi-dark office. As he stood off to one side, Agent Sinclair, hands on her hips, stared straight at him.

He said, "Hello, Agent Sinclair."

Sinclair cocked her head. "You're late."

"I know," he said, as he removed the bag from across his shoulder and held it in front of him.

"Well, you're here now, that's something," she said. "Throw your bag on the chair."

Price placed his bag on the seat, removed his suit jacket, and draped it over the armchair. He pulled over another chair from a corner and sat.

When she spoke, it was with a warm, almost husky voice, something he'd failed to catch before, but now he considered it as attractive and sexy.

Why is that? he thought. Maybe it would have something to do with the way she dressed?

Now, without her Class A Army jacket, he guessed a thirty-six with a C cup size under her tight-fitting white blouse and her uniform skirt topping over her knees. He admired her fine chiseled runner's legs and great looking knees. She was wearing nylons and plain, black, lace-up, military-issued shoes. She wasn't tall, but trim, highly attractive and sexy, almost leaving him breathless, as she walked behind her desk and sat.

The room was heating up, or is that me, he thought.

Breathe in, breathe out slowly, he told himself.

His mind wandered for a second as he spied food on her desk.

His eyes shifted to the half-eaten quiche. "Are you going to eat the rest of that?" he asked.

"No, but I guess you can," she said with a grin.

"You bet I would. Thanks, I haven't eaten a bite in several hours."

"So, help me out here," she asked. "How long you've been with Military Intelligence?"

In between bites, he said, "I'm not with MI."

She pondered this for only a moment. "Oh, so, who are you associated with?"

"DIA."

"The Defense Intelligence Agency?"

He nodded. "Guilty as charged."

She paused and groaned. "*Shit*, a civilian?"

Agent Tom Price, snapping the fingers of his left hand, grinned and said, "Right again."

She took this information with her usual equanimity as she set her eyes on this handsome man. He looked like a man that attracts women rather effortlessly. But he also appeared to be an unsophisticated, rustic kind of man. That aside, she stared straight at him and, just as quickly, averted her gaze elsewhere.

Already, she heard alarms going off in her head.

She said, "This is getting better by the minute. And you likened this to a terrorist plot?"

"Why I'm here with you," he replied as he finished the food and wiped his mouth with the back of his hand. "Will never know, until we get into it."

"Right, okay." Her eyebrows rose; nothing yet seemed to connect to that crazy theory. She glanced away. "I've had no signs that terrorists were involved."

"Well, you've heard the saying," Price said, "A terrorist to one, a freedom fighter to another."

She put her head down and sighed.

With her office door left open, the CID secretary stood at the threshold holding a file folder. Clearing her throat, she waited for Agent Sinclair to raise her head her way. "I have a folder for you, Ms. Sinclair."

Sinclair said, "Agent Price, get that, would you?"

With a shallow breath he stood and walked to the door, smiled at the secretary, and held out his hand for the thick and bulky folder.

As Agent Sinclair observed him turning and moving toward her desk, she was struck by his fine chiseled features, brilliant blue eyes, and blond hair. He seemed to project self-confidence and manliness, more than male bluster. But what caught her full attention was that he favored a slight limp in his step. Not too pronounced, but there, almost as if he was trying hard not to show it.

As he moved toward her, Agent Price stopped and placed the folder on top of the desk, just by her left hand. As she made to grab it, for an instant, their hands touched. And rather quickly, they both withdrew their hands. She averted her stare. As she pulled the folder toward her, undid the clasp holding it together, and opened it, her thoughts turned to her upcoming date.

Agent Price said nothing. But something stirred deep down inside his soul.

He shook his head. What went through his mind was crazy and dumb. She was too much of a sophisticated woman to have anything to do with the likes of him. Plus, he didn't know if she was dating anyone. But it wouldn't hurt to find out though, in the event there wasn't one.

It stunned Agent Sinclair for a moment. Forgotten was her silliness when she'd touched his hand, as the first sheet of paper she opened had her name written on the folded sheet. It was from her father—*Belle*, was handwritten on the face of the sheet.

She cocked an eyebrow as she unfolded the sheet, the note being short and to the point.

Hi Belle, trust no one!

Agent Sinclair fell silent. And thought about what her father had written.

"You seem to favor a limp," she said, changing her chain of thought about what her father meant by trusting no one, and stared straight at Price. "You need time with that?"

For a moment, Tom Price appeared surprised by her question, and then he smiled. "Oh, it's nothing. Fell on the stairs during our chase."

Sinclair said nothing and returned to the folder.

Deliberately slow, Sinclair paged through all the reports, going from one to the other and placing them in some order on her desk, along with solid investigative notes by the responding MPs at the crime scenes and from the on-call CID agent who arrived thereafter at the scene.

The task was arduous. But it needed to be done. She was looking for any commonality, any connection to suggest who may have committed the kidnappings and the murders.

And, included in the reports, was the request to have the two murdered youth's remains remanded to the military for autopsy examination at the Landstuhl Regional Medical Center, She would have to attend the autopsy. So, the only connection, which she had already known, was that all the children were family members of highly placed military officers in the command, which included:

Fifteen-year-old Lisa M. Shaffer, Father, Lieutenant General James Earl Shaffer—Assistant Deputy Commander EUCOM, Stuttgart

Seventeen-year-old Janet L. Rodgers, Father, Brigadier General Thomas D. Rodgers—Special Operations Command, Europe, Stuttgart.

Sixteen-year-old Helen Chapman, Father, Brigadier General Earl C. Chapman–EUCOM Chief-of-Staff, Stuttgart.

Eighteen-year-old Duane E. Hartmann, Father, Brigadier General Phillip R. Hartmann - 17th Army Air Missile Command, Stuttgart.

The investigative notes by German police, MPs, and the initial CID report that was marked Top Secret, all narrated the findings as a blank for physical evidence, and not one bullet casing was recovered, nor any latent prints found, except for the prints of the deceased.

There was nothing new she hadn't already known, and nothing that would shed new light into her investigation. And, obviously, nothing to suggest a terrorist act, so far that is. So, she was going in blind.

What else is new? she thought.

Coughing and grimacing, Sinclair rose from her chair and paced her office. One thought kept repeating itself over and over—it was only a simple kidnapping, nothing more. However, according to the instructions left at the scene by the perps, it was clear no ransom was demanded. And that further instructions would be forthcoming . . . what was that all about?

She wasn't feeling confident going in so far . . . no, not at all. In fact, the only theory that made any sense to her was the kidnapping itself, and that the victims were at the wrong place, wrong time. As a cop that made perfect sense.

Agent Price didn't say a word. No use interfering with her chain of thought, at least for the time being.

Agent Sinclair strode back behind her desk, sat down, and pulled out the sheet that listed the names of those kidnapped and the names of their parents. Clearly, something about it had drawn her attention. She looked it over not once but twice. Something wasn't clicking in her mind; she didn't know what it was. She was feeling a slight little tingling sensation run up her spine; she felt something big may be at work here.

Sinclair leaned back in her chair, and still with the sheet in her hand, she looked over at Agent Price and smiled as she remembered the people he works for—DIA.

Leaning forward in her chair, she waved the sheet of paper at him. "Here, take this and tell me what you make of it."

Agent Price stood, leaned over the desk, took the sheet being offered to him, sat back down, and began reading through it. Not once but twice, slowly shaking his head.

For a long moment, there was nothing but silence.

"Christ!" he said.

"What, what?"

Tom Price hesitated. "Look at where these generals work."

"I did, and?"

Agent Price nodded, rubbed his head with the palm of his left hand, took a deep breath, and exhaled with an air for the dramatic. "We may have a problem, or not. But let me take this to my office and check it out. I'll keep you posted."

"You're not going to clue me in on your thoughts, are you?"

"I don't want to look like a complete idiot with you, so no. I'll keep it to myself for now."

With a deep breath, she nodded and said, "*Shit*. Okay."

"You have anything else?"

"Yes, get yourself ready to go."

"Where are we heading?"

"Crime scene where Helen Chapman was snatched. Who knows, we may have better luck."

Snapping his fingers, he said, "You're the boss."

"Answer me this. Why do you keep snapping your fingers?"

"Oh, that. A habit that never went away."

She shrugged, shook her head, and said, "Keep it under control, would you?"

Smiling, he snapped his fingers and said, "Sure enough."

Sinclair shook her head again.

Donning her Army jacket once again, Agent Sinclair opened a drawer on her desk, pulled out her assigned Beretta M9 9mm pistol, locked in a round, and tucked it at the small of her back. She removed a set of cuffs and stored them in her purse.

Agent Price didn't need to be told; he already guessed what he needed to do. Grabbing his backpack, he pulled out his Colt 1911A1 .45 caliber automatic pistol and extra magazines, clipped his holster to his belt, jacked in a live round, and holstered his big gun. His Colt wasn't Government issue for DIA agents, but he preferred it over Sinclair's peashooter.

They were ready for any eventuality.

Ten minutes later, with Agent Sinclair driving and Tom Price in the passenger seat, she maneuvered her assigned military vehicle, a 4 door, 2017 black Chevy, from her parking space, drove through the main gate, and headed east.

A black Lincoln Navigator slowly pulled up behind them and stayed four car lengths behind the Chevy.

She drove through the midst of a dense country road as tall trees blocked the late afternoon sun on either side of the two-lane road. With enough daylight left to complete a search, they arrived at the crime scene thirty minutes later.

The first thing Agent Sinclair observed was the complete isolation of the area. The trees were massive. She guessed seventy-feet tall with large branches that extended above the road. It was an eerie sensation. Reducing her speed, she steered over to the side of the road and pulled to a stop. No houses were visible for miles, and they did not encounter any traffic either.

Yes, a perfect ambush spot, she thought.

Still in the car, Sinclair pulled out a set of photographs that showed exactly where the VW Bug was and where in relation to the VW Billy Ackers' body was found. Another set of photos showed the body by the left side of the VW.

As she was reviewing the set of photos, they failed to detect the presence of another vehicle, a black Lincoln Navigator, as it pulled over and came to stop about half a klick down the road from the Chevy. The only occupant was a heavy-set black man, who retrieved a pair of binoculars from his tote bag, aimed it at the two investigators, adjusted the lenses, and waited to catch sight of whatever they may come up with. His information was that the area had been cleared after the operation, so there wasn't anything for them to find.

With knowledge that the police had searched the area, Agent Price considered this a waste of time, but didn't say so to her, keeping his thoughts to himself for the time being. He wasn't a cop, so this line of investigation was hers . . . and he didn't agree with it. He wanted to get to his office and do a little digging on those generals. He didn't look at her, but he kept glancing out his window.

Setting his gaze on her he finally asked, "What now?", with a little edge in his voice.

Agent Sinclair returned the photos to their folder and placed it on her lap for now. The way he asked wasn't lost on her.

But she only smiled.

She was beginning to believe he was getting annoyed with her line of investigation. Good, she thought.

Sinclair gave him a single, brusque shake of her head. "Let's get out and look around."

Putting the folder on the back seat, she unbuckled her seatbelt.

He asked before he opened his door, "What do you expect to find that others hadn't?"

A pause, as she glanced at him. "I'll let you know," she said, "the moment I find it."

Agent Tom Price took this without a reply.

They opened their doors and got out. She closed her door, walked toward the back of the Chevy, and opened its trunk. She rummaged through a small briefcase, pulled out four clear zip-lock bags, along with two sets of flashlights, and as Price joined her, she gave him two of the bags, along with a flashlight.

"If you find anything," she said, "try not to use your bare hands in handling it and place it in the bag."

Price gave Sinclair a curt nod and stuffed the bags in his pants pocket.

"So, here's the way I see this," she said. "Damage to the VW showed that at least two vehicles were involved in order to force the VW off the road—one in front and the other in the back. Billy Ackers, Helen Chapman's boyfriend, got out of the car." As she set the scene in her mind, she walked away from her Chevy, and stood where she thought the perps were when they'd approached Ackers. "And apparently, that's when the perps opened fire, killing him."

"Aha," Price said.

"So, in relation to the body," she said, "let's take a side of the road each and walk through it and see what we can find."

Back and forth they walked, illuminating the ground with the light beam off their flashlights. They searched both sides of the road. After about twenty minutes of fruitless searching, Agent Price stopped and turned his gaze on Sinclair.

"This is getting us nowhere," he said. "We've been at this for twenty minutes and have found nothing. Let's call this off and head on back."

She said, "I'm not happy having you scrutinize my investigation."

He said, "Oh, come on for Christ's sake."

"So, this is why I work alone," she said. "And now you're getting in my way."

"Uh, *shit*, Sinclair, Christ almighty."

She walked toward the area behind and to the left side of the road, from where she guessed the perps shot. As she began a fifth try in the same area, she stopped, something had caught her eyes . . . something that reflected off her flashlight beam for a second.

On hands and knees beside the object, she turned the beam back and forth over it. To her surprise, it looked like a shell casing. She quickly yelled out to Price, "Hey, get over here! I need you to witness this."

"Find something? A bottle top, maybe," he said, rather sarcastically.

Stopping, he stood above her. "So, tell me . . . what did you find?"

"Shine your light over this area," she said.

"Okay, now what?"

Now, with both her hands free, she could brush away grass and dirt from around the object. She pulled out a zip-lock bag, a pencil, and her phone from her shirt pocket. With her phone, she snapped a picture of the casing and, with the pencil, she gently removed the surrounding dirt, exposing it. It appeared to be from a small-bore gun. A 9mm or .380 ACP, she wasn't sure. Again, using the pencil, she inserted it into the casing. Lifting it from the ground and standing, she let Price witness the find.

"So, what do you think?"

"What a stroke of luck, Sinclair."

"Our first piece of actual physical evidence," she said smiling.

With the zip-lock bag in hand, she placed the casing into it and skewered Agent Price with her stare. He glanced away, and when he did, he caught sight of an SUV parked down the road with its engine running and white smoke trailing from its tailpipes. He was unable to make out who was in it. Too far. He didn't even hear its engine running.

With the bag safely in her pocket, Sinclair followed his gaze. Something in the way he looked caught her attention. As her eyes came in focus, she made out the SUV.

"What do you think about that?" Price asked.

"We've been followed and watched, that's what I think."

"Yeah, me too!"

"Let's get back in the car and see what they want."

"Sounds like a plan," he said, snapping his fingers.

The driver of the Lincoln, with the driver's side window rolled down halfway, was able to distinguish exactly what they were up to. Through the binoculars, he was able to make out the female removing something from the ground and placing it in a bag. "Oh *shit*," he said, as he turned away, grabbed for his cell phone from the passenger seat, dialed, raised it to his ear, and waited.

When it was answered, he heard Alpha speaking. *"What do you have to report, Bravo?"*

"Sir, they found something."

A brief pause.

Alpha said, *"Did you have time to see what it was?"*

"No, sir, I was too far to see what they found. Only that it was a small object. I believe they found a bullet casing, sir."

"Oh," Alpha said, sounding annoyed but not concerned.

"What do you want me to do, sir?"

"Retrieve whatever they found, no matter the cost."

"Do you want me to eliminate them?"

"That's the general idea, Bravo."

Bravo nodded, swallowed, and ended the conversation. He pulled out his M-4 Carbine Assault Rifle, drew back the slide, making sure a round was chambered, turned the selector switch to full automatic fire, and placed it on his lap. He waited for the Chevy to pull away before he made his move.

As the sun was slowly setting in the west, Sinclair reached for her Beretta 9mm and placed it on her lap. She wasn't sure if she needed it, but better to be prepared than not. Agent Price acknowledging what she had done, said, "Ah *shit*." And removing his Colt .45 ACP and holding it in his right hand, he stared straight ahead. Not what he wanted, a fight, but if push comes to shove, he was prepared to kick some ass. Oh yeah!

Shifting into drive, and with her foot on the brake, Sinclair glanced behind her. And, there, perfectly framed against the dying sun, was the black SUV. She glanced over at Price. When he looked back at her, he had a smile on his handsome face.

"You ready?" she whispered. "Hope this turns out well for both of us."

She pulled out onto the road, drove up about ten feet, twisted the steering hard to the left, and accomplished a 180-degree turn on burning rubber.

Now, they were facing the SUV.

"Damn," he said, "that was so cool."

"Thanks, learned it from my Dad."

"Ah, a while back I looked over your personnel file."

"And?"

"Well, is there anything you can't do?"

"None I'm aware of," she said with a smile.

At that moment, they set their full attention on the SUV.

—Chapter Five—

A gent Sinclair stiffened for a moment, her eyes lit up. For in front of her, less than a quarter of a mile straight ahead, the SUV was pointed straight at them. She relaxed and prepared herself for the inevitable.

She'd brought the Chevy to a stop as soon as she completed the turnabout. With the Chevy in low gear, foot on the brakes, both hands on the steering wheel, she watched as the SUV shot forward coming straight for them! Yard by yard, the SUV closed the distance. Releasing her foot on the brakes, she stomped down on the accelerator. With stretching, burning tires, the Chevy responded, as it shot forward, ready to meet the threat head-on.

It was a reckless answer to the driver of the SUV, who wasn't expecting her to respond in kind.

So be it. Recklessness was her only way to counter and confront his action.

Agent Price's face was a mask. He gave nothing away to show he was scared shitless.

In an instant, the stutter of automatic weapons fire cut through the air. Agent Price, with his window already rolled down, and bringing his 'A' game, stuck his Colt out the window and opened fire on the SUV. Sinclair hesitated for a moment. She understood what her next step was—stop the killer before they collided. "But how?" she muttered.

Price kept staring at Sinclair and back to the SUV. "Did you say something?"

"No."

They stood to lose their lives in the next few seconds, however, she would fight until her dying breath. Agent Sinclair hoped it wouldn't come to that.

Neither agent's gaze left the oncoming vehicle.

Agent Sinclair, with her 9mm on her lap, picked it up with her left hand, stuck it outside the window and unloaded five continuous rounds into the cab of the oncoming SUV.

It only took a nano-second for both vehicles to close the gap on each other.

The peaceful, quiet scene was instantly turned into a killing ground as automatic weapon fire flew, whistling death through the air, into the Chevy, and all around them.

The firing stopped for a brief second.

They stared at each other for about one breath and concentrated back on the SUV.

A second later, another burst of fire from the SUV struck the Chevy, peppering the windshield with so many bullet holes she was unable to see through it. Bullets thudded onto the hood of the Chevy and the ground in front. As she moved her head slightly left, another bullet whistled past—too damn close to taking her head off and thudded into the rear window, shattering it to pieces.

"That . . . was too fucking close!" she muttered.

Having ejected a spent magazine, Price quickly replaced a new one, cocked back the slide, and was ready to fire once again. Glancing over at Sinclair, he saw what Sinclair was about to do. "Don't play chicken with him, Sinclair!" he yelled out to her. "Cut across the driver's side and let me shoot the son-of-a-bitch."

Sinclair's Chevy would not withstand the impact the big SUV would no doubt deliver. That thought ran through her mind even as Price warned her.

Agent Price sustained a gunshot wound on his left shoulder, and as the impact jerked him back on the seat he roared, "son-of-a-bitch!", as blood seeped down his arm.

Sinclair yelled, "Are you hit?"

Price, sweeping off a large coating of broken glass from about his jacket and shirt, said, "It's nothing, a flesh wound, keep going."

All at once, she saw her chance and did as Price suggested. The SUV was prepared to collide head-on, but she wasn't. At the point when the two vehicles would collide, she swerved away, making a hard right. She was a little too late in her maneuver as the SUV struck a glancing blow to the left side of the Chevy, sending it spinning off to the left.

The spinning was heaven sent.

Gaining control of the spinning Chevy, Agent Sinclair kept it close to the side of the SUV. And, as the SUV driver's window appeared, and before streaking on by, Agent Sinclair released her right hand off the steering wheel, quickly picked up her 9mm, and watched as the SUV's driver glanced down at her. Firing across her body, she unloaded the rest of her magazine at him.

And, in that same instant, Agent Price pointed his Colt through the driver's window as he too peppered the driver.

With full control of the Chevy again, she screeched to a complete stop just as Price reloaded his Colt. Wheeling around in her seat, Sinclair looked for the SUV.

"Where the hell is he?" she said. "See him anywhere?"

"I see taillights way up ahead," he said. "We may have wounded the driver, or he would stay to finish us."

She said, "I'm sure we put a couple of bullets into him."

"Yeah!"

Sinclair turned the car around and took off after the SUV.

The attack had only lasted less than a minute—and the chase was on.

But it wasn't to be.

Try as she would, she wasn't able to catch up to the SUV. Ten minutes later, they reached a fork in the road—one left, one right. They looked and did not catch any taillights from either side.

Sinclair pulled off to the side of the road and reloaded her weapon.

Agent Price opened his door and, swinging his legs out, stood with a wince and walked a few feet away from the car. Removing his jacket, he slid his hand down his back-pocket and came away with a handkerchief. He tied it around the wound, stopping for now the flow of blood. With the bullet still lodged in his arm and no way to remove it, he didn't spend time worrying about it. He'd been shot before while serving in Afghanistan, entrenched with US Special Forces Operators. Nothing to worry about, for now, he figured.

Agent Sinclair came up behind him. "How you doing?"

"I'll be alright. A little prick, bleeding stopped, nothing to worry about."

She smiled. "Who said I was worried."

He just grinned.

She said, "Well, let's head on back and let a doctor look you over." She turned to face him. "That's enough excitement for one night, don't you think?"

Turning to face her head-on, he said, "I'm getting the distinct impression that someone . . . doesn't want us on this case."

She said, "I have to agree. We need to keep a better watch on our . . . *Six*."

"Bet your ass I will," he said grinning.

* * *

With her back against the damp wall, stretched out on the cold damp floor, Helen Chapman woke and realized her bindings had been removed. When was that done? She had no inkling. They may have drugged her bread or water and entered her cell when she unconscious. She still was in darkness, but over to her left, her eyes caught the glitter of light—small, but there.

The very subdued lighting came from the wall on her left, down by the ground. It was a small opening where someone pushed through a plate of hard bread, a little meat, and water to wash it all down. When they came with the food, she tried yelling and talking, but no one replied. No one entered her small dungeon since being thrown in it while she was awake. No one called out her name. But several hours ago, she sensed far away crying and the rattle of keys. Followed by silence once again.

She cried again and, wiping her tears, she was cognizant of all the details since Billy was killed. She thought so much of her father, now worried sick about her. And it was all her fault. If she hadn't gone out that night, all this wouldn't have happened, she reasoned. She remembered when her mother passed, how hard her father had reacted.

At one point, she stood and walked the circumference of her cell and figured she was in a ten-by-ten room. Her examination revealed only a small door, no windows, nothing to suggest where she was being kept.

She was never a brave girl and never wanted to do the things her father wanted of her: fishing, hunting and shooting, among other activities. She wanted to be alone. Well now she was, and the loneliness and isolation were taking their toll on her. She wished now she'd followed his request.

Her continued sense of loneliness caused her heart to thunder in her chest, her mind befogged with the terrors of the unknown, as sleep, at the moment, was unthinkable.

She developed an uncontrollable bout of coughing that she attributed to the coldness. They had removed her jacket, leaving her with her thin blouse to keep her warm. No shoes either. She lay on the cold hard floor and, when sleep finally came, she fell into a fitful restless sleep, dreaming the worst.

In three separate cells, resembling Helen's, and down a long wide cavern, as dark as night, were three other captives. The cavern's entrance was narrow but, down the passage, it grew larger. It was cold in the hallways of the cavern. With the loss of all time, they were unable to tell how long they'd been in their cells.

Why were they kept in cells? Who had done this, and most important, will they be killed? These were their thoughts that kept running through their minds, hour after hour. They felt like trapped rats.

Desperation, fear, and the sense of helplessness had helped them fall into a fitful sleep.

In one cell was Lisa Schaffer, described as an exquisite, petite, young woman and the best looking of the girls being held.

It was to this cell that two men walked carrying a lantern. At the door of her cell, one inserted a key and unlocked it. They walked in and closed the door behind them. The one with the lantern placed it by the door and eyed the fifteen-year-old. The black-clad guards stood side by side a few feet from her.

Scared, she asked, "What do you want? Please leave me alone!"

One guard, a tall black man licking his lips, replied, "You, baby."

She went speechless, aghast, and her eyes lit up wide.

They were at her feet, and to her horror, she became aware of what they planned to do.

She yelled and screamed and tried to push away from them.

The other guard looked down at her body and said, "Scream all you want, honey, no one's going to hear ya."

But someone did.

Helen Chapman sat straight; something woke her. Her head cocked to one side, listening. Someone was yelling and screaming, but she wasn't sure. It had sounded as if it came from far away—a little louder than a whisper.

Chapman yelled at the top of her voice, hoping someone would respond. No one did.

Then she wondered whether there were others like her in cells, being held for purposes unknown. She kept praying she would get to see her father again and end her nightmare.

Cradling her head in her arms, she stretched back on the hard, cold floor. She kept her eyes wide open, but sleep finally overcame her.

* * *

Sergeant Alfonso White, the driver of the black Lincoln Navigator, an ex-US Army Ranger, was shot four times: left arm, right shoulder, upper chest, and a scalp wound on his left side. He was bleeding and needed to get back to the rest of the group. However, he guessed, in his current state, he wouldn't make it that far.

White reached across his seat and found his cell phone. Ready to dial, the cell phone sounded. He recognized the number and accepted the call. An angry voice buzzed in the earpiece, *"Why haven't you reported in, Bravo?"*

"Been hit bad, sir. Don't think I'll be able to make it."

"Where are you?"

White gave him his approximate location and turned on the phone's GPS function.

Alpha said, *"I'll have someone sent to you."*

"Thank you, sir."

Without panic, or even mild concern, he was slowly dying. His heart rate was slowly decreasing. His time was almost up. Funny, he lived through three tours in Afghanistan and Iraq, wounded twice, and for what, to die here all alone.

He turned his gaze upwards toward the setting sun as he felt himself growing weak from loss of blood.

His one thought was of his late wife. "Honey, I'm coming to be with you soon."

He leaned back on his seat and waited.

* * *

Two hours later, another Lincoln Navigator pulled up behind White's SUV. Two young looking men and an older man, comprising Charlie Team, emerged from the vehicle, with holstered 9mm Glocks at their sides and dressed in casual clothing. The older man, a dark-skinned fellow with a scar on his face, approached the driver's side door of White's vehicle, while the two younger men kept watch.

As he opened the door, he found White slumped over the steering wheel. He checked his pulse and confirmed White's passing. Walking around toward the passenger side, he opened the door, and removed all weapons, cell phone, and anything else that would identify White. He removed the license plates. Then back around to the body, he removed White's wallet, and stored the items in his SUV. From the passenger side, he opened the door and pulled out a can of gasoline.

Back to White's vehicle, he splashed the Navigator with the gas, and threw gas onto White's body. After emptying the gas can, he stood back and pulled out his cigarette lighter, threw it into the cab of the SUV and watched as it burst into flames.

With the flames engulfing the vehicle and satisfied with his work, they got back into the SUV and drove away from the scene.

* * *

And, at the moment that Sergeant Alfonso White's SUV went up in flames, Alpha-Two Colonel Godfrey Randall, the second in command of the complex and operations, and Major Edward Ross, in charge of Delta team performing their mission, wearing their battle dressed uniforms, stood in the communications room in the upper floor of the missile silo. Nearby, a uniformed radio operator, Corporal Raul Sanchez continued to monitor the operations unfolding miles away, as Sanchez, whispered into his headset microphone:

"—Charlie Team, advise your present situation—"

"—Roger, Charlie Team reports Bravo has been neutralized—"

"—Roger that. Return to base—"

"—Delta Team, report your progress—"

"—Roger, Delta Team leader with teams 1, 2, and 3 are airborne and should arrive in position in ten minutes—"

"—Roger, advise once you're landed—"

"—Copy that—"

One-hundred-fifty miles east of Stuttgart, the Sikorsky UH-60 Blackhawk copter, armed with missiles, rockets, machine guns and 20mm cannons, and with its low detectability and outstanding nap-of-the-earth capabilities, flew over the late evening German landscape in relative silence.

The helicopter's cabin provided for eleven fully equipped troops. But today it carried nine black-clad fully equipped combat troops under the command of Captain Earl Chambers, the Delta team leader and his three teams. Armed with M-4 combat assault weapons with its M203 over and under grenade launcher and other assorted weapons, they all knew what the mission entailed.

Decreasing its air speed, the pilot keyed his mic and informed the Delta Team Leader that they were within three minutes from target.

The target was the US Army Theatre Logistics Support Center, which housed the Army's ammunition depot at Miesau, Germany, located approximately 156 miles east of Stuttgart.

Prior arrangements were made with a low-level air-controller at the base with the monetary compensation in the sum of twenty-thousand dollars for his part in the operations—that of allowing the Blackhawk's landing authorization.

"Blackhawk 619'ner request landing instruction, over," the pilot said over the mic, as it neared the depot outside perimeter and with the control tower within visual sight.

"*Copy that, 619'ner,*" a voice replied over his earpiece. "*Authorization for landing is confirmed, over.*"

"Roger that."

Once over the logistics support base, the copter flew another mile and spotted the depot's main entrance to the facility. Before touching ground, the pilot brought the helicopter into hovering position a few seconds and slowly brought it down in a whirlwind of sand two hundred yards away.

At the moment the chopper's tires touched the ground, nine troopers leaped out and ran about twenty paces from the chopper, as Team-One assumed combat security posture with their weapons pointing to the outside of the Blackhawk, as the other two teams ran to within twenty feet of the main entrance.

No sentries were stationed in the depot, and there was only a two-man motorized unit that patrolled the outer perimeter of the depot. Minutes after landing, a light-armored Humvee vehicle rounded the far corner to the depot with its headlights on high beam—the patrol unit.

As the patrol approached the helicopter and as it stopped in front of it, Teams 2 and 3, surrounded the Humvee, opened both its front doors, and shot and killed the two guards before uttering a single word. The only sound came from the suppressors attached to their weapons. With the quiet kill over, they ran to their assigned positions. Delta Team already knew the lay of the depot. They'd trained in a mock situational environment a week in advance.

Once in place, they waited for their orders.

"—Delta Team to base—" Captain Earl Chambers spoke into his mic.

"—Go, Delta, this is base—"

"—Landed, two guards neutralized, no other problems—"

"—Roger, Delta Team. All teams report—"

"—Team one—"

"—Roger, in position awaiting orders—"

"—Team two—"

"—Roger, Team two in position awaiting orders—"

"—Team three—"

"—Roger, Team three in position awaiting orders—"

"—Roger, Delta teams stand by for further orders—"

Sanchez slowly turned and faced Alpha-Two who was standing just to the right and behind him.

"Sir," Sanchez said, "all teams are in place and waiting your instructions."

"Give them the go-ahead, corporal."

"Yes, sir."

Back facing his communications array, Sanchez keyed his mic. "All Teams proceed as planned. The operation is a go."

"—Roger that, Delta Team confirmation received and understood—"

Alpha-Two said, "Corporal, continue to monitor their progress and report to Major Ross once they've completed their mission and are airborne."

"Yes, sir."

A minute later, team-two approached the gate. A trooper, carrying a pair of bolt cutters, stepped to the gate, cut through the gate's chains that secured the doors, and opened the six-foot high gates to either side as teams three and one entered the depot. They knew where they needed to go.

Running along the main street, they came to a bunker with many warning signs and some with nuclear signs and symbols. The bunker's entrance had an electronic door access control device with a deadbolt keypad. Another trooper attached a device to it, hooked up two pairs of blue and red wires to the timing device, and when the three blinking lights turned green, he disarmed it. They pushed the doors in and walked through.

They found the section housing exactly what they had come for. Their prize was two B61-12 Nuclear "Smart" bombs out of four in view. Each weighed 3kg and was capable of penetrating fortified structures several meters underground. Also taken were two 50-kiloton bullet-shaped silver warheads and two guided tail kit assemblys for GPS guidance. Once they loaded the bombs and the assembly kits onto a truck, they drove it to the copter. Loading them on took fifteen minutes.

They waited for one last trooper assigned to neutralize the air-controller. He arrived within two minutes as the copter was warming up for lifting.

Slowly the helicopter rose and, achieving sufficient altitude, the pilot turned it heading west.

"—Delta leader to base—"

"—Base here, Delta leader—"

"—Roger, airborne with two packages—"

"—Roger that—"

—Chapter Six—

At twenty minutes past nine that same evening, Agent Jacqueline Sinclair, dressed in an elegant red Maxi V neck Chiffon cocktail dress, and Captain Jeffrey Cory, in his best black suit and white shirt—the Company Commander of a local Stuttgart-based Logistics Readiness Company and in-country for the last year—were sitting at a table of the prestigious Christophorus Restaurant just off of Porscheplatz, in the city of Stuttgart.

When he'd picked her up at her apartment, just before nine, her beauty spellbound him. "You're looking wonderful and exquisite. The dress flatters every inch of you."

"Thank you," she said with a smile.

Then she put her head down as Cory held her hand.

She looked up at him, giving him a warm smile.

He leaned in slowly, reached out, and held her in his embrace. They kissed passionately for a long minute; as one, they melted into each other.

Sinclair broke her trance first. Breathless, she sighed, "I think we should go."

Cory didn't reply right away. "Yes . . . yes, I think we should."

At the restaurant, Captain Cory planned a nice quiet evening together with soft romantic music playing in the back from a live three-piece band. It wasn't the first time he'd set foot in the restaurant, so he was sure what this high-class establishment offered.

When the waiter came, he ordered them both the Schwartz Rinderroula Roulade, a special beef entrée, served with mashed potatoes, sautéed in butter and sour cream. For drinks, he ordered a bottle of J.J. Prum, Wehlener Sonneauhi Riesling, a white wine, perfect with its fresh fruity delicate flavor, served chilled.

The meal, he hoped wouldn't be too filling but just enough to get them through. He had other plans for them later in the evening once they were in his apartment, and he didn't want a heavy meal to spoil things.

After the waiter brought the wine, he poured both of their glasses. The Captain lifted his glass to her. "To the most beautiful woman I've ever had the most profound pleasure of knowing," he said, taking a sip of the wine.

"You're certain I'm as beautiful as you say?" she asked, blushing.

"Nothing in life is certain. But, in this, I am."

Sinclair grinned and reached for her glass of wine.

After their meals, she asked, "Do you have any other plans for us tonight?"

"Yes, but I have only one question," he replied. "Would you like to come up to my place for a nightcap?"

She said, "Unh-uh, let's go to mine."

* * *

It was almost 10:30 when she unlocked the door to her apartment; she pushed Cory through and started taking off his suit jacket and untucking his shirt, as he too was doing the same to her dress. He fumbled for the zipper and quickly unzipped her.

Slamming the door closed behind them, he pulled down her dress, exposing her bra, and as he reached to undo the bra's clasps, a loud knocking came from the front door.

She nuzzled him away. "Who the hell . . .?"

"Oh, for Christ's sake" . . . Straightening out her dress, she approached the door and, opening it a crack, saw Agent Price with his hands in his pockets wearing a solemn face.

She then held the door wide open, and they stared at each other for a second.

"Well, look at you," he said arching his brow as he stared at her dress. "Beautiful, am I disturbing something?"

"What do you want, Price? And how the hell did you get my address?" Sinclair said, confused by his appearance.

"I want you, Sinclair," he said, as in a whisper, "but not in the way I would care for right now."

"What?"

"Never mind," he said, shrugging.

From inside the apartment, Captain Jeffrey Cory yelled out, "Who the blazes is at the door at this time of night, Belle?"

She said, "Hang on, Jeffrey. It's my partner."

"Belle?" Price asked arching a brow.

"Never mind that."

"I need to talk to you," Price said. "There's been a development in the case."

"You know," she said, "I have a phone, right?"

"Yes, I do. But this is more fun."

Sinclair frowned. "*Shit*, come in then. Hey, shouldn't you be lying in bed after the bullet was removed from your arm?" she asked.

"Yeah, about that," he said. "Doc wanted to place my arm in a sling, but I didn't want him to."

She nodded and shrugged.

"Jeffrey, this is Agent Tom Price, we work together," she said by way of an introduction.

Price glanced over at Jeffrey Cory, as if he'd seen him for the first time. "Sorry to mess up your evening, dude," he said, not unsympathetically.

"Yeah," Cory said, with an edge to his voice. "State what you came for and leave."

Disregarding his tone of voice and what he'd said, Agent Price glanced at Sinclair.

"The German police found our SUV from tonight, dead body and all. Thought maybe we go on over before they impound it."

"Holy *shit*, damn right, I'll go."

She turned to face the Captain. "Sorry, Jeffrey, work. Please call me tomorrow."

"*Shit!*" Cory said.

Agent Price cracked a small smile as he turned away from them. His question as to a boyfriend was answered.

Cory stared at Price. Then something she'd said finally hit him. He said, "Hey, wait . . . what bullet?"

A half hour later as she drove fast across the city, heading east, she glanced over at Agent Price.

"Ah, Price," she asked. "How did you get my address?"

A ghost of a smile spread across his face as he sat in the passenger seat. "I made a few calls, here and there."

"Oh, was one of those to my father?"

Price cocked his head away from her. "Ain't telling," he said.

Without another word, Sinclair already knew he'd called her father. No one else at her office would have given him her address.

When they arrived, German police and US Army military police were on the scene along with a coroner's vehicle, as personnel crawled all over the SUV, collecting what evidence they could find. Several men wearing plastic gloves and holding evidence bags moved away from the burned-out vehicle as Sinclair and Price approached, and coming to a stop, she parked behind an MP squad car.

Even before getting out of their car, their eyes fell to the SUV for a moment.

Price said, "Think that's the one?"

"Well," she replied, "not too many Lincoln's in this part of the woods."

Getting out of her new Chevy, Sinclair approached an MP, showed him her shield, ducked under the yellow tape surrounding the scene, and told Price to follow her. There was no wind to bring the unmistakable stench of decaying, burned human flesh to their nostrils. Only when they were close to the SUV did they breathe in its unpleasant but unique smell. But it was the same lingering horror they'd both encountered back in the war.

Something they would never get used to.

Approaching the senior MP, she asked, "So, what have you found so far, Sergeant?"

"Not much, ma'am," the Sergeant said. "The body is unrecognizable, only that it's a male."

"Thanks. I'll take it from here, Sergeant," she said. "Oh, do any of the German police speak English?"

"Yes, ma'am. Two of them do."

She approached one of the German policemen. "Do you speak English?"

"Yes, I do."

"Good, I would like to be present once your people conduct an autopsy on the body. Here is my card; can someone please call me at the listed number?"

"Will do what we can, fraulein," the officer said with a smile.

Returning his smile, she replied, "Vielen Dank, thank you so much."

Agent Sinclair reached into her pockets and pulled out a notebook and a pencil and jotted down her observations. The moment she finished, she joined Price at the front of the SUV, and did a complete walk around it.

She said, "See what I see so far?"

"Oh, yeah, just a burned-out SUV with a dead body in it."

"*Shit*, I keep forgetting you're not a cop," she said. "Okay, there are no license plates, and none lying on the ground. The back window is riddled with bullet holes and the windshield too."

"Okay, and?"

"Let's look inside."

"Oh, come on, do we have to?"

"Why don't you go stay with the MPs?"

"Good idea," he said as he walked away from her.

Fetching a sigh, Sinclair pocketed her notebook and pencil.

She'd already guessed she wouldn't find much of anything in the vehicle, but she needed to go through the motions anyway.

Coming around to the front of the vehicle, she stared inside through the open driver's door. Everything was charred to a crisp, all black. She donned a pair of blue-colored plastic gloves and searched the body for anything to identify it with—front pocket, back pockets, nothing, not even a wallet.

Shit, she thought, so far someone had cleaned out the body pretty well. Next, she stepped on the running board and looked deeper into the cab. During the attack on her and Price, the guy used automatic firing mode when he'd started shooting. So, searching with only her eyes, she did not come up with any bullet casings. There were no weapons left in the cab either.

"They were very thorough," she muttered.

Coming down from the running board, she started walking to the left side of the windshield, the part that housed a silver metal strip about three inches long and about half-an-inch wide—the VIN or vehicle identification number plate. But she only found a large burned out hole in its place.

"Fuck," she said under her breath.

Bending and kneeling, she rummaged around on the ground, next to the burned-out front tire.

She yelled out, "Hey, Price, bring me a flashlight from my bag."

Once Price brought over the flashlight, he kneeled down beside her. "What are we looking for?"

She said, "Silver strip of metal with the VIN number to the SUV."

As he swung the flashlight through, its beam struck something shining for a second.

"There," she said. "There, toward my right side."

Price said, "Okay, I see it."

Extending her arm through, Sinclair could not reach it. Then lying prone on the ground, she pushed herself closer and was able to retrieve the silver metal. Shifting her gaze some, she caught sight of another piece of thick silvery metal underneath some burned out plastic.

Once again reaching out, she grabbed the item with two fingers and pulled it away from the burned metal pieces. In her hand, she could see it was a Zippo cigarette lighter. She straightened herself back up, pulled out two plastic bags from her pocket, placed the items in separate bags, and transferred them into her pocket, before making sure no one was watching. She wanted her own lab to scan through it.

Getting back to Agent Price, they walked toward the MPs.

Reaching them, and stopping by the MP Sergeant, she said, "I want a full report once you get back to the MP station."

"Yes, ma'am."

As Agents Price and Sinclair walked back to her Chevy, Price said, "You know, as an afterthought, whatever someone is cooking up, it's a hell of a lot more important than you or I could imagine."

"I hope you're wrong, for both our sakes."

Then back in her Chevy, they headed to the CID office to write her report and submit the evidence to the crime lab.

—Chapter Seven—

Nazi Missile Launch Facility–the Silo
One-hundred-forty-one Miles East of Stuttgart, Germany

"There comes a time, when 'We' the people cannot timidly abide or stand idly on the sidelines as our government cannot or will not protect American citizens from the corrupt and or terrorist nations around the globe," he said as his baritone voice echoed throughout and carried across the large room. "I quote from the words of Julius Caesar: 'The difference between a republic and an empire is the loyalty of one's army.'

"Gentlemen, all of you gathered here tonight," he continued, looking around at the faces of his seven staff officers, "it was a disgrace, and the indecisiveness on the part of our government, including our great military generals, not to act in a timely and direct manner in requesting the release of my son . . . but not just my son, others that are being held by that regime.

"Time after time I'd requested our leaders in the White House and the State Department to have my son released from captivity by the North Korean Government. The EUCOM command and its generals are just as much at fault as the North Koreans for the capture, torture, and ultimate death of my son, as they persistently refused to intervene through military and or diplomatic channels."

There was a short pause as he looked at those gathered around the large conference room. They were there more for the money than for the speaker's revenge, but they all also owed their loyalty and trust to him.

"All of you here are being compensated in the amount of one million dollars each for your assistance and loyalty. We have faithfully served our government through the years. Some of you have lost loved ones, some have issues and complaints. I'm here to help with all that. You have all pledged to assist me in my endeavor, and for that I am grateful."

The conference room located underground in an old abandoned Nazi missile silo, used in the development of the V-2 rocket program, was the perfect place he'd chosen to begin his plans. The silo complex was underground and surrounded by two-foot-thick walls of solid granite. It used only one gate for vehicles and personnel coming in or going out.

A quarter of a mile into the complex was a ramp leading down into a large cavern that housed vehicles and equipment. A large wide winding path led to the main storage room and, to the right, a larger tunnel leading to the personnel living quarters.

Sitting around a huge oaken desk were his staff officers, seven all highly loyal men, combat tested, one and all. And, under their command, twenty men and women, vehicles, and highly sophisticated radio and communications equipment, weapons, and ammunition, which made up the bulk of the force under the command and control of Alpha.

Alpha, his current name, and a former Army brigadier general named Thomas Randolph Scott, had been assigned as a staff officer at USEUCOM, Stuttgart, Germany until his retirement following the death of his son, Jason Randolph Scott. And, for the past two years, he'd waited patiently as he planned, coordinated, and recruited loyal ex-soldiers from several units which he'd commanded.

He buried his wife just days after their son's burial; she had committed suicide, unable to cope after the death of their son. With no other living family left, he turned his full attention to his task. His task did not call for the deaths of American servicemen, unless it was necessary, but he would make a few of them pay in other ways.

It wasn't revenge per se, to the General. No eye for an eye, a tooth for a tooth, or the law of retaliation. No. This was blood for blood! And he would collect every ounce he could.

"Gentlemen, now that phase one is complete," he continued, "we set our tasks posthaste into phase two."

At the mention of phase two, all eyes centered on the general.

They all knew what phase two entailed. They waited for confirmation and or additions and deletions to the proposed plan.

As this was being discussed, from a darkened room in a smaller office, a soldier in military uniform was listening to chatter while wearing a radio headset and seated cross-legged in front of his computer communications array. Information was being relayed on the German Police radio band, about a burned-out SUV and a burned-out body found with it. He relayed the information to another soldier in the room, his runner, who immediately stood from his chair and ran to the conference room.

Once there, he saw his superior officer, and quickly coming up to him, whispered his information into his ear.

The officer, a major, stood and said, "Sir, German authorities found the SUV and the body of Sergeant White."

General Scott stared at the staff officer for a moment. "Was everything removed from the body and the vehicle that could be traced back to us?"

The colonel on his right replied. "Yes, sir, it was."

"Then, everything is going according to plan," the general said.

"Sir," the colonel said. "I have some other business you should know which requires your action."

"What is it, Colonel?"

"Sir," he said while standing. "It's been reported that one of our female captives has been molested by two of our men."

The staff member to the right of the general leaned over and whispered in the General's ear. "We have the two waiting just outside the conference room, sir."

"Very well, bring them in. And Captain Rose," he said to another staff member who stood and glanced at his commander, "would you approach, please."

Captain Jerome Rose, a tall, powerfully built young man, with a bull neck and broad shoulders and wearing a low-slung holstered Beretta 9mm on his right hip, hastily made his way toward the general. Once there, Rose stood behind and to the left of the general and waited.

The two accused men entered the conference room. Both were blindfolded, with hands tied behind their backs, as two guards on either side escorted them with guns at the ready.

"Sir," the colonel said. "These two men stand accused of repeatedly raping a fifteen-year-old female hostage."

Kneeling behind and to the left of the general, the two prisoners faced the assembled officers, heads held to the ground. And behind them stood Captain Rose, with his Beretta held in his right hand ready to carry out his order, if and when it came.

The General said, "You all know the penalty for disobeying my orders written into your contracts; none of our captives were to be harmed, unless I say so."

No one said anything.

"Captain," the General said, "Please begin."

Standing behind one, then the other prisoner, Captain Rose removed their blindfolds. He lifted his weapon, held it about two inches from the back of the first prisoner's head, and fired one round. It was loud and sudden, *Boom!,* the prisoner's body convulsed and shuddered from the impact of the steel-jacketed 9mm hollow-point bullet, as the front of his head exploded in a burst of red, with skin and brain matter spraying onto the ground in front of the body. Slowly, it collapsed in a heap to the ground.

The second prisoner having seen his partner killed, yelled his lungs out, and tried to rise. Forced down by his guards, Captain Rose came up behind him, lifted his gun, and fired. The prisoner suffered the same fate.

After the bodies had been removed, the meeting continued as if nothing had happened.

Once Phase-Two had been talked about back and forth between them, the signal to move forward was given.

"Sir," the colonel said, "There is one more point of business at hand, that of CID Agent Jacqueline Sinclair and her partner Agent Tom Price. What would you have us do with them?"

The General asked, "Do you have something in mind, Colonel?"

"Yes, sir, with your permission, I have a sergeant, a sniper, Ranger trained, proficient in killing, and well versed in surveillance that could keep tabs on those two, and if they get too close to our operations, he's authorized to kill them and anyone else privy to our interest."

"Very well, set it in motion and keep me informed."

A brief silence.

"Is there any other business at hand?" the general asked.

The colonel, the General's second in command, said, "Sir, the two items and all the equipment for it arrived this evening."

"Excellent, Colonel," Scott said, "just what I needed to hear. Please have our two technicians begin their work on them."

"I have already taken care of it, sir."

"Also, Colonel, activate Operational Order D and advise our operative to start close surveillance on Agent Sinclair," Alpha said, and added, "With two pair of eyes on her, I should know what her moves will be and prepare for them."

"Yes, sir."

—Chapter Eight—

Friday - August 9

With a brilliant early autumn morning, the air crisp and the sky a cloudless blue, they were clear to fly.

The helicopter lifted gently and hovered a few feet above the helipad for an instant, as the pilot checked in with the air traffic control tower. The chopper taxied along and, within seconds, as it slowly gathered speed and height, it took to the skies.

The teardrop-shaped Bell OH-58 Kiowa copter named after a Native American tribe, nicknamed the LOH or Light Observation Helicopter and in service since 1968, had been used for the first time during the Vietnam War to draw out ground fire for the elite Cobra helicopter gunships.

But today it carried one government agent. Although the copter was unarmed for this trip, its distinctive wop-wop-wop sound thundered through the early morning silence over the German landscape at a safe cruising speed of one-hundred-fifty-five mph.

The agent needed to be at the LRMC, Landstuhl Regional Hospital Center, in Kaiserslautern by eight that morning. He checked the time on his instrument panel - seven o'clock. He should have her there in thirty minutes at his present cruising speed.

The pilot turned to his occupant, a woman in civilian dress, and said over the mic. "Should have you there about seven-thirty, ma'am."

"Thank you," Agent Jacqueline Sinclair said through her helmet's mic.

With sufficient time to go through what she and Agent Price had discovered so far, she placed her briefcase on her lap, and pulled out her iPad. Poking through the tablet, she reviewed the photos of the two deceased American dependents shot and killed at the crime scenes. But with nothing else to see, nothing to find, the autopsy and what it would reveal were the only clues beyond going through photos and reports.

She shrugged but continued to review the reports.

At exactly seven-thirty-two they arrived on top of the hospital helipad. The pilot mentioned to his passenger that he'd be waiting for her return trip, no matter how long she stayed.

She nodded and, removing her flight helmet, she left it on the seat, grabbed her briefcase, and stepped out of the Kiowa.

A female hospital staff member met her and escorted her into the hospital.

The LRMC opened in 1953 and is the largest American hospital outside the United States in the German state of Rheinland-Pfalz, six miles west of Kaiserslautern and three miles south of Ramstein Air Force Base.

It provides primary and tertiary specialized care and hospitalization and medical treatment for over fifty-two thousand local American military personnel and their families. It also provides specialized care for over two-hundred-thousand additional American personnel and their families in the European Theater of Operations.

The staff of the hospital comprises fifty percent Army, fifteen percent Air Force, and thirty-five percent civilian personnel. The hospital has over one-hundred physicians, two-hundred nurses, forty Medical Service Corps officers, nine-hundred enlisted personnel, and five-hundred civilian employees.

Serving as the primary medical treatment center for injuries during Operations Desert Shield and Storm, the facility has also treated non-military personnel injuries and is also the treatment point for hundreds of Bosnian refugees injured in the 1994 Sarajevo marketplace bombing, along with the treatment of American and Kenyan victims of the 1998 U.S. Embassy bombing in Nairobi. Also treated, those injured during Operation Enduring Freedom in Afghanistan, and Operation Iraqi Freedom.

Today, Sinclair will witness two autopsies.

Not a shrinking violet, she'd witnessed her share of autopsies in her career. But seeing one ranked low on her list of things to do in an investigation.

And now, back-to-back autopsies were staring her in the face.

Her combat experiences dealing with shot-up bodies gave her a distinct advantage when in an autopsy room. Most agents shy away from it. She'd dealt with violent sudden death scenes and bloody corpses. No problem. But the ever-detached method used in the autopsy room sent a chill up her spine. It's how they took apart the bodies that turned her off. Like as if you'd tuned into Doctor Frankenstein at work—creepy. However, it was a necessary evil that needed to be done, and she understood that.

Each body part needed to be categorized, labeled, and photographed and, in most cases, weighed. Over the years, you got used to all the grim work they did, or you didn't. You have got to have a morbid constitution in the first place to become a forensic pathologist, she reasoned.

Sinclair was dressed in a clinical white gown, with two other people, both alive and kicking, waiting on her. One the pathologist, another the assistant, as two white-sheet-covered bodies lay on the slab waited to be cut-up, dissected, and measured.

Throughout the autopsy, the conducting pathologist recorded all her findings through a microphone held by wire from the ceiling, positioned just above the body being worked upon.

An hour slowly passed, when the body of seventeen-year-old Billy Ackers was ruled a homicide, killed by twelve 9mm steel-jacketed hollow point slugs to various parts of his upper torso, and one, the cause of death, to the head. All the slugs were bagged, labeled, and handed to the investigating officer, Agent Sinclair, for further forensic examination.

The second autopsy on the body of the fifteen-year-old Dennis Jackson began. Again, nothing unusual, and as in the first autopsy, also ruled a homicide. Jackson, who sustained multiple gunshots to the lower extremity, had ten 9mm slugs pulled from the body and were determined to be of the same caliber bullets that had been pulled-out from Ackers. The cause of death, a single shot to the head.

"The autopsies of Billy Ackers and Dennis Jackson are complete," the pathologist finally said into the microphone.

Agent Sinclair checked her watch: 10:30. She'd witnessed back-to-back autopsies, and in her estimation, it took way too long.

Pulling off her gown, facemask and gloves, she dropped them into a dirty clothes bin by the swinging double doors that led into the autopsy room. Then, Agent Sinclair stepped outside the room for a breath of fresh air and into a small waiting lobby, looking for something to drink. The two pathologists followed her out.

Two couples waited for the pathologists in the waiting area, and when they saw them, they all stood and walked up to meet them.

Agent Sinclair, standing by a beverage dispenser with a Coke can in hand saw both women crying, while the men, grieving, appeared shaken, disturbed, and hurt. Holding the two women tight against them, the men tried comforting and calming them.

Once they left, Sinclair walked up to the assistant pathologist and asked, "Who are those people?"

She turned to the Agent and said, "Parents of the deceased."

Sinclair then understood. And understood their pain. Hell, she'd gone through it herself.

Sighing, she knew firsthand what they'd experienced. The emotional anxiety of it still vivid and real to her even though it'd been well over seven years since she'd lost her mother to breast cancer that metastasized to the rest of her body. She loved her mother, but her suffering became too unbearable to watch. When she succumbed to the illness, she felt relieved; relieved that she suffered no more but feeling the pain of losing her early in her young life. She had still not gotten over it, and neither had her father. Her father's face flashed before her then. Sinclair didn't know what she would do if she lost him too.

She'd been close to her mother, always there when Sinclair needed her the most and always giving her sage advice that guided her through the turbulent times known as life.

The Agent remained standing, still deep in thought, for another few minutes. Then, shaking her head, she broke away from her reminiscing.

Sinclair slowly nodded and swallowed.

With the back of her hand she wiped at tears that formed on her eyes.

After she finished her Coke, and with a long sigh, she glanced at her watch—time to get back to work.

The bullets extracted from the bodies needed to be analyzed to determine the weapons used, and if possible, traced back to the killers.

After retrieving her briefcase, she took a slow walk, clearing her mind.

"Yes," she said . . . "a lot of work to do."

In the meantime, she'd debated on staying overnight and leaving early the following day. Putting off her shopping for the last three months, she needed a little time off too.

So, her decision hadn't been all that difficult. She would stay; facial, massage, and shopping for clothes were her aim for the day. And talking on the phone with Captain Cory was also planned.

After advising the copter pilot she'll see him in the morning, she left for the local BOQ Bachelor Officer's Quarters lodging for a night's stay—a hot shower followed by a little fun. But first, she called her father and told him of her plans.

—Chapter Nine—

Missile Silo

The Nazi era Missile Launch Facility, built in 1941, was a vertical cylindrical structure constructed underground and, protecting its main entrance, was a large above-ground double blast door.

Other entrances into the facility consisted of two guarded manholes on either side of the complex, which led into the old missile storage areas. It connected most of the rooms. These storage rooms consisted of a metal door, with no windows.

The deserted silo had overgrown with vegetation, almost to where the entrance itself made it invisible to prying eyes. Purchased two years ago by ex-Brigadier General Thomas R. Scott, known as Alpha under an assumed name, and through a business conglomerate, untraceable to him, unless one dug deep and long.

It also boasted a command-and-control room, the CAC.

In one of the underground rooms, situated at the other end of the complex, stood the CAC and, sitting behind a metal gray desk with phones, a desk-top computer and staring at the monitor, was a stocky no-necked individual, dressed in BDU's, Battle Dress Uniform.

General Scott's second in command, Alpha-Two.

Colonel Godfrey Randall, known as "Alpha-Two", shouldered command responsibilities, including the operational aspects of all three phases of the Alpha's main battle plan. With Phase-One drawing to a close, work and coordination began on Phase-Two.

But Phase-Three required the utmost attention. Everything needed to come together in order for the battle plan to succeed. The equipment and materials for the project had already arrived, and he had two technicians already working on them. A lot more needed to be done before Phase-Three became operational.

The first part of Phase-Two was the delivery of the message to the four generals who maintained total operational control of their area of responsibilities; they would be the unwilling part of the plan. Their guaranteed cooperation rested on the lives of their children. That part of the operation fell to four of his staff members, all highly trained ex-Special Forces operatives, with a special set of skills unique to each.

They'd been tasked to maintain strict surveillance of the targeted generals to ensure complete cooperation, ensuring they not pass vital information as presented in the message, to anyone.

Part-two would come as soon as they received confirmation that all the generals complied and operated in total secrecy.

Alpha-Two, a combat veteran of both theaters of operation, served two tours of duty in both Afghanistan and Iraq. An old man at sixty-seven, he had a round, weather-beaten face, attesting to the continued extreme exposure to the hot environment of the East. With straight-backed black hair and gray at the temples, he stood six-feet tall, broad shouldered, and with huge-calloused hands.

Colonel Godfrey H. Randall, discharged from the US Army just short of twenty-six years of service for conduct unbecoming an officer and charged with the illegal sale of US Army weapons and ammunition, had been sentenced to twenty years in confinement but served only ten of those years. Stripped of his full-bird colonel rank and the forfeiture of all pay and allowances and no visible means of supporting his family, his wife filed for divorce and took their four children with her.

Approached by BG Scott two years ago, he immediately accepted his offer and pay.

With the final contents of the message approved by him and assurances that four copies were made, they were ready!

Finally, the four soldiers' instruction called for their departure at 11:00 hours, the next day.

* * *

The field offices of the Defense Intelligence Agency or DIA were located at the United States Consulate at number forty-five LeitzStrasse, Stuttgart.

Although not on the official directory of the consulate, they were below ground on its second floor. Only six personnel, all civilians, manned the office twenty-four-seven, with one duty agent posted after duty hours and during the weekends.

It was a nice Friday morning, too nice to be in his office, Agent Price thought. What with Agent Sinclair out at Landstuhl hospital attending to the autopsies, he was alone, except for the on-duty Agent Jaime J. Vargas, a highly experienced agent, sitting across the hall.

When he stepped off the elevator, he went straight to his office, located two doors down a wide hallway. He arrived very early and started to work on the list, seeking information on the four generals, and how they fit into the kidnappings, besides being the parents. Something told him the children and their parents' work were somehow connected. He had to find that connection and then find out why them.

He secretly hoped one of his old friends would help him out.

With the Provost Marshal's warning in the back of his mind about not requesting outside agency assistance, he discarded it and made some calls.

He glanced at his watch. Forty minutes had passed, and he was back to square one. Price, with a slight hesitation, made up his mind and placed a call to his last friend who worked at the CIA.

He opened a small notebook that lay on top of his desk by his phone. As he paged through it, he found her number and placed the call, not sure if her number remained active after the last time they were together. His one fear about calling her had to do with their heated separation.

They'd been a couple for three years, and she wanted something more, and he felt a little scared about having that type of commitment. No, not ready for that. However, when she'd thrown all his belongings out the window and told him she didn't want to see or speak to him again, he knew the end had arrived in their relationship.

Agent Price shifted in his chair while waiting for the call to go through and thought of her, an analyst and profiler for the agency. Judith-Mary Mason was twenty-three when they met five years ago, when, straight out of college, she'd been recruited by the CIA because of her dedicated academic work in the field of analytical reasoning and her dissertations on intelligence gathering procedures. A highly intelligent woman with one drawback; she missed out in the common sense department. He'd always being drawn to smart, capable women.

So, he kept his fingers crossed as the phone buzzed in his ear. He pinned his trust that she still lived and worked in Washington; if her cell number is still active after all these years; if she wouldn't hang-up on him.

A lot of ifs to surmount.

But damn, what the hell, nothing ventured, nothing gained, right?

Drumming the fingers of one hand restlessly against the side of the desk, he heard from the other end of the line her soft unmistakable voice, almost a soft purr.

She said, "Hello."

For an instant he just blinked as he listened to her voice once again.

Clearing his throat, Price didn't answer at once, but heard himself say, *act cool, Tom, act cool.*

"Hi, Judith, it's me, Tom Price."

Only silence on the other end. Then he heard a long sigh.

"Jesus. Is that really you, Tom? How are you?"

Act cool kept going through his mind, as old memories flashed through to his consciousness of good times on the beach and in bed. Is there still some sexual tension lingering between them? No, he didn't think so, not with him at least. But he remembered how free they were in exploring and acting out their sexual fantasies.

"Yes, it's me, doing okay for now, ah, and working."

She said, "If you're calling about a possible get-together, you're so late."

Intrigued and curious at the same time, he asked, "Oh, why is that?"

After a short pause, she said, "I'm engaged. Date set for and all."

"That's great news. Congratulations," he said almost feeling relieved at the news. "Who's the lucky man?"

"Someone you don't know."

Leaning back in his chair, he asked, "I see. Are you happy, Judith?"

"Ah, yes . . . yes I am."

"I'm thrilled for you," he said. "Hope married life agrees with you."

"So, I've been hearing your working for the DIA now," she said. "Is that why you're calling, something to do about a case you're working on?"

"Yes, it's the reason I called," he said, noting how quickly she caught on to him. "Damn but it seems like nothing escapes you; I need your help though."

"Okay, tell me all about it."

Price started from the beginning. The kidnapping and the murders, the list of generals, their brush with death, and everything they'd uncovered so far. But he left out one important part, the connection between parents and children. He'd wait for her revelations if there were any forthcoming.

Just have to wait it out, he thought.

"My partner," Price said, "is attending to the autopsies for the two dependent victims as we speak."

"Okay, tell you what," she said, "this is a onetime deal, and I do this for old times' sake." She paused and then said, "Fax me all you have, include that list of yours, and let me see what I can dig up, and I'll shoot you an email as soon as I find something."

"Thank you, Judith. Don't know how to repay you."

She took a deep breath, sighed, and said, "Oh, I'll find a way."

Then, after ending the call, he leaned slightly forward in his chair, ran a hand over his hair, and frowning, muttered, "Wonder what she meant by that?"

—Chapter Ten—

The Silo, That Morning, August 9

At 11:00 hours, the steel-reinforced double-doors leading into the huge storage area of the missile silo slowly opened and, as the doors clanged, fully extended against the sides of the opening, four white late model four-door Chevy Malibu's, each with one occupant, the drivers, slowly emerged and made their way through.

Their destination was Patch Barracks Kaserne, EUCOM military installation, Stuttgart.

A few minutes later and, after making their way through the six-foot chain-link fence-gate left opened for their departure, they drove west for over twenty minutes. They then pulled slowly to the side of the curb and stopped about half a mile from the main autobahn leading to Stuttgart.

The lead vehicle's driver, Captain Jim Steel, the Team-leader in this operation, paused, pressed his throat microphone wrapped around his neck, and whispered into everyone's comm's:

"—All units maintain your two-mile distance between vehicles. Units report in sequence—"

With a finger of his left hand, he touched the earbud on his left ear and waited for their reply.

"—Unit-One, copy and understood—"

"—Unit-Two, copy and understood—"

"—Unit-Three, copy and understood—"

"—Roger and good luck, out—"

They had all been designated separate quarters or a house on the installation and knew the exact layout of those quarters. It was to be a simple in and out scenario that involved a ten-minute interval to complete. But they also charged the Captain with two other places for which he'd be responsible. One of those was the office of CID Agent Sinclair.

Checking for any oncoming traffic, Captain Steel slowly pulled away with a screech of rubber from the curb, heading for the autobahn A5, then to the 81, and onto the 831 to their ultimate destination.

* * *

At that moment, a Bell OH-58 Kiowa helicopter touched ground on the back lawn of the Provost Marshal's office, at Kelley Barracks, Stuttgart.

As the helicopter powered down, Special Agent Jacqueline Sinclair stepped out and felt pleasantly surprised when the PM, her father, waited for her.

As she cleared the rotating rotors of the copter, she approached and stopped in front of him, rendering a hand salute. She said, "Hello, sir."

Returning her salute and giving her a wink, he said, "We have lots to talk about, honey. Let's walk and do that in my office."

"Yes, Dad."

"So, how was your trip?"

"It was so-so," she said, "Learned a lot though."

"Good. I have lunch prepared for us."

"That will be a great. I'm famished."

"Good, thought you would be."

"Oh, Dad, I have several pieces of bags in the copter, I really need to get them to my apartment."

"Tell you what, I'll have my driver take those in for you."

"Thank you."

With a smile on his lips, he said, "Anything for my little girl."

"So, Dad, what brings you out of your office? You didn't come out to be with your daughter, did you?"

"You're knowing me way too well, Belle."

"I should," she said, "been around you all my life."

He glanced at her as they walked into the building. "Yeah, guess you have at that."

Ten minutes later, they were sitting across from each other in his office as his secretary came in carrying a covered serving platter.

After the secretary set the platter on the coffee table between the PM and his daughter, she left and returned with a pitcher of ice tea and glanced at them with a smile, saying, "Enjoy, you two."

With the secretary gone, Sinclair lifted the cover on the serving plate as she reacted to all the cheeseburgers and onion-rings.

"Mmm, they look so good, Dad," Sinclair said, as she picked one up. "You remembered how much I love cheeseburgers."

"Yeah, I remember they'd always been one of your weaknesses, that and pizza."

In between bites she said, "Now who knows whom better?"

For several minutes they ate burger after burger and the onion-rings and gulped down the iced tea, enjoying each other's company. Their conversation so far had been about family and old memories about her mother and his wife as they smiled, joked, and laughed.

They lapsed into silence, each with their own thoughts.

Sinclair sat still in her father's office. It was a very comfortable office, fully furnished, and with the chandelier overhead, the lights gave off a warm cozy glow. Nothing like her office lighting, she thought.

She poured herself one last glass of tea and stared at her father. "So, Dad, what's the story?"

His eyes seemed to bore through her rather than at her

"Would you tell me what you've got so far," he asked, "and where you think your investigation is leading you?"

She shrugged. "What I've got is theories, all unfounded, speculation, and conjecture, guesses, all leading nowhere."

He said nothing but waited on her to elaborate, as he noticed the slight irritation in her voice.

Slowly, as she gathered her thoughts, she closed her eyes momentarily. A second later, she opened them and looked at him.

"Well, to begin with," she said, as she cleared her throat, "I chased a soldier down the stairs in your hallway after I called him out for staring at me and Agent Price. I had to call for back-up from the MPs. Something about him didn't sit right with me. He acted rather suspicious to begin with and, when I called him out, he rabbits and disappears. Later on, Price and I went to the scene of Chapman's abduction. There, I found a bullet casing. I could make out a print but won't know if it's any good until the lab pulls it. While there, a lone gunman attacked us in an SUV."

Pausing long enough to make out his expression, she gazed at him and realized his state of shock. With eyelids wide, his mouth slightly opened, the PM felt pained.

"I—" the PM began, his mouth opened and closed. "Oh crap! Anyone hurt. . . you weren't hurt, were you?"

"No, Dad. Please take it easy. Agent Price got a bullet to his shoulder. But he'll be alright."

After the initial shock wore off, he said, "I'm sorry, please continue."

"Well, after his attempt to kill us failed, we tried to give chase to the SUV, but he got away too."

A momentary silence fell between them.

Breaking the silence, she said, "We received a report that the German police found the SUV engulfed in flames with the driver in it, burned to a crisp. When we arrived, I couldn't make any identification on the gunman, but I was able to retrieve the VIN number plate and a Zippo lighter I believe was used to set the SUV and the body on fire. I've yet to send them to the lab. Two of the numbers on the VIN were almost unreadable. The lab should be able to get the rest of the numbers."

She paused for a second.

She continued. "The autopsy of the two victims showed that they were shot with 9mm steel-jacketed hollow point ammunition. The ammunition is civilian grade, not a military issue, which would make it almost impossible to track their origin. I may have to contact the FBI. Need them to track the ammo for us. I still have the ammo in my possession. Again, hoping the lab can give me a make and model of the weapon used. I'll have them sent to the lab, as soon I get to my office."

Her father was listening carefully as she went on. "About the four generals whose dependents have been taken, I and Agent Price think there is a connection as to the purpose of the kidnappings. We have a tangible suspicion that may or may not pan out. Agent Price is following up on that lead. We should have something tomorrow."

She paused and said, "That's where I stand so far, Dad."

"First thing, Belle," he said with a stern voice, "no FBI involvement, yet. We'll cross that bridge if and when we come to it. Understood?"

With a sigh she nodded.

"So, what's your next move?" her father asked.

"Back to the office, meet up with Price," she said, as she placed her glass on the table and glanced back at him. "And make appointments to speak with those four general officers and their family members. Maybe they can provide something that can be of help to me, but I'm not keeping my fingers crossed."

The PM stood and paced back and forth, his steps uncertain, as he tilted his head slightly to the floor, scratching his neck. With his arms held behind his back, he paused his pacing and faced his daughter, organizing his thoughts.

Bringing his arms in front of him and taking in a deep breath, he gazed at his daughter while smoothing his strong hands down the sides of his uniform. Colonel Sinclair was a powerful man, physically as well as being the PM. But with his daughter he was Dad. When she'd mentioned they'd been attacked, he was debating whether to remove her from the investigation.

This was getting a little out of hand, and the investigation had only started. What should I do? he asked himself. But he already knew the answer to that. Nothing. If he tried to get her off it, she would resent his decision and still continue with the investigation. He knew how strong-minded she could get. She was a great cop and a better detective. And that's what made this even harder.

With a certain regret, he sat back down across from her and said, "I'm concerned about you, Belle. When you were in Afghanistan, I worried. Then when I was notified you suffered combat wounds, I thought I'd lost you. Look, I understand, Belle, but..."

"Don't, Dad," she cut him off. "Please don't. I can take care of myself, really."

"Damn, I realize that too."

She shook her head, understanding the feelings that were going through him. The feeling of fear and regret if something tragic would befall her.

"Please, Dad," she said, "try not to worry so much. You and I will be together for a long time to come."

With a deep sigh, he said, "Okay, okay, I won't worry . . . too much."

A short silence fell between them.

Colonel Sinclair sighed and glanced at his daughter. "You should know from what stock you're made from, Belle."

Sinclair rolled her eyes, knowing full well what her father would say. She knew better than to quiet her father from what he wanted to say to her. She'd known the history of her ancestors. Ever since high school, she'd researched the Sinclair Clan, and was in awe of the rich history associated with the name Sinclair.

Her father said. "Stories handed from father to son, and now from me to you, tell that we go back to the 1300s to Henry I, Sinclair of Orkney, Baron of Roslin and Lord of Shetland. He was a Scottish explorer nobleman. The Sinclair Clan has been well respected throughout the centuries. They won and were awarded property and lands and involved in the battles during the Wars of Independence and are first mentioned in the invasion of England with William the Conqueror. So, there you are, Belle, your courage, fortitude and sense of combat stems from our ancestors, all the way through their arrival in the New World and through our battles for freedom throughout the history of this great nation."

Belle frowned. "Yes, I know, Dad. You've told me the history hundreds of times."

"I know, honey. And you know why I've kept them alive through you?"

"So that I'll never forget where I came from?"

"Guess I've told you that too."

Nodding, she cracked a smile. "Yes, Dad."

The Colonel laughed. "It's why I have complete confidence in you and your ability to take care of yourself."

Sinclair stood up, walked over to her father, and said, "Thanks, Dad, it's very reassuring."

He stood, embraced his daughter, and kissed her on the forehead.

With deep sighs they separated and, as he stared into her eyes, he said, "Okay, now I put on my PM hat."

Sinclair nodded.

She said, "Yes, sir." She understood perfectly what that meant. Official business was at hand.

Sitting back behind his desk, Colonel Sinclair opened the center drawer, pulled out a folder with a control and cover sheet with red colored borders written on it and stamped in bold black letters, 'Top Secret' centered on the folder. As he flipped it open, he scanned it, then paged through another file, extracted a sheet from it, closed the folder, and set the file on top of the folder.

The USAREUR Chief submitted the report to military intelligence or MI in Wiesbaden, on his request.

Sinclair watched him walk around and sit behind his desk; watched as he took the folder from his desk; watched as he removed a sheet from the folder and placed it on top of it. Then she slowly raised her head, and their eyes locked.

Before he spoke, the PM's desktop phone rang. With a twitch of annoyance, he lifted the receiver and asked, "What is it, Mary?"

"*It's from the EUCOM's office, his adjutant Colonel Phillip Quarles, sir,*" came the reply from his secretary on the other end of the line.

"Tell him . . . tell him, I'll call back in a few minutes. I'm in a very important conference."

Slowly he cradled the receiver, returned it, and as he leaned back in his chair, his eyes moved slowly—willingly—to his daughter who kept staring back at him.

"I'm sorry about that, honey."

"It's ok, Dad."

Agent Sinclair waited for him to open the conversation about the folder on his desk, but his question momentarily threw her for a loop.

Clearing his throat, he said, "It's about the four generals, Belle. I've been looking through their areas of responsibilities. You mentioned that you're looking into a possible connection as to the purpose of the kidnappings. You also said you have tangible suspicions. Please elaborate on that?"

She wasn't shocked at his question. Eventually, someone would ask that same thing.

"Yes, sir," she said. "I'm not familiar with the generals' duties, or what they're responsible for, but I suspect and what Agent Price suspects—although he didn't come right out and say so—is that they're using the children as leverage so someone could pry information from them for whatever nefarious reasons they may have. I don't believe a ransom will be asked for, but something will be. What that is, is unclear at the present time. As for those two victims, they were at the wrong place, wrong time, and they got killed for it."

"Does anyone one else share your suspicions?"

"No, sir, I don't think so."

"Very well."

The Provost Marshal was set on revealing what the contents of the Top Secret folder entailed, but now he thought better of it. He'll wait to find out what further information Belle would be able to dig up, then act accordingly, but not before.

As he slipped the exposed sheet of paper back in its folder, he stood, walked around his desk, and stopped in front of his daughter. "Whatever you find out about any connections, please inform me first."

"Yes, sir."

With a nod and a wink, he said, "You're dismissed, Agent Sinclair."

She cocked her head to the side. Something was wrong. And she guessed it's something he was not prepared to tell her. Whatever reasons he may have for keeping the information from her, she figured it had to do with national security; there wasn't any other explanation for his behavior, because he knew she wouldn't be a security risk, that's a fact. She peeked over at the file and noticed the control cover was marked 'Top Secret.'

She gave him a sideward glance and walked out of his office.

Outside the PM building, she reached into her purse and pulled out her phone.

She waited a moment before dialing as she let her eyes drift shut and stood there for a few minutes. What the hell happened back there? She turned it over thoughtfully in her mind. It would seem he was about to tell her some big secret from which he had backed away. Not like him to be so reticent with the information he had. No, not like him at all.

Sinclair opened her eyes, glanced at her phone, clicked on the text message box, and found Price's number. Instead of dialing, she typed across the keyboard:

Meet me at my office in an hour. And don't be late.

His reply took a minute as she heard the pinging of his return text. She read:

I'll be there as soon as I can, waiting on a phone call or an email.

She took a shallow breath, returned her phone to her purse, started walking to her office, and did not notice a white Chevy parked across the Post Exchange parking lot watching her. The Chevy's driver followed her all the way to the CID building and watched as she disappeared inside. The Chevy's driver parked, turned off the engine and waited.

* * *

As soon as his daughter left his office, the Provost Marshal lifted his phone, dialed the CID office, AIC Chief Phillip R. Jones, and waited. Once he heard Jones pick up on the other end of the line, he said, "I need you at my office as soon as possible."

"Yes, sir," Jones said without asking any questions. "I'll be there in a few minutes."

It took Jones twelve minutes.

Standing at ease in front of the PM's desk, he waited for the Colonel to speak. He watched as the PM reached, opened the center drawer of his desk and pulled out a folder marked Top Secret. Opening it, he slipped out a sheet of paper.

With the sheet in hand, the PM said, "Take this and don't let it out of your sight. I'm detailing you to start an inquiry on the overall nature of the duties the men listed on the sheet have; what they're responsible for and who they specifically command. I don't want command structure crap; I want as much as you can get without rousing suspicion from anyone you connect with. And you'll report to me and me alone. Is this understood, Chief Jones?"

"Yes, sir, I'll get on it right away."

The moment Chief Jones departed, the PM leaned back in his chair and muttered, "Damn, I hope I'm wrong about this."

He needed at least two confirmations of what he suspected. His daughter could put that together for him and so would Chief Jones. Confirmation is what he so desperately was seeking before he went to the EUCOM commander.

The PM was acting under the assumption that somehow someone was setting into motion some type of mission aimed at the USEUCOM Commander and maybe some of his staff. It was a wild theory, but it was the only viable one so far. He mused that the General may have fallen out of favor among his staff officers.

Then he remembered the call from Colonel Phillip Quarles, at the EUCOM's office.

"Mary," he spoke through the open door of his office to his secretary, "please put me through to the EUCOM's office, and get Phillip Quarles on the line. Tell him I'm returning his call."

"Yes, sir," Mary replied.

Slowly, he turned around in his chair, facing the tall book cabinet stocked with military books on tactics and deployment of assets in the field of battle and the Iraq War strategy in four different volumes behind him. Once facing the bookshelves, his eyes took in the two framed photos, one of his daughter and the other of his late wife.

He stared at his beloved wife Lilith, who always wore a warm, kind smile, no matter the circumstances. He missed her smile and the warm gentleness of her. "Jesus, how I miss you, honey," he said, almost in a whisper.

Turning back around, he heard his secretary on the intercom. "Sir, I have Colonel Quarles on line one."

Committing the memory of his wife to the recesses of his mind, he lifted the receiver to his ear, pushed the blinking amber colored button on his phone, and said, "Hello, Phillip, you called earlier. What's up?"

"*Hi, Richard, I have to be brief,*" came the reply on the other end. "*The General wants a one-on-one update on the investigation of the kidnapped dependents. He needs to see you ASAP.*"

"Okay, advise him I'll be there in fifteen minutes."

"*Will do.*"

Colonel Richard Sinclair, facing his computer screen, pulled his keyboard toward him, and typed a memo for record addressed to the EUCOM Commander. Once he'd finished, he placed it in a folder, grabbed his hat, and walked out of his office.

In an office four doors down the hallway from that of the Provost Marshal and marked as the communications equipment and storage room, a solitary soldier was sitting behind a desk with a pair of earphones on as he adjusted two dials on his listening and recording devices. The bugs he'd placed in the PM's office were coming in loud and clear.

They recorded every word.

The soldier, of medium height, dark tan, skinny, and wearing BDU's, removed his earphones, picked up his cell phone, and dialed a direct number. Sergeant Richard Stevens waited.

"*Alpha,*" he heard a moment later through his phone's earpiece. "*What have you to report?*"

"Sir," Sergeant Stevens said, "Agent Sinclair is investigating the true nature of your plan. Also, the PM has detailed Chief Jones, to conduct inquiries as to the full duties of the four generals. And the EUCOM Commander has requested a sit-in with the PM. Also, the CID crime lab will be receiving a cigarette lighter found at the burned-out SUV, and they also found the VIN identification of the SUV. Agent Sinclair has the bullets extracted from the two bodies and forwarded them to the Crime Lab."

"*Good,*" came the response. "*Stay on your post.*"

"Yes, sir."

* * *

At 1300 hours, a white four door Chevy Malibu with the U.S. Army Europe USAREUR license plates approached the main gate to Kelley Barracks Kaserne. Several vehicles were ahead of the Chevy as it slowly waited its turn to enter.

At the gate, as he was stopped by the MP, he presented his military ID card and was allowed to proceed.

Fifteen minutes later a second Malibu approached the gate; the driver showed his military ID card and was also allowed to proceed on through. Another, and a fourth Chevy Malibu were also allowed to proceed unchallenged. Why would they be challenged at all? All the vehicles and the drivers had the proper authority to enter the military installation.

On the other end of the Kaserne, the driver of the Chevy parked in the CID building's assigned parking lot and waited for Agent Sinclair and Agent Price, who arrived within the last twenty minutes, to leave the building.

The driver, ex-Sergeant Larry Kincaid, a tall, stocky, deeply tanned thirty-year-old from Amarillo, a small sleepy-eyed town in the central highlands of Texas where hunting and fishing were the norm, was an Army sniper who served three tours of duty in both Iraq and Afghanistan. With confirmed kills numbering over forty-eight, he was known for his dead accuracy with his MK14 battle rifle. It was the same rifle he had locked up in the trunk of the Chevy. And among his weapons of choice was his Glock-26 subcompact with his unattached Osprey 40k suppressor, held in his shoulder rig holster, and his backup weapon a Smith & Wesson .38 Special holstered on his right ankle.

Six months ago, he swore he'd not be doing this kind of work ever again. But now, with his wife diagnosed with cancer and having no other means of support to pay for all the doctors and hospital bills, they left him with no choice but to accept the offer they had given him.

Once he accepted, a partial payment had been deposited to his checking account, which he used to pay off some of his bills.

His job now was to keep close surveillance on Special Agent Jacqueline Sinclair and DIA Agent Tom Price. And when and if the command to eliminate them was given, he would be ready.

He had no compulsion about killing another human being. Rather, it came almost as second nature to the Sergeant. He could turn it on and off. It came that simple to him.

As he reached for his phone to call his wife, it buzzed with an incoming call.

With the phone in hand, the ID on the screen was that of Alpha. Placing it to his ear, he said, "Yes, sir?"

"Have a job for you. Stand by, and I'll send you the information."

Two minutes later, his phone pinged as a message showed on the screen, it read:

Subject—Chief of CID Jones —Photo included, off post quarters address listed.

Immediate elimination—Do not engage subject while on the Kaserne—Repeat DO NOT engage in the Kaserne.

Sergeant Kincaid studied the photo, checked the address, and listing it on his GPS device, the sniper sighed and nodded, continued to wait as the thought of why he shouldn't engage the CID Chief in the Kaserne revolved in his line of thinking.

But then he reasoned the why. The installation would be placed in lock-down mode the moment the killing was broadcasted to the military police. He would be trapped. So, it was good advice to handle it from the subject's off-post quarters.

Kincaid shrugged and, nodding, glanced over at the CID building.

Well, the *when* to eliminate the Chief would depend on the subject.

No use thinking hard about it, he thought, as he dialed his wife's cell number.

—Chapter Eleven—

Saturday, August 10

At about 1:30 p.m., at the quarters of Lieutenant General James Earl Shaffer, a white Chevy was parked toward the back of the two-story officers living quarters for the better part of ten minutes.

The General's quarters, situated in a cul-de-sac, was carefully tended and maintained, and outward appearances suggested no one was home. He saw no cars in the driveway nor parked in the back. But appearances could be deceiving.

"This has to be done by the numbers," the driver muttered.

The driver, a tall, stocky blond-haired man, wearing a blue shirt, jeans, and a baseball cap, opened the driver's door and climbed out, closing it behind him. With an identification card that showed his photo clipped to his shirt pocket, it identified him as a building inspector for the Post Engineers.

With a toolbox and clipboard in hand, he walked toward the front door. Once there, he knocked twice and waited.

Two minutes later, a medium height fortyish woman opened the door.

First thing he noticed was the woman oozed sophistication, and she had a certain savoir-faire about her that was unmistakable. She was dressed in a simple white blouse and tight-fitting jeans. Her blue eyes and long, blond, flowing hair was done in a curly 'do style haircut. She reminded him of a young, classy Christie Brinkley.

"Good afternoon, ma'am," he said as he showed her his ID. "I'm from the Post Engineers building inspector's office."

She said glancing at his ID, "Yes, what do you need?"

"Well, ma'am, they listed your quarters on our quarterly inspection sheet, and I'd like your permission to conduct it."

"Come in please. How long will you be?" she asked closing the door once he was inside. "I have guests coming shortly."

"I won't take too long, ma'am, fifteen minutes, tops."

"Okay, I'll be in the kitchen if you need me."

"Thank you."

The first place he moved to was the den. There, he kneeled as if inspecting the electrical outlets. Opening his toolbox, he pulled out a small tan envelope containing a thumb-drive and placed it in front of the desktop computer. Under the desk he placed a highly sophisticated miniature voice-activated listening device—a bug. Next, he moved upstairs and placed another bug in the bedroom under the nightstand. He did the same to each room he came to. Checking his watch, it read 1:40. He'd made good time.

At the front door, he yelled out, "All finished, ma'am. I'm leaving now."

Not hearing a response, he opened the door. General Shaffer stood on the other side of the door, reaching to grasp the door's handle.

"Hello, sir, I finished inspecting your quarters," he said, showing his ID.

"All okay?"

"Yes, sir, no deficiencies were found."

"Well, that's good to know. Thank you."

"You're welcome, sir."

He walked back to the Chevy. Once he was behind the steering wheel, he opened a large box that was on the passenger seat, pulled out an antenna that he hooked to the top of the open driver's window, adjusted a couple of dials on the listening and recording instruments, and placed earphones over his head. Fiddling with another knob, he picked up the conversation from the house, loud and clear.

Detaching the antenna and placing it on the passenger seat, he inserted the ignition key, fired up the engine, and, with the gear shift in drive, he pulled away from the back of the house, as he whistled the Army's "caissons" tune.

At that same moment at the quarters of Brigadier General Earl C. Chapman, Brigadier Generals Thomas D. Rogers and Phillip R. Hartman, the same scenario was being played out: bugs and thumb drives being left.

All four of the drivers, drove to the Provost Marshal's building, each carrying large boxes. Then one by one, once inside, they climbed the stairs to the second floor, found the communications and storage room, made contact with Sergeant Richard Stevens, and left the boxes in his care.

When their mission was completed, the three white Chevrolet Malibus exited the Kaserne. That left the Team-leader Captain Jim Steel. He had two other places to attend to. But for what he had been tasked, he'd needed to wait until after duty hours, in the late evening. So, he had time to kill as it was.

A few seconds later, his phone rang.

Reaching the car's console, he picked it up. The screen registered the name—Alpha.

"Yes, sir," Captain Steel said.

"The bug for Chief Jones, forget about placing it."

"Yes, sir."

"Well, that leaves me with Agent Sinclair's office," he said to himself after severing the connection.

* * *

Agent Tom Price took a long swig of his beer, and glanced over to Agent Sinclair, who was studiously staring at her computer as the glow of its screen reflected onto her face. He saw her absently, and without looking, reach across her computer keyboard, grasp her bottle of beer, raise it to her lips, take a sip, and return to her computer.

Sinclair, he thought, was so focused on the task in front of her she may have forgotten he was sitting across from her.

Price had brought along a six-pack of Kapuziner-Weissbier, his favorite beer since being assigned to his German post, in case they had to work overtime. The beer had what he called a fluffy shade of white cloud-like head, and it wasn't overpowering. And she insisted on opening a bottle before that, to his delight.

Agent Price smiled at her antics and shook his head. He was at the verge of enjoying being around her. He wasn't seeing anyone lately, and she was the type of woman he'd always dreamed of. And now that she was in front of him, he vowed to have an honest to goodness date with her, as soon as he mustered up the courage to ask.

Hell, he knew she was going out with that captain of hers, but he really didn't think she was taking him too seriously. At least that's what he said to himself.

He sighed, as he scanned over to set his eyes on her beautiful face once more.

"Someday," he muttered to himself, as his eyes finally glanced away.

The CID building was once again deserted, not even the secretary was in. The two other field agents were out on cases, and the chief was nowhere to be found. Reason she was having a beer—no one to catch her at it. And it was a Saturday, a non-workday—so much the better.

With his laptop sitting on the edge of her desk, he too was busy going through his email accounts, hoping he'd see the information he'd asked for from his CIA contact and friend Judith-Mary Mason, an analyst with the agency.

And there it was in his personal email account. Where he knew it would be.

Clicking on the link, it opened. Scanning through the brief message he read:

Hi Tom, I've exhausted my contacts and did what little I could on the computer and was unable to get any connections nor establish exactly what these men do in the command. However, I ran into something very interesting. It has to do with their security clearances. And you won't believe it. They are as high as one can get. It's the reason I couldn't get anywhere with this. You see, they possess top crypto clearances, and are need-to-know basis only. And my clearance doesn't go that high.

Sorry Tom. Good luck.

Best,

Judith

"Ah, damn!" Price said as he shut-down his computer.

He was still thinking about the email when Sinclair spoke out his name.

Price hesitated, and said, "Shit!"

"What's wrong, Agent Price?"

"Gee, for once can you call me Tom, please." His voice sounded slightly agitated. "We've been working together for the last few days, got shot at, and ran after a suspect. I mean, if it's not too much of an imposition."

"Ok . . . Tom, so, what's wrong? You seem upset about something."

"Upset isn't what I'm feeling. Try discouraged, or maybe disheartened. Yeah, yeah that's it, disheartening."

"What are you talking about?"

"I had a friend in the CIA, an analyst, try to dig up information about those four generals. But she was unable to because . . . "

"What?. . . Wait," she said cutting him off, confused and shaking her head. "What did you do? You were told not to have any outside agency involved in our investigation."

Staring down on her, he said, "I had to do it. I couldn't find anything out on my own, not even with my contacts, and Judith was the only hope I had left. But, please don't worry she won't say a thing about it."

"Oh, you took an awful long chance," she said, shaking her head once more, "and then not telling me beforehand just undermines our trust. I just don't know what else to say. Except, you and I have to build a trust and work together. At least until I prove otherwise this may just be a simple kidnapping and nothing more. And that in itself is proving to be difficult, too."

"I understand. It won't happen again, cross my heart and hope to die."

She said, "Okay, we'll see. So, what did she find out?"

"That they have top crypto clearances," he said, and then paused, letting that sink in. "You do know what that means, right?"

"Yes, they are involved with the responsibilities involving national security matters. They and a select few just like them."

He asked, "Yes, but what exactly are they involved with in those plans?"

"I don't know the answer to that."

"Okay then, what next?" he asked.

"Well the lab was able to lift a half print from the bullet casing and a full print from the Zippo lighter. The friction ridge print or latent print found on the bullet casing was blurred. Usually with a half print it could make identification exhausting work, so I don't think they can come up with anything usable. The print from the Zippo lighter is being run. How long they will take, is anyone's guess."

"So far then, we've struck out with our evidence, we have no location where the children are being held, and we're at an impasse in trying to find some connection with these generals," Tom said, sounding discouraged.

"Look at it this way. We know a little more than when we first started."

"Yeah," he replied. "That's one way of looking at it."

"My biggest concern is for those children," she said. "And not knowing if they're going to be released or killed must prey on their minds day and night."

"So, my question again is," he said, sipping his beer, "what do we do now?"

"Well," she replied, "I've made appointments for later this evening to interview our generals and their dependents at their quarters."

He asked, "Ok, so, when do we start?"

Dropping her empty beer bottle into her waste can she said, "Six tonight."

Price took a quick glance at his watch. It read 2:30.

Agent Sinclair said, "In the meantime, mind telling me what your theory is on the generals?"

"Well," Price replied. "The children kidnapped are a means to an end. What the end is, I can only speculate. But think about this, maybe just maybe to have the generals do something specific, something connected with munitions ordnances. To be specific, last week, I went through a report which showed a large shipment of munitions and supplies was shipped and is being stored at the Miesau Depot. But get this, in the shipment manifest, four nuclear 'smart bombs' were delivered as well. Not an unusual occurrence, you say, right? Many various munitions are stored there day in day out."

With a wan smile and a roll of her eyes, she said, "I don't get the connection."

"Come on, think about it." Price hesitated a second. "This could be a theft of one or two of those bombs, which they can sell on the black market for huge amounts of money."

"Interesting theory," she said leaning back on her seat and crossing her arms across her chest. "I'll have one of our agents do an inventory of the place. It's a shot in the dark."

Price sighed. Rubbing his chin, he said, "Yeah, but at this stage of the game, what do we have to lose?"

She nodded and was now torn between letting her father know Price's theory and not telling him until later on when she received the inventory list. Shaking her head, she picked up her cell phone from the desk, decided he should know immediately, and dialed his number.

* * *

The late afternoon was peaceful, and the drive took less than eight minutes. Colonel Sinclair drove his candy-apple red 1969 Chevy Camaro instead of walking as, with his windows down, he let the wind blow through the car and onto his face while he enjoyed the drive.

He was thinking of maybe getting back on the dating scene and figured it was just about time for that when his phone buzzed. He picked it up and noticed the screen read Belle. He pushed the accept button and placed the phone to his ear.

"Hi there, Belle," he said. "What are you up to, honey?"

"Dad, it's not a social call. I have information I need to share with you."

"Shoot then, what's it about?"

"Agent Price, Tom that is, has a reasonable theory concerning a possible connection. He hypothesizes that maybe the connection is for the theft of munitions stored at the Miesau Depot."

"That doesn't make any sense, Belle."

"Yes, Dad, on the face of it, yes, it doesn't. But Price found out that four nuclear 'smart' bombs are stored there."

A long silence.

She knew he was digesting this new information.

The Colonel thought about it. A flood of questions streamed through his mind, but one scenario had to do with possible black-market activities, and those bombs would fetch a pretty penny on the open market. Was that what all this was about?, he asked himself.

He shook his head; he just didn't know.

"I'm having an agent conduct an inventory," Agent Sinclair said.

"Good idea. Keep me posted."

"Yes, Dad."

"So, you two are on a first name basis now, I see."

"It was time, Dad."

"Okay, honey," he said, cutting the connection, smiling.

This new information was not on his memo for the general, he thought. But he'd have to convey such to him.

He arrived at the headquarters of the EUCOM office in Patch Barracks ahead of time. Colonel Sinclair was always early to any event or conference he had ever attended. The old Army motto 'hurry up and wait' was the foundation of his character and one that the Army had ingrained in him.

He saw several free parking spaces close to the main entrance. After he'd parked and left his car, he started for the building.

The four-story building loomed just ahead, and he'd remembered reading about Patch Barracks. The Kaserne or barracks in German, was named after Husterhoeh Kurmarker. It had been built between 1936 and 1937 and housed a Panzer Battalion until December 1945 when it became an American installation.

Approaching the building, he walked through the double glass doors to the EUCOM headquarters. He stopped and checked his watch.

Five minutes to spare, he told himself, yes sir, right on time.

The EUCOM Commander, General Bradford S. Roland, had been in command for the last four years. He'd only seen the general twice since they had promoted him to the post as the Provost Marshal but had shared phone conversations about ongoing investigations and crime reports. So now it would be three times. "And maybe one time too many?" he told himself, "too early to tell, though."

In the huge lobby, he turned left to the banks of elevators, waited and, as the doors swung out, he stepped in and pressed the fourth-floor button, as his thoughts turned to his daughter. She was all he had left of his prior married life. "Just hope you're okay, honey," he muttered.

Then the elevator dinged, the doors opened and, stepping out onto a long hallway, he turned left. After a minute, he faced the office of the commanding general. Then, for a second, as he stood there, he muttered, "Hope all goes well in there for me." He swung open the tall, solid-wood door and walked into a large lobby.

The office lobby was lit from a hanging chandelier. Two walls had built-in bookcases and were jammed full of books. In a corner just by the entrance door, a secretary was sitting behind her desk, staring at her computer screen, and was busy typing away on her keyboard. She was a serious looking woman, with skin the color of alabaster, pale and white, with shortcut black hair. But she was honest and quite decent and friendly. He'd met her before on his prior visits.

The secretary, Monica Potter, was a fiftyish lady, and married to an Army active-duty Sergeant-Major from one of the logistics commands.

Potter looked up from the computer screen and flashed him a warm, friendly smile and said, "Hi, Colonel Sinclair, the General is expecting you, please go right in."

"Thank you, Mrs. Potter."

Walking toward the right side of Monica Potter, he saw the General's half-open door. Slowly, he approached it and pushed it open as he stared into the office of the EUCOM commander.

General Bradford S. Roland sat at the far side of his office and just in front of his large picture windows, behind his large oaken desk. The room was at a cool, comfortable temperature. The only items of interest on his desk were a laptop computer, a phone, and the intercom system, and a tall mug of some beverage with a small rising steam coming from it, coffee he assumed. He was dressed in his Class A uniform without his jacket that hung on a wooden coat rack by the front door and where Sinclair just hung his cap.

The four-star General was a well-proportioned man of sixty-six and just a little shy of six feet tall. He was a man with years marked across his face, ageless, but well preserved, deceivingly youthful, but the Iraq and Afghanistan Wars had taken a toll on his life. A Texan native from Abilene and with a family of seven, his children grown and moved away, it only left him alone with his wife and lifelong partner, Jane-Marie Morrison.

"Come on in, Richard, pour yourself a cup of coffee and sit," the general said in his deep Texas twang accent.

"Thank you, sir," Sinclair said, as he walked over to the table to the right of the front door. He poured himself a cup of black, steaming coffee.

As he walked with the cup of coffee and his folder to an armchair by the General's desk, he came around to the front and sat. General Roland asked him, "How's your daughter coming along with the case?"

Richard Sinclair smiled to himself. So then, right to the point, he thought.

The Colonel leaned slightly forward on his chair. "Well, sir, she's gone through a lot since I assigned her the case and learned a great deal in the short period."

The General nodded once. "Oh, tell me about it."

Standing, the Colonel opened his folder, removed the memo from it, and handed it over to General Roland.

"What is this, Richard?"

"It's a memo, sir, detailing all that has transpired so far in Special Agent Sinclair's investigation. But there're some facts not listed that came to my attention just after I've written it, sir."

"I'll read it after I get your report, so shoot, Colonel."

Sitting back down, he leaned back in his seat, took a drink of his coffee, and laid it down on the coffee table to his right.

The Colonel's eyes narrowed some, his mind concentrating. Slowly, he reiterated exactly what his daughter had reported to him; her harrowing escape from a killer, the chase in his building, finding the shooter burned to a crisp, the evidence found at the scene, of learning of the theory placed by Agent Price on the possible motive behind the kidnappings, and of the bombs.

The General scratched his head and, nodding, said, "Do you think Agent Price's theory has any footing, Richard?"

"I don't think is has, but it's one way of looking at it. Black marketing activities in the command have increased over the years. It would seem like a reasonable leap, sir."

The General shook his head. "I wouldn't put too much stock in his theory, Colonel. Nevertheless, an incident happened on Saturday morning at the Miesau Depot, which quite frankly stinks of hell and high water. According to the report, an enlisted air-traffic controller was found dead at his post. They suspect cause of death to be a gunshot wound to the head. And they also found two roving guards, dead too. Whether this has anything to do with black marketing, is what I want your agent to find out."

"Yes, sir, I'll get her on it."

The General stood, which the Colonel took as the end of the meeting.

"Good, anything else to report?"

"No, sir."

—Chapter Twelve—

Agents Price and Sinclair knew that in a short time, they'd be conducting four interviews. So, discarding the beers, they both grabbed two cups of hot, steaming coffee from the lobby and settled into their seats in her office. Price, spending about twenty minutes doing random work on his computer, glanced over at Agent Sinclair as she worked on-and-off on her computer and also saw her working her phone, answering some calls and placing some.

One of those calls was from the Provost Marshal.

After the conversation with her father, Sinclair stared over at Agent Price. Her mind delved on his theory of black-marketing operations. What if he was right? But why involve four generals? And, to do what? Things didn't seem to fit. Still, it seemed too early to say if Agent Price may have been correct all along.

Glancing at Agent Price, she said, "The PM just detailed me to investigate the death of a military traffic controller at the munitions depot, two dead guards, and any connections with possible black-marketing operations. He also said that he doesn't think a connection can be made with the killings."

Agent Price's eyes snapped up to hers. "Damn, I knew I was right," he said.

Sinclair blinked a few times, her face not giving away anything she was thinking about the whole thing. "Not so fast there, Tom, we still haven't made that connection, if there is one."

"Yeah, okay, so, why kill an air-traffic controller and those two guards?"

Agent Sinclair turned in her squeaking chair and shrugged. "Well, my thoughts on that are that they may have been killed to silence them."

"Silence them about what?"

Churning the question over on her mind, she replied, "Perhaps, from telling of a possible unauthorized chopper landing."

"Yeah, that makes sense."

"Also, when I spoke to my Dad," she said, "I let him know that I'd placed Agent Alex West to liaison with the MPs and CID personnel who conducted the initial investigation and to start an inventory."

And then, her email program dinged on a new email. Going through them, she opened one that read, *Crime Lab Report.* With her full attention on the report, she clicked on it and waited for it to open. When it did, she read:

Findings: On the latent print lifted from one solid-steel Zippo lighter, showed a well-defined print. It was undetermined which hand the print came from or which digit. With the print lifted, they made a complete computer search through Federal and Military databases. A match found on the DOD and DOA data personnel files showed it came from the subject listed below:

Subject: Staff Sergeant Alan NMN Meadows, Age: fifty-five, Sex: Male, Race: White

DOB: 8/27/1962 Height: 5'10" Weight: 180 1bs, Eyes: Brown, Hair: Brown

Scars: Thee inch scar on left side of face.

Tattoos: 1st Cavalry Division Patch, left shoulder

Alan Meadows was dishonorably discharged and dropped from the rolls as a deserter. Charged with the unlawful possession of a loaded firearm in a military installation, possession of a controlled substance —heroin, and he's suspected of murder by local authorities.

Alan Meadows fled the United States and is suspected to be in Italy.

Meadows' last assignment was as a covert operator specializing in explosives and working in conjunction with the CIA and Special Operations forces in Iraq and Afghanistan.

He's classified as an expert in small arms weapons.

Nothing else follows.

Agent Sinclair, sighing, sat back on her seat after reading the report and seeing Meadows' mugshot; she ran a hand through her hair.

She said glancing over at Price, "Well, the lab identified the owner of the Zippo lighter. It belongs to a discharged Staff Sergeant, an expert in explosives. He's not living in the US and is suspected to be somewhere in Italy."

"So, at least we know he's here in Germany, working for someone. So, what do you think?" he asked.

"Think?" she replied. "About what?"

"About Meadows."

"Mercenary comes to mind."

"Just what I was thinking, and he doesn't sound like a nice guy."

Once again, her email site pinged. Sinclair glanced over at the computer screen, moved her mouse over the link, and clicked on it. As it opened, she read:

Autopsy report on a 'John Doe,' found burned in a vehicle:

Damn! Now she was pissed. The German authorities didn't bother to call her on the autopsy. Not very professional on their part. Although she actually didn't want to attend another.

At least they sent their results through channels. And the report was in German with an English translation.

They had conducted it in a German hospital the day before. As Sinclair read through the English translation, she found it contained nothing worthwhile. Going down through the report, she read that the initial evidence showed that the cause of death resulted from a small caliber gunshot wound to the chest, possibly a 9mm round that entered about two inches from the heart, transecting the spinal column, and exiting through the back. It also noted several gunshot wounds on the body but not life-threatening.

She noticed, with a smile, that it was she and not Price that killed their attacker.

She read on. In the next paragraph, the report stated that as far as identification, no fingerprints were lifted because of the skin being burned.

The third paragraph said that besides charring on the surface, they had subjected the body to an accelerant, which caused it to disintegrate. But they had extracted DNA from the center of a tooth and from bone marrow. Further, it said, examination of the head showed the brain was intact and blood was able to be drawn from it. The DNA, once analyzed, was run through the German DNA criminal computers system for a possible match.

They found none.

Further down the email, she read: The CID crime lab had received the DNA strips.

Now she needed to wait on the DNA strips to be analyzed and run through their databases, which she suspected could very well yield a match.

She was working under the assumption that whoever was running the operation had hired ex-military as mercenaries. So, it wouldn't come as a surprise to learn that the burned corpse was also ex-military as well.

Once again, a lot of physical evidence, which so far had not yielded a single clue in identifying those responsible for the kidnappings, the death of two innocent bystanders, nor where the children were being held.

A *big fat zero,* she told herself, shaking her head.

Sinclair shrugged.

"I've received the autopsy results," she said, "on our would-be killer."

"Anything of interest?" he asked.

"The German authorities," she replied, "could not make an identification on the corpse, but they drew DNA from the body. My lab received the DNA strips, and they will run it ASAP."

"Another mercenary is my guess."

She nodded to Price. "My guess as well."

Now, as the time was drawing closer to the start of their interviews, she mused on the possibilities that the families could not shed any light on the case. But she had to go through the motions. Further, it would show that the CID was doing everything possible to get their children back.

She blinked twice and checked her watch. It read half-past five. It was time to go.

She stood and reached for her holstered Beretta 9mm sitting on top of her desk. She picked it up, removed the gun, and felt the all too familiar feel and how perfectly it formed in her hand. Thumbing the magazine release, she ejected it, made sure it was full, snapped it back into the weapon, jacked a live round, holstered it, and clipped the holster onto her belt on her right side.

She remembered the times her father used to take her along to the firing ranges during her teen years. He'd introduced her to the Colt .45 and his Glock 19. Her vivid recollection on that first day, when she fired off two rounds from the Colt, she'd missed both shots on the target. She couldn't control the weapon's up and down movement and its strong sharp recoil. However, with the Glock, she felt it settle in her small hand and, when she fired it, with its mild recoil, she was able to control it a lot better than the Colt.

She stared over at Price, who was smiling at her.

She smiled back and said, "Time to go."

Then two occurrences happened that were completely unknown to both of them.

—Chapter Thirteen—

He ate his dinner in silence. Now that they had activated him, he was waiting to make sure Special Agent Sinclair was not home-bound soon. Earlier, he'd been given the okay to proceed by those who watched her.

Once he'd finished, he stood and picked up a small black gym bag, tucked a SIG Sauer P320 chambered for the .45 caliber ammunition to the small of his back, picked up the bag, and slipped on a thin, brown, leather jacket.

Turning off all the lights to his apartment, he opened his front door, closed it, and walked down the hall to the stairs, and to his waiting 2017 black Alpha Romero Stelvio coupe.

Sitting behind the wheel, he knew what route he'd travel to get to her apartment. He turned over the engine. As it purred to life, he shifted to drive and pulled away from the parking lot. As he hung a right from the corner of Pascal Strasse and Kurmarker Strasse, he took another right and proceeded to the A831 Autobahn.

Twenty minutes later he reached Sinclair's two-story apartment building. He knew Sinclair had the first-floor unit.

With his car parked in the back of the building, he waited to see if anyone came out to investigate.

Satisfied no one was about or spying on him, he opened his door and slid out of the car, taking along his black bag, and locked it. Slowly, acting as if he had all the time in the world, he crossed the street and continued his leisurely pace to the side of the apartment building.

And as darkness covered his path, he stopped and vaulted a low stone wall that surrounded the complex and made his way slowly to her apartment's back door balcony.

Kneeling and removing a set of burglary tools from a small pouch, he removed two thin-bladed instruments, inserted them into the lock, and within seconds he'd opened the door a crack.

Standing back up, he looked about him and then pushed the door open and walked inside. Reaching into his pocket, he took out a small penlight, turned it on and surveyed the apartment. Slowly going through the house, he noted that the duplex apartment was completely new with some antique and some modern furniture. The fitted kitchen was replete with cooking accessories.

The bedroom had a large double-wide bed and to this he made his way first. There he opened his bag, pulled out a small listening device, and attached it to the bottom of the nightstand. Walking back into the living room, he placed another bug on the back of her TV set.

Satisfied with his work, he came to the balcony, opened the door, made sure it was locked from the inside, and made his way back over the stone wall, where he came to a complete stop. For just behind his car, a German police patrol car with warning lights on was parked. A patrolman was inspecting the inside of his car with a flashlight.

Son of a bitch, he told himself, as he slowly removed his Sig, attached the suppressor, and approached the officer.

His vehicle couldn't be seen anywhere near Sinclair's apartment.

"Sie schreiben was passiert, Offizier?" he asked, "What's happening, officer?", once he stopped almost in front of him. Suddenly, just as the officer reacted to his presence, the burglar raised his right arm half-way and fired three quick, successive, almost-silent rounds into the man's chest. The instant the officer seemed to fall, the burglar reached out and held him upright, pulling the body toward the back of the patrol car. From the officer's utility belt, he found his keys, unlocked the trunk, placed the body in it, and closed the trunk's lid.

Two minutes later, the burglar slipped into his car, and slowly pulled away.

* * *

General James Earl Shaffer was just finishing up his dinner and, with a glass of red wine, was preparing to enjoy his favorite activity—relaxing with a glass of wine and reading one of his favorite classical books "Pride & Prejudice" by Jane Austen. It was his way of not letting his anger and frustration get the better of him since his daughter was taken. His wife was not adapting as well.

Walking into his small nook-like reading room, it was the perfect place to read. He always kept it comfortable with sufficient lighting but not overpowering his eyes. He walked in. On the far side of the wall was a bookcase of six shelves, each fully stacked. Two armchairs and a desk with his laptop computer and phone complemented the room.

Sitting behind his desk, he set down his glass of wine, when a small envelope by his computer caught his eye.

He picked up the tan envelope. It certainly wasn't his. Maybe his wife placed it there. Curious as to the contents, he opened it and out slid a small thumb drive, as well as a short type-written note. As he palmed the drive, he read the note, which mentioned that there were two files, two videos, and one of those was of his daughter.

Sitting bolt upright in his chair and taking the drive, he inserted the silver-tipped end into an USB port of his laptop, waited for it to populate on his screen and, within seconds, he was able to make out the two files.

With shaking hands, he first clicked on the video file marked with his daughter's name and gasped as his daughter's image appeared on the screen. She was blindfolded, her arms tied in front of her, as she sat on a chair.

A tall guard, wearing all black, with a balaclava over his head, and holding a gun to her head, held a microphone to her face, while two other guards stood in the shadows by a door.

"I have a mic next to your face," the guard told the girl, "And a gun to your head. Say anything about this place, and I'll put a bullet to your head. So, say hi to your daddy."

"Daddy, help me. Oh God, please, Daddy, help me."

General Shaffer hesitated. With pain in his heart as he focused his attention on his only child tied and blindfolded, he came to the realization that he was useless at the moment. There wasn't anything he could have done to help his child. Nothing! But the only thing he could do was to see what they wanted from him.

The image disappeared.

He returned to her video and turned it on again, as tears flowed, and he held back his pent-up emotions of rage.

From behind him, he did not see his wife had come into the reading room and stand behind him, staring at the image of her daughter on his computer screen.

"Oh my God, my baby, my baby!" she yelled uncontrollably, as she clasped her arms tightly across her chest. "What have they done to you?" she cried at the top of her lungs.

General Shaffer, clicking off the child's image, stood and held his wife tightly in his arms as she struggled and screamed. Crying, she lay limp in his arms. He pulled away slightly and said, "Honey, we can't say anything about this to anyone. If we do, we'll never see her alive again. Do you understand?"

She nodded and fell back onto a chair behind her, as she held her face in her hands, sobbing.

"They want me for something," he said, sitting back down in front of his computer, "and the sooner I do as they ask, the sooner we can have her back."

Clicking on the next file, he stared at a face he thought he'd never see again. He knew him well, having served together as it was. Until the North Korean Government killed his son. He was a staff officer at USEUCOM headquarters, Brigadier General Thomas Randolph Scott, retired.

General Scott was sitting in a small lit room, behind a gray metal desk, surrounded by computers and communications array. He was staring into the camera.

"Hello, Earl," General Scott said, "I trust you're well. Your daughter is well too. But how she continues to be that way is strictly up to you. You follow my instructions to the letter, and you'll get her back in one piece. Otherwise . . . well, let's just say, she won't be feeling anything."

Scott continued. "Here is what I want you to do; I need you to adjust the War Plan information strategy implementation order OPLAN-8009. Instead of striking Iran, I want it to reflect North Korea and include an aerial strike plan and have it approved by the Special Operations Command, General Thomas Rodgers the chief of staff, General Earl Chapman and General Phillip Hartmann 17th Army Missile command. The plan will call for the bombing run of the North Korean capital."

A slight pause.

He continued. "The moment the plan is approved, you will dial the number you see on the screen and advise as to the plan's approval. Later, you will get the date and time it will be implemented."

Another pause.

General Scott spoke. "I can't overemphasize the role you have in front of you, Earl. Your daughter's life hangs in the balance. If you fail in this, I will send her back to you in pieces. Hope to hear from you soon, Earl. By the way, you have a week from today to get this done."

The image faded, leaving a white screen on his computer monitor.

Inwardly, Schaffer let his rage go. *"Bastard. You son of a bitch!"*

From her chair, Mrs. Shaffer swallowed and said, "Oh my *God*!"

* * *

In the residences of General Rodgers, Chapman, and Hartmann, they also opened envelopes with almost the exact same videos and the same notes.

But in the quarters of General Chapman, once he'd seen the videos, he decided to forward a copy of the two attachments to the Provost Marshal's Office through his government-issued email. He thought the PM wouldn't be in his office until Monday and hoped he could do something, because, as it was, he was useless at the moment to help his daughter. And if they learned that he had done the opposite to his instruction, he'd probably not see his daughter alive again.

He anguished over his decision repeatedly. But arriving at his conclusion, he had no other alternative. Someone needs to know what this was all about and what better person than the PM. It was his duty as much as anything to have it done, even though the life of his child hung in the balance.

So, he kept it to himself. He'd probably regret it, but what else could he do?

Then he heard a knock on his front door.

—Chapter Fourteen—

Back to Kelley Barracks and with darkness shrouding the otherwise darkened streets, Sergeant Larry Kincaid checked his watch; it read 5:45.

It was almost time to attend to his new assignment.

Throughout the sniper's surveillance of the CID office, he'd watched as Agents Sinclair and Tom Price climbed into her car and drove off. They were not his concern for now.

Pulling his cellphone, he called Captain Steel's number. The moment it was answered, he let the captain know that the CID office would be deserted for the next few hours. His placing of a bug in Sinclair's office would go without a hitch, and he closed his phone.

After keeping watch for about thirty minutes, he turned over the car's engine, pulled away from the curb, and headed out the front gate.

His destination was about a twenty-mile ride to a house in the town of Sonnenberg. But first, before he'd exited the gate, he turned off into the Post Exchange area and drove through the Dunkin Donuts drive-thru. He was working on an empty stomach. So, with a large mug of strong black coffee and three donuts, he steered the Chevy for the gate.

* * *

Fifteen minutes later, he parked the Chevy off to the side of the road, a quarter of a mile past the two-story brick house, situated in a large wooded area. Through several large oak trees, he could just make out the house. Two yellow bug-lights burned on either side in front of the double garage doors.

At that precise moment, Captain Steel broke into the CID office and placed a bug under Sinclair's desk. Once he'd finished, he drove back to the silo.

* * *

Kincaid observed only two cars parked in its driveway.

That was a hell of a good sign.

Cautiously, he waited for about half an hour as he maintained surveillance on CID Jones' house. He saw a light on in one of the upstairs bedrooms and dim lighting in what he assumed could be a den or living room. No one came in or out.

Taking a penlight from his hip pocket and, making sure it was operational, he switched it on and, as a stream of light came on, he turned it off and returned it to his pocket. Turning off the ignition, he opened his car door and slipped out. The house had been built around a small forest of large trees, and the nearest neighbor was maybe a third of a mile to the right of Jones' property.

Slowly and silently, he walked the circumference of the property that had no retaining walls or fences. There were no dogs out to impede his progress either. The window with the light on the ground floor was slightly ajar. But he discarded the thought of going through it.

Flitting around the back of the house, he reached for his penlight and turned it on and approached a back door. To his surprise, as he turned the door-knob, he found it unsecured.

Perfect, he told himself.

For a minute or two, he made no movements as he turned off his penlight and shoved it into his pocket. From the outside, the house seemed completely still. But he knew that at least two people were inside.

From another pocket, he removed his custom-made Osprey 40k suppressor and, drawing his Glock 26, screwed it to his weapon. Slowly he turned the door's knob and, as he pushed it open, it made no sound. He found himself in a darkened kitchen. And guiding himself with the help of hallway lights that filtered through onto the wooden floor, he proceeded into the short hallway and a set of closed French doors on his left. To his right, was a set of stairs leading up to the second-floor bedrooms.

Light also filtered through the French doors.

Keeping to the walls of the hallway, he made his way to the doors. Peering around the door jamb, he saw someone sitting behind a desk at a laptop computer that he could just make out with his back toward him. And only a small table lamp that provided some light to the room.

Quietly, he turned the knob and, opening it just enough to get inside, he walked in. Keeping within the darkness of the room, he made his way to the left of the person sitting behind the desk; yet unknowing someone else was in there with him.

So engrossed was Chief Jones that he failed to see or hear the stranger in the den sit in a chair just to the left of him. But as he turned around in his chair, he saw him and gasped.

"Who the hell . . ."

"Let's keep it down, shall we," Kincaid said almost in a whisper, "we don't want the little lady to come down and cause a scene. It wouldn't end well for her."

"What do you want?" Jones said, when suddenly, he stood and reached for the weapon he still had clipped to his holster on his right hip, not having removed it when he came home. It was his one and only desperate move.

As he drew his Beretta 9mm and before he took aim, he saw the flash of a gun from the stranger. The force of the slug slammed into his shoulder and forcibly punched him back onto his chair, causing him to lose the grasp of his gun as it tumbled across the floor.

"Now, now, let's have none of that," Kincaid said, shaking his head and wagging his index finger at him.

Getting up from his chair, Kincaid came around the desk, picked up Jones's gun, and slowly backed up around to the front of the desk.

Kincaid frowned. "Now that that's over and done with, why don't you tell me where you're hiding the list, and I'll let you live."

Jones shook his head, and said, "What list? I don't know what you're talking about. And if I did, you're going to kill me, anyway."

"Hardball eh," Kincaid said smiling. "Okay, well, think of what I could do to your wife upstairs, besides killing her first that is."

Again, Jones shook his head.

Kincaid smiled lightly. "Okay, I'll give you to the count of three, and afterward, I'll just tie you up and have some fun with your wife."

"One."

Nothing.

A few seconds passed.

"Two."

On the verge of passing out, Jones said, "Okay, okay. "It's in the top right drawer."

Silence from Kincaid.

"Did . . . did you hear me?"

Not saying a word, with the faintest of smiles, Kincaid skewered Jones with his stare, walked around to the right of the desk, opened the top drawer, rifled through it, and found what he was looking for. Unplugging the computer, he slammed it onto the floor.

Sorting through the broken parts of the laptop, he pulled the hard drive from it and placed it in his pocket.

Suddenly, from upstairs a woman's voice yelled out, "Honey, what's that racket? I'm coming down."

"Please don't hurt her," Jones begged.

Listening to her footsteps coming down the stairs, Kincaid waited until she was just coming into the den with his Glock at the ready.

"Honey, run!" Jones cried out, just as she walked through the French doors.

But it was too late.

Quickly, Kincaid took aim and fired off four rounds as a line of silent whispering death thudded into her chest, the impact of the 9mm steel-jacketed hollow point rounds flipping her over onto her back.

Moaning with pain, she was still alive as she hit the floor. Sprawled out on her back, with blood seeping through her mouth, her blood quickly draining onto the floor all around and underneath her, she tried calling out her husband's name, but only gurgling sounds escaped her lips.

"Rachael!" he screamed, as he leaped from his chair, his wound and the gunman an afterthought.

But Kincaid turned as Jones stood from the chair. Taking careful aim and before Jones took a step forward, he fired one last round that impacted Jones on the side of his head. As blood and brain matter exploded from the other side of his head, it spattered onto the wall, as he too tumbled onto the floor dead.

Walking over to Jones' body, he removed the spent magazine and inserted a fresh one. Then, jacking in a live round, he leveled the Glock at Jones' body and fired off three slugs into his chest.

Approaching the body of the wife, she followed his movements with blood tears streaming from her eyes and, as she tried to form a word, he fired three more rounds into her body.

"Well," he said, "that's taken care of."

He walked back to the chair he'd been sitting on, pulled out his cell phone, and dialed Alpha-Two's direct number.

Letting it ring several times, he heard the voice on the other side. *"Report,"* Alpha-Two said.

"Sir, Jones has been terminated. I have the list and his hard drive."

"Good work," Colonel Godfrey Randall replied. *"Were there any complications?"*

"No, sir, none at all."

"Continue with mission. You know what to do with the list and hard drive."

—Chapter Fifteen—

Agent Jacqueline Sinclair and Agent Tom Price paused at the front door of General Earl C. Chapman's quarters. It was 6:15, fifteen minutes late for their six o'clock appointment, when she knocked once. And taking back a step or two, they waited. A weak, gentle, cool breeze seemed to settle onto her face, while the dying embers of the sun's rays quickly disappeared into the night behind them.

With a slow deep breath, Sinclair stepped up to the door once again and, as she raised her hand to knock a second time, the door opened slowly. When she palmed her credentials, Sinclair was taken aback by the person holding the door for them. She was of medium height, wearing a low-cut, V-neck, long, flowing, gold-colored evening dress, as her long, blond hair cascaded onto her shoulders. She wore gold-toned, textured, hoop earrings. And, Sinclair admitted, she was beautiful.

Agent Price raised his brows and, stunned by her beauty, was unable to take his eyes off her.

However, Agent Sinclair's face remained expressionless. The countenance of a professional interrogator about to conduct her interview with possible witnesses—her cop face, as she called it.

Showing her badge, Sinclair flipped open the credential case. The woman scrutinized it without taking hold of it.

"Ma'am, I'm Special Agent Sinclair, with the CID," she said. "This is my partner, Agent Price. We have an appointment with the General."

"Yes, of course, he is expecting you," she said in a low voice, almost in a whisper, not surprised that the police were at her door. "The General is in the den. Please follow me."

Closing the door behind them, she came around to the front, and proceeded down a narrow hallway to the last room on their left—the den.

As they walked through the hallway, Sinclair noticed the absence of sufficient lighting throughout. The dim lighting, she thought, may have showed their concern and worry for his kidnapped child. She was reminded of a saying by Maya Angelou; 'Nothing can dim the light which shines from within.'

The woman said, as if for emphasis, as she stopped just short of the den, "I'm Mrs. Castillo, a friend of the family. As you can see, we're about ready to attend a late-night outing. How long do you think you'll be?" she asked.

Sinclair replied, "Shouldn't take more than twenty minutes."

Satisfied with her answer, Mrs. Castillo opened the sliding doors, led them into a warm, beautifully kept den, which accommodated a fireplace and endless shelves of books, and walked in.

It was a combination den and library, Sinclair observed.

"Thomas, the agents are here," Mrs. Castillo said.

Sinclair turned her gaze on the General.

He was a tall, handsome man with a slight paunch but nothing to call him overweight, with black hair graying at the temples. He wore a black three-piece suit, white shirt, black bowtie, and black shoes. In her estimation, he didn't appear to be agonizing over his missing daughter. But appearances can be deceiving. "We all handle stress in our own way," she told herself.

General Chapman was sitting in an armchair, with a glass of wine, when they walked in. Standing, he placed his glass on top of a glass-top end table and walked over to them, extending his hand.

"Welcome to my house. Would you care for a glass of wine?" he asked.

"Oh, no sir, thank you," Sinclair said, shaking his hand.

Price shook his head.

The General said, "Then, please have a seat."

With Castillo standing by his side, he sat back in his armchair and crossed his legs. Sinclair and Price sat in a very comfortable leather two-cushion sofa facing them.

Sinclair, pulling out her leather flip-top notebook and a pen from her purse, said, "Sir, when was the last time you saw your daughter?"

"Let me start by pointing out to you that it's been days since my daughter had been kidnapped," he said as he glanced to a photograph of his daughter on the fireplace mantel, "and I'm now getting a visit from CID? Your chief will hear from me."

Agent Sinclair glimpsed over at Agent Price and saw him holding eye contact with Chapman. She saw Price's low-brow stare and was about to offer a possible rebuff to Chapman's remark.

As she eyed Price, Sinclair coughed once and, slowly shaking her head, shot him a stressed look.

Agent Price nodded once, understanding the look.

Tense silence for a moment.

Then Sinclair said, "That's your prerogative, sir, but we're here now. I would hope you can shed some light into her kidnapping by answering my questions."

The General stared at Sinclair for a moment, then lowered his gaze. "Very well, to your question," he said. "It was several nights ago; I saw her through my living room window. I heard a door closing and went to investigate. As I pulled away the curtain, I saw her walk away from the house and get into a car belonging to her boyfriend." He went silent for a second. "That was the last time I saw her."

Sinclair said, "So, she's done this kind of thing before, leaving the house without your consent?"

"Yes, always with her boyfriend."

"How long would she stay out for?"

"Sometimes for the weekend," he replied, "sometimes less."

"I see. So, you're accustomed to her coming and going?"

General Chapman looked up at Castillo and then back to Sinclair.

Ignoring the question, he said, "Agent . . ."

"Sinclair," she said.

"Agent Sinclair," he responded by saying, "I'm sure you've read the note left by her kidnappers, of not involving the police. Having said that, I couldn't do it. I called the assistant deputy commander. When he mentioned his child Lisa had also been kidnapped, he called the Provost Marshal direct." He paused. "That's why I mentioned the length of time you people got around to interviewing me."

"I see," Sinclair said. "Do you recall when you called the deputy commander?"

General Chapman sighed. "The night we received the information of my daughter's boyfriend's death."

Sinclair nodded.

Agent Sinclair smiled thinly and, taking a deep breath, she knew full well that nothing else was to be gained by the interview. She closed her notebook and glanced at the general.

"Is there anything else," she asked, "you'd like to add, sir, ma'am?"

Sinclair almost missed it. It was Castillo's eyes that opened wide on Sinclair's last question. Curiously, both Chapman and Castillo glanced at each other almost, she thought, as if there was something she wanted to say. She noticed Chapman gently shaking his head at her.

It wasn't very perceptible, but Sinclair hadn't taken her eyes from them throughout their interview. It seemed to her that they were holding back on something. What exactly it was, she wasn't sure. It was their eyes and the way they looked at each other which suggested they weren't forthcoming with some information.

General Chapman asked, "Has your investigation developed any clues as to where they're holding her?"

"We're working on some clues as we speak. Nothing concrete, but, the moment we do, you'll be the first to know. I give you my word."

"Very well, thank you, Agent Sinclair."

A short pause.

The General asked, "Agent Sinclair, are you in any way related to the Provost Marshal, Colonel Richard Sinclair?"

"Yes sir, he's my father."

"Remarkable!"

Ten minutes later they were sitting in her car.

"So, what ya thinking, Sinclair?" Price asked when he noticed how quiet she'd become.

"Nothing really," she replied, "only that toward the end there, I felt as if . . . maybe they were holding back on us."

"I got that impression as well."

"You did?" She sounded a little surprised.

"Hey, I'm not a cop, but I know when someone's lying to me."

"Yeah, okay," she said. "Despite that, what could they know to cause them not to speak to us?"

"Could very well be that someone has gotten their attention in a bad way?"

"Like, maybe, more than having their child kidnapped?"

"Point taken."

A slight pause.

"Hey," he said, "you handled yourself very well in there."

"Just doing my job."

"Aha," he said, nodding.

She said, "I noticed you were getting a little under the weather with the General."

"Yeah, he was getting on my nerves. Good thing you backed me away, or I could've said something that I would regret later."

She just smiled, inserted her key into the ignition, fired up the Chevy, and placed it in drive.

"Where to now?" he asked.

"General Shaffer's quarters."

Pulling out of the General's driveway, she pointed the car onto the main road.

Seconds later, a white Chevy pulled out from the curb four houses down from them and slowly kept its distance from the two agents.

* * *

Less than two hours later, while sitting back in her office, and after they'd interviewed the remaining three Generals, Sinclair sighed and sat in silence for several minutes.

She let Agent Price leave for the night, although he would be available in case anything came up.

She needed to be alone and try to wrap her head around all that had transpired so far.

Throughout her interviews, she'd felt frustration and anxiety sweep over her.

The attitude and closed mouth that Chapman had with her, was reflected in the other Generals too. She felt it was possibly connected to the children. She surmised that whatever it was, it could imperil their lives. It was the only explanation. But what could it be? She just didn't know.

Then her computer email program dinged. It was an email from the crime lab that she clicked on. She read:

Results of the VIN plate submitted for analysis showed the following:

a. The plate submitted with two undefined numbers that were unable to be read with the naked eye. It was determined that a microscopic examination was necessary.

b. During the microstructure analysis of the metal strip to study the structure of material under magnification and, after a careful spray of chemicals, we were able to discern the full numbers and lettering on the metal.

c. VIN number is as follows: YVXWM6AN4AE215441

d. We submitted the VIN number to the investigated section for cross references to establish ownership. Report pending.

Finally, this was some excellent news. Now all she had to do was wait for the results.

Calling it a night, Sinclair decided that a hot bath and a possible night with Captain Cory would do her some good. "Hell," she muttered. "I had to make it up to him somehow."

A few minutes later, as she pulled away from the CID office, the same Chevy that had been following her every move slowly pulled away from the curb from across the street and began shadowing her again.

Arriving at her off-post apartment, Sinclair parked her car and, as she got out, she saw from the corner of her right eye, a white Chevy slowly gliding past her vehicle. Although she tried to keep a visual on the driver, she was unable to because of the tinted windows.

As it passed her, she frowned.

Throughout her drive, she believed she was being followed, although she wasn't sure. "Was it that Chevy?" she asked herself. She decided that she was getting somewhat paranoid, seeing shadows everywhere.

"Need to keep a sharp eye out," she said, as she walked toward her front door.

A few minutes later, Sergeant Larry Kincaid pulled his Chevy over into a darkened parking area. He stopped, turned off his engine, and set himself to wait until he made sure no lights were on in her apartment. He wanted to get a bite to eat before he resumed the surveillance. However, he had to make sure she was all snuggled up tight in bed fast asleep before he did. He knew he was going to be relieved in four hours and couldn't wait to get into his own bed.

He was positioned in such a way that he had a clear line-of-sight to her balcony window.

Earlier, he thought she'd *made him* as he drove past her parked car, though he wasn't too sure. "Must be extra careful next time," he said to himself.

Kincaid rubbed his hands together and was deciding on what to order at a restaurant he passed on his way to the apartment when his phone chirped on an encrypted text message.

Grabbing the phone from the center console and staring at the screen, he saw it was from Alpha-Two. Pressing two buttons, he finally got the encryption program working. He read:

NEW ASSIGNMENT: Immediate termination of Agent Sinclair; agent too close to our plans; Report once the assignment is complete.

He read it once and once again. Satisfied, he responded with his understanding and sent it on its way.

He closed his red-rimmed eyes and, shaking his head, he muttered, "Damn, there goes dinner for now."

Opening and reaching into the glove-compartment, he grabbed his sound suppressor, pulled his Glock 26, screwed in the suppressor, pulled back the slide, making sure a round was chambered, and tucked it into his belt on his right side. Making sure his knife-sheath was positioned horizontally on the small of his back, he inserted his combat knife into the sheath. And lastly, he made sure his Springfield Armory 911 .380ACP was holstered down his right leg. He'd already had prior knowledge of Agent Sinclair's combat experiences, and he wasn't taking any chances with her.

He'd decided not to wait any longer. As he opened his car door, he slid out and rose to his full height, checked and made sure no one was about, and then slowly made his way across to the apartment, as a light rain started to fall about him.

"Damn, just my luck," he said extending his arms, palms turned upward, as the rain spattered onto his hands.

He stopped as he heard a car's engine come to life and saw it when its headlights flashed on. With senses fully alert, he slowly started walking again and saw the car pull away and pass him, going the other way.

The rain started falling a little harder. He looked up at the rain and let it fall on his face. Then glancing back down, he continued.

As he crossed the street onto the opposite sidewalk, he approached the front of the apartment with its porch lights on. The surrounding area was bathed in darkness. So, using it as cover, he slowly made his way around the back of the two-story duplex apartment building, which didn't appear to have a balcony light.

He jumped a small, low, stone wall and, once on the other side, made his way to her back door. He turned the knob, but it was locked. Moving to his left, a window was visible. Once there, he saw that it was slightly open.

—Chapter Sixteen—

A t approximately nine-thirty, Jacqueline Sinclair unlocked her apartment door, slowly pushed it inward, closed it behind her, and momentarily leaned back on it. Her thoughts turned to the Chevy she'd seen earlier.

Agent Sinclair couldn't put her finger on why she kept thinking of it. She'd felt throughout her investigation that she'd been followed, and it irked her consciousness. "Did they maybe—just maybe—accidently show their hand? And can that be them?" she asked herself.

Sinclair had the uncanny sensation of being exposed.

"Christ. There's only one way to find out," she muttered.

Staring into open space, she started thinking, and smiled.

Shrugging, she walked into her bedroom, removed her clothing, and slipped into a pair of jeans, a white blouse, and her Army-issued black shoes.

Next, in the bathroom, walking into her glass shower enclosure, Sinclair opened the glass-pane door, turned on the hot water, and closed it behind her. The impulse to suddenly hop into the shower, wash the day's dirt off, and climb into bed struck her. But she had other ideas. When the glass fogged up sufficiently, her preparations continued.

Stepping back into her bedroom, she drew her Beretta M9, ejected the magazine, checked the load, snapped it back in, jacked a round down the tube, set the safety off, and tucked it on the small of her back. Going into her kitchen, she opened the pantry and found on the second shelf a bag of mixed hard-shell nuts she'd been saving, but now she had another use for them.

Opening the bag, she walked back to the front door and sprinkled a few of the nuts about four inches on the floor in front of the door. Then, she did the same to her balcony door and the two windows.

She made sure the table lamp in the living room was left on, the bedroom's overhead lights and the bathroom's vanity lights as well. She wanted eye contact with whoever entered instead of shadows in the dark.

Taking her cell phone, she opened the walk-in closet in her bedroom, left the door slightly ajar, kneeled and braced herself against the wall, and turned off her phone. She didn't need any distractions or interruption at any crucial point.

With her arms about her knees, Sinclair waited and listened.

* * *

At the same time this was happening, on the other side of town in Patch Barracks, at the quarters of Colonel Richard Sinclair, the Colonel felt exhausted.

He'd spent the day playing a round of golf, and now he'd just finished his last glass of gin on the rocks and was reading a book. And, as the effects of his gin started to kick in, he felt himself falling asleep in his easy chair.

Heading into his bedroom, he took a shower and prepared for bed. He always made it a point to shower twice a day, in the mornings and evenings. A practice he shared with his late wife. He'd remember with a smile the fun they had and the sex they both enjoyed while in the shower.

As he stood under the hot steaming water, his thoughts revolved around his daughter Belle and how she was faring with her interviews. No use worrying about it, he thought, she would keep him apprised of any irregularities if any, that she may turn up.

Finishing his shower, the Colonel toweled off and pulled on a pair of pajamas. He walked into the kitchen, prepared another glass of gin, and headed to his laptop on his desk in the den.

Sitting behind his desk with his back to the double styled picture windows, he sat listening for a moment to the wind and rain tapping the windows. Then he opened his laptop's browser, signed in to his assigned military email account, took a long pull of his gin, and waited for it to populate. Once he logged in, he scrolled through several messages when he came across one that caught his eye.

It was from General Chapman . . .

Suddenly a sharp crack pierced the night as a bullet took to flight. A split second later, it came crashing through the Colonel's window. Colonel Sinclair was thrown violently forward as his forehead struck the hardwood of his desk. Blood immediately started to soak the front and back of his pajama's top, and now blood congealed in an ever-expanding pattern on the desktop.

An all-out howling sound pierced the night as the wind blew through the shattered window.

Through the eye-piece of his telescopic sight mounted on top of his SOPMOD M4 rifle, he watched as the bullet's trajectory traveled its estimated distance of 660 feet or an eighth of a mile, crashed through the window, and saw his target he knew to be the Provost Marshal, disappear from his optical sight.

Seconds later, several of the Colonel's dogs and those of his neighbors barked insistently and loudly.

Captain Jacob Rose, a young solidly built ex-Army Ranger and sniper, dressed in black and lying atop a metal Conex-container, covered from the elements with a poncho, rose, threw his weapon onto the grassy ground below him, and jumped down. Then, retrieving his rifle, he ran to his Chevy, slid in, turned over the engine, and pulled away fast, heading out of the Kaserne before the warning bells went off.

It took ten minutes of driving through the rain to get to the gate. To his delight, he noticed it was still open and, with a sigh he watched as the MP waved him through. He hung a right onto the main drag and headed for the missile silo.

His assignment from Alpha now was terminated.

Twenty minutes later, the MP gate guard had been alerted to secure the gate—no one in, or out.

* * *

When several minutes had gone by, Sinclair thought maybe she'd been wrong.

Moments later, as Kincaid slowly pulled the window open, he soundlessly slipped inside and, as he pulled out his Glock 26, she heard the cracking of nuts at the living room window.

Someone was now in her apartment!

For several moments, there were no movements. Whatever her intruder was thinking or doing, she hadn't moved a muscle. The rain outside was getting louder, and that could become a problem. It was hindering her ability to listen to the person's movements. Her only alternative was to wait it out at least until an opening was presented to her.

Smiling wanly, her nerves jangled and her heart beat steadily and loudly inside her chest, Sinclair felt a surge of energy run though her body. The same feelings she'd experienced in combat years ago. It was the Flight or Fight syndrome. In this case, Sinclair wasn't prepared to run away.

Seconds flew by, when she heard a distinct sound she knew came from the noisy hinges of her bedroom door, as it was slowly being pushed open. Leaving the door slightly ajar, her gamble was that the creaking hinges would work in her favor.

The gamble paid off!

Peeking between the louvers of the closet door, she saw a tall man wearing a black military uniform holding a handgun out in front of him, as he crept in noisily, making his way through her bedroom and heading straight to the shower.

When he reached the bathroom's open door, he'd stopped as he saw hot steam escape through the enclosure's top, heard the shower water running, saw the foggy glass, and raised his weapon.

* * *

This was the moment she'd waited for!

Without a sound, Sinclair made her way out of the closet, and crept toward the open bathroom door with her 9mm held double fisted and aimed in front of her.

When Kincaid stepped forward, he opened the glass door, saw no one in it and, in the same breath, immediately dropped to his knees and spun around, his weapon at the ready. Catching a quick glimpse of her at the door, he squeezed off two successive shots.

With wide-open eyes, Sinclair watched the intruder move almost in a blur of motion and threw herself to the right side while cutting loose with a shot of her own that whisked the intruder's left shoulder. Landing hard on her right side behind her bed, the shock caused her to lose the grasp of her weapon just as a volley of bullets whistled past.

Her gun clattered away from her.

Now, she was defenseless against his weapon.

She quickly stood and crawled across her bed, stood by the wall, and waited for the intruder to show himself in the bedroom.

Sergeant Kincaid, knowing she was armed, rose slowly as he gripped his weapon two-fisted, made his way to the door's threshold, took a cautious step, and peered into the bedroom. Not seeing his target and leading with his weapon, he took another cautious step into the bedroom.

Suddenly—with shocking suddenness—Agent Sinclair bent low, leaped, and dived at him, bringing them down in a *thump* on the hard wooden floor with Sinclair on top and Kincaid losing the grip of his handgun.

They rolled and rolled on the floor, as they both gave and took blows to their heads and bodies.

Sinclair and Kincaid finally untangled themselves, stood, and faced off.

And without a word from either side, Kincaid, a close-quarter combat expert, sprang toward her as he unleashed a flurry of quick blows, with fists as hard as rocks, driving her toward the far wall of the living room.

One-two-three steps she took ever backwards in the face of his onslaught. With her martial arts training kicking in, she blocked and parried almost all his strikes, absorbed some as blood from a possible broken nose flew, as the thought of a bladed instrument could make its way into the fight kept running through her mind.

They were evenly matched, but he outweighed her and was a lot stronger. She didn't let that deter her, as she quickly wiped at her nose and spit out a blood clot.

And then she saw her assailant reach behind him and pull an Army Combat knife–a K-Bar with seven inches of deadly steel.

Quickly stepping in toward her, he lunged the blade's point, aimed at her mid-section. Blocking the thrust, she spun away, twisted around, and connected with a clenched fist onto his knife arm, sending the knife clattering to the floor.

Taking a step back, and with a burst of speed, she pivoted on her left foot, spun, and delivered a front kick that connected solidly onto his solar plexus, stunning him momentarily and driving him back half a step.

However, it was nothing to the trained, hardened killer.

Suddenly, with speed and accuracy, he grabbed her left arm the moment she'd finished the kick and pulled her into him.

Sinclair let him pull her in and, using his momentum, she twisted to his inside and brought up her left arm, bent the elbow, and struck a nasty, heavy, elbow strike into his exposed cheekbone.

She heard it crack under the strike, as he howled in pain.

Then twisting away, she grounded her left foot and, with her right, executed a thrust kick to his front kneecap that also broke with a loud resounding *crack*. Not stopping her attack, with her left foot still grounded, she threw her right foot high, whipping around so fast in a spinning roundhouse kick that the heel of her foot swooshed in the air as—*whack*—it connected with the side of his head.

Sergeant Kincaid was thrown back, landed hard on his buttocks, and crawled up to his knees.

Walking up to the limp figure who was slowly shaking his head, she clenched a fist and, with a *whack,* struck the side of his head, sending him sprawling onto the floor moaning with pain, as blood flowed down his face.

Swaying and staggering backwards, she bent down and, supporting herself with her elbows on her knees, she gasped, coughing and spitting blood.

Turning her back on the intruder, she moved away from him, headed to her bed looking for her weapon . . . just as Sergeant Kincaid, slowly clearing his head and getting back onto his knees, pulled his .380ACP from his ankle holster and with shaking hands, slowly took careful aim at her back.

And just as Kincaid was pulling the trigger . . .

. . . her front door exploded inward and, standing there with his Colt held out in front of him, was Agent Price. In a wink of an eye he took in the scene and fired three quick rounds at the figure on bent knees. And, as the rounds flew with deadly accuracy, Kincaid's gun came alive, as a slug went flying toward Price missing his head by mere inches as he heard it whistle by him.

Sinclair dropped flat to the floor away from the line of fire, while Kincaid's chest was hammered with the three slugs. And as Kincaid's body shook with the impact of the heavy caliber bullets, he finally sprawled on his side, dead.

Taking a quick glance at the corpse, Sinclair stood and gazed at Price, shocked by his appearance in her apartment, but also relieved.

"What the fuck . . . are you doing here, Price?" she asked.

Agent Tom Price smiled wryly. "Saving your ass, it would seem," he replied. "Heard all the commotion, busted right in, and saved you; you know, like a knight in shining armor."

"No, damn ass," she said, making her way to him. "Why are you *here?*"

"Hey, listen, are you okay?"

"A few bruises here and there, maybe a broken nose, but I'll be ok."

"So, who's the stiff there?" he said, slightly inclining his head toward the corpse.

"Don't know yet," she said. "So, answer my question. Why are you here?"

"I need you to calm down and gather yourself, I have some bad news."

"What?"

Price frowned. "Christ, there's no way to say this," he replied, "so here it is. Your father has been shot. They found him in his quarters . . ."

With shock and disbelief, she felt her heart sink. A blurted "*What,*" she cut him off. "When, is *he . . .?*"

"No," he said, before she finished her sentence. "He's in the operating room right now."

Sinclair felt the breath rush out of her. She flinched and swallowed hard. "Let's go!" Sinclair said. "You drive."

On their way out of the apartment, she said, "Don't start thinking I owe you anything for tonight."

"Never crossed my mind," he said, lying under his breath.

* * *

In Sergeant Richard Stevens' office, just by the office of the Provost Marshal, in his communications equipment and storage room, he'd listened to the bug placed in Agent Sinclair's apartment. Knowing full well of the mission to terminate her, it made him take notice, as he sat straighter in his chair.

The sounds of a commotion and gunfire were heard loud and clear. After several moments, he heard a loud bang and more shots. Then, after a moment of silence, he picked up the conversation between Agents Sinclair and Price. Stevens knew then that Sergeant Larry Kincaid failed in his mission, and it had cost him his life.

He also overheard that the take-down of the Provost Marshal, did not go as planned either. Somehow the PM was still alive!

So now, both Sinclair's have escaped their well-planned assassination attempts.

Unhooking from his communications array, he removed his earphones and placed a call to Alpha. He already knew Alpha would not be thrilled with the news.

The phone rang several times and was picked up on the final ring.

"Alpha," came the all-too-familiar voice.

Clearing his throat, the sergeant said, "Sir, the attempts on both of the Sinclair's have failed. Sergeant Kincaid was killed, and Colonel Sinclair survived."

There was a long pause.

Sergeant Stevens could feel the palpable tension and anger transmitted through the line. He waited, tense, listening, knowing the plan had not been laid out carefully enough, and it all unraveled in the space of a few minutes.

Then he heard the reply. *They did what they could under the circumstances. Thank you for your report.*

"Yes, sir."

On then was out of the apartment. She added "Don't see
thinking I owe you anything, thing for tonight."

"Never toss and turning," she said, firm under his breath.

—Chapter Seventeen—

A doctor, wearing scrubs and pulling down a facemask, pushed open the doors to the waiting room of the US Army Health Care emergency room clinic at Kelly Barracks. He stopped, looked around, walked over, and stopped once again, as two individuals stood and approached him. "Are you the daughter of Colonel Sinclair?" he asked as soon as Sinclair stopped in front of him.

"Yes, yes, I am. How is my father, doctor?" Agent Sinclair asked.

"He's in a coma, but stable. He'd lost a great deal of blood. With the bullet extracted, we won't know how well he'll be until he wakes. The bullet hit and broke a rib causing it to miss his heart by mere millimeters. He's in the surgical intensive care unit, if you'd like to see him. He's not out of the woods yet. Although, we're sure he'll pull through."

"Thank God. Yes, I'd like to see him."

"I can only allow two visitors in to see him at a time," the doctor said as he looked at the individuals in the waiting room.

Price said, "I'm right behind you, Sinclair."

Several MPs and the on-call CID Agent were there along with Agent Price, who stood next to her. Sinclair asked CID Agent Alex West, the agent on the scene, to stay until she got back. She wanted his progress report on the shooting, and that of the MPs as well and also his notes on the inventory and deaths at the depot. She needed to keep abreast of any new developments, but especially the identification of any suspects.

With Agent Price following, they walked through the double doors.

Moments later, Agent Sinclair sat by her father's bed, as two MPs guarded them outside the intensive care unit. She held on to her father's hand, softly caressing and kissing him.

She observed several medical charts and x-rays placed in a carrier at the foot of the bed. Then she laid eyes on her father. He was very pale, almost white. He had an IV in his right arm, a nasal mask fitted to his nostrils, and he was covered with a white sheet and a blanket up to his chest.

As Agent Price stood behind her with his hand on her shoulder, a doctor wearing hospital whites, white shirt, and a dark tie with a stethoscope around his neck, walked in. Price and Sinclair looked over at him as he pulled a chart from the carrier. Slowly, he opened it and started making entries and lifting through the pages. Then as his gaze fell on them, as if he'd just seen them for the first time, he closed the chart.

"Hi, I'm the admitting doctor," he said with a hint of an English accent. "Just checking in."

She asked, "Doctor, is there anything else we should know . . . about his condition?"

The doctor replied, "The only thing I can add is that the wound was clean, and he required no major operation."

"With the bullet, doctor," Sinclair said, "we require it for evidence."

"Yes, of course," he replied. "they have already delivered it to the MPs."

"Thank you, doctor," she said, nodding.

Once the doctor left, Price said, "Sinclair, they tried taking you out and tried to kill your father too. Only one way I read this. They, whoever *they* are, think we're close to exposing them. It only stands to reason."

She rose from her chair and slowly faced him, and, laying a hand on his shoulder, said, "Let's talk about this later, ok?"

"Oh. I'm sorry. I was just trying to help."

"I know you are. Thank you."

After about twenty minutes, Agent Sinclair rose from beside her father's bed and turned to Price. "It's time to get back to work and find out who's doing all this."

Agent Price acknowledged her with a nod. "Right behind you," he said.

Agent Sinclair walked and stopped at the threshold of the intensive care unit, glanced back at her father, brushed away strands of hair from her crying eyes, stared, and blew him a kiss. Then, with a sigh, she relaxed her shoulders and turned away from her father.

Sinclair knew she was leaving her father in expert hands, and with the MPs maintaining security, they both walked back to the waiting room.

Once there, the MPs and CID Agent Alex West, stood and approached each other. And from the other end of the waiting room, Captain Jeffrey Cory entered, spied Agent Sinclair, and called her name.

Sinclair turned to look at him, and as they approached each other, they met in a warm embrace, gently kissed, and parted.

Agent Price slowly turned away from them with a sigh, unable to keep his eyes on them.

"Thanks for coming, Jeffrey," she said. "Glad you're here."

"What happened to you?" he said as he looked at her, his eyes glinting with anger and concern. "My God, your face!" She had a swollen eye, blood stained her white blouse, and her nose was puffy.

"It's nothing," she replied. "You should see the other guy."

His eyes narrowed. "Don't know if I should laugh or take you seriously."

Sinclair smiled and said nothing.

They just stood together in silence for a second, maybe two.

Holding on to her hand, Cory said, "As soon as I heard what had happened to your father, I came right over."

She shot him a perplexed look.

"Wait a second. How did you hear about it?" she asked her voice small, low. She knew full well that news of the shooting would not be broadcasted within the Kaserne.

Captain Cory hesitated, keeping his voice cool and even, and shrugging, he said, "Oh, that, I was talking to an MP patrolman a while ago . . . heard it through his car radio."

Her eyes narrowed somewhat in surprise. Something about his answer just wasn't ringing true. However, she was glad to be with him.

"I'll be working late tonight," she said. "So, why don't you call me in the morning, and we'll have breakfast together, okay?"

"Whatever you say," Cory said in a measured tone. "Call you about 10-ish?"

Agent Sinclair was reflecting on Cory's statement of how he'd learned of the shooting when she heard him talking to her.

She replied, "What? . . . Oh, that's fine."

When she'd turned away, he watched her leave, and Captain Cory with a slight turn of his head, heard a little voice inside him say, "Did she? Na, how could she?" Then he realized, she couldn't have.

He thought to himself—not wanting to voice it aloud—be careful what you say.

Captain Cory roused himself, walked out of the waiting room and back to his car.

—Chapter Eighteen—

Missile Launch Facility – The Silo

Amid a placid lake and the thick forests of Stuttgart's central highlands, and deep within the bowels of the missile launch facility, approximately five stories underground, are four of the old missile storage caves—a hundred-feet deep. Each located on the bottom of the silo. One cave housed the cadre of soldiers, and in others, a large kitchen and two bathrooms. Another housed vehicles and equipment. Three others housed senior officers, their offices, and living accommodations. A series of huge industrial floodlights spaced throughout the tunnels provided all the lighting necessary. If the lights were to go off, a person wouldn't be able to see his hands held out in front of him.

One cave was being used to house two B61-12 nuclear "smart" bombs. The black-tipped, orange and silver-colored bombs with three tail-fins carried a fifty-kiloton capacity explosives and a B61-4 warhead. Each smart bomb weighed seven-hundred pounds measuring thirteen inches in diameter, eleven feet from nose to fin-tip, capable of earth-penetration.

They enclosed the cave in clear plastic sheeting top to bottom and around the entrance. Two workmen wearing yellow, fully closed, protective hazmat suits, covered from top to bottom with full face gas masks, were engaged in preparing the B61-12 bombs for eventual use. They also wore film dosimeter badges, used for monitoring cumulative radiation dosage.

The bombs were positioned on two large wooden tables; both had their front housing removed and their control hatch open. Beside the bombs, there were two large open metal cases that contained the control module to each.

At the entrance to the cave, two men were following the preparations, Colonel Godfrey Randall, the second in command, and Brigadier General Thomas R. Scott, commander, with keen interest. Everything hinged on the exact calibrations of the bombs.

Colonel Randall hadn't slept well for the last few days, considering the planning and execution of his commander's plans rested on his shoulders. His eyelids were heavy, but they were at the crucial point where the plan, if it were to succeed, had to be flawlessly executed.

He shifted, his knees hurting. Not accustomed to the hard concrete ground of the caves. Shifting his gaze, he stared at the General on his right, who hadn't said a word —which was surprising given how crucial this point of the plan was, he thought—before turning back toward the two workers and the bombs. The General appeared calm and collected, with his arms behind his back and a smile that played upon his lips. He wore camouflaged fatigues, with a .45 handgun holstered on his right hip, his hair combed straight back and cut to military regulations. A tall straight back and imposing figure, he let no distractions impair his thinking and resolve.

Not wavering from the two workers, the General finally asked, "Have they increased the accuracy and payload as per my instructions?"

The colonel hesitated. "Yes sir, they have," he replied. "They still have to define the early warning system, adjust the enhanced target recognition aptitudes signature, and adjust the guiding standoff system as well."

"Excellent. And how long will that take them?"

Randall turned and faced the general. "They mentioned it would take about two days, sir."

The general nodded. "And have we identified which B-2 Stealth bomber we will utilize and from where we will take possession?"

Colonel Randall closed his eyes for a moment and reopened them. "No, sir. We won't know that until we take possession of OPLAN-8009."

"Have you identified the two pilots who will take control of the bomber?"

"Yes sir, I have," Randall replied, "both will arrive shortly. When we have access to the OPLAN I will brief them and have them transported to the craft's location."

General Scott nodded and stared at the Colonel and shifted his gaze once more at the two workers. "Carry on, Colonel," he said as he walked away.

* * *

Later that evening
Special Agent Jacqueline Sinclair pushed open the door to her office and turned on the lights and, with Tom Price followed by Alex West, they entered. Alex West had been in her office a time or two in the past and found it as cozy as a tomb—no pictures nor anything else—just bare walls, a desk, and some chairs.

As Agent Sinclair took a seat behind her desk, she logged into her computer and opened her email program. Agent West, with two pizza boxes and a six-pack of beer, drifted across the office and placed the pizza boxes and beer on her desk, pulled up a chair, and sat.

Agent West, two years older than Price, about the same age as Sinclair, and divorced for well over three years, had no children. His ex-wife, a blue-eyed blond working her way through college when they met, had been a barfly in Columbus, Georgia, and he so enjoyed his single life. With two years left on his enlistment, he was hoping to land a job with the US Secret Service.

Tom Price sat with his arms crossed imperially, like a general officer, about ready to offer a speech to an attentive audience at some college. He stared over at Sinclair busy on her computer. Then he looked over at Agent West.

"I'm hungry. What say we eat?" Price said as he flashed Sinclair a questioning gaze. Not getting a reaction, he stood and reached over for a slice of pizza and a beer.

Agent West said, "Thought no one would ask."

Agent Sinclair with a slight frown, stopped what she was doing, reached across, and grabbed a slice of pizza, as Price popped the top of a beer bottle for her. And, with throbbing pain to her face, she reached over to the left-hand drawer of her desk, rummaged through it, and pulled out a bottle of aspirins. Tilting the bottle, she palmed four pills and, with her beer, swallowed all four.

Satisfied that should keep the pain down some and, between bites of her pizza, she checked her watch. It was getting late. She glanced at the two agents, then at the pizza boxes and beer, a small smile etched across her lips.

"Eat up, guys," she said with a giggle. "Afterward, we need to discuss our options here, and see where we can go with this investigation. Also, I need to find out who shot my father. With all that's happened, it's my top priority. And, Alex, I need to hear your report on what you found at the ammo depot."

They slowly devoured the two boxes of pizza and washed it all down with their beers. Sinclair was back on her computer. Checking her emails, she'd hoped the results of the lab's findings on the bullet casings and those extracted from the two teenage victims were completed.

Scrolling through several emails, she hesitated on two sent from the Defense Forensic Science Center or DFSC, formerly called the USACIL or US Army Criminal Investigation Laboratory, in Forest Park, Georgia, and a third email, further down her email list, reflected the results of the VIN number investigation. The lab had worked around the clock on her inquiries, she thought; although, she'd marked all the evidence as a top priority.

Reading through the three emails, her face beamed. She said, "Most curious: looks like we got lucky—paydirt, fellows. More baffling is the result of the VIN number on the SUV that got burned..." Sinclair's voiced trailed away.

"What did they find out?" West asked.

After a brief silence, Sinclair frowned.

Price gazed at her and said, "So, Sinclair, what's the story?"

Turning away from her computer screen, she gazed at the two agents and, taking a deep breath, said, "Well, the lab was able to identify the type of weapon used on our assault. They determined that the weapon used was a military issue M4 assault rifle and the lot it came from. Seems those weapons had been purchased through normal channels and delivered to the US Army Logistics Readiness Command in Baumholder, Germany and further shipped through channels on a purchase order from the 113th Logistics Company, here in Stuttgart."

"Okay, wait a second," Tom Price said, "you said, they determined the weapon used was an M4, right? They got that from a shell casing. How was it done?"

"Micro-stamping," Agent Sinclair replied. "It's the technique whereby all military weapons have an endeavor to give firearms a unique mark on the firing pin. It can then be traced to an exact gun just from the casing."

"Got to remember that," Price said with a smile, "for future use."

Sinclair collected her thoughts and remembered that it was the same company that Captain Cory was assigned as its commander. Her feelings for Cory were strong, loving the way he was always fussing about her. The way they kissed and their lovemaking. But now, she felt total disbelief and pain. What if it involved him? she thought. Pushing it out of her mind, at least until they had proof of his involvement, if there were any found, she got back to work.

She lowered her eyes and then, raising them again, she looked at the two agents waiting on her.

Sinclair went on. "The lab searched through the National Crime Information Center database, the NCIC. And there was a CID report on the thief. It listed that particular lot of weapons as not reaching their intended final destination. They were stolen nine months ago in route somewhere between Baumholder and Stuttgart."

She stopped once more.

"Very interesting," Agent Price said.

Both Sinclair and Agent West turned to gaze at Price.

"What's so interesting about stolen weapons?" West asked.

Sinclair answered for Price. "It's the unit my boyfriend is the commander of."

"Oh," West said. "You don't think . . ."

"Yeah," Price said cutting him off, as he stared at Sinclair with a somewhat strange expression passing over his face. "Think there's something to that, Sinclair?"

Sinclair waited, as she tried to find an answer to his question.

Then, instead, she responded with, "Well, if you found that interesting, this next piece of information should really give us time to think about your question, Tom."

"Shoot!" Tom Price said nodding.

"The VIN number to the burned-out vehicle," she began, "belongs on a 2017 Lincoln Navigator, black 4-door. It was also submitted to the Investigative Section for further follow-up cross investigation. The results are that the vehicle was shipped to the Logistics Readiness Command, and another Purchase Order, PO, was submitted for the purchase of four of the Lincoln Navigators. They shipped the vehicles to the 113th Logistics Company."

She paused, letting the information sink in.

Agent Price nodded slowly, as a *hummm* escaped his lips.

West said, "Holy *shit*, no way, wait . . ."

Sinclair waved her hand. "Hang on, there's more," she said, and continued. "The vehicles never reached the 113th. They were stolen about the same time as the rifles."

"Who reported the thefts?" Agent Alex West asked.

"The 113th Commander . . . Captain Jeffrey Cory!" She finally felt a little dazed, as if somebody had just sucker-punched her in the gut. She hoped Cory wasn't involved. However, she had to look at it professionally—the way a cop looks at a possible suspect: with facts.

Agents Price and West did not reply.

"Let's move on, shall we?" she said, gazing over at Agent West. "Tell me what you discovered in your investigation at the ammo depot, Alex?"

Sinclair looked at West sharply and waited for his report.

"Well," West said, "I learned a few things while I was there."

He paused, gathering up his thoughts in order.

"Oh, like what?" Sinclair asked noticing his slight hesitation.

"Well, for one, the air-traffic controller had been shot in the head. Small bore hole, a nine-millimeter round, maybe. The reason for it, I suspect, so he wouldn't be able to identify his killer."

Sinclair asked, "Did you recover a shell casing?"

"No," Agent West said and added, "What was most interesting was when I along with the depot personnel and conducted our inventory. Hell, Sinclair, we found two nuclear smart bombs missing from the inventory!"

"Holy *shit*, God damn!" Price said not feeling at all surprised. "I knew it had something to do with those bombs."

Sinclair shook her head. She leaned in her chair and said, "Anything else?"

"Yeah, I developed a witness of sorts."

"Who's the witness?" Price asked.

"According to the witness," West began, "a Sergeant Allen Corvallis, an MP patrolman, noticed a helicopter flying over his patrol area. He didn't give it any thought until he saw it land in the ammo site."

Here, he stopped for a second.

"Although," he continued, "when he decided to investigate, he was dispatched on a domestic disturbance call. It wasn't until two hours later, that the Sergeant drove onto the depot site to see what had become of the chopper. That's when he found a military vehicle with its doors wide open and two dead guards inside. Both riddled with bullets."

He paused for another moment.

"Then later he found the dead air-controller. The sergeant also found on the ground near the entrance to the site, marks of where a chopper had landed. He surmised it may have been the same chopper he'd seen earlier that night, but he wasn't sure. That's all I've got on the matter."

Tom Price shook his head. "Is it rare for choppers to land by the entrance to the depot?"

"I put that question to the Depot personnel," West said, "and the answer was, helicopters are prohibited from landing on or near the site."

Sinclair said, "So, we can say for sure, that the chopper was there for only one thing, the bombs."

Both Agents Price and West slowly nodded.

"And we now know why the killers picked up their ammo brass," Price said. "They wanted to mask the stolen weapons. They didn't want them traced back to them or where they came from."

A brief silence settled between them, each wrapped up in their own thoughts.

It was Agent Sinclair that broke the silence.

She picked up her beer and, downing the last of it, she asked, "Did anyone go through my apartment and identify my would-be killer?"

Alex West looked up and gazed at Sinclair. "Ah, CID Agent Jaime Vargas, two MP patrols, and the German police are at the crime scene as we speak, Sinclair. Probably won't be finished until later in the morning."

Price chimed in, swallowed, and clearing his throat, said, "Well, since it was me that broke down your apartment door, why don't you stay over at my place for the time being?"

"Let's talk about that after we're finished here, okay?" she said.

Price nodded. Deep down, he hoped she'd take him up on his offer.

"Several things I need accomplished later this morning," Agent Sinclair said, as she counted them out with her fingers. "First, we have to go through my father's quarters, see what we can come up with. Second, we'll call in Captain Cory and find out about his stolen weapons and the stolen vehicles as well."

"By the way, talking about your father's quarters," Agent Alex West said in a matter-of- fact tone. "Agent Vargas called me direct about his findings so far. He mentioned that the only sign a crime had been committed was the large amount of blood on your father's desk. Nothing else seemed disturbed."

Sinclair cocked her head. "Oh, I'm sure he's doing a thorough job. I'll still conduct by own investigation."

West chuckled and said, "No doubt. Need help, just let me know."

She paused a second or two and gazed over at Agent Price and smiled. "And Tom, if you have an extra bed, I'll like to take you up on your offer."

Price grinned. "Sure, no problem. You can sleep in my bedroom, I'll take the sofa," Price said not showing his excitement at the prospect of having her stay at his apartment.

She glanced at Price for a moment. Then she took the last bite of her pizza and gave him a little crooked smile as she held a questioning stare.

Agent Tom Price dropped his eyes and nodded. A sensation of giddiness came over him.

* * *

Sergeant Richard Stevens picked up the conversation through Agent's Sinclair bug placed in her office. Picking up his cell phone, he dialed Alpha's number. As soon as it was picked up, he said, "Sir, bad news to report."

"Go on, Sergeant, please state your report," General Scott said.

"Yes, sir. Agent Sinclair has identified our weapons and traced them to the 113th Logistics Company, including our four Lincoln Navigators. They suspect Captain Jeffrey Cory of maybe having knowledge of our weapons and vehicles."

"Did they come out and say that, Sergeant?"

"Not in so many words, sir. They want to interview Captain Cory sometime today."

A slight pause.

"And sir, they also know of the bombs," Sergeant Stevens said.

"Anything else, Sergeant?"

"Yes, sir, Agent Sinclair will be staying with Agent Price at his off-post quarters. Where that is, is unknown at the present. We just don't have that information, yet. Further, sir, Sergeant Larry Kincaid died at the hand of Agent Sinclair in her apartment."

"Thank you, Sergeant."

* * *

In Brigadier General Thomas R. Scott's office, in the silo, along with Colonel Godfrey Randall, the matter of Agent Sinclair and Price was being discussed.

Sitting behind his desk, in his well-lit office, surrounded by two large computer screens off to the left side of his desk, with an array of communications equipment behind him and two land-line telephones on his right-hand side, and while he held a framed photograph of his only son, Jason Scott, he'd listened to the report being made by Colonel Randall, his second in command.

His thoughts were always of his son, and how those responsible would pay for causing his untimely death. Only twenty-six at the time of his death, he would've turned twenty-seven next month; he felt a cold tear form. He wouldn't let it fall. No, his crying days were all behind him now. Now, their blood was the only thing that would satisfy his craving for revenge. He knew nothing he could do would bring his son back, but he would have his pound of flesh and blood.

When he graduated from West Point, so many years ago, never in his wildest dreams did he ever figure he'd go against the government he served for over thirty years. Throughout his military career, from commanding an infantry company, and battalion commander in Vietnam and Iraq, then Afghanistan, his sole responsibilities were for his men under him, and the mission. He never let politics sway neither his judgment nor his ability to carry out his orders. At least, not until the death of his son.

As the Colonel spoke, General Scott was thinking of the OPLAN he so needed to set the next phase of his plan in motion. Two individuals frustrated his plans—Agent Sinclair and Agent Price. He could not allow them to get too close to learning his ultimate plan.

Placing the photograph of his son back on his desk, he tried not to think of him and, gazing over at his second in command, he paid attention to his narrative of current events.

"So, with Sergeants Kincaid and White's deaths, we have no one watching the two agents—except for one. The bug in Sinclair's office is still being monitored by Sergeant Stevens. And as you know, sir, they've traced both our weapons and the Lincoln Navigators to Captain Jeffrey Cory's unit. Only time will tell if they connect all of our equipment. It can only have one possible end—being traced here to us."

General Scott shook his head. "On that point, unless the FBI gets involved, there isn't any possible way this facility can be traced to me by the two agents."

Colonel Randall nodded. "Understood, sir."

There was a brief silence.

General Scott said, "Those two agents seemed to be working hard in identifying us, in an attempt to rescue our prisoners and to derail our plans. It's time to put an end to their meddling, once and for all."

"Yes, sir, I agree."

"Who do you have that can put an end to them, Colonel?"

"We have several qualified soldiers, sir. Though, the ones capable of handling the assignment would be Captain Jim Steel and his crew, sir."

"Very well, since we have no address of Agent Price's residence, have them post themselves at the Provost Marshal's hospital. Those two would come to visit sometime soon. I want complete termination of them both, Colonel."

"Yes, sir, I'll set that in motion."

"And Colonel," Scott added as he leaned on his desk and gazed at him. "Your men have failed me in the past; make sure they succeed this time."

"Sir," Colonel Randall said. He didn't need to say anything further; *Failure will not be tolerated, or else!* the General's gaze said.

—Chapter Nineteen—

Sunday, August 11th

It was a twilight sunrise. That part of the early morning as the sky was brightening, and the sun not yet visible, when Agent Tom Price pushed open the door leading into his apartment and a rush of excitement swept through him. And having this beautiful woman sharing his apartment and his bedroom, he thought, gave him a small measure of hope. Hope? Christ, he thought, hope for what? he asked himself. Nothing will happen, he kept thinking. This was just pure friendship. Comrades in arms. She was his partner, nothing more, right? If something *were* to happen between them, that would be icing on the cake, he imagined with a smile.

The sun was now breaking through to the early Sunday morning. Pushing open the door, he stepped aside to let Agent Sinclair walk through, as from somewhere inside a clock chimed the hour of six, with a soft low tone playing a Whittington melody. It had a lovely and soothing effect to the ear, which he loved.

As she entered his one-bedroom apartment, she paused for a moment, as Price gently closed the door behind her. And as he gestured for her to walk through a narrow hallway, he brushed against her backside. She turned, took a deep breath, smiled, and followed him through the hallway as if nothing had happened.

Agent Tom Price paused at the end of the hallway, flipped on the overhead kitchen light, turned to face her and, smiling, said, "Well, come on in and make yourself at home."

At a large picture window, Price drew back the curtains, letting the sunlight flood in to an otherwise darkened living room. Turning back to her, he smiled. "Please, have a seat while I get the bed ready for you."

"You have a nice place, Tom," Sinclair said. "And thanks for letting me stay here for the day."

"Hey, no need to thank me. What are partners for, if not to help each other, right?"

"That's so sweet."

She sat on the sofa and yawned, as tiredness and fatigue slowly started taking its toll on her body, but still thinking of what lay in store for them in the coming days and thinking of her father still in a coma. Nothing else seemed to occupy her mind as much as her father's condition. Everything else was secondary.

As Sinclair sat waiting on Price, she noticed the one-bedroom apartment furnished in a modern motif, with brown and white colored furniture. The open living and dining area were equipped with a high quality fitted kitchen, with what appeared to her to be brand new appliances. The bedroom was reached from the rear of the apartment.

A few minutes later, Price called to her from the bedroom, "All ready for you, Sinclair."

Sinclair slowly made her way to the bedroom, stopped at the threshold and gazed at a lovely king-size bed. Walking into the room, she halted again at the bathroom door and saw an inviting shower with a stylish bathtub.

Turning back to Price, she said, "Very nice."

He said, "I've laid out one of my gym shorts and a large T-shirt for you, and if you want to shower first, I've placed some clean towels for you as well."

"You're very sweet, Tom. I won't forget this."

Price said nothing, just smiled and nodded.

A few awkward moments passed between them as they stared at each other. Sinclair was the first to blink, as she quickly looked somewhere else.

As he turned and faced away from her stare, he said, "It's all yours. Think I'll leave you now. Sleep well. I'll be in the living room if you need anything."

She just smiled.

Another awkward second passed.

"Okay . . . I'll close the door behind me," Price said as he walked out of the bedroom.

Assuring herself the door was closed, she pulled off her clothing, removed her bra and panties, and shuffled to the shower. Turning on the hot water, with her aching muscles pleading for her to get in, she entered the tub and closed the shower curtains, and just let the hot water cascade down her body for several moments. Quickly lathering, she washed the blood from her face and hair. Rinsing off, she felt alive once more. As if the shower had cleansed the night's deadly encounter from her body.

She toweled off and wrapped the towel around her hair. Walking back into the bedroom, she picked up the shorts he'd left on the bed, pulled those on, and slipped into Tom's T-shirt.

After fifteen minutes more or less, and not hearing the shower running, Price assumed Sinclair had finished. So, with a white metal first-aid kit under his left arm, he walked toward the bedroom. With a deep breath, he stepped up to her door and knocked. After a few seconds, the door opened, and she stood in front of him, wearing his shorts and T-shirt and looking so damn beautiful as he could see her fully erect nipples outlined through the T-shirt.

He stood there, silent for a second. Then he raised his eyes to her and, as she stared back, his thoughts revolved to her wounds that needed attending before they became infected.

"Hi, ah, Sinclair—" Tom Price, didn't quite know how to address what he wanted to do as he showed her the first-aid kit. "Can I look at your wounds?"

Agent Sinclair nodded mutely and allowed him into the bedroom and, as she walked behind him toward the edge of the bed, she sat. He felt like when in his teens, he'd visited his girlfriend in her bedroom for the first time. His heart was racing. He felt like smiling but didn't. His lips moved and only a very low whisper came out.

"Did you say something, Tom?"

'No, no, I didn't."

"Okay. I'm all yours, Tom."

If only that was true, he thought, and felt his pulse quickening.

Though, with parted lips, he tried to form the word *okay,* only a small amount of air came rushing out.

He was a basket case, and he knew it.

Sitting on the edge of the bed alongside Sinclair, he placed the first-aid kit on the bed, opened it, and removed an antibiotic ointment. Sliding up closer to her, he wanted to reach over, take her in his embrace, and kiss her, but thought better of it.

With a deep sigh he woke up from his fantasy, knowing full well that could never be.

Now, with the bleeding all but stopped, he applied the ointment to several cuts and abrasions to both sides of her face and, with a gauze pad, he taped it to a small but deep cut on her right cheek. With the redness and swelling under control, he felt better now that he'd thought of it.

As Tom Price gently administered the ointment, she looked deep into his eyes and felt a slight stirring deep down in her bosom, which she couldn't explain. And as he looked at her, she could sense he was starting to feel something for her. But she felt it was not wise to do anything to tip the balance of their friendship.

"There, all done," Price said, as he returned all the bandages and ointment to the kit, closed it, and stood.

"Thank you, Tom." Sinclair also stood and faced him; her eyes locked onto his.

As he got nearer to her, he stopped the moment she turned away.

He said, "Okay. Hope you have a few good hours of sleep."

Once Price had gone, she fell onto the king-size bed that was covered with plain white sheets and a blue blanket, draped the blanket over her, placed her head on the pillow, and was fast asleep within ten minutes. Her last thought was of her father.

In the living room, Agent Tom Price pulled down a blanket from his hallway closet and an extra pillow, ambled over to his sofa and, still fully clothed, covered himself, but wasn't able to fall right to sleep. His thoughts kept drifting back to Sinclair, in his bedroom, by herself, sleeping on his bed. Oh my!

As his eyes started closing, deep down in the pit of his stomach, he felt a warm fluttery sensation he hadn't felt in years for any woman. Slowly sleep came, as his subconscious mind imagined her with her head resting on his chest, just after having their first sexual encounter. But sleep finally overtook him, and he fell into that slow wave deep sleep.

Agent Price, as if from far away, kept hearing ringing bells. He slowly stirred from his sound slumber and placed his pillow over his head, trying to snuff out the ringing. But it was no use. Frustrated over the annoying interruption to his sleep, he turned over on the sofa, and rolled off it, landing on the floor with a loud *thump* as his head hit the hardwood flooring.

Startled out of his wits, he quickly got to his feet, turned around twice, didn't see anyone, scratched his head, and heard his cell phone ringing and ringing.

"Son of a bitch, who the hell is calling so damn early in the morning," he asked himself, rubbing the side of head. Then he glanced at his wall clock: almost 10:45 in the morning. Damn, so much for getting a much-needed sleep.

With the phone still ringing, he picked it up from the coffee table. Clicking on the accept-call button, he heard a strong male voice on the other end.

"Hello, sir."

"This better be a national disaster, if not, this had better wait until tomorrow."

There was a long sigh. "Agent Price, we've been trying to reach Agent Sinclair for over an hour. Can you advise me of her whereabouts, sir?"

"She's here with me, in my apartment. What's up?"

"Please let her know her father is asking for her. He just woke up from his coma."

"How's he doing?"

"He's fine but wants to talk to her."

"No problem. We'll be at the hospital in thirty minutes, if not sooner."

"Thank you, sir, I'll let him know."

Agent Price clicked off his phone and slipped it into this pocket. Then he ambled over to the kitchen, opened his refrigerator, and pulled out a jug of orange juice. He poured himself half a glass and prepared himself to wake Sinclair.

Reaching his bedroom door, he lightly knocked twice and, not hearing any response, he slowly opened it and gently walked in. He stopped at the foot of the bed. As he moved a little closer, he softly called out her name. Nothing. Then he dragged the sheets and stopped, again nothing. *Shit,* he thought, *I'm not going to scare the hell out of her, but I need to wake her.* As he stood there contemplating his next move, he felt like a jerk for what he was about to do. So, raising his tone he called out her name again, while gently shaking her.

She stirred and sat straight up wide awake, tilted her head to the side, and gazed at him. "What the hell, Tom," she asked, "what's going on, is it time to get going?"

Price ignored her questions. "Listen, your father woke from his coma and wants to see you right away."

For a moment she was motionless, absorbing what he'd just said. Then with a smile, she leaped out of bed.

"Sinclair," Price said, "let me look at your cuts and bruises and bandage them up a little before we leave, and that eye still looks puffy."

"No time, I need to get to my apartment and get a clean set of clothing," Sinclair said.

"Well, let me get dressed, and we'll be on our way."

* * *

They made good time.

Despite the light falling rain and the cool breeze, they were fully prepared. The four special operators and ex-Special Forces team members that made up Captain Jim Steel's crew, were briefed earlier on their assignment, that of putting down CID Agent Sinclair and DIA Agent Tom Price, at all cost!

The men had formed a cohesive close-knit team, each highly trained and motivated. Not just by the promise of pay, but by their commitment to each other; each had the other's back, no matter what the mission or the dangers it presented.

They were a hard-hitting strike force unto itself. Each member was trained in hand-to-hand combat, weapons specialist, tactical munitions trained and certified. Killers all, enjoying the hunt and the gratification it derived. These were men that served their country in its hour of need. They also once did extrajudicial killings or "wet-work" that the CIA or other three-letter word intelligence outfits couldn't or wouldn't.

Captain Jim, as the men called him, was a born killer. Prior to US Army service, he was a hired killer for a New York City mob from the age of fourteen, growing up in the family itself. He had twenty-three confirmed kills, including women and children. At seventeen, he changed his last name from Bonanno to Steel. A distant relative to the New York City crime family, he made a name for himself, while never once being caught or suspected of the killings. Then, at the age of eighteen, he volunteered for the US Army.

They'd arrived in two white four-door Chevrolets, with two men each. Captain Steel's vehicle was parked upfront in the parking lot to the US Army Health Clinic, Kelly Barracks. The second Chevy was parked by the emergency room entrance parking area.

If the possibility arose and Jim Steel did not see the two agents enter the hospital, one man was detailed inside the clinic to watch for the two agents. They had every contingency covered. Photographs of both agents were in their smart phones for easy identification. They noticed MP patrols in and around the clinic and one parked MP patrol car at the entrance. These were of no concern to him or his crew. The plans he'd devised didn't include shooting it out with the MPs on the installation.

Captain Jim Steel fished out his lighter and a pack of Marlboro cigarettes, stuck one between his lips and lit it and tried to relax as he rolled down his window a crack. He didn't know how long the wait would be. It already had been a long night and a long drive too. As he sat back in the car's seat, he surveyed the area for any possible dangers. His partner, Alvin Jones, a tall black man wearing sunglasses, shifted his gaze left and right, ready for any eventuality.

It was an easy assignment. Captain Jim Steel was well aware of the efforts to eliminate the two agents and their outcome, yet he was completely unperturbed. His plan was simple in its execution.

He and his team would not fail.

—Chapter Twenty—

OP-CENTER, USAEUCOM Headquarters, Patch Barracks, Stuttgart, Germany, 11:00 a.m. Sunday, August 11

Lieutenant General James Earl Shaffer, Assistant Deputy Commander, EUCOM was the first to arrive at the OP-CENTER, a highly secured facility located in the bowels of the USAEUCOM headquarters building.

The OP-CENTER contained only one large room, which housed an array of large screen monitors mounted on three walls, and a wide assortment of communications equipment. Several telephones sat on the desk at each sitting area. By each of the four walls, there were several computers each connected to three or more monitors. In the center of the room stood a massive oak desk, and enough space to seat at least twelve staff personnel in new leather armchairs.

In times of Europe-wide alerts, there would be many military personnel all going about their assigned jobs, that of monitoring ongoing exercises. In the event of a National alert crisis, the OP-CENTER was responsible for the operational implementation of three operational war plans.

Those war plans included but were not limited to: strategic bombing runs on prearranged targets of interest, as set forth in the plan; assignments of first strike operatives from Special Forces, Delta and Ranger units; and intelligence gathering missions, by Military Intelligence, and operatives selected by the CIA and DIA agencies to conduct any covert operations necessary for the completion of assigned missions.

The plans could be implemented in whole, or in part, depending on the operational requirements, as prescribed by the Pentagon, the USAEUCOM Commander, or his designated officer. General Shaffer was the designated officer, responsible only to the EUCOM Commander. Their center was one of several worldwide linked to the Pentagon's OP-CENTER, in Washington, DC.

There were military personnel staffing the OP-CENTER around the clock, and two armed Military Police officers with M4 assault weapons and M9 pistols posted top-side, as well as to the entrance of an elevator directly facing the center, twenty-four hours a day, seven days a week.

Another MP stood by the entrance into the center proper. The MPs had prior knowledge of a scheduled meeting for that day. The MP charged with the overall control of the center had been instructed not to disturb those conducting their meeting within the room.

Approaching the main entrance to the EUCOM headquarters building, after leaving his parked vehicle, General Shaffer, carrying a leather attaché case, heard his name being yelled out behind him. "James, hold on, right behind you."

Coming to a stop, Shaffer turned and saw General Phillip Hartmann slowly making his way toward him. Both of them were dressed in two-piece business suits, Shaffer in light blue and Hartmann in black.

"I see you've come too, James," General Hartmann said, his voice gravelly, with a Southern twang to it.

Glancing at Hartmann, General Shaffer shook his head. "Did I . . . have a choice?" he asked with a deadpan look.

General Hartmann nodded. "I guess we all didn't."

"Are the others coming?"

"Well, they said they'd be here."

Shaffer took a deep breath. "Good, let's head on down, then."

"Are those the war plans in your case?"

"Yes, to include, the most important one of the three."

Walking side by side, they entered the building and headed to an elevator marked "private" on their far-left side of a bank of elevators, as two MPs stood guard.

Showing their military IDs and special OP-CENTER ID to the MP, General Shaffer held his OP ID to a scanner on the left side of the elevator, and the door opened. Once they were inside, the doors closed, and they slowly descended four levels. Reaching the fourth level, the doors opened onto a long wide walkway. An MP stood guard there as well. The end of the walkway featured a set of double glass doors, into which the OP-CENTER was visible through the glass.

As they approached the glass doors, General Shaffer once again placed his OP ID onto a scanner and waited. As the doors opened, the interior lights came on automatically, the lights giving a certain ambiance to the interior. General Shaffer's hard-sole half boots' heels thumped softly on the carpet as he entered the room. And as General Hartmann followed through, the doors closed behind them, as the MP stood guard outside and to the left of the glass door.

Walking around toward the front of the large desk, General Shaffer placed his attaché case on the desktop and snapped the two locking switches. Once the case was open, he pulled out a white and orange-bordered cover sheet and a folder marked "Secret Crypto OP-Plan 8009," dated March 2016. He opened the folder and laid several white sheets of typed papers on the desk. Closing his case, he set it on the floor beside his right foot.

In the meantime, General Hartmann sat to Shaffer's left, as they waited for Generals Earl Chapman and Thomas Rodgers to arrive before starting the meeting.

* * *

Special Agent Jacqueline Sinclair, having changed to a white blouse, a blue windbreaker, jeans, and brown cowboy boots, and Agent Tom Price, with a tan sports coat over a white T-shirt, and jeans, arrived at Kelly Barracks Health Clinic, forty-five minutes later.

Tom Price had parked his car, a black late-model BMW coupe, toward the rear of the clinic and entered through the backdoor. Once inside they headed toward the front only to find CID Agent Alex West sitting in the waiting room.

The Agent, in a one-piece black business suit and open collar white shirt, no tie, was sitting reading a magazine and, as he looked up, he noticed Sinclair and Price enter from the back of the clinic. He stood and walked over to meet them.

"My God," Agent West said, his voice low and edged with concern. "What the hell happened to your face, Sinclair?"

With a dry chuckle and a smile, she said, "Tell you later."

"Anyway, I've been waiting for you two, ever since I found out your father was awake," Alex West said once they stopped in front of each other.

Sinclair said, "Thank you for coming, Alex."

Agent Tom Price extended his hand out to West in a handshake. "Nice seeing you again, Alex."

Alex West replied, shaking Price's hand, "You too, Tom."

Seconds later, together they walked to the clinic's recovery rooms toward the side of the building.

And, toward the back in the waiting room, a tallish slender guy in a black leather jacket over a black T-shirt and dark jeans, sat reading a *Stars and Stripes* newspaper and casually glanced over to the three individuals.

The guy, once the three left the waiting area, stood and walked outside the clinic, pulled out his cell phone, and called Captain Steel.

"Sir," he said once he heard Steel's voice on the other end. "They came through the back, both of them. And they have a third person with them."

Jim Steel said, *"Set up somewhere in the back and wait and see what type of vehicle they get into. Then get back to your partner."*

The guy replied, "Yes, sir."

After pocketing his phone, he reentered the clinic, walked toward the back door, and stepped outside. Checking the parking lot, he noted several parked cars. He'd hope to just find *that* one car. But no dice, there were too many. Then, walking back inside he found a chair in the waiting room and sat to wait.

* * *

In the clinic recovery room, in a secured private bedroom guarded by two armed MPs, Agent Jacqueline Sinclair and Agent Tom Price were sitting by Colonel Sinclair's bed, while Agent Alex West stood behind them. The PM was wide awake, sitting up and sipping orange juice through a straw from a plastic cup, as Sinclair held his free hand.

After the initial shock of his daughter's bruises and puffy eye had worn off, Colonel Sinclair asked, "What the hell happened to you, Belle?"

"Someone tried to kill me in my apartment. Price pumped three into him."

Colonel Sinclair looked at Price in a different light. He'd have to thank him for saving his little girl's life.

It was that part of the morning, exactly twelve o'clock in the middle of day, when the sun was at its highest point in the sky, a mild day for the month of August. A cool misty rain and wind started to fall outside the recovery room windows.

He'd just awakened from his coma over an hour ago. His throat felt tight and dry, and the orange juice wasn't helping. He wished he had a shot of bourbon to soothe his throat and calm his nerves and his mood.

"What time is it?" he asked as he glanced over at his daughter.

"It's twelve o'clock, Dad."

"It's got to be five o'clock somewhere, honey," Colonel Sinclair said with a wink and a smile.

"Why do you say that?" she asked, trying to smile back. Already she knew what was coming.

"A shot of bourbon or two could help more than this juice."

Agent Sinclair held his hand a little tighter. "Dad, you know you can't have any liquor, right? Anyway, not just yet."

Colonel Sinclair shook his head. "You're no fun, honey."

"Dad, what happened?" his daughter whispered, voicing both Price and West's concerns, too.

The PM didn't answer right away. Instead, he gently squeezed his daughter's hand and stared at her for a few seconds.

"I don't know," the Colonel finally answered slowly. "One moment I'm at my computer and the next pain, then total blackout."

Not surprised by his answer, Belle cleared her throat and dabbed at a tear from her eye. "You had a brush with death, Dad, and you lived through it. I don't know what to think if you were to—"

Colonel Sinclair inclined his head and quickly said, "I'm here, Belle."

Agent Jacqueline Belle Sinclair nodded.

"Right now, I have something to say," Colonel Sinclair slowly said. "I need you and Tom to do three things before you continue with this investigation. So, stop whatever you're doing and follow my directions."

Agent Price took a deep breath. "What's this about, sir?"

Both Belle and West cocked an ear, waiting for him to elaborate.

However, Belle's expression was unchanged as she stared at her father.

"There've been certain times when I felt like someone's been listening to my office conversations. Call it a gut feeling if you would. So, first, I need a clean sweep of my office to be done for listening devices. I suspect someone may have placed a bug somewhere in there," he said not making eye contact with them. "Then do a sweep of my quarters. And, Belle, sweep your office as well. Last, get my computer and bring it to me. I think it holds the key to all this."

This time it was Agent West that said, "What do you mean, sir?"

"Well, before I was shot, I was about to open an email with two attachments," he said. "I was curious, since it came from General Chapman's private email account. I was about to open it when the lights went out."

Agent Price said, "And you suspect . . . ah, the email to contain what exactly?"

"If I knew that, I would tell you, Agent Price."

Price looked away, slightly annoyed at his own question. "Yes, sir."

"Belle, once at my quarters, have a patrol bring me my cell phone. I feel naked without it."

Belle nodded. "Of course, Dad."

"Also, call my secretary and have her get my deputy PM over here. I have things for him to do. Also, Belle, get a hold of your AIC, let him know I need to see him today. While in my office, I set Jones on a detail to find some information for me. I urgently need to talk to him. They won't release me until tomorrow, that is, if I'm up to it."

"Yes, sir."

"Now, I would like to be left alone. I'm tired and would like to sleep awhile."

Agent Sinclair stood, kissed her father, turned, and said, "Let's go, guys; we have a lot of work to do."

Once they'd walked out of the clinic, Agent Alex West said, "We have the scanners back at the office, Sinclair. I'll meet you there."

"Roger that, Alex," Sinclair acknowledged.

The moment they were in his car, Agent Price turned to Sinclair. "You didn't fill your father in on what happened so far, Sinclair."

"Yeah, about that," she said, "I didn't feel like troubling him with the results of our investigation just yet."

"Understood."

Once he had his car in motion, Agent Alex West slowly pulled out of the clinic parking lot, while Agent Price, with Sinclair in the passenger seat, fell in line behind West's car and headed toward the CID office.

As both vehicles pulled out onto the main road, Captain Jim Steel's crew followed.

—Chapter Twenty-One—

The OP-CENTER, 12:30 p.m.

It had taken them thirty minutes.

But now that all four generals sat around the conference table, they got down to business.

With their children's lives hanging in the balance, they were all in agreement—this needed to be done. It was the only way to have the children back home again. The CID was not any closer to rescuing their children from the clutches of General Thomas Scott and his henchmen.

They all knew that once their involvement became public, their military careers ended, and they would all be facing the threat of possible prison time. But none of that mattered to them. They thought only of their children. Nothing, not even the possible loss of millions of innocent lives, could deter their fierce determination to carry out the task at hand.

All four of them confessed to the possibility of a third world war if this plan was carried through to completion. However, not even that worried them as much as the lives of their kids. They would do anything and everything to affect their release.

Laid out in front of each of them were sheets of the total OP-PLAN that General Thomas Scott needed to have amended to reflect the new changes. These modifications involved the total number of the strike force, with the capabilities and assignment of certain provisions, assigning aircraft designation and type, and location of that aircraft and its armaments. The tentative dates and times changed as well, as per general instructions and requirements, and alerting those responsible for its implementation. It would be General Scott's determination when implementation of the plan would begin.

The changes circumvented and bypassed presidential approval to implement the operational first strike plan!

They also changed the other three OP-PLANS to reflect the new adjustments. These changes were instrumental to the effectiveness of General Scott's plan. If they failed to submit it, Scott would immediately be made aware of it. They couldn't take that chance.

With Lieutenant General James Shaffer, the Assistant Deputy Commander, EUCOM, the leader of the four, they worked throughout the day, accepting or adding information, tables, and minute details. But, once they'd finished, the plan would be complete and all that would be left was to have it written out and placed in motion.

Once the OP-PLAN was ready, General Shaffer would call the number provided to him and inform General Scott that it had been accomplished and then await his implementation order.

—Chapter Twenty-Two —

The Silo—Control and Command Center (CAC), 1:15 p.m.

aptain Jacob Rose, a tall man, powerfully built with a bull neck and broad shoulders, was designated by Colonel Godfrey Randall, the second in command, as the main security or bodyguard to General Scott, his commander.

Colonel Randall hand-picked the captain out of all his staff officers for his unique set of skills—killing without remorse and getting the job done at all cost. Jacob Rose was a killer with an abnormal psychological gratification in killing another human being. The colonel pieced together this young man's past from his military records and through his interview of the captain.

And what Colonel Randall found suited the young captain very well in the position.

Captain Rose was subjected to psychological abuse from the age of six by both his parents and a drunkard abusive uncle. They would mete out discipline to the child that was both wicked and inhumane. However, at twelve, using his father's gun, he killed both of his parents point blank and his uncle in their sleep. Afterward he set the house on fire. The authorities ruled the fire accidental and the killing as a burglary gone wrong, with young Rose as the sole survivor.

Moving about from one foster care to another, Rose, at eighteen, joined the Army and, after hard work, became qualified to be a Ranger, then a Special Forces operative in both theaters of war. As a sniper, he excelled at his craft and enjoyed killing in the same vein as he made love to women.

Three years ago, on his return home from Afghanistan and, while celebrating his return, he became involved in a brutal bar fight. According to the local police, Rose used a broken beer bottle and killed all four of his attackers. Although the police ruled it self-defense, others didn't see it that way, and Rose faced a murder charge. Later acquitted of all charges, Jacob Rose disappeared.

A little over two years ago, Colonel Randall and three other men found Captain Rose impoverished, face down in a gutter, drunk. After several days of rehabilitation, they offered him a job. Shortly thereafter, Rose was classified a deserter by the US Army.

Now, his new mission, was to assist Captain Steel's team as needed for possible backup.

Having loaded a Lincoln Navigator with two unique shoulder held weapons, his Beretta 9mm, and suppressor, he departed the Silo that afternoon.

* * *

It was nearly 1:45 p.m. when Agent Sinclair, Price, and West shuffled into the CID building. They'd first stopped off at the PX food court and ordered cheeseburgers, fries and sodas to take back to the office. Sinclair and Price hadn't eaten breakfast, and Agent West had only a large coffee earlier in the morning. They were all famished.

As they parked, they picked up their food and proceeded toward the back door. Sinclair pulled out her keys and, once at the door, opened it, and all three walked inside.

Two white Chevys slowly pulled into the front of the CID building. One car to the left and the other to the right side of the parking lot. They pulled in ass-backward and waited, keeping vigil on both sides of the building, watching through their rear-view mirrors.

Inside the building, Agent West had already retrieved two of the hand-held scanners. All three had agreed to not say a single word during the search for listening devices.

Sinclair and Price sat and devoured their burgers as Agent West turned on a scanner and went through, inch-by-inch, her office, without success, until he waved it slowly around her desk. There, the scanner picked by a steady beeping signal.

Setting down the scanner, Agent West dropped to his knees and looked under the desk. Sticking out from the rear left side was a black 2x2 inch bug with a small antenna jutting out from a corner. Removing it, he stood, dropped the bug on the floor and, with his shoe, stomped hard on the plastic case, shattering it into pieces. Then he went through the office once more, but he detected no further bugs.

West, when he'd finished, settled himself in a chair, and glanced over at Sinclair and Price. "We're good to go, Sinclair."

"So, they have monitored us all this time," Sinclair observed. "I wonder how much they know about our investigation. I'm so fucking pissed."

Price raised an eyebrow. "Yeah, me too. There's no way of telling what they've picked up, and when."

Sinclair nodded. "Yeah, well, now we know the why they wanted us out of the picture. They'd stayed one-step ahead of us all this time. Maybe now, we'll have the advantage."

"Yeah, but for how long?" Agent Alex West asked.

"Good question, Alex," Sinclair replied. "We just don't know. Guess playing it by ear would seem the most prudent thing to do now."

In one hand, she held the rest of her burger. In the other, she picked up her desk phone and placed a call to her AIC, Chief Jones, at his home. Dialing, she took the last bite of the burger. The phone rang several times without an answer. She tried calling Jones' cell phone, which went straight to voice mail. No answer there either.

"That's strange," she said returning the receiver. "I'm getting no answer from Chief Jones' home or his cell phone. He's always home about this time of the day and has his cell on him at all times."

Price asked, "What do you want to do?"

"Let's go have a visit." Sinclair replied. "Something tells me all may not be right at his house. Let's hope I'm wrong."

Price took a deep breath. "You know, Sinclair, your father did mention that he'd sent your chief to gather some type of information. And if your father's office got bugged, they would know that. Don't you think?"

A momentary pause as she let that sink in.

"*Shit* yeah," Sinclair said, "no use standing around. . . *hell*, we need to get to his quarters, ASAP!"

Locking up the office behind her, Sinclair, Price and Alex West used one car for the drive. Agent Price volunteered to drive his car. They quickly walked to his car and, with Sinclair in the front passenger seat and Alex West behind her in the back, they all hoped against hope there wasn't anything wrong with Chief Jones.

Once they were all in Price's BMW coupe, he turned the key in the ignition, shifted to drive, and slowly pulled away.

Checking the time on her cell phone, it read 2:35. Then she redialed Jones' quarters a second time, but after several rings, she still wasn't getting an answer. She also tried his cell phone once more, but like before, nothing. *Just hope they're driving somewhere or out shopping*, she thought.

From the front of the CID building, Captain Steel saw the BMW pull away from the back of the building, coming toward the front, and saw three persons in the car. Through his throat mic, he said, "Get ready, men."

Once the BMW was on the main street and with a sufficient distance between them, they locked step behind the BMW.

* * *

Underground caves - The Silo

She'd been crying off and on for several hours.

The girl's eyes were deep pools, dark as night. Her long hair coming down over her shoulders was a tangled mess. She hurt in the worst places of her body and not just her heart and soul. Her clothing was stained in blood, her blood. And the bloodstained panties lay in a corner, as a reminder of what they represented—rape! Her dress had been stripped in tatters, barely covering her body.

She shivered in the coldness of her cell, unable to find any source of warmth. She didn't know if it was night or day outside. Her cell was always dark!

The only thought running through her tired mind was, were they coming to rape her again? She couldn't bear it any longer. The mere thought of it brought terror and agonizing dread. It kept her awake, unable to sleep or to close her eyes.

The rape had mushroomed in her mind to the point she couldn't take it any longer. She vowed it wouldn't happen again.

Given up on any rescue from her father or anyone else, it was useless to think anyone knew where she was. Knowing what they could do next terrified her waking hours. The feeling of being alone for the first time in her life and having no one to turn to—no one, brought her to tears.

The outer corners of her eyes turned upward to the wooden rafters above her. Without necessitation, she knew what she needed to do and, walking to a pail she'd use to urinate into, she spilled it over and placed it under the rafter above her. Sitting on the hard, cold floor, she removed her shoelaces and joined them into one. Stepping on the pail, she threw a line over the rafter and caught it on the other end. After making a noose, Lisa Shaffer placed it around her neck.

For a moment she stood, staring at nothing and, with anguished pain and tears flowing down her eyes, she said in a hoarse, raspy voice, "I love you, Daddy, Mommy."

Then, standing tippy toed on the pail, the fifteen-year-old Lisa M. Shaffer, daughter of General James Shaffer, kicked the pail out from under her. And as she swung back and forth, tears ran down her face, her eyes bulged, and closed for the very last time.

A few minutes later, the laces gave out and her body dropped onto the cold, hard floor.

—Chapter Twenty-Three—

A light rain was starting to fall and, with heavy traffic on the road, it took him almost twice the normal time to make the long drive to Stuttgart. The forecast called for showers off and on for the rest of the day with temperatures in the mid-seventies and light to moderate sustained winds.

Captain Jacob Rose arrived at his destination and checked his watch, 3:00 p.m. "Hell, I'd still made good time," he muttered. The two-story apartment in the Heusteigviertel district was on one of the four corners.

This apartment complex encircled and wrapped around the whole street and, within walking distance to the creative district, included a Rathaus and a Markplatz. Landmarks in the area also included a museum, Hegelhaus, and the Kaufhaus Breuninger, and offered everything from bakeries to exclusive restaurants. He noticed those were a stone's throw away from the apartment. The nearest tram and bus stops he observed were in the immediate vicinity, and he saw the main train station a few minutes away as he drove through the area.

Keeping his speed below twenty, he continued to drive around the block, scouting for any possible shooting sites within an area that wasn't so populated. But none presented itself.

As he drove, the light rain tapped against his windshield as his wipers kept a steady slow beat. Rose observed a throng of people clustered together shopping in an open Markplatz or market area, or walking and riding bicycles, some with umbrellas but most without. Traffic was heavy as well. Across from the apartment complex was an open park, jam-packed with families with children and pets. Not even the light rain that now turned to drizzle could keep them away.

This is not good, he thought, quickly realizing there could be severe collateral damage and entirely too many witnesses. That would be the result if he implemented his plan here and now. His idea was to fire one of his M72, 66mm LAWs rocket into the car while his target drove through the dense area.

He scratched that idea.

Coming around toward his intended victim's front door, he drove through an adjacent parking lot and found a space without obstructions to his target's front door. What he saw brought a tiny smile to his lips. Parked parallel to the front door was a black Alpha Romero Stelvio coupe, which he knew belonged to the target. It confirmed his victim's presence. Sliding into the vacant space, as he turned off the engine, the rain stopped.

Opening his cell phone, Jacob Rose scrolled through his photo application, found the target's photograph and studiously examined and memorized his features and closed the phone.

Pulling one of three rolled marijuana joints from his shirt pocket, he placed it between his lips. Striking a match with his thumb, he lit it and inhaled the strong smoke, then, holding it for a few seconds, he exhaled and tried to relax.

* * *

With the rain subsiding, Agent Price drove in silence, as he kept an eye on Sinclair, fast asleep next to him. They had been through a lot the last couple of days, more so *her*, getting singled out to be killed, and himself too. He admired the way she handled herself when they attacked in her apartment. It was a testament to her training and wits. What a remarkable woman. A woman like that only comes into this world once in a hundred years. Amazon comes to mind and so did warrior princess, come to think of it, he thought with a smile.

Agent Tom Price sighed. "What a woman," he said to himself.

It was 3:30 in the afternoon, as he checked his watch. He'd been driving for about forty-five minutes, give or take. They were in route to CID Chief Jones' off-post quarters, in Sonnenberg, a town eight more miles away. Traffic was light and only a few cars were behind him to contend with. With barely any oncoming traffic, he kept it within the speed limit.

With Agent Alex West sound asleep in the back, he drove into the small town of Sonnenberg and gently touched Sinclair's arm, waking her. She jerked awake, reached for her gun, but relaxed once she stared at Tom Price and saw the smile that played across his lips.

"How long have I slept?" she asked, as she sat back on her seat and rubbed her face.

"All the way," Price replied.

"Where are we?"

"Arriving into the town of Sonnenberg," Tom Price said. "It's your turn to navigate."

"Okay, let's see. Oh, right, go through the town for about a mile," she said, stretching and stifling a yawn. "Once you pass the Sonnenberg Castle, hang a left. His house is in the sticks about a quarter of a mile further on, on the left side."

Agent Price shifted his large frame in his seat and gazed at her. "How often have you visited his house?" he asked.

"Once or twice, so please drive slow."

"No problem."

Sinclair turned on her seat and faced behind her. "Hey, Alex, wake up, we're almost there."

"Yeah, yeah, I'm up," Agent West said, yawning.

Ten minutes later, they were traveling East on Bettlehecker Strasse, as tall trees grew on both sides of the road. There were several lakes and the road twisted here and there as low wooded hills appeared from both sides.

"Easy now. Tom," Sinclair said, "the entrance should be just around the next bend."

"Okay."

"There it is," she said, pointing to her left. "Hang a left onto the driveway."

When he made the turn, he saw a long driveway leading to a darkened two-story house with lighting coming from a front room on the left side of the house, bathinh its glow only on a part of the outside grounds. Bordering on both sides of the driveway were wooden fences. Parked in the driveway, Sinclair noticed two cars, one owned by Chief Jones and the other by his wife.

Six cars behind Sinclair's party, Captain Steel and his team followed. He didn't turn into the driveway, giving sufficient time for Sinclair and her agents to enter the house.

They pulled to the side of the road, stopped, and waited.

* * *

At 3:45, the front door to his target's apartment opened.

The apartment itself was a two-story complex with a second-story balcony. Built with brick masonry and blocks with a layer of stucco applied then painted brown, it was an upscale dwelling for upper-class residents.

The man, wearing a two-piece gray suit, stood just outside the door, locked it, turned around, and walked down the short flight of stairs to the street.

Through his windshield, Captain Rose identified his target as that of Captain Jeffrey Cory. Why did they want him dead? He didn't ask. His job was clear. He scanned the area, but it was not yet conducive for a killing zone. He must wait and see if Jeffrey Cory gets into his car, then the plan would be to follow and wait for the opportunity to strike.

"Yeah, play it by ear, Jacob," he said to himself.

Then he heard a faint steady vibration from his cell phone lying on the car's center console. Picking it up, he saw the text on the screen, it read: *check with possible backup to Captain Steel's crew once you've completed your task.* He didn't need reminding.

After a few seconds, Jeffrey Cory stopped and stood on the street landing of his apartment complex. He breathed in the crisp cool air, turned right, and started walking as if he had no care in the world. He didn't know that, in the next few minutes, his fate would be sealed.

As Cory passed his car, Jacob Rose pulled his Beretta 9mm from his shoulder holster, reached into the glove compartment and pulled out a suppressor. Screwing it onto the Beretta, he holstered it, fixed his jacket, and opened the SUV's door.

Damn, he was looking forward to using the LAWs rocket.

"*Shit*, scratch that idea," he muttered.

After locking his SUV, he casually crossed the street and followed his prey. He was not yet in a hurry. This needed to be done slowly. Preferring Cory to have gotten into his car, it would've done the trick. However, he had to play the hand that was dealt.

Jeffrey Cory moved up the street; he wasn't in any hurry. Having made reservations at a restaurant three blocks away for four o'clock, he had plenty of time.

Jacob Rose, being too far to do anything, quickened his pace, gaining little by little. When he was about a hundred feet away, more or less, he started to increase his speed yet again—sixty, then fifty-feet. His target hadn't bothered to look behind him, and that was good, Rose thought.

Just within twenty-feet, Rose scanned the area. Traffic had thinned somewhat, and there wasn't anyone within a half a block of their position, which suited him well.

His next plan of action took less than a second to put together in his mind. And, as he was about ten-feet behind his prey, Rose pulled his 9mm, pointed it at Cory's back, fired four quick shots into his back and one to the back of his head, as a car with its horn blaring passed on the street, muffling the sound from his suppressor even more.

Jeffrey Cory never saw his killer. With the bullets' impact, he was violently flung forward as the front of his head exploded. Then two twists of his body later, he fell face down on the hard concrete. No one had witnessed the kill. It was a clean and straightforward affair, by Rose's estimation.

Perfect in every way, he thought, with a slight smile. Jacob Rose was very proud of himself.

Quickly, he walked past his felled target. A block further on, he turned away, crossed the street, walked around the block, and finally got back to his waiting Lincoln.

Once in his SUV, the rain started falling without warning. He dug into his pocket, pulled out his cell phone, and dialed Captain Jim Steel's number from memory. Once he heard Steel on the other end he said, "I'm finished here, Jim. Need my help?"

Jim Steel replied, *"I could use another hand or two."*

"Good, give me the address, and I'll input it into the Lincoln's navigation."

Once he had the address plotted, it showed travel time of twelve minutes.

"Hey, I'm close to you," Jacob Rose said, "I'll be there in about twelve minutes, should be fun."

* * *

As Sinclair opened the car door, she swung her legs around and stepped out of the car. Standing and facing west, out in the distance, she noticed low, dark, heavy, rain clouds. It was blowing their way at a steady pace. It was just a matter of time, she reasoned, before it came down on them.

Stepping out of the car, Price and West stared at the house, then at Sinclair.

West said, "I've got a bad feeling about this, Sinclair."

Agent Price said, "Yeah, I'm getting bad vibes too."

"I have to agree with you guys, something is not right," Sinclair said nodding her agreement. "With only one light on in the house, cars parked, and no one answering the phones, yeah, something's off."

This was no coincidence, and it was plain spooky too. Worst, it made no sense. Sinclair was having second thoughts about entering the house. But it needed to be done.

Agent Price said, "So, what do you want to do?"

"What we came here for," she replied. "Let's take this nice and easy and cautious."

Drawing her Berretta and holding it down by her right side, she waited on them.

"*Shit*, that *cautious* eh, okay then," Price said, watching her draw her weapon.

Tom Price walked to the back of his car, opened the trunk, reached in, and grabbed his Mossberg 20GA shotgun with a handful of shells. Then, inserting seven rounds into the shotgun's breach, he pulled back the slide, jacked a round in the chamber, thumbed off the safety, pocketed the extra shells, and closed the trunk lid.

Agent Tom Price grunted. "I'm ready."

Walking shoulder to shoulder with Agent Sinclair, Agent West asked, "What do you think we'll find?"

Sinclair replied, shrugging and shaking her head, "I don't know, something, anything, hell, maybe nothing at all. We'll see."

"*Shit,*" West said. Pulling his 9mm, he slid back the slide, jacked a live round into the chamber, and held it by his side. He was uncomfortable pulling his weapon. Ever since he became an accredited special agent, he'd never pulled it or shot anyone in the line of duty. But, he reasoned, there's always a first time.

As they walked up the driveway leading to the front door, Agent West asked, "Don't you guys think this is a little over-kill?"

"We're just being cautious, Alex," Sinclair said. "No telling who is inside that house. It's better to be safe than sorry."

Agent Alex West nodded. But the other two didn't share his feeling of dismay. He felt this was not going to end well. "Yeah, sure, I guess you're right."

Using the lighting from the side of the house, they approached the front door. The outside of the house was in darkness, except for dozens of fireflies about the ground giving off their usual yellow sunlight glow, as sunlight refused to shine through the tall, leafed overhang trees that seemed to cover the wooded landscape. It was like a virtual forest, giving off a dark and creepy sensation, you'd read about in a horror story.

First to reach the door, Sinclair stopped, for the door was slightly ajar. Slowly pushing it wide open, she entered the foyer and stopped as Price and West halted behind her.

"What wrong, Sinclair?" Price whispered, almost in her ear.

"There's a body down the hallway by the stairs."

Hurrying, she approached the body and identified the remains as Mrs. Jones, Rachael Jones, wife to Chief Jones. Sinclair saw dried blood on her eyes and mouth, with caked dried blood on both sides of the body and underneath her. And, on both sides of the body, pools of dried blood had soaked the partial carpet. Her chest had three bullet holes. Sinclair felt for a pulse but knew there wasn't one.

Agent Alex West asked, "Who is she, Sinclair?"

"It's Mrs. Jones, and she's been dead quite a while."

Taking quick charge, Sinclair said, "Alex, take upstairs, Tom, take the den, and I'll check the rest of the house. Someone may still be here, so watch yourselves."

"Copy that," Price said walking off into the den, as West started up the stairs.

Suddenly, Price yelled out to Sinclair, "Better get in here, Sinclair. I believe I found your chief!"

Quickly, Sinclair entered the den, and there, on the side of his desk was her chief, lying in a pool of blood. Walking up to the body, she saw the side of his head had been blown away.

A brief silence.

Sinclair shook her head. "Christ, someone is covering up their tracks. Whatever my Dad put Jones to do, someone didn't want him to look into."

"You want me to search the place?"

"Don't think that'll be necessary. Whatever they or he came for, they must've gotten their hands on it."

They heard someone coming down the stairs and met Agent West before he entered the den. "All clear upstairs . . . wait, is that our chief?" he said pointing, as he saw the body in the den.

"Yeah, dead too, I'm afraid," Price replied.

Shaking his head, Alex West said, "*Jesus H. Christ*, Sinclair, what have we gotten ourselves into?"

"Alex, calm down, okay?" Sinclair said. "Listen, stand guard by the den's window, in case someone drives up."

"Roger that, Chief," he said.

"What did you say?" she asked, shocked at his response.

"I'm only stating a fact, Sinclair," West said. "You're Chief now."

Sinclair frowned. "Damn," was all she could bring herself to say.

Shaking her head and sighing, she glanced over at Price. "Tom, let's check out the rest of the house."

* * *

An old woman who had been walking her dog found Captain Jeffrey Cory's body at about 4:15 the same afternoon after he'd been gunned down.

It was the end of the workday and the exhausted Gretel Afflenbach needed to be home before her husband returned and, with Aldo, her German Pointer, taking his time, there'd be hell to pay if she got home and did not have dinner ready.

With the streets wet from the small amount of rain that fell earlier, Gretel came around the block and stopped, pulling Aldo hard, telling him to stop. For just ahead of her, she saw what she believed was a human body lying halfway into the street about halfway up from her. She couldn't say what it was really, without her glasses. Reaching into her jacket pocket, she pulled out a wire-framed, thick-lens pair of glasses, set it on, and glanced once again toward the body.

"Oh . . . Mein . . . Gott!" she said, slowly approaching the body. She quickly glanced around for anyone else that could help the poor man, but she was alone and, once again, she stopped; for she saw blood pooled around the body.

Then she jumped back a step, her heart leaping in her throat, and screamed hard and loud.

Gretel's dog Aldo sniffed at the body, calmly backed up from it, and sat.

—Chapter Twenty-Four—

At the very moment Agent Price found Chief Jones' corpse, Captain Steel's team of four black-clad men, armed with M4A1 rifles with attached M203 grenade launchers, began their approach to the house. And, walking side by side with Jim Steel, was Captain Jacob Rose who'd arrived just in time for the assault on the current occupants. Rose shouldered one of his LAWs rocket and his sidearm.

Slowly they split into two teams, one to the left and the other to the right, and, with dusk approaching, they used the darkness for cover, stopping just about a hundred yards toward the front of the two-story house. They'd already planned their attack. The team on the right would have one person work his way to the back and gain entrance. The other would work his way toward the right side of the house and find a side door, if present, and, if not, then gain entry through a side window.

One of Steel's team members would work his way around the other side of the house. And, with Rose's 66mm LAWs rocket, it would be fired into the room with the lights on.

Once he gave his signal, the teams broke away, heading to their positions, just as Jacob Rose slung off his rocket launcher. Then, grasping it with both hands, Rose slid them slightly apart and, as it locked into position, he placed it on his shoulder and, raising the sights, Rose aimed down range to the lit window.

"I'm ready, Jim," he said to Steel.

"Hang on just a little while longer, Jacob."

"I'm hanging."

Captain Steel waited for several minutes for his men to get into their positions. Then he gave Rose the go-head.

"Roger," Rose said as he pulled the trigger. And, with a loud booming sound, the rocket streaked through the air with great accuracy towards the lit-up window.

A second later, a terrifying boom came from the side of the house, as a grenade fired from an M203 grenade launcher plowed through the back door and exploded into hundreds of pieces. A minute later, a side window blew apart, as another grenade from another M203 grenade wreaked its destruction.

Rising swiftly to their feet, Steel and Jacob Rose started running toward the front door.

Then, without warning, a single loud clap of thunder broke through and a lightning bolt cracked across the sky. An instant later, the rain fell in torrents.

—Chapter Twenty-Five—

It was dark and stormy; the rain fell unabated, as the 66mm HEAT warhead of the LAWs rocket streaked through the air, at a speed of 475fps!

As he stared out the closed window, Agent Alex West saw it coming right towards him.

"Holy shit!" was all he could say.

Spinning away from the window, he started running.

However, it was too late.

As the rocket's nose-cone impacted, the closed window blew apart into dust. The fragments and incendiary produced a blinding orange and white light that destroyed half of the interior of the den, along with Agent Alex West, when the blast lifted him into the air. As metal fragments of the grenade flew at tremendous velocity, West was struck on his upper and lower torso cutting him in half.

Agents Sinclair and Price had just cleared the kitchen, when the den blew. Running into the hallway, they stopped dead in their tracks.

"We're under attack!" Price said.

"You think?"

"Alex!" Sinclair yelled into the den. But, in the back of her mind, she already suspected the worst.

No answer.

Just the howling wind blowing through the den's window answered her.

"Goddamn!" Sinclair said, shaking her head, knowing he could already be dead.

With no time to enter the den and see for themselves, when suddenly . . .

. . . They immediately turned as the back door blew apart and a side window. Hearing the explosions, Sinclair, quickly staring over at Price, said, "Take the side window. I'll take the back door. And don't get yourself killed. I've already lost one partner."

Sinclair slowly headed to the back door, while Tom Price started running to the side window. With white dust clouds hanging throughout the lower portion of the house, it was getting hard to breathe, and visibility was poor. Just as she rounded a corner, Sinclair reached the back door, or what was left of it, and confronted a black-clad intruder slowly making his way inside, his assault rifle pointing the way.

Sinclair wasted no time. With her 9mm already pointing straight out in front of her, she unleashed a deadly accurate barrage at the guy. But as her rounds impacted on his chest, there was no visible effect.

"*Shit, body armor,*" she muttered, taking cover behind a door, as a stream of automatic fire ripped into the wall inches from her position.

The intruder kept shooting in automatic fire mode. As the bullets riddled the wall behind and above where she'd sought shelter, she kneeled behind it.

Contingency plans coursed through her mind. She didn't have enough time to think about it; she just reacted. With her back against the wall and, hearing the intruder slowly walking forward, she leaned forward, threw her body on the ground facing the guy, and, once she had the target in her sights, she quickly fired four rounds into his upper body. One round found the intruder's face, killing him as her weapon locked on an empty magazine.

Sinclair swept to her feet in one fluid, graceful motion, while ejecting the empty magazine. Then, reaching behind her to an ammo pouch holding two extra magazines, she quickly pulled one and rammed it into the pistol grip, and let the slide ram forward, jacking in a live round. Then she said, "That's one down and no telling how many more to go."

Holding her weapon double-fisted and pointing it at the ground, she heard automatic weapon fire coming from the front door and the side window.

Instead of running to the front door, she headed to the side window to help Price.

Halfway through the hallway, she heard crunching footsteps behind her.

Oh, hell no! Sinclair thought to herself as her eyes widened in surprise. *Someone else was coming through the back door!*

She was caught in the middle of some sort of nightmare.

And, before she could turn, several bullets came whistling toward her. A bullet grazed her left shoulder, while others sailed to her left and right. Left with only one option, and without conscious thought, she threw herself on the ground, turned, and faced her attacker. Taking quick aim at the person's upper body and knowing full well they were wearing body armor, she unleashed the rest of her magazine at the figure creeping forward from the back entrance.

One or two of her rounds struck center of his head, and he was thrown backward and stopped by the impact of her bullets to his lower body, dead before he hit the ground. Releasing the empty magazine, she reached behind her and pulled out her last magazine.

Shrugging off this attack, Sinclair struggled to collect her wits, and slowly headed to the side window and Tom Price, as she chambered a live round to her weapon.

* * *

Agent Tom Price, reaching the side window, came to a sudden stop and froze at the threshold to an open door but darkened room.

He faced a large anteroom and, through the heavy dust, he saw several pieces of furniture covered with white sheets; it was a storage room for old or maybe new furniture. The floor was wood and covered with plaster chips, wood particles, and dust, and the walls to his side were bare. He took this all in with an instant glance. Through the thick white dust, he saw a tall, black-clad man climbing through what they left of the window on the left side of the room.

In a blur of motion, Price stepped into the room and met the man head-on. Not having his weapon out in front of him cost him precious seconds—and nearly his life. For just as Price raised his weapon to fire, the man in black aimed and fired his assault weapon first and with a sustained burst at the faint dark figure in front of him, raking Price up and down.

One bullet sailed off to Tom Price's left side and impacted the doorframe mere inches from him. Another bullet nicked his left shoulder, twisting him. The third grazed his right leg, knocking him to his knees. Rolling away from the side of the door, Tom Price raised and pointed his shotgun at the figure walking towards him through the dust, just as the man in black fired once more. Price working the pump, cut loose with three blasts of his own from his 20GA shotgun.

The rounds slammed into the attacker's chest and lower torso, flinging him backwards and almost throwing him back through the window. The man was sprawled half in half out of the window and was still breathing. Price rose and, limping his way forward, jacked a shell into the chamber and pumped a round into the upturned face.

"Asshole, that's for shooting at me."

Then hearing running footsteps behind him, he twirled around so fast that he lost his balance and landed on the floor in a sitting position with his shotgun pointed at the doorway.

"Hey, you okay?" he heard Sinclair ask from the edge of the doorway.

"Come on ahead."

Strolling into the room, she could just make out Price through the dim light and through the dust in the air, sitting on the floor. As she approached him, she saw he was bleeding from a gunshot wound. She holstered her weapon, ready to help him stand.

"Can you walk, Tom?"

"Yeah, I can. It's not that bad, I think."

"We got them coming through the front door. We can't go upstairs. No way of telling how many are still outside. Think we should make a stand here. What do you think?"

"Sounds like a plan, could use a little rest."

Watching Price, she felt he would be of no use in an open confrontation.

"Here, let me help you," she said wrapping her arms around his waist, helping him up, and leading him to a dark corner of the room.

Just as she was letting him down, he felt her face touching his cheeks. She turned her face slightly toward him and, without a moment's hesitation, he turned and kissed her on her lips.

Dropping him on the floor, she said, "Are you crazy? What was that for?"

"In case I don't make it out of here."

"In case you do, what then?"

"Cross that bridge when and if we get to it, I guess."

He then asked, "Like the kiss?"

"Had better," she said, turning away, not letting him see her smile.

Seconds later, over the wind blowing through the demolished window, they thought they heard footsteps slowly approaching down the hallway.

* * *

Without a word, with weapons drawn and pointing straight ahead, Captains Rose and Steel slowly made their way through the hallway, passing the corpse of one of their team members and a woman's corpse. Coming to a stop by the entrance to the den, Rose smiled at his handiwork.

With one on the left, the other on the right side of the hallway they walked, trying to listen for the location of whoever was still alive in the house, if anyone. Coming to the stairs, Steel pointed at Rose, then at the stairs. Rose caught on and started moving to the first landing and made his way up the stairs, as Steel, watching him make his way up, resumed his way down the hallway.

The wind outside was strong and the rain came down in sheets, almost muffling his footsteps on the hardwood flooring. Steel continued on, pausing here and there, listening. The only sounds seemed to be coming from an open door further down toward the end of the hallway, as the racket of howling winds blew into the hallway from where, he assumed, one of his men blew through the window.

He continued on and stopped short of reaching the door on his right and leaned on the wall, listening.

Shit! There was only one-way to do this, he thought, go straight in and continue shooting. It was his only recourse. He needed to see this through to the end.

Steel, with years of special operations missions under his belt, suspected that whoever was still alive was in the room and waiting for whomever to walk through that door. Not having a stun-grenade on him, he was left with no choice but to storm the room and hope he was wrong.

Sinclair and Price waited just in the far-left corner of the room behind a sofa. Sitting with their backs up against it, they checked their ammo supply. Sinclair had just replaced her last magazine, while Price only had two rounds left in his shotgun and one full magazine in his .45ACP.

Sinclair hoped it was sufficient; if not, they were dead.

In the interim, Sinclair tried to stop the flow of blood from Price's arm and leg, and checked out her shoulder too, but noticed it wasn't bleeding. They waited for whomever to come barreling through. They knew it would not be a good guy. Hell, no one knew of the battle that raged on in the house. Therefore, whoever came through would do it firing.

They stared at each and smiled. Sinclair was of the opinion maybe one of them, or both, would not make it. She prayed it wasn't so, as her thoughts turned to her father.

Moments later, Sinclair peeked around the side of the sofa and stared at the door's entrance into the room when she saw a blur of a figure, rushing into the room firing his assault weapon on full auto left and right of him, then taking cover behind a small desk on his right.

She fired two shots to where the figure took shelter and missed, while Price on the other side of the sofa, fired the last of his ammo from his shotgun at the figure's blur motion before it found cover.

Conserving her ammo supply, Sinclair slowly rose to the top of the sofa and aimed at the spot she thought the figure would pop out of, while Price, with his Colt .45, came around the sofa, raised himself over it, and waited for the figure to show. They had both corners of the desk covered.

Now it was a waiting game.

Captain Steel ejected his spent magazine for a full one, stood and opened fire toward the two ends of the sofa.

At the precise moment that Steel rose to his full height, Sinclair saw him silhouetted against the window's light, a black-clad figure and, without hesitation, she fired her gun, while to the other side of the sofa, Price opened up his Colt .45.

"Tom, shoot higher, body armor!" Sinclair yelled out to Price.

With Steel firing at Sinclair's position, it gave Price a fleeting chance. Taking aim, he fired two rounds into where he thought was a figure's head and watched as both shots struck Steel, blowing away the side of his head, as he collapsed on the floor, dead.

From the top landing of the second floor, Captain Rose heard shots being fired downstairs. Taking cover, he waited to see who walked through the hallway. Not showing himself until the last possible moment, just to be sure, he told himself.

* * *

Sinclair and Price stood, while Price leaned on the sofa for support. Sinclair walked over to the body just to make sure it was dead. Satisfying herself, she walked over to Tom Price.

She said, "Here, let me help you."

"I think I can manage, Sinclair."

"Suit yourself, then."

"Thanks anyway. You think there's more of 'em?"

"If they were, they would have attacked alongside that one," she said inclining her head to the corpse.

"Yeah, guess you're right. How about we get out of here?"

"Let's get to the front and decide what to do next."

"Hey, we work well together."

She said with a hint of a smile, "Not well, but maybe good is a better word for it."

They walked side by side, Price limping along with his left arm hanging down beside him, while his right hand still grasped his

Colt. Sinclair ejected her magazine and saw she only had three rounds left and one in the chamber.

Down the hallway they went, past the stairs and the body of Mrs. Jones. On their left, the front door was a few feet ahead of them.

Suddenly, as they walked side by side toward the front door, they heard a cracking noise behind them and, with weapons drawn, they spun around almost as one and watched as Captain Rose rounded the corner from the stairs. In unison, without thinking, they both opened fire. The noise of their combined weapons was especially loud in the confines of the hallway.

Slug after slug found their mark on the target that was still standing in front of them. Then Rose's trigger finger fired off his weapon into the floor. Believing he may have body armor, Special Agent Jacqueline Sinclair raised her weapon sights to head level of the target and fired off her remaining ammunition.

Rose's body danced as the bullets thumped into his chest. Slowly, with each impact, he was being driven backwards, when his head exploded in a gore of blood and brain matter, and then his body sank to the floor, dead.

"Jesus H. Christ, another one!" Tom Price said. "Don't these guys ever quit?"

"Let's hope that's the last of them."

"Roger that."

As they reached the front door, Sinclair heard her cell phone ringing in her pocket. Her hand went to it and, as she pulled it out, saw that it was a call from her father.

"Hi, Dad."

"Hi, yourself, Belle" the Colonel replied. "Just called to see how you'd made out with Chief Jones, honey."

Finding a dry place to sit, she filled him in on all that had transpired in the house.

"What can I do to help?" he asked.

"Could you call the MPs and the German police and an ambulance?" she asked. "We'll wait here for them."

"I will, honey, stay safe."

"Love you, Dad."

"Back at you, honey."

—Chapter Twenty-Six—

Sunday, August 11th, 7:55 p.m.

It was late that evening when the German Federal police concluded their investigation and as a German television news truck pulled into Chief' Jones' driveway, or tried to, the German police on request of the military police and the on-call CID agent, stopped and turned them away with the excuse of it being a matter of national security.

With the MPs squad leader, patrol supervisor, two military policemen at the scene, and CID Agent Jaime Vargas, the on-call duty agent attesting to the identity of the two agents, the matter was referred to the military for their jurisdiction and continued investigation..

Agent Vargas knew that Sinclair was the temporary acting chief, at least until CID Command assigned a permanent one, so he'd better stay in her good graces. One never knew from where a next promotion could materialize.

Once treated for non-life-threatening wounds by the German medics, they considered Agent Price completely able to stand on his own two feet, with Agent Sinclair the lucky one of the two, sustaining a flesh wound to her left shoulder.

An hour later Sinclair and Price drove away from the crime scene or, as Sinclair would describe it—the killing field. *Jesus, what else can it be*, Sinclair thought. Not even in her combat days, had she seen nor been involved in so much killing.

With Jacqueline Sinclair sitting in the passenger seat and Tom Price driving, she shifted irritably. Pain shot through her legs and her left arm. Raising her arm and slowly rotating it, she tried working out the tightness and the kinks.

Sinclair inclined her head and sighed, trying to drive away the pain. She thought of all the havoc done in Jones' house and those that died. First, Chief Jones, his wife, CID Agent Alex West, a friend and close partner in the office, along with those she and Tom killed in self-defense. One thing was certain; they had followed her to Chief Jones' home. Of that, there was no doubt.

She ran through the events of the last few days.

At the onset of her investigation, her objectives were clear. First, find and rescue the kidnapped children. Second, bring to justice those responsible. The only Intel she'd had to work with was sketchy—the notes left at the kidnapping scenes. They suggested that more instructions would be was forthcoming. Did the generals, in fact, already receive those instructions and, if so, how? Why didn't the generals come forth with the information? The evidence she'd gathered at the scene, the possible identification of the weapons used, and where they may have come from, not to mention the vehicles. All suspicions, up to this point. And who was the figurehead in the 113th that knew about those thefts? Was it Captain Cory? Too early to tell, she figured.

It was also disturbing that even the parents of the kidnapped children had, without a doubt, clammed up, offering her no leads, assuming any existed for her to follow. The two stolen smart bombs portended even greater catastrophic events to happen. And, if that were the case, where and when would it happen? She didn't believe anymore that it was a black-market operation. And, with the missing smart bombs, it was just a matter of time before her father called in the FBI. Knowing her father, however, he wasn't about to relinquish his authority to them without a fight.

That being said, those questions she pondered paled in comparison to why she and Price were marked for death. Did they, whoever they were, think they were getting close to their operations? Close to knowing what their plans really entailed? And, ultimately, were the children still alive?

It was only a matter of time before she had the answers to those questions.

And, if what happened back at the house was any indication, that she and Price and now her father were marked—*were more hired killers coming after them again?* she asked herself.

This wasn't any run-of-the-mill criminal investigation. This was looking like what Tom Price once suggested—a terrorist plot.

Allowing herself to think in that possible scenario, made her believe that maybe a time schedule was being worked on. How much time did they have left, until *it*, whenever *it* was, came blowing up in their faces?

It was becoming clear that she and Price were keeping them off balance and guessing what she and Tom had gleaned from her investigation. Now that the "bugs" were found, would they attempt, yet again, to kill her and Tom? If they were, she would be prepared for their next encounter.

Time—was it playing in her favor? Or theirs. Would she have enough time to stop them before their plan bore fruit?

Only time itself would tell.

Another thought that crossed her mind was her father's request to have his computer examined. Sinclair thought that maybe her father could've been right. Could there really be something in his computer that held some evidence as to whom *they* might be?

She shrugged and glanced over at Agent Price. "Tom, we're going to my father's quarters. Something I need to get from there. And while we're there, scan for bugs. I still have Alex's scanner in the back seat. So, let's go there first."

"I thought you wanted to get something to eat and get a change of clothes."

She nodded slowly. "Yeah well, that's going to wait. This is more important."

There was a brief silence.

"You're the boss," he said with a smile, as he quickly glanced at her.

* * *

The Silo - The Communications Room

It already had been twenty minutes since they last reported in. So, when Captain Steel and his team did not report within their next prescribed time frame, Corporal Raul Sanchez, monitoring the communications from Steel's team, thought he'd better call them and get a sit-rep, a Situational Report. But he then thought better of it. He didn't want to disrupt them in any way. So, he gave them an additional ten minutes before he'd call.

In the meantime, he hadn't received his usual call from Captain Rose either. He knew Rose was to team-up with Steel's team if called. So why hadn't he called in too? Strange!

Turning on his iPod, he slipped on the earbuds and listened to his favorite country music artist *Alan Jackson*. Then he stood up and paced his office back and forth, as he held his arms locked behind his back. True, he thought this could be nothing, but again, it could be something. But it could be worse. Worse than what? he asked himself.

He turned off his iPod. The music just didn't help relieve the tension that kept steadily mounting.

Sanchez was squinting at his wall clock, as he slowly counted down the minutes . . . 8 . . . 9 . . . 10. Grabbing his chair, he sat down and called Steel's call-sign. He broke squelch on his mic and said, "Charlie Team, this is base, come in."

Nothing, just static from his headphones.

Calling once again, he said, "Charlie Team, this is base, report."

He gave a slow count of ten and then called Captain Rose's call sign.

"Echo Team, this is base, report your situation, over."

The only thing he was receiving was static through his headphones.

He tried once again, but again it was the same thing, static.

Removing his headphones, he shook his head and said, "Man, oh man. He will not like this." Picking up the desk phone receiver, he dialed his CO. After a few rings, Colonel Godfrey picked up.

"*Colonel Godfrey here.*"

"Sir, we may have some problems with Captain Steel's team and that of Captain Rose. They have both failed to report in."

"I'll be right down."

"Yes, sir," Sanchez said.

"Damn, why was he coming to the commo room?" Sanchez muttered, "when I just told him all that I could?"

As he finished and replaced the receiver, he heard, coming through his police scanner, the German Police being sent to investigate gunshots and loud explosions coming from the vicinity of the area where Steel's team was operating. Could that be them? And what of Captain Rose, was he with Steel's team too? But all that was not his concern, his job was communications. Let the powers that be worry about it, he thought.

* * *

The moon was at its mid-sky, that part when the moon is farthest from the horizon, when Agent Tom Price pulled into the main gate of Patch Barracks military installation. With their identification confirmed, the MP gate guard waved them through.

And following Agent Sinclair's directions, he proceeded straight to Colonel Sinclair's quarters.

Prior to their arrival onto Patch Barracks, Tom Price, on the recommendation of Sinclair, had, throughout the long drive, kept watch behind them for a possible tail. At one point, he'd turned off from the Autobahn, parked, and turned off his headlights, as they sat motionless, waiting for any passing vehicle they thought could be a possible threat. Twice, he'd changed direction on the Autobahn and, when he was on the side-roads, he would double-back. But try as he would, he couldn't see anyone that looked suspicious.

They were keeping an eye out not just toward the front, but to their rear as well. They would not be taken by surprise again.

Driving in an area referred to in military jargon as "Officers Row," that part of the installation where family housing was reserved for high-ranking military officers and their families, they passed row after row of cookie-cutter housing units—two-story brick homes painted the same white and yellow colors—Agent Sinclair pointed out her father's quarters as being the third up the way on the right side of the road.

Agent Price, as he approached the quarters, turned onto its driveway and came to a stop behind a 1969 Chevy Camaro, parked ass-end. The Colonel's quarters were like any of the two-story brick homes, with two picture windows on the front and an open detached garage on its right side.

As Price shut down the engine, Sinclair turned in her seat, reached out behind her, and grabbed Agent Alex West's scanner from the back seat. Then, opening her door she slid out, as did Price, and both walked toward the front door and stopped as a sign that read, 'Colonel Sinclair,' on the front door showed whose quarters they were calling on.

Pulling out her set of keys from her pocket that included a key to her father's quarters, given to her in case she ever wanted to move in, she inserted it into the upper dead-bolt lock, twisted the key, turned the knob, and slowly pushed the door inwards. Then, leading the way inside, they stepped onto the foyer, as Price closed the door behind him.

Turning on the lights from a switch on the right-side wall, Sinclair led the way to her father's den. At the threshold, she stopped and switched on the den's lights and, for a moment, she realized the close shave with death her father had gone through. The window through which the would-be assassin's bullet plowed through, striking her father, remained uncovered. From her position, she saw her father's desk and, still, she didn't make a move to enter.

Tom Price cleared his throat and asked, "You want me to do this?"

She stared at the window and didn't say a word. Then she eyed her father's desk. From her position and, through the den's lighting, it was sufficient for her to see and treat this as a crime scene, as she eyed the central pool of blood on the desk. Then, her thoughts revolved to the window once again. Before she left the house, she thought, she would have to cover it up. She just couldn't leave it that way.

A long silence fell between them.

Price, retaining his patient face, gently touched her arm and said, "Sinclair?"

Price's voice seemed to break through her thoughts. She slowly shook her head, glanced at him, and, in a soft whisper, said,

"What? Oh, yes, sorry. Let's remain quiet until I do a scan of the room, okay?"

"No problem. I'll stay here."

Turning on the scanner, she walked into the den. Back and forth, she moved, waving the scanner out in front of her. Sinclair slowly continued in this manner until she'd methodically covered the width and length of the den. But nothing seemed to move the signal that would signify a bug.

Then, she approached the wooden desk. She scanned the desk phone and the computer, nothing there. Bending at the knees, she was about to scan there when the signal on the scanner warned of a bug within its vicinity.

Then, waving at Price to approach her, she turned off the device, placed it on the desk, and, reaching into her pocket, she pulled out her cell phone. Using its flashlight app, she turned it on, and shone its light under the desk.

She found the bug, a 2x2 inch square black plastic cube, with a small antenna sticking out from a side, with a tiny red LED light blinking on and off. She grasped the cube, removed it, stood back up, and showed it to Tom Price, who was standing right beside her.

Dropping the cube on the floor, she stepped hard on it and heard it crack open. Then, she stomped on it again and watched as the red light blinked for the last time.

"Tom," Sinclair said. "Try to get my Dad's computer turned on. I'm going to sweep the rest of the house for any more bugs."

"Roger that."

However, after twenty minutes, they both struck out; Sinclair had found no other listening devices, and Price was unable to get into the computer—it was password-protected.

"Sinclair, I can't get into the computer," Price yelled out looking at the computer screen, thinking she wasn't yet in the room.

"Why are you yelling?" Sinclair asked once she was at the side of the desk.

He said, "Oh, there you are, sorry. It's no use, it's password-protected."

"Here, let me try," she said, turning the laptop around on the desk and stopping once it was facing her.

After several attempts at the password had failed, she typed the word, BELLE, and the computer responded as it opened onto the Windows operating interface main page.

With a hint of a smile, the first thing she did was look into her father's email account and open that. She scrolled through the 102 emails and found the one she was looking for: the email from General Chapman.

Clicking on the email, she waited a second until it was ready on another screen. What she saw were two video files, one named Helen Chapman and the other marked Alpha.

Clicking on the file labeled Helen Chapman, Sinclair waited until the computer's video application recognized the video format and, as Price watched over her shoulder, the video started to play automatically. What they saw was both shocking and telling.

Tom Price took in a deep breath, realizing what he was looking at. "Eh, Goddamn, is that . . .?"

Sinclair said, cutting him off, "Yeah, we're looking at Helen Chapman, one of our kidnapped victims."

The background video was dark, but it provided enough lighting to make out Helen Chapman, blindfolded and tied to a chair. A tall guard wearing all black, with a balaclava hood over his head and holding a gun to her head, had a microphone shoved to her face. They warned not to say a word about where she was being held. Then with a chilling desperate plea, Helen Chapman spoke to her father. *"Daddy, help me. Oh God, Daddy, help me!"*

Then the image just disappeared.

Sinclair could not imagine what the four victims were going though or the torment the general was enduring. Her motherly instincts rose to the surface. Now, knowing what she'd just seen, she knew *why* the four generals had clammed up on her. After watching the video of their child with a gun to her head, blindfolded and all tied up, it would give any parent second thoughts. The hope of getting them back alive was the only thought the parents were concerned with and damned be the law.

Don't blame them one bit, Sinclair thought.

Then she clicked on the second file video, and she saw a face she hadn't seen in well over three years. A face she'd once had the pleasure of knowing, during her father's promotion, and *he* being the presenter during ceremonies at USAEUCOM headquarters.

That face belonged to Brigadier General Thomas Scott.

After listening through the file, she finally had to agree that this was a homegrown terrorist plot to undermine the United States and its allies that could bring the world to the brink of World War Three. It was chilling and frightening as well, Sinclair thought. Her father needed to have this information immediately.

Tom Price stared at the image of General Scott and then at Sinclair and asked, "You know who that is, don't you?"

"Yes, yes, I'm afraid I do."

"Who is he?"

"A long-time friend of my father," she slowly replied, contemplatively.

"Shit!"

Now, Sinclair and Price felt they knew who was behind the operation and the sinister plotting of the events that transpired in the last few days that could unfold in the days to follow.

But they still didn't know the whereabouts of the children or General Scott's base of operations.

Those were details she and Price would have to find out, and soon!

Sinclair was hedging her bets on Captain Cory, her captain, to fill in all the answers to her questions. She was prepared to get her answers, one way or another!

Price stared at Sinclair, his face flushed. "My boss needs to have this information, ASAP."

"I agree, Tom," she said, shrugging. "But first, though, we have to get this information to my father. At this junction, I imagine the FBI would have to be brought in."

"Yeah," Tom Price said, shaking his head. "And you know who else? The President of the United States."

Sinclair turned a withering gaze back at Price but didn't say a word. Then, she walked over to her father's liquor cabinet, pulled out a bottle of Jim Beam whiskey and two Fairbanks whiskey tumblers, poured three fingers' worth, gave one to Tom, and lifted her glass.

Sinclair toasted, "To whatever comes our way next."

Sinclair and Price both downed their drinks. Pouring another round, Sinclair stared over at Tom Price and smiled.

"You know that kiss you gave me?"

"Eh, yeah, and?"

She said, staring him down, "Well, is that the best you can do?"

In answer, Tom Price placed his glass on the wooden desk, came and took Sinclair into his arms, and was ready to give her a kiss, when she gently pushed him away and said, "Not now, but later, maybe."

"You're a big tease," he said, feeling already flustered.

Sinclair shrugged, poker face in place, as she tilted her head back and downed her glass once again. Then, Sinclair closed her eyes, visualizing him kissing her and holding her tight against his firm hard body, but then she opened her eyes and was all business once again.

Wanting to get a shower and a change of clothing, she asked Tom Price to drop her off at her apartment. Knowing she couldn't stay at her place until they repaired her front door, she wanted to pack a suitcase, pick up her car, and drive back to her father's quarters. She was planning to stay at her father's place.

Part Two

Order of Battle

—Chapter Twenty-Seven—

Monday, August 12th

Back at her father's place, Jacqueline Sinclair, deciding to cover the window through which her father had been shot, grabbed a small sheet of plywood, nails, and a hammer from the garage, and boarded it up the best she could. "At least the wind won't be blowing through it anymore," she muttered.

Once done, she grew restless and started pacing. Finding where her father kept his best stock of liquor, she found a half-empty bottle of Harper's Kentucky bourbon, poured herself a tall glass, and gulped it down. She refilled her glass then huddled in a corner of her father's couch.

It should keep her asleep, she thought.

With the window boarded up, it was quiet once again. Sitting in the den's darkness and placing the empty glass on the side-table, her thoughts turned toward her father; cheerful thoughts of her past together with her mother, traveling all over the world, leaving her old friends behind for new ones along the way. It was a military way of life she'd grown to love.

Sinclair's shoulders slumped. "I love you, Mom, Dad." Sinclair felt tears welling up and slowly closed her eyes.

Having finished her bourbon, she rose and walked toward the room she knew her father kept ready if and when she would return.

Stripping naked, she looked in the mirror and didn't like what she saw. Her face looked as if a Mack truck had run her over. The swelling above her left eye had gone down considerably, but the cuts about her face looked about healed. A slight reddish scar on the right side of the forehead would need more time to heal. Maybe the shower will do her some good.

Sinclair pondered one thing or another about her time with Tom Price as she showered. Once finished, she toweled herself down, wrapped another towel around her hair, and donned a nightgown. Once her hair had dried, she entered the bedroom and lay down to sleep.

Tossing and turning, she found sleep elusive, her mind shifting to one person, Tom Price. *Why him?* she thought. She couldn't put her finger on it, but she was feeling a stronger bond she hadn't felt in a long time. Not even with Captain Cory.

Sleep overtook her and her dream was of Price.

In her dream, they were standing close to each other, and he wore only his shorts, and she a white nightgown, opened in the front. She saw herself sliding out of her gown, now naked and moving closer to him as her breasts touched his hard, chiseled chest and, whispering in his ear, "I need you inside me!"

He still wore his underwear, and as her hand slid down inside, she felt him very firm. Her breathing became labored; seeing herself as he picked her up and carried to the bedroom, she moaned, sighing, "Oh, so strong." And, as he gently set her on her bed, she removed his underwear. Crawling on all fours, and lying on top of her, she felt a rush of heat inside her body as he entered her, thrusting deep into her...

Then she woke straight up.

She heard several sharp raps at her front door, and it jarred her awake. Glancing at her cell phone, it was six o'clock in the morning!

She'd slept four hours straight.

Again, she heard more raps, but had not moved to rise out of bed. Her dream was too vivid. It was a dream she'd never had before with anyone. Never thought she could and thinking that it would never become a reality. She would never allow herself, valuing his friendship above everything.

The knocking didn't stop. "Okay, damn it! I'm coming," Sinclair yelled as she slid from the bed, donned a robe, and grabbed her Beretta 9mm from the nightstand.

She came to the door with heavy legs, her eyes watery from lack of sleep. She could've slept another few hours, except for whoever the asshole was, trying to knock down the door.

Glancing through the glass partition of the door, she saw an MP standing, waiting.

"What the hell?" she muttered, her eyes widened in surprise.

Sinclair grasped the cold brass knob, turned it, and pulled open the door.

Standing in the cold windy morning, the MP was bathed in light from the yellow porch lights. The MP was a First Lieutenant, the OIC, Officer-in-charge of the on-duty MP squad.

"Ah, are you Special Agent Sinclair?" the MP Officer asked with a hint of a smile on his handsome face.

"Yes, what's up, Lieutenant?" Sinclair asked wrapping her arms around the front of her robe as she shrugged, a little embarrassed and a little cold, too.

"Well, I've been instructed to inform you that the assistant Provost Marshal would like for you to report to his office . . . as soon as you can."

She leaned against the door and pondered the summons. How the hell did the assistant PM know where to find her? Only two people knew, her father and Tom Price. And only one reason she was being called—a meeting with him and his staff—to bring those in command up to speed on her investigation. That sounded reasonable and not at all surprising after all that had gone down last night. But why at six in the morning? Damn! Couldn't they wait an extra three or four hours? Christ!

She sighed. "Please let him know I'll be there in an hour."

"Yes, ma'am."

Back in her bedroom, dressed in blue jeans, a white blouse and plum-colored Totes storm sport jacket, Sinclair reached for her cell phone from the nightstand. Dialing Jeffrey Cory's number, she let it ring and, not getting an answer, left a message asking him to call her back, then she hung up. This was not like him. He always answered, no matter what he was doing.

Something must be wrong. What? She didn't know.

Wanting to call her father next before her meeting, she debated placing the call because of the early hour. No, she'll wait. Last night, she'd transferred the email from General Scott from her father's computer onto a thumb-drive, which she pocketed. She wanted to show her father first before she showed it to anyone else.

Thirty minutes later, she was in her car and on her way to see the Assistant PM.

Sinclair arrived on the second floor of the Provost Marshal's Office on Patch Barracks and was processed through the new security desk where a heavyset MP stood. Having her ID checked and cleared, they allowed her to proceed. They'd installed the new checkpoint in response to the attacks on the PM and the fatal attack on the life of CID Chief Jones.

Down the hallway, two MPs still guarded the main doors to the PM's Office. Once there, she again surrendered her ID and, several moments later, she pushed through into the main waiting room.

Mary Elders, her father's secretary smiled as she entered, and waved her to a chair. "Belle, they want you to wait until they finish their conference."

"*They?*" Sinclair asked surprised. "Who are *they*, Mary?"

"Sorry, honey, can't tell."

Ten minutes later, the intercom buzzed, and Sinclair heard someone say something she couldn't make out.

"Belle, honey, you're to go in now."

Agent Sinclair shrugged and stood. Walking past Mary Elders, Elders winked at her, and Sinclair pushed through the double doors into her father's office.

Closing the doors behind her, she turned back around and, to her astonishment and surprise, sitting behind his desk was her father in civilian clothing, with his arm in a sling and, as she took her first step in, three men stood and faced her.

Besides her astonishment, she felt let down, because no one told her they had discharged him from the hospital.

Agent Sinclair walked forward and stopped in front of her father's desk. "Sir, you're supposed to be in the hospital."

"Talk about that later, Belle," he said. "I want you to meet these two gentlemen first. You know Major Stephen Whitehall, my Assistant PM."

She nodded to the major.

The major bowed his head slightly and said, "Glad to see you in one piece, agent."

"Agent Sinclair, please meet FBI Special Agents Daniel Russell, and Jesse Martinez," her father said, glancing over at the two men. "Both from the Regional Security Office or RSO Terrorist Task Force from our embassy in Frankfurt. The Embassy Attaché out of Berlin assigned them to investigate the two stolen smart bombs, among other duties."

Agent Sinclair nodded to the two agents.

The taller of the two men, broad shouldered, about six-foot-tall, with thinning blond hair, approached her and extended his hand as a smile creased his face. He was dressed in a gray two-piece suit, red tie, and white shirt.

"I'm Daniel Russell," he said. "But, since we will work in conjunction to each other, call me Dan. I've heard so much about you, agent. Your exploits so far are the stuff of a mystery novel."

Agent Martinez, the senior of the two, tall, slender, dressed in a dark two-piece suit, his face tan and angular with a trimmed mustache came forward, smiled, held out his hand, and in a soft-spoken voice said, "Don't mind my partner, he's a romantic at heart. I'm proud to meet you after what your father has said about you."

Reaching out to shake his hand, Sinclair shook her head and said, "Thank you."

FBI Agent Daniel Russell, the closest to Agent Sinclair, gave up his seat to her and, pulling another chair, sat and faced the PM. Once Agent Martinez took a seat, Colonel Sinclair broke into a gentle smile, as he watched the two FBI agents interact with his daughter. They didn't mention the scars on her face, or the swollen eye. *I bet they wanted to, but were too damn civil to even ask,* he thought.

Colonel Richard Sinclair, in a detached weary manner, after all the introductions, leaned back in his chair, and glanced at his daughter.

"Belle, I called the FBI and filled them in on what your investigation has turned up so far. I need you to fill in the gaps and inform them of any new developments you may have uncovered as far as how the stolen bombs relate to your investigation."

"Yes, sir," she said. "Would you rather I start from the beginning? This way, you'll have the full picture of what I've had uncovered so far."

Agent Martinez said with both hands in his pockets, "The beginning would seem the best place to start."

Then, all eyes turned on her.

Nodding, she closed her eyes, getting her thoughts in order and, opening them, she glanced first at the two FBI agents, at her father, once again back at the agents. Slowly, speaking in a clipped, measured matter-of-fact tone, she recited the events of the last few days since starting her investigation.

The FBI agents listened without interrupting her, as Agent Russell jotting down his notes from his investigative notebook, would quickly glance at her, and then back to his notebook again jotting down his notes.

When she came to their involvement in the shootings, her brush with the killer in her apartment, and her and Agent Price getting attacked at CID Jones' home, the two agents glanced at each other, and shook their heads. They were doubtful that both her and Price could have survived the attacks she'd mentioned and lived to tell of it. Could she had embellished the story somewhat in her favor? But if she had, why? It was a question better left for later.

She hadn't spoken long, maybe about three minutes, and, once finished, she looked away, glancing at her father, waiting for questions she knew would come. However, one thing she held back was the contents of the thumb-drive she held in her possession. She wanted her father to look at it first, before the FBI knew of its existence. She knew she was keeping valued evidence from their hands, but this was a military investigation.

Sinclair crossed a leg and waited in silence to hear what their questions would be.

The first question they asked wouldn't have been her first, she reasoned.

It was Agent Russell who raised his head and stared at her as he asked, "Do you have anyone that would make you believe you'd suspect of perpetrating the theft of those bombs, Agent Sinclair?"

She glanced once at her father, then met Agent Russell's stare. Hell, they knew the answer to that question, or they wouldn't have asked, she thought. Still, she played along. "I may have a lead that I hadn't had the time to follow up on."

"Would that be Captain Jeffrey Cory, commander of the 113th Logistics Company?" Agent Martinez asked.

"Yes," she replied.

"We'll work that lead for you, Agent Sinclair," Agent Martinez said. "We are of the understanding that you and Captain Cory have been . . . dating. Is this true?"

For a moment, her eyes flashed at her father. "Dad, I'm being interrogated now?"

The FBI agents went silent as they stared at Colonel Sinclair and at his daughter.

Colonel Sinclair smiled at his daughter. "No, Belle, you're not. Please, let them do their work and answer the question so we can move on."

Turning back to Agent Martinez, she tried to control her anger. "You seem to know a great deal about my affairs, agent."

"I see you're reluctant to speak of it, Agent Sinclair," Agent Martinez said.

"So, he was more than . . . a dating partner?" Agent Russell chimed in.

Sinclair did not reply immediately, as her eyes lingered on Agent Russell for a moment.

Finally, she said, "There is no reason to deny it. Yes, we're romantically involved."

Agent Martinez said, "And when was it that you may have suspected Captain Cory of possibly having knowledge of the two stolen bombs, the stolen weapons, and vehicles that may have come through his unit?"

"Agent Price and I pieced it all together and came up with Cory being the logical suspect. As I mentioned, I tried getting in contact with him, but he hasn't returned my calls."

"No doubt," Agent Martinez said sarcastically.

Agent Sinclair was about to give him a piece of her mind, when her father, not amused at their questioning, stood up from his desk. "I think that's enough for now, agents. I need to be alone with Agent Sinclair. Please keep me informed of your progress. Have a good day."

* * *

Once the FBI Agents departed, Colonel Sinclair poured a cup of coffee for himself and one for his daughter, strode back to the front of his desk, as Belle grasped the coffee cup her father offered and took a seat beside him.

Sipping on his warm coffee, he stared at her. He knew she was pissed at him. He'd grown accustomed to it, and not just from her but from her mother too. Therefore, this wasn't anything new.

"Don't be mad at me, Belle," he said, smiling.

"Jesus, Dad. How could you let them get away with talking to me like I was a suspect?"

"They were just doing their job, honey, like you would've done, if the sides were reversed."

Belle looked at him. "Yeah, Dad. I'm not as mad as I should be. You didn't even call me that you were out of the hospital."

"It was a spur of the moment. Things needed to move along faster and, with me in the hospital, I couldn't do much."

"Okay, Dad."

Sipping his coffee, he said, "What of Captain Cory? Have you heard anything back?'

"No, and I'm worried something may have happened. If it involved him, then he may be in grave danger. People seem to die or disappear that have information worthwhile to say."

"I have to agree with you, Belle."

There was a brief silence.

Then she pulled the thumb-drive from her pocket and extended it toward him. "I went home to your quarters and downloaded the email General Chapman sent you. It's in the drive. And, Dad, you will not like what's on it."

* * *

Communications and Storage Room second floor, Provost Marshal building, Patch Barracks

He couldn't explain what had gone wrong.

He'd checked and rechecked his equipment and couldn't find anything to account for it.

Sergeant Richard Stevens, with his earphones on and turning dial after dial on his equipment, was trying to make out what was being said in the PM's office. Earlier, he'd seen the Assistant PM and the PM and the PMs Secretary arrive. Then a half hour later, two civilian-dressed men arrived too.

But, it was later on, when Agent Sinclair walked through the double doors of the PM's office that made him think of reporting this to the powers that be.

Shaking his head, he removed the useless earphones and dialed Colonel Godfrey Randall's number. On the second ring, the colonel picked up and said, "Report, Sergeant."

"Sir, for the last hour, a conference has been held in the PM's Office. The Provost Marshal and his assistant along with two unknown men with Agent Sinclair are in attendance. No one has since left."

"What was the conference about, Sergeant?"

"That's another reason why I'm calling, sir," Sergeant Stevens said. "There seems to be a problem with the bug. I'm not getting anything from it."

"I see. They found the bug, Sergeant."

"Yes, sir, it's what I've been thinking too."

"Make plans to install another soon. In the meantime, describe the two unknown men."

"Sir, they wore civilian suits and I would hazard a guess and say, extra CID or FBI."

"Thank you for that assessment, Sergeant. Report once you install a new bug."

"Yes, sir."

—Chapter Twenty-Eight—

"**T**here's something you have to see, Father."

Agent Sinclair stood and walked around her father's desk. Facing his laptop, she opened it and waited for it to turn on. After a minute or two, she inserted the thumb-drive into an USB port, as her father raised an inquiring eyebrow.

The colonel made a small gesture with his hand. "Is this the email General Chapman sent me?"

Belle slowly nodded. "Yes, sir, it is. Dad, once the files appear on the screen, you'll see two video files, click on the one marked Helen Chapman first."

Agent Sinclair watched as her father sat forward on his chair, moved his mouse pointer to the video marked Helen Chapman, and then she ambled over for some hot coffee Mrs. Elders made earlier, who wasn't the only one up very early this Monday morning.

With a coffee cup in hand, she sat and leaned back on the chair and watched her father's reaction to the videos as she sipped her coffee.

His eyes lit up once he saw Helen Chapman, whom he'd known since she was twelve, blindfolded with a gun to her head, asking for her father's help. Colonel Sinclair knew just what had run through General Chapman's thoughts when he saw his daughter: do whatever it took to get her back, safe and sound. It's what he would do, if the shoe were on the other foot.

After the video had played through, Colonel Sinclair leaned back on his chair and took a deep breath.

Nodding he said, "Interesting." Then, staring at his daughter with a frown, he said, "And quite disturbing, too. Do you have any ideas where they may have hidden her away?"

Shaking her head, she said, "No, not yet. But if you find that interesting, wait until you see the second video."

Clicking on the second video and, as it slowly opened, he noticed the almost total darkness in which they filmed it, suspecting it could be in some type of cavern or darkened room. As it played out, he went rigid with shock and disbelief to see an all too familiar face, one that he'd all but forgotten. Then he concentrated on the substance of the video itself, and what was being said.

With the mention of OPLAN-8009, he straightened upright in his chair, conscious of the extent the plan represented, and the effects it may bring if unleashed. It was a first-strike plan!

After viewing the video a second time, the colonel slowly shook his head. For a long moment, he sat stock-still, unbelieving what he had seen. He ran his hand over his hair. His lips moved slowly.

Feeling a sudden welling of anger slowly building, he spoke in a cold, hard voice. "Jesus Christ, that was Tom Scott. I can't believe it. He was a good friend, one of the best."

The colonel remembered the parties and celebrating one thing or another with General Scott's family, the BBQs at his home, the promotion party, Scott pinning the eagle of full bird colonel on him. Those were days he remembered: Fun times, great times.

Then with his son's death in North Korea, there was a marked change that came over Scott and, after taking his son's body back stateside, Colonel Sinclair heard he'd retired from the Army. Then, learning from some of his friends of Tom's wife suicide, it seemed like too much for Tom.

Colonel Sinclair couldn't imagine the pain, anxiety, and the feeling of helplessness Tom Scott must have gone through with the tragic loss of both his wife and only son.

That was the last time he'd heard about his friend until now.

However, Tom's dream to exact revenge on North Korea was unbelievable and reckless, which could only lead to his ultimate death or imprisonment for life. Now he understood why kidnapping of the children was a vital part of Scott's plan. But would he release them once the plan was complete, or would he have them killed? No telling what Scott would do in his state of mind. The children were Belle's first task, and the rest really depended on DIA, the FBI, and the Secret Service.

Only thing left for him to do was to report his findings to General Roland, the EUCOM Commander. Second thing he had to do was to inform the FBI of a possible second lead for them to follow up on. Maybe the FBI could come up with some information to help them locate the kidnapped children and recover the two stolen bombs. It was a long shot. But so far, it was the only one they had.

Colonel Sinclair sat in his chair, feeling an unpleasant sense of helplessness come over him. If Scott's plan was carried out to its conclusion, World War Three would be the result.

It was getting warm inside his office.

He looked up.

The Provost Marshal wiped his brow with the back of his hand and took a deep breath. "Belle, honey, tell me what you plan on doing next?"

She closed her eyes a moment, gathering her thoughts before she replied. Opening them, she looked around slowly. Then they settled on her father. Her eyes sharply narrowed.

Agent Sinclair rose and walked over to him, stopping by the side of his desk. Just for a moment, she stiffened, as if she was coming to attention, unwilling to take her eyes from her father. "First thing, Dad, I need to find out why Captain Cory has not been answering my calls. I think something has happened to him."

"You can't do that, Belle. So far, that's the FBI's ground game now. They will not like you poking around asking questions, looking for him."

"I don't give a damn what they like or don't. No matter what he's done or not done, I still care about him, Dad."

"You were always a stubborn child, now a full-grown woman, you haven't changed a lick. Go on then, see what you can find out. I have pressing matters I need to attend to."

As she stood there, smiling, she said, "Thank you, Dad."

"Oh, by the way, what's your next course of action once you find out about Captain Cory?"

"I'll have to wait and see where my leads take me."

He nodded. "Okay. Make sure you have Agent Price by your side."

"I'm ahead of you there, sir."

Agent Sinclair turned and walked out of his office, stopped at the threshold, blew her father a kiss and, as he shook his head, he picked up his office phone.

Not in any hurry, Sinclair walked out of the building.

As the sun slowly moved upward into the early Monday morning sky, Agent Sinclair stopped, leaned on the driver's side door to her car, and inhaled the crisp August air. Admiring the beauty of an early sunrise, she slowly tilted her head and closed her eyes for a moment as the cool August winds caressed her face.

"Good morning sunshine, the world says hello," she muttered remembering words to a long-forgotten song. It's great to be alive she thought and, thinking if she wasn't successful in putting an end to the horror that awaited them in the next few days, what they left the world with during the subsequent world war would be unimaginable. What with China and North Korea having a mutual defense treaty, this would mean China would come to its defense, as would Russia; the beginning of the Third World War would ultimately be assured.

It was a frightening prospect, she thought.

Then slipping behind the wheel, she sat in the Chevy but didn't start it.

She sighed. Reaching for her purse, she pulled out her cell phone and dialed Agent Tom Price's number.

It rang several times, and, on the fourth ring, she heard a heavy-sleepy voice come on the line.

"*Come on, it's Monday and my day off. Whoever you are, this better be good.*"

"Tom? It's me, Sinclair."

There was a pause, Price shook his head to clear it. "*Damn it, Sinclair, don't you ever sleep?*"

"Are you wide awake?"

"*I am now.*"

"I need your help, partner."

There was another pause. When it came on again, it sounded intrigued. *"Okay, I'm up. What's this about?"*

"Meet me in my office in an hour, and I'll tell you then."

Tom Price took a deep breath. *"I'm on my way."*

Belle slowly shut her cell phone and prayed that what she was thinking wasn't so. Then, inserting her key into the ignition, she started the car and pulled off onto the main drag.

* * *

They sat in their car, windows rolled down, outside the Provost Marshal's building, both lighting up cigarettes before they started the investigation.

FBI Special Agent Martinez turned to his partner, Daniel Russell. "What do you make of Agent Sinclair?"

Russell glanced at Martinez with a smile. "Beautiful comes to mind."

"No, Dan, I mean what do you make of her?" Agent Martinez said.

Special Agent Jesse Martinez was the lead investigator and senior of the two and was the section chief of the anti-terrorist task force assigned to the Frankfurt embassy. With a team of twelve highly trained and capable agents, they were ready to respond to any crises anywhere in Southern Germany or beyond. And since the attack on 9/11, they provided his force with the best in weaponry and tactics training available.

After a short silence, Russell sighed, looked out his window, and glanced at Martinez.

Russell replied, "Well, if everything said about her is true, she may not wait for us to find out about Jeffrey Cory's involvement. I wouldn't put it past her to try beating us to him."

"Yeah, it's what I've been thinking."

"So, you want to head out to his company first or his off-post quarters?"

Martinez shook his head. "Neither for now. We haven't had breakfast since we arrived. Breakfast first, then his company and his quarters. . . let's worry about Sinclair later."

"Breakfast sounds about right."

Flipping their cigarette butts out their windows, with Agent Russell behind the wheel, he started up the engine, placed the car in drive, and headed to the Post Exchange cafeteria.

* * *

The Silo - Underground holding cells
Lucas moved slowly as he favored his right knee that was giving him trouble. It was the same knee he took a bullet in during his first and last deployment to Afghanistan when ambushed and coming under heavy fire. The bullet crashed his knee and, since then, he walked with a metal prosthetic device. If it hadn't been for two nearby gunships, he wouldn't be here bellyaching about it, he thought.

With the coldness of the caverns and his breath flaring in the cold, he stuffed a hand in his pocket and, with the other, he pushed an iron and metal cart loaded with food and water for his captives, with only the dim lights guiding his way.

On most days in the early morning hours he would deliver the food, except on those days when he wasn't drunk on his ass and forgotten his duties, which occasionally he did. By his reckoning, he'd missed three straight days.

Having finished delivering the food to two of the captives, he was able to pick up their empty metal plates and filled them, then shoved it through the small hole in the door's bottom. He didn't know, nor care to know, their names.

With only two left, two girls, he came around the corner to one pathway, and stopped at a door. He saw the plate still there filled with food. It was a miracle the rats hadn't eaten it by now. His instructions were clear, if the captives don't eat, he needed to open the cell, check on them, and make sure they were still alive.

"*Shit,*" he muttered. Once or twice before, he entered a cell, and the stink and stench were too much for even him. No, he wasn't fond of opening the cells. But what if something had happened to this one? he thought. There would be hell and high water to pay, yes, sir.

Helen Chapman, in the cell down from where Lucas had stopped, knew that her jailer was out there now, making his rounds with the food. It'd been days since last he came, and now she was ready, ready to at least get to talk to him. In her cell, she heard the clattering of wheels, as it moved outside. Then she believed she heard it stop. The sixteen-year-old Chapman guessed others could be locked up with her in the darkness but couldn't hear them.

Outside Lisa Shaffer's cell, Lucas knocked several times, but didn't hear any noises from inside. "Ah, shit, she's making me open the damn cell," he muttered. Slowly, he pulled his key tied from around his neck, and, inserting and turning the key, he slowly pushed the heavy iron door open. As his eyes grew accustomed to the darkness, he saw a figure sprawled out on the ground in the center of the cell.

"Hey, hey, are you okay?" he asked, almost shouting. Then raising his voice a little louder, he repeated it. Getting no response, he moved closer to the figure and stopped about a foot away from it. Using his foot, he jabbed at it but got no response. Kneeling beside the girl, he placed his finger on her neck, looking for a pulse, but didn't find one.

"Oh, fuck, am I going to pay for this mess. This bitch is dead," he said. "Damn, now I have to check the last girl. Hope she's alive."

"Jesus H. Christ," he said, almost yelling as he walked out of the cell heading toward the last of his captives. He could just see someone putting a bullet to the back of his head. He would not outlive this one, he thought.

Helen Chapman walked over to the side of the door. She thought she heard someone yelling and coming closer to her cell. Then, she heard someone stop on the other side of the door. Something told her not to say a word. She figured, once the guard did not see the plate shoved through the slot, he would say something.

He didn't.

Quickly she walked back to a corner where she'd slept and grabbed her plate and, as quickly, came back to the door. Something wasn't right, she thought, for just as she leaned up against the side of the wall, she heard a key being inserted, and the lock being turned. Staying in the darkness, she saw the door opening and someone entering her cell.

This was her only chance.

Not thinking it through—if she had, she surely wouldn't have done it—she slowly came away from the wall, and, as the guard took another step inside, she tapped his shoulder. When Lucas turned facing her, Helen Chapman mustered all the strength in her young, tired, and aching body and thrust the edge of the plate into Lucas' throat.

The plate penetrated though his trachea, cutting off his breathing and crushing his windpipe. Making gagging noises and holding his throat, Lucas slumped to the ground dying, thrashed about for a few seconds, when his body went limp, and died.

Helen Chapman dropped to her knees, unable to stand, and heaved whatever she still had. She closed her eyes, not wanting to see the body next to her. Then, slowly at first, she realized the cell door was open. Escape seemed at her fingertips. Standing back up, with no shoes, and only in a thin blouse and jeans, Helen made her way through the door.

Which way? she thought. *Left or right?* She stood there in the darkness debating, breathing hard, feeling her lungs explode with excitement, trying to stay alive. No telling how long she had before the alarm went off.

Taking a few steps, she walked the way Lucas had used coming in. A few minutes later, she rounded a corner and stopped when she saw an open door.

Quickly walking to the door, she saw it was another cell, just like her own and, lying in the center of it, was a figure of what she believed was that of a woman. Walking inside the cell, she took the time to see if she was alive but saw that she wasn't. *Poor thing*, she thought. Helen kneeled and turned her around face up and saw either a rope or laces tied around her neck. She had been young, and another prisoner just like her.

Helen Chapman, without a word, walked back to the pathway, turned right and slowly made her way through.

Twenty minutes later, after rounding a corner, she stopped. There was lighting coming from a shaft way down through the cavern. Not seeing anyone about, slowly at first, then running, she made the shaft and saw metal ladder rungs leading straight up and could make out faint lighting, as if from far away.

Stepping on the first rung, she grasped the top one and started climbing and climbing.

—Chapter Twenty-Nine—

A s soon as Agent Price entered the CID building, two MPs met him at the entrance. While one checked his ID, the other called over to Agent Sinclair's office for confirmation of his visit.

The building had an unusual silence to it that was slightly unnerving to him.

Giving her secretary the day off, Sinclair and CID Agent Timothy Jenkins, along with the MPs remained in the building.

Agent Jenkins was a short, wiry man of thirty-two, fair-skinned with long dark sandy hair, almost down to his shoulders. He wore a mustache and short beard, allowed because of his last investigation, and was slightly overweight, but all muscle. His specialty was in deep undercover narcotics investigations, but he also served as on-call Agent from time to time.

Now that she was the Acting Chief, she'd detailed Agent Jenkins to be on-call and to pick up any and all cases, and, if he needed, to contact Agent Vargas, whom she had given the day off, for assistance. With the deaths of Agent West and Chief Jones, she was shorthanded.

Tom Price moved through the echoing corridor to Sinclair's office.

It was exactly eight in the morning when Price cracked open the door to Sinclair's office. Walking on through, he closed the door behind him and saw her standing by her desk dressed in jeans, dark blouse, and a leather jacket and loading a small backpack with some ammo magazines.

Leaning up against the door, he said, "Hey, you expecting some trouble wherever you're planning to go?"

"Glad you can make it. Well, I'd rather be prepared. No telling if we meet up with some of General Scott's goons along the way."

"Okay. So, what's the story?"

"Tell you on the way. Let's go."

"Yeah, okay," he said, opening the door for her. "So, where are we heading exactly?"

"To my boyfriend's apartment," she said.

"Oh boy," he chuckled. "This is going to be fun."

"Cory is missing, and I feel as if something may have happened to him."

"I . . ." Price didn't quite know how to respond to that. "Sorry," was all he could say.

There I go again, putting my foot in my mouth, Price said to himself.

They fell silent.

Without saying a word to each other, they hurried through the building, then onto the parking lot and her car. As she took in the coolness of the early morning wind, it refreshed and gave her energy to take on her day.

At her car, Agent Sinclair took a last look around to make sure there was no one near them or any car that may look suspicious to her. Then, taking a deep breath, she unlocked the door and slipped into the driver's seat. As Price sat in the passenger seat, he waited for her to put the car in motion and reveal her intentions.

They pulled out onto the main drag and drove out of the installation. She glanced over at Price, then back out the windshield. "The FBI are now involved in our investigation, Tom."

Tom Price gave a curt nod. "I see."

Earlier, while at her office, Sinclair had called Jeffrey Cory's unit. From the unit clerk who answered, she learned that Cory hadn't been to work nor had he called. According to the clerk, he didn't know when his commander would report for duty.

That, in itself, was strange, she thought, shaking her head. Strange, because it wasn't like him not to report in even if he wasn't reporting for duty.

They drove on in silence, each with their own thoughts.

* * *

The Silo - Underground holding cells
It was Sebastian Cruz's turn to walk through the cavern and make his rounds. He was to make three full turns of the underground caverns every hour, making sure the captives were secure, until relieved of his duties by the next guard.

Twenty minutes into his watch, Cruz, a tall Hispanic man with a stocky build and short, curly, black hair, made his slow way past the first and second of the prisoners' cells. He walked up to each door and physically checked the lock, making sure all was as it should be.

Satisfied, he moved on.

The next two were about a quarter of a mile further on and around a bend, and it would take him a few minutes to get there. But, before he did, he leaned his weapon against the rock wall and lit a cigarette, as he was in no hurry. Hell, he thought, his prisoners weren't going anywhere.

Once he finished his smoke, Cruz picked up his weapon and proceeded on his rounds and, as he passed one of the three missile tubes, he thought he'd heard squeaking noises inside it. Rats maybe, he thought, "*Shit*, there are plenty of those in here," he muttered. Not hearing it again, he kept on walking.

A few minutes later, as he rounded the bend, he came to a stop. Something was wrong. A cell door was wide open, and it shouldn't be, he told himself. Raising his weapon, he slowly approached the cell, glancing left and right, then down the cavern. Coming to the door, he stepped inside and saw a body sprawled on the ground.

"Hey, you there, are you okay?"

Not getting a response, he calmly walked over, kneeled by the body, and knew instinctively that the woman was dead.

"Madre de Dios," he said, crossing himself and backing out of the cell.

Standing on the cavern pathway next to the cell's door, he pulled out his hand-held radio. Pressing the talk button and, in a somewhat calm voice, he said, "Unit Six to base, over."

"*Unit Six, this is base, go.*"

"Roger, base, I have a situation down here with one of the captives, over."

"Roger that. Explain the situation, over."

"One captive is dead, over."

"Six, repeat your last, over."

"Roger, found a captive, female, dead in her cell, over."

"Roger, understood, a captive is dead, over."

"Roger, base, over."

"Roger, Six, please standby."

Several minutes later, Cruz's orders were to check the remaining cells and report his findings. They were sending two additional guards.

"Nothing for the other guards to do, except get in my way," Cruz muttered to himself.

Since he was closer to the next cell, he made his way there.

Ahead, the cells, each separated by over a thousand yards apart were not visible through the darkness. Cruz wasn't able to make out the cell, not until he was within a few yards and, to his astonishment, he saw that cell door open too.

Once again, he brought his weapon to bear and slowly approached the cell. Inside the entrance, he saw another body. He took a quick glance inside and noticed that the prisoner was missing. Pulling out his flashlight, he shone the beam to the corpse, and saw that it was Lucas, the meal-delivering guy, dead. Shining his light through the cell, he made sure his prisoner wasn't hiding in some corner.

"Oh *shit,* they are not going to like this," he said, pulling out his radio yet again.

Then he remembered the noise he'd heard from the missile tube and, running back as fast as he could, he thought maybe the prisoner was hiding out there. Worth the look, he thought.

Before arriving at the missile tube, he was met by the two guards sent to help.

Stopping in front of them, he said, "I got two dead bodies and an escaped prisoner. One of you call base, give him the rundown and have a guard waiting on top, in case she tries to make a run for it into the woods."

After a brief silence and, as one of them pulled out his radio, Cruz said, "You, come with me, I need to check out the missile tube."

Once at the tube, Cruz pulled out his flashlight, shined it up through the tube, and caught sight of a shadow all the way at the top. "She's up there."

Turning to the guard by his side, Cruz said, "Shine your light up the tube while I go up after her."

She was at the last rung, standing there listening for any possible sounds above and below her. She didn't know if the hatch above was her way to escape; and if it was locked, then what? She was about to extend a hand toward the hatch when suddenly . . .she heard what she thought was shuffling and yelling coming from far below her, through the darkness of what she thought was a manhole, but in reality was one of the of three missile launch tubes.

It was becoming clear to her that they knew she'd escaped, but did they know where she'd gone? That was the question running through her mind. Not moving a muscle, alone and terrified that they would find her, she began to pray. "*Oh God, help me, please help me.*"

Then silence for a moment. *Did they leave or were they still down below me?* she kept thinking.

Escape was Helen's constant thought. But how?

Then she heard some more yelling far below. A light stabbed through the darkness and caught her in its beam. She heard the yelling again, but couldn't make out what was being said

Oh hell, they found me! Helen thought. She would rather die than get caught again.

Helen Chapman began to cry and wiped at her tear-filled eyes. Terrified, dizzy, and confused, she was unable to concentrate, almost to the point of losing her footing on the rung. Focus, she tried to tell herself, stay calm, or you will die.

Chapman drew in a deep breath and slowly exhaled.

Suddenly, she remembered the hatch above her and she stopped crying.

She glanced up at what she figured to be an iron hatch with a circular wheel and a handle at one corner. With her eyes adjusting to the total darkness, she saw it much better and immediately knew it would turn like unscrewing a cap. Grasping the handle, she slowly began turning and was being rewarded by feeling it slightly move. Little by little, she agonizingly continued turning the wheel.

As she concentrated on the wheel, she thought she'd heard clattering noises and felt vibrations of the ladder's handles, and then she realized what they were . . .

Oh my God, someone was climbing the ladder, Helen mumbled to herself. *Then go faster, hurry, turn that wheel!*

Just then, she'd felt the wheel click and stop on metal, felt the hatch open slightly, and she saw sunlight filtering through a small gap. Helen was almost blinded by the bright sunlight as she momentarily turned her gaze away from the light.

Pushing the hatch open as far as it could, she heard it clang on metal. She once again felt the sun shining on her head as her eyes became accustomed to the harsh sunlight. Crying again, this time for joy, she pulled herself through the hole and into a forest of tall leafy trees and knee-high tall grass.

She got to her feet, staggered, and weaved her way through the trees, then from behind her a shot rang out, and she saw wood splinter off the side of a tree on her left, as the bullet narrowly missed her. Quickly, she looked behind her and saw two men, one of whom was pointing a rifle at her, and she started running.

"Run, Helen, run!" she heard herself yell.

Coming to a chain-link fence, she stopped. She would have to climb, she thought. Then, glancing down, she saw a large enough hole through which she could crawl. Parting the chain-links further apart, she crawled to the other side.

Back on her feet, she started running again, hard.

Hearing the loud boom of another gunshot seconds later, Helen felt it strike her left shoulder. She moaned as the pain shot through her brain. *Oh my God, they shot me!* Her mouth was wide open. The shock and impact of the bullet spun her around as she almost fell to the ground. She tried to gain control, but she stumbled and, taking three steps, she momentarily lost her footing and fell down a steep ledge that pushed her, rolling over and over. She clawed at the empty air as she plunged down into a cold, wide stream.

Once she came to a stop, and, on her knees, she touched her left shoulder, came away with blood, and felt it seep down her arm. Helen wanted to scream but was too shocked to do so. Barely able to get back up and already weak from loss of blood, she heard noises coming from the top of the hill.

Were they coming after her? Did they see her? She had no idea. Thinking they would come down the hill, she, slowly and as quietly as she could, crawled through the stream, turning her head now and then, trying to hear if they were approaching her position.

Further down the stream, she rose, did a 360-degree turn, and not seeing anyone behind her, grabbed at her injured shoulder, holding on to it, trying to staunch the flow of blood, and began to walk, crossing the steam onto the opposite bank, conscious of still being hunted.

Minutes later, she stopped, exhausted. A moment later, she thought she heard a noise behind her. Wheeling around, she spied a gunman through the thick forest—a silhouette against the sun. She turned around and took off as fast as she could.

As she swerved around some thick trees, more gunshots rang out, but none came near her.

Helen ran as fast as her legs would go.

—Chapter Thirty—

The military police Desk Sergeant at Patch Barracks received the call from the Stuttgart German Police at 0900 hours, Monday morning, of a US military soldier found dead on a sidewalk.

By way of the German Police interpreter assigned for duty with the MPs, the Desk Sergeant was able to receive the information to start the paperwork. First, the identification had been made possible from the deceased's military ID found on his person. Second, according to the German Police investigators, the victim had been found face-down on a public street and had been shot several times from behind. Third, the cause of death was a gunshot wound to the victim's head. They'll keep the body of Captain Cory on ice, they mentioned, until it can be released to US authorities. No autopsy had yet been performed because of pending notification of the US military.

Knowing that protocol called for an SIR, *Serious Incident Report*, the Desk Sergeant set himself on preparing it and of notifying the on-call CID agent, including the Provost Marshal. The Desk Sergeant also dispatched an MP patrol along with the MP Duty Officer to the hospital where the victim was being kept to assist with the German Federal Police investigators and the CID agent with their investigation.

The PM's secretary received the call from the MP Duty Officer at 10:15. She stood, walked into Colonel Sinclair's office and, with a no-nonsense grace, she relayed the information to the PM.

Sinclair muttered something she couldn't understand.

"Did you say something, sir?"

"She will not like this."

"I suspect she won't, sir," she said.

He nodded, remembering how happy she was with the captain. "Thank you, Mary."

Colonel Sinclair took in a deep breath and sat back in his chair. He knew this information would upset his daughter or maybe worse. Should he call her? he asked himself. *Or, should I wait for her to call me?*

It was a tough decision.

In the meantime, he called the FBI, instead, and got them up to date on this new development and of the contents of the videos.

Then he slowly nodded. "I'll wait to hear from her," he muttered.

It would be easier that way, he thought.

* * *

From somewhere, the town clock chimed eleven. The sounds carried as if from afar, muted but audible from inside Sinclair's car. Agent Tom Price stretched and sat back on his seat as his fingertips worked the kinks from his neck. Then he checked his wristwatch and made sure it was running on time. His Seiko piece given to him by his father was dead on, he noticed.

The street was bustling with people heading toward the Markplatz, which was filling up with early morning grocery shoppers. Heavy trucks and passenger cars zipped along the busy street, with mothers walking their children, and stores opening for the day as a few small children, not yet of school age, played on the sidewalk, their mothers keeping a watchful eye. These were scenes that played out all over Germany. It was a normal Monday, for a normal German street.

Agent Jacqueline Sinclair sat forward on her seat, arms resting atop the steering wheel and looking straight ahead toward Jeffrey Cory's apartment complex. She noticed his car parked out in front, which would suggest Cory was possibly inside.

But, if he is in his apartment, then why isn't he answering my calls? she asked herself.

Having arrived a few minutes before, she wanted to make certain the FBI hadn't beaten her there. She'd delayed telling Price of her meeting with the FBI until after going through Cory's apartment and then after—on a one-on-one basis—talking with her boyfriend. She wanted to make sure he told her of his possible involvement in her investigation, before she read him his Miranda rights, if she went down that route. She told herself, she would try to keep her emotions in check during her questioning.

Keeping watch for several minutes, she waited, hoping the FBI hadn't already been inside Cory's apartment.

After several minutes and satisfied they were alone, Sinclair glanced at Price. "Hey, time to go."

"Right behind you," Price replied.

They slipped out of the car, closed their doors, and sashayed across the street, while dodging oncoming traffic. Once they gained the sidewalk, they proceeded up the stairs and stopped in front of Cory's front door.

"You wouldn't have a key, would you?" Tom Price said with a smile.

"No, I wouldn't. But what I do have should do the trick," Sinclair replied.

Reaching into her hip pocket, she came away with a small rolled leather case she packed for this possible situation. Unfolding it, she removed a set of burglar picks, inserted two into the lock, and within seconds had the door unlocked. They walked in and closed the door behind them as she shoved the leather case back into her hip pocket.

Captain Cory kept a neat household, Tom Price thought, from what he had seen so far. The place wasn't large enough for one person let alone two. There was a small picture window toward the front of the unit. Walking toward the back, Price pulled away the curtains, and saw, with the apartment being on the ground floor, it had a small paved alley out back.

Agent Price turned back toward the center of the apartment and noticed Sinclair hadn't said a word since they'd entered. She was busy going through the residence inch by inch. But it wasn't like her to be quiet for so long, he thought.

Is it this place, or am I reading too much into this? he asked himself. He was a little concerned for her and, if he wasn't careful, his true feelings would show through. It just wasn't the time or place to express his feelings, he told himself.

Not knowing her inner feelings for Jeffrey Cory, Price was unable to read her. She was a woman hyperaware of everything around her and extremely self-assured. The only times he'd seen her let go of herself, even for an instant, was around her father. She was a tough cookie, he mused.

He was thinking he'd never be able to understand her—as much as any man can understand a woman. And, by all intents and purposes, he wasn't an expert on *them*.

Sinclair stopped at the threshold of his bedroom. Glancing inside, she saw his tousled bed and clothing thrown in a heap on the floor by the bed. Turning back to the living room, she approached Cory's computer desk. His laptop was open and powered up. She fingered the internal mouse and moved her finger around the pad, waking it from its sleep-mode.

Suddenly, the creak of an opening door broke their concentration. With their backs to the front door, Sinclair and Price reacted as one, wheeling around with weapons drawn. Stopped at the door, FBI Agents Martinez and Russell also had their weapons drawn and pointing straight at them.

A few seconds passed, or more. No one said a word.

Agent Price, without dropping his gaze from the two suited intruders, said, "Drop your weapons, we're American agents."

Sinclair quickly glanced at Price. "Tom, easy there, partner, they're FBI."

"*FBI* . . . Jesus Christ, you all scared the shit out of me," Tom Price said, lowering the point of his weapon. "I could've shot you guys."

Agent Jesse Martinez stared at Price. "Nah, I don't think so."

Price glanced over at Sinclair and said, "You know these guys?"

"Yes, we had the pleasure of meeting earlier," Sinclair replied.

Holstering their weapons, both FBI agents slowly walked into the apartment. Agent Daniel Russell noticed the open laptop and moved to close it while tucking it under his arm.

Staring at Sinclair, Agent Russell said, "You were told, Agent Sinclair, that we would handle Captain Cory."

"Yeah," Sinclair said, also holstering her weapon. "We were in the neighborhood, so I thought I'd check on my boyfriend. You got a problem with that?"

Agent Martinez shook his head. "Did you find anything worth *our* while?"

"Didn't have the time to go through it," she said, not being truthful.

Martinez said. "We'll take possession of the computer and, once we go through it, we'll share its information. But, in the meantime, the German police found Captain Cory. We just left the hospital where his body is being kept."

She blinked once, twice.

"Wait, his *body*, is he . . . dead?" she asked, glancing once at Martinez then at Russell.

Suddenly she stiffened and, for a slight moment, she just stood there.

The FBI agents stood still and continued to fix her with a level gaze.

Agent Price watched as her gaze moved away from the two agents. Then he reached over to take her hand, but she brushed him away. "Sinclair," he whispered.

Sinclair gave a single, brusque shake of her head, shrugged, took a deep breath and, clearing her throat she asked, "He's dead?" her voice filled with sadness.

Agent Price took a step away from Sinclair, realizing he was hovering.

"I hate to be the bearer of bad news, Agent," Martinez said.

"My condolences," Agent Russell said, glancing at her. "The MPs have notified your father."

Still staring at Sinclair, Price saw the fire in her eyes and a deadpan face as she arched her brows for a second. He was going to say something but thought better of it. Sometimes it pays just not to say anything, he thought.

Then her face changed to that of a professional criminal investigator carrying on with her investigation. "Let's go, Tom."

Agent Price took this without replying. Then, without so much as a glance at the FBI agents, Sinclair just walked out of the apartment, as Tom Price, with a curt nod to the agents, followed her out.

Once back in her car, she sat staring off into dead space for a few seconds, as her heart beat fast and a tear began to flow down her cheek. She wiped at it with the palm of her hand.

Then, with apparent calmness, she turned to Price and, drawing in a sharp breath, she said in a low voice, "Let's return to my office. We have a lot of work to do."

"Sinclair," he said, keeping his voice low. "If you want to talk about—"

Sinclair raised her right hand. "Let's not talk about that right now."

He nodded.

Reaching into her jacket pocket, she took out her cell phone and dialed her father's private cell number. On the third ring, he picked up.

"Belle, are you alright?" he asked with concern in his voice.

"Yes, Dad, I just learned that Captain Cory is dead, I—"

"I know, honey; I was waiting for you to call."

"Do you know how he died?"

"Yes, according to the MP's, Captain Cory was shot several times in the back, and—listen, do you need to hear this now?"

"Yes, Dad, please."

"Okay," he said, clearing his throat. "The cause of death was a gunshot to the back of his head."

"*Jesus,* he was assassinated, Dad!" she said, her voice raising an octave. "He was killed because he knew too much!"

"What are you planning on doing, Belle?"

"Price and I are heading back to the office, and, once I figure on what to pursue next, I'll call you."

"Be careful, honey. These people are playing by their own set of rules."

"When I find them, I'll be playing with my own rules, Dad!"

—Chapter Thirty-One—

It was after 11:00 a.m. when they took a breather. Roberts sat on a rock and placed his M4 rifle across his lap, while Sergeant Colin Cooper remained standing, scanning the thick forest and cocking an ear trying to listen for any sounds from the escaped prisoner.

Corporal Brian Roberts was a large man, wide with a pulpy face and a stern expression. He wore his black hair long, falling over his shoulders, as he wiped the back of his hand across his wet forehead. He wore Army camouflage fatigues and a throat mic. Every twenty minutes, he'd been reporting their progress back to the Silo.

Glancing down on Roberts, Cooper said, "Come on, let's keep moving, we can't let her get too far ahead of us. You know our orders, alive or dead. Makes no difference to them."

"Yeah, yeah, I know," Roberts muttered. "But it's time for my report."

"Well, get on with it then."

With his mic on, and the talk button clipped along with the two-way radio onto his utility belt, he depressed the talk or broadcast button.

"—Bravo One to base, over—" he whispered and waited for the reply.

Seconds later, he heard through his earbud the reply from base.

"—Come in, Bravo One, this is base, over—"

"—Roger, Base, subject wounded. Still tracking, should have subject soon, over—"

"—Roger, copy, soon to have subject?—"

"—Affirmative, Base—"

"—Roger, advise once accomplished, over—"

"—Roger Base, Bravo One, out—"

Slowly, Roberts stood and, holding his rifle down by his side, followed Cooper, who was already way ahead of him.

"Hey, wait up," Roberts said.

"Get your fat ass in gear, dude."

Cooper, a tall black man, lean and fit, his hair cut short and wearing a full growth of beard, mustache, and sunglasses, wanted to catch up with her before anyone came across either of them. He knew he'd shot the girl, as they now followed her faint blood trail.

They were in a forested area with an oppressive canopy of evergreens loomed above the forest floor. While still following her blood trail, at one point they came to an abandoned half-timbered house, but her trail angled away back into the forest.

Cooper scanned the area and the ground. He found some blood that looked fresh. Bending, Cooper lifted his sunglasses over his head and brushed a finger across the blood.

"It's fresh alright," he muttered, wiping his finger on his pants leg.

Rising and returning his shades over his eyes, he waited for Roberts to meet up with him. "She's not too far ahead of us now, maybe ten or twenty minutes, heading east."

"Need to end this soon. I've had no breakfast or coffee," Roberts said, shaking his head.

"Won't be long," Cooper said. "She's lost a lot of blood. We'll find her dead before too long."

* * *

It was twenty minutes later when they heard faint scraping noises ahead of them. Cooper motioning in hand signals told Roberts to take the flank. As they moved quietly forward, and moving in concert to each other, Cooper could sense that they were almost on top of her.

They moved soundlessly through the tall grass and among the tall evergreens, keeping low in the shadows as much as they could, while holding their weapons pointing straight ahead, ready to fire.

Not far ahead of the two guards, Helen Chapman, dazed and wobbling, stopped and, with constant thoughts of those following her, squatted barefoot and tired beside a large fallen log and hugged herself, trying to get some warmth.

There, she rested panting among the tall-forested trees in which she had taken a brief refuge from those that chased her.

Her shoulder throbbed with pain, and she couldn't stop the flow of blood. She was thirsty, cold, and miserable. Her body was bruised with several cuts and abrasions, and her clothing was badly torn. She was almost completely soaked in blood. Her heart was beating a mile a minute.

If I stay resting, would I have the strength to get back up? That thought ran through her mind and, besides the guards tracking her, this was all too frightening.

Will I ever get out of this nightmare alive?

She didn't know, but she wasn't ready to give up yet. She'd come this far, and she'd see this to the end or die trying, she told herself.

The air itself was cool and fresh. She was outdoors, a major improvement from the cave she'd been holed up in for days.

Her thoughts turned to her father.

I miss you so much, Dad. I miss how you nursed me when I was sick, the times you held me when I cried. I love you, Daddy.

She had no idea how long she could stay resting until they found her. Then she remembered fragments of the lessons her father tried to teach her about survival since she'd reached the age of fourteen. She really hadn't paid too much attention to him, wanting instead to be with her friends. But things he'd mentioned slowly came to the forefront of her long-forgotten memories.

Brightening up some, she remembered what he'd said about wounds. Then, the sixteen-year-old tore up strips of her blouse and started using them as bandages.

The good thing about her wound was that the bullet seemed to have passed through her arm. She could feel the exit wound on the other side. She winced when she tried to lift it, but the pain was too intense. It was like white-hot needles stabbing through her shoulder.

She believed she'd sustained a broken bone. After wrapping the last of the strips, she had stopped the bleeding. And she did not find any bones breaking through the skin. Was that a sign of not having broken any bones? She didn't know.

Not knowing if they were still following her, she assumed they were and tried to keep from giving her position away by not moving about too much.

Then, other things her father said came rushing back. Things like what to do when being followed, how to gain the upper hand in case someone grabbed you. Things that she could use in case they came upon her. It was worth a try, she thought.

"What's the worst they could do, besides killing me?" she muttered.

So, her mind wrapped around the idea of setting up some type of ambush. Then what? There were two of them and armed. What did she have to arm herself with?

"Nothing at all," she muttered.

In her condition, she just didn't know if that was even workable. Hell, she thought, it could get her killed. She quickly discarded that idea.

She lay back on the fallen tree, oh so alone as, closing her eyes, she sighed.

"I'm sounding like my father," she muttered.

And she did the one thing she hadn't been able to do since she was taken. She smiled.

Minutes later, she thought she'd heard the snapping of twigs and the rustling of bushes coming from somewhere behind her. Then, more slight noises from the far side, and she realized they'd broken off, coming at her from two different directions.

Getting up, she did so soundlessly and, glancing left and right, she moved straight ahead through the high bushes and trees to keep concealed as much as possible. Far ahead of her, she thought she could hear rushing water. Walking as fast she could, she heard them now.

They were getting closer!

With a smothered scream, Helen, sprinting for her life, ran and ran, not worried anymore about keeping quiet!

Suddenly, coming into a clearing, she stopped. Panting, almost out of breath, she moved forward slowly and found herself on a steep mountain ledge and, far below her, was a fast-moving river.

Quickly glancing around and behind her, she knew she had no other place to go except down. Maintaining her self-possession in the face of this new danger, she neither cried out nor moved a muscle.

Then she glanced back down the mountain and suddenly heard the unmistakable crack of a rifle's booming sound, and she felt a bullet graze her forehead. The girl felt the pain, and her hand instinctively flew to her head and came away with blood, while at the same time, her body spun from the impact of the bullet. Then, her arms went up over her head, as darkness overtook her conscious thought and, as she toppled over the ledge, she lost consciousness.

Moments later, both guards came to a stop on the ledge and stared down into the river.

Roberts asked, "You see her? 'Cause I don't."

"That's a long way down, dude," Cooper replied. "That river is moving fast, and I don't think she's alive, not with my bullet striking her head, and that fall would've done her in."

Roberts said, "Yeah, ya had the clear shot, I didn't."

They both kept staring down, waiting for her to pop her head out of the water, not saying a word.

They caught no sight of her.

"So, what ya wanna do?" Roberts asked, breaking the silence.

Sergeant Cooper's answer came in less than a second. "I say she's dead. Report that and let's get on back."

"Words I wanted to hear."

Two minutes later, once Roberts made the report to base, they turned their backs and started walking the way they'd came.

* * *

The CAC, Missile Silo
They gave Colonel Godfrey Randall the good news, the escaped prisoner—Helen Chapman—was dead. With that having been taken care of, it was just another piece of information he would report to his commander as soon as he stepped into the CAC.

No use waking him just yet, he thought.

The CAC was bright with the hot lights, and there was an unmistakable muskiness in the air. Then, as he hummed, he opened a drawer on his left side, pulled out a bottle of Johnny Walker Red, and poured a large amount of the liquid into a tall glass sitting on his desk. Smiling with the good news, he lifted the glass with a rough hand and took a quick drink, then another, feeling euphoric.

More good news had arrived earlier today as well. The OPLAN-8009, which he'd been waiting on, had been transmitted and received. He had already gone through the initial plan and found it concise down to the last detail. Yet more good news, the technicians working on the bombs had nearly completed their work.

But he had also received a setback of sorts on the placing of another bug into the office of the Provost Marshal. His man was unable to place a second bug. This needed to be accomplished post-haste, he realized.

Now, having knowledge as to the base the B-2 Bomber was to be available from and its tail number, he would plan the next phase. There were forthcoming challenges, but none that couldn't be surmounted.

Then he heard someone knocking on his office door.

The Colonel already knew who they were. It was the pilot that will fly the Stealth bomber and his gunner—there for their briefing and orders.

These two men were active-duty, Air Force personnel, both wanted for crimes against the military and both recruited six months ago.

Major Craig Thornton was under investigation by the AFOSTO or Air Force Office of Special Investigations and charged in the stabbing death of a fellow officer in a possible hate crime and the death of his own wife. Seems the major caught his wife in bed with a black officer. While on bail, personnel of the Silo approached him and offered a large sum of money and transportation to any part of the world in exchange for his cooperation and his ability to fly a B-2 Bomber.

Captain Jack King had gone AWOL and was placed on the rolls as a deserter. According to his file, Captain King was a dealer in narcotics and charged with its distribution and use while on a military installation. With no family ties to speak off, he'd gone AWOL. Personnel of the Silo found King in a Los Angeles Skid Row and also offered a large sum of money and transportation to any country he so desired for his invaluable expertise in operating the weapons system aboard a B-2 Bomber.

It had taken time and money to find them. But, shortly, it would pay itself off.

Both individuals had been quartered in the Silo and now were ready to be given their orders.

—Chapter Thirty-Two—

FBI Special Agent Jesse Martinez sat forward behind his desk, studying the video files supplied to him from the Provost Marshal's office, as his partner Agent Dan Russell sat across from him. Russell, sitting back in the chair, with a phone's receiver up against his ear, listened to what was being relayed to him.

Staring over his monitor, Martinez momentarily made eye contact with Russell, who gave him a smile as if to say, *"I'm making progress."* With a thumbs up, they both returned to work.

Martinez had the video of Helen Chapman open as the glow of the computer screen shone on his face. Taking careful notes, he jotted down the conditions of the cave-like atmosphere and, from that reference, he surmised that the video may have been from somewhere underground, although, because of the darkness and poor lighting, he could not identify any background objects.

But a more careful analysis was needed to conclude his assumption of an underground haven. As for the girl, he didn't see any evidence that would show she was in harm's way, at least not yet. And she wasn't his focus.

He felt for her plight though, having two teenage daughters of his own, but he had bigger fish to fry.

The American Consulate in Stuttgart is situated across from the offices of the Defense Intelligence Agency, DIA. DIA agent Tom Price wasn't present, having left earlier in the day. That left one other agent manning that office, if the FBI agents needed to coordinate anything with them.

Not concerned with the staff of DIA, the FBI agents were conducting their own investigations into the thefts of the bombs and, with the received information referencing General Scott, they had their hands full.

No legwork here, no pounding the pavement for clues, no questioning of subjects or suspects. This, so far, was an electronic investigative effort, with Dan going through the late Captain Cory's computer and sending inquiries through the proper channels and to Quantico, Virginia. This type of investigation could take days or months. They both knew that time was not on their side. Something big was about to happen, and time wasn't standing still for them.

With two separate computers and two banks of phones, supplied by DIA, they coordinated every single shred of evidence and electronic statements through the NCAVC, The National Center for the Analysis of Violent Crime, and the CIRG, Critical Incident Response Group, at headquarters in Quantico. Located at the FBI Academy, the NCAVC was established in May 1994 and was designed to provide rapid assistance to incidents of a crisis nature. It's composed of diverse units that provide operational support and conduct research in related areas. It furnishes expertise in cases involving abduction or mysterious disappearance of children, crime scene analysis, profiling, as well as other tactics.

Clicking on the second video, Martinez was able to watch General Scott's interactions. This would be a valuable piece of information to the Behavioral section of the FBI to form a clear, precise profile of General Scott. The experts could then take apart Scott's life, his holdings, his bank accounts, and any property he may have anywhere in the world. It was just a matter of time until he received the results, and it could lead to significant trails they could follow.

They labeled their request urgent, time sensitive.

Phone call after call they answered, writing all the information, but, as yet, no definitive leads had been identified.

Agent Martinez glanced at the computer screen, barely blinking. Hell, he knew there would be endless hours that lay ahead of them. And, being just past twelve, he decided on some much-needed lunch. They had been working ever since leaving the PM's Office and just after having breakfast.

Then he glanced over at Dan Russell and watched as Dan cradled the receiver, saved whatever he had on his computer, and was ready to dial another number, when Martinez said, as he pushed with his arms and stood, "Hey, how's about some lunch?"

Russell smiled. And, with his soft-spoken Georgia accent, he said, "You're, eh, buying, right?"

"Is it my turn?"

Pushing off with his arms and standing up, he said, "Damn right it is, boss. Like to keep you honest."

"Okay, let's go then. Work can wait an hour. When we return, let's hope we have some good news waiting for us."

* * *

Thirty minutes after arriving at her office, Agent Sinclair and Tom Price were back on the road and navigating through the streets of downtown Stuttgart. It had started to rain. The windshield wipers slapped away at the heavy rain. Tentatively, Price agreed on her next course of action. And he believed she'd not made a valid point in wanting to go back to Jeffrey Cory's place.

Traffic was heavy for this time of the day and, with the rain steadily falling, traffic was almost bumper-to-bumper. Her Chevy was the only American-made vehicle on the streets that they could make out, what with so many brand names as Mercedes-Benz, Audi, Porsche, and Alfa Romeo that didn't seem as unusual for a large city like Stuttgart.

"So, tell me again why you want to look through Cory's place?" Price asked from the passenger seat.

"Are you questioning me again, Tom?" Sinclair asked as she sounded her horn and passed a slow-moving car.

"No, I'm not questioning you. But we both know the FBI went through his apartment, and all they came up with was his computer, that we almost came away with."

A dead silence.

They exchanged a quick look. As he glanced at Sinclair, surprised, there was a little sadness in his eyes.

Sighing, Sinclair said, "We need to find something, *Christ*, anything with which to go on. I have no leads to follow except him. Maybe in death he has something to say that he wouldn't if he was still alive. A person who has been in contact with whoever and who has been pulling his strings doesn't keep vital information just in his computer. And I bet the FBI will come up empty-handed with it. Still, it's worth the shot."

"A long shot, if you ask me."

"Listen, if I didn't need you to come with me, I wouldn't have called you. But I do need you, Tom. We work well together."

He hung his head. "Not... great?"

She shook her head and smiled. "Don't push it."

* * *

Fifteen minutes later, they arrived.

The rain had slackened off some as she rolled the Chevy to a gentle stop and parked across the street from Cory's apartment. Exiting the car, they began walking, crossed the street and stopped once they reached the steps. Climbing the four steps, Sinclair immediately noticed something was off with the door. The doorframe was pulled off its top and center hinges and pushed closed, but not all the way. Someone had broken into the apartment. That was obvious.

The question is, are *they* or *him* inside?

Sinclair let Price see the damage done. Then, without a word, she pulled her weapon, as did Price. Slowly pushing with her shoulder, Sinclair opened the door a few feet. Without a sound, she pushed some more, just enough so she could get her body through. Once she was in, Price soundlessly followed and entered the apartment.

Standing shoulder to shoulder with their backs to the door, they started to spill left and right when, all of a sudden, a figure stepped out of the bedroom, saw them, stopped and, reaching behind his back, pulled a weapon and instantly fired two shots in their direction! Not waiting to see if he hit anyone, he immediately turned and ran to the back door. As he ran, he fired another shot at the glass-paneled door shattering it to pieces.

The moment they saw the figure stepping out of the bedroom, they froze for a second and, with the echo of gunshots, both Sinclair and Price dropped to the floor, knees bent. They heard the whistling noise of the two rounds as they flew over their heads and crashed into the door behind them.

Without a second's hesitation, Sinclair fired off a shot that grazed the running figure's left arm. Then, as if they had not shot him, the would-be burglar ran through the door onto a balcony and, without losing a step, vaulted a three-foot high balcony railing onto a small alleyway.

Just mere seconds may have passed.

In a heartbeat, Sinclair, in a flash of motion, ran to the back, jumped through the back door, and also vaulted the railing, just clearing it, landed with bent knees onto the alleyway and, straightening, she gave chase.

Tom Price, taken off guard by the intruder and by the time he fired a shot, the figure disappeared from his sight. Regaining his senses and his wits, Price immediately ran to the front door. Pushing himself through and out to the street, he hoped to catch sight of the fleeing figure in case he doubled back around the front of the apartment.

Sinclair sprinted through the alleyway, saw an open gate, ran through, and paused on the street corner as she glanced east and west along the narrow street. The rain wasn't helping her any, falling in sheets all around her. Wiping her eyes, she finally caught sight of a figure walking fast heading west.

It has to be him! The thought flashed through her mind.

Sinclair ran after him.

She pulled out her cell phone and quickly dialed the German police number, set as a favorite, as she ran.

"Polizeistation, Stuttgart, Ja," came the response. *"Offizier Heinz."*

"This is a CID Military Police officer. In pursuit of a male fleeing suspect near the Heusteigviertel district. Request your assistance. The suspect is armed and dangerous."

"I have a patrol in the vicinity; I will dispatch the patrol. Please keep me informed as to your location."

As Sinclair pocketed the phone, she saw the figure had slowed and veered around a corner. The man had not bothered to glance behind him, yet. Gradually, Sinclair had closed the gap between them. And, as she also rounded the corner, the man sensing someone behind him, turned, saw her, and fired two shots her way. One pinged off a wall, showering her with plaster pieces, the other went flying off to her right side.

Sinclair took cover against a wall and, with gun in hand, she raised it and let loose three quick shots at the running figure. All of them missed.

Shrugging off his attempt on either slowing her down or killing her, Sinclair doubled her efforts.

A moment later, she heard the loud squealing of tires and the *crump*, *crump* sounds of a vehicle hitting another. Still running, she came to an abrupt stop as she entered a four-lane street. And, there, ahead of her, she saw a two-car collision and a sprawled body, unmoving, illuminated by a car's headlights. A German police patrol car was one of the damaged cars.

Jogging over to the body, she noticed the man was conscious as she heard him moan with pain. His head was bloody as the blood, mixed with the rain, dripped onto the street, making it look more damaging than what it seemed. He was on his back, one leg canted to his side, broken, she thought. She felt around him for his gun but couldn't find it. Then she searched him for his wallet and found it. She had the distinct impression of having seen the man before.

Two German police officers approached her. After Sinclair identified herself to the two patrol officers, one of them called for an ambulance and another patrol car.

A few seconds later, Tom Price came running onto the scene.

Going through the man's wallet, Sinclair found a military ID card made out to a Sergeant Richard Stevens. The photo of Sergeant Stevens struck a chord in her memory. Then she remembered who this guy was. She remembered the chase through the PM's building of a tall skinny man who had been shadowing her and Price.

Going through the rest of the man's pockets, she found a cell phone, shoved that in her pocket along with the wallet, but kept the military ID in her hand.

As Price stopped by her side, she said, "Here, take a look at this ID, and tell me if you'd seen him before."

Taking the ID, he looked it over and remembered the description of a man he'd seen before. "If my memory serves me well, and it does, I think that's the guy we chased over at the PM's Office the other day."

"Yeah, I agree. One and the same."

Once the ambulance arrived and transported her suspect to the nearest German hospital, Sinclair called the MP Desk Sergeant at Patch Barracks and instructed him to dispatch a patrol and take over from the German police in guarding her prisoner and reporting to her his condition.

In the meantime, Sinclair planned to return to the apartment. She needed to see what information Sergeant Stevens was so intent on discovering. Could it be that valuable, she thought, to send someone after it? Or was someone just being cautious, covering up a loose end?

She'd know soon enough.

With the rain turning to a slight drizzle, both Sinclair and Price walked back to the apartment. When they arrived, they immediately noticed the place had been ransacked, furniture turned over, bookcases overturned. Things that they failed to notice due to being shot at and almost taken by surprise.

As Price took over the living room and kitchen, Sinclair concentrated on the bedroom.

Entering Cory's bedroom, the first thing that caught her attention was the bed, overturned, and the lights turned on, with drawn curtains.

Standing in the center of the suite, she methodically turned counterclockwise ever slowly, staring at one corner then the other at this and that, stopping, evaluating, and then back again, turning this time clockwise and repeating the process.

Subconsciously, Sinclair was walking the grid of a crime scene.

Something was off. She could sense it but was unable to see it.

Then it hit her.

Something along the far-left sidewall that shouldn't be. That was the only spot in the bedroom that seemed to her to be out of sync with the rest of the room. Closing her eyes, she tried to visualize it in her mind. Then shaking her head, she slowly walked to that spot.

She came to a stop about two feet from the wall.

Then she saw it, the one thing that stood out from the rest. The air duct cover. It was painted white, yet someone had removed the screws and replaced them, and in the process scraped the paint on all the screwheads.

Approaching the grill cover, she saw residue of paint flakes on the floor just under the grill. She then pulled out her pocketknife and slowly removed each screw.

"Yeah," she muttered as she worked, "this recently happened."

Agent Tom Price had already finished in the living room and had found nothing of value. He stood at the threshold of the bedroom, leaning up against the doorjamb, arms crossed over his chest, not saying a word, as he watched Sinclair at work.

After finally having all the screws removed, Sinclair pulled on the metal screen and felt it give way under her hands. Placing the grill off to one side, she ran her hand on all four corners of the duct. Then she stopped, as her hand touched something, a package maybe, taped to the upper right-hand corner. Grasping the package, she yanked hard, and it came away in her hand. Slowly, she retrieved her hand, stood, and noticed Price staring at her. "Nothing better to do?" she asked.

"Just watching you work, Sinclair," Price said adding, "You're one lucky cop."

"Luck has nothing to do with it."

With the package in hand, she walked toward the living room. There, they found two chairs and sat at the dining table as she unraveled the package. With all the packing removed, the mysterious package contained a small black book with a thick rubber band securing it closed.

"Well, well, let's see what we have here," Sinclair said.

Removing the rubber band, Sinclair leafed through the book, and smiled.

"Okay," Price said, "wanna share what you're reading, partner."

"There are notes, names, telephone numbers, and times and places of weapons shipments. I think we hit the jackpot, Tom."

"Guess I owe you an apology for not backing you."

"No problem, Tom. Don't sweat the small stuff, as my Dad would say."

"What now? Do you inform the FBI or keep it to ourselves?"

"Tempting, isn't it?" she replied. "But for now, let's keep it our secret. I started this investigation, and I'll see it through to the end."

—Chapter Thirty-Three—

Colonel Richard L. Sinclair had been steadily working the phones, and keeping the EUCOM Commander abreast on the ongoing investigations between the FBI and the CID, primarily his daughter's investigation. And now, he was having his reservations about Belle's continuance, as he believed her to be too emotionally involved.

With the death of Captain Jeffrey Cory, whom Belle had fallen in love with, he felt she could be a liability. Hell, he knew how she could get when someone she knew was killed. He was of the same temperament. He feared her reaction could bring discredit to the Army and the CID.

He wasn't saying she would, he thought. But a person under stress is liable to do things unnecessarily cruel and unlawful. He was thinking of her self-interest and her welfare.

He would just have to see how she responds to his questioning on the matter. And how gentle should he be with her? He could give her a direct order, but what would that mean to their father and daughter relationship? There was a strong bond between them since her mother had passed, and he certainly didn't want to see that destroyed.

In the meantime, he developed a disturbing piece of information.

Through his many military and civilian contacts, he learned of an impending high-level conference with the North Korean

President Pak-Un-Nam and the United States President Richard Bradley, in Pyongyang.

Knowing the situation with OPLAN-8009 activation and its scenario, General Scott's mission seemed to coincide with the visit of the US President. Or did it? Was this just a coincidence or shrewd planning by General Scott? Was this his plan all along? And how did he know about the planned visit so far in advance?

There were too many questions, too few answers—or none at all.

With the OPLAN activated a few hours ago and its fail-safe mechanism in motion, there was no one that could cancel its ultimate conclusion. And as far as the bomber was concerned, both pilots understood they were to ignore all orders given after a confirmed war plan was set in motion—no one could stop it!

This was a first-strike scenario. A war plan set and approved. But there were others measures that, when put in play, could at least counter some the OPLAN's operational parameters.

Coordination and top-level meetings would convene, and decisions would be made. And that was out of his hands.

Now, he waited for his daughter to arrive.

* * *

It was exactly two in the afternoon when Agent Jacqueline Sinclair and Agent Tom Price cracked open the door to the Provost Marshal's Office.

Earlier, she'd received a call from her father that he wanted her and Price to report to him within the hour. With no explanations given, Sinclair tried to drill him on the *why*, he had rebuffed her questions, and told her he would explain once they'd arrived.

He sounded pissed about something, she thought, remembering back to his phone call.

Did he find out about the book? And, if he did, who told him? Or was this something to do with the investigation the FBI was conducting? Hell, no use trying to figure it out.

I'll just have to wait and see, she thought.

Stepping through the lobby and into her father's office, Sinclair walked right up to his desk as Price stopped three feet behind her.

"Is this formal or informal, sir?" Sinclair asked, standing with her arms behind her back.

"Christ, honey, just take a seat, the both of you, okay?"

She tried to smile but failed.

"Yes, Dad," Sinclair replied as she turned around and winked at Price, who had already pulled up a chair and sat staring at her and the colonel. Price was ready for anything. This had all the markings of them being pulled from the investigation, he thought, so why the informal father and daughter routine? But he kept his mouth shut. *Let's see where this leads*, he mused.

Drawing in a deep breath, Sinclair grabbed a seat, sat back, and crossed a leg. "Okay, Dad, shoot. What's this all about?"

"Straight to the point, okay then," the PM said, almost in a whisper.

Colonel Sinclair glanced at Belle, then at Agent Price. His office felt warmer than usual as a bead of sweat started forming on his forehead. This was going to be difficult. He had no alternative. And when he'd talked with the EUCOM commander, he had also expressed his concern about Belle. His commander's pressing question was: can she continue on the way she has, or will she jeopardize the investigation by going off half-cocked?

It was a reasonable question his commander put forth. And one that stabbed directly into his heart. Ultimately, he reasoned, it was a question he had also asked himself.

To make matters worse, left with making the final decision, Colonel Sinclair agonized over whether to pull her off or keep her on the investigation. And now, formally assigned as the Acting Chief of the Stuttgart CID field office by CID Command, she had matters that needed attention, as befitting an officer's position of authority.

Placing his hands on his desk, he pushed off and stood tall and sad. Sad, because if she didn't answer in the way he thought, he would be left with making the biggest decision of his life and having his only daughter's anger sour their happiness together. He knew his daughter, knew she could be vindictive, and it would a very long time before she would come around again.

He was caught in a catch twenty-two.

Slowly making his way around the desk, he stopped midway and sat on its edge, as he glanced straight into his daughter's eyes.

"Belle, honey," he said, arching his brows, "it's time to figure out your involvement with the investigation. Command and I are of the accord that we should pull you as lead investigator and have another agent continue the case with Agent Price."

She flushed as she looked at her father's eyes. "I thought we were straight on this matter, Father? Didn't we once talk about this?"

"Yes, yes, we did," he said. "But the concern is that you're involved personally since the tragic death of Captain Cory."

It would seem to Agent Price, as he stared at them both, that the careful bond that kept them together was suddenly drawing to a close. Once again, not saying anything on her behalf, he kept silent, observing more than engaging. It wasn't his place to ridicule or do anything at this stage. He'll just sit back and, if asked for his opinion, then he'll give it, although, he was with her all the way.

Agent Sinclair was careful in what she would say to her father, as her eyes widened, knowing that the next few words she spoke could spell her being pulled from the lead investigator position. Slowly, her thoughts came together.

Then, standing, she approached her father and, standing very close to him, she reached out and gently held his hand in hers.

"If you take me off this case, Dad," she said. "It means you and Command don't have any faith in me as a CID investigator." Her tone now had a slight edge to it. "I'm capable of setting my own personal boundaries with my heart, Father. I'm the better judge of that than you, Dad. I'm a professional in every sense of the word. Haven't I proven myself repeatedly that I do my job honorably and completely to the letter of the book? I've never let my personal life interfere with my work. You know that to be true. When have I ever failed you?"

Then, with her head held low, she continued. "And where was I when Mom died, Dad?"

Colonel Sinclair stiffened, as he raised his right hand, stopping her.

For just a moment, he stood there, staring her down. "That's enough, Belle."

Pulling his hand away from hers and standing, Colonel Sinclair walked back around his desk and sat with his arms around his chest as he stared at his daughter and Agent Price, a small tear flowing down his cheek. This, as the mention of his late wife struck a chord in his heart.

Colonel Richard Sinclair drew in a deep breath, reached over to the left-hand drawer, opened it, and pulled out a half-full bottle of *Crown Royal XR Extra* whiskey and three glasses.

Pouring the whiskey into the tall glasses, he said, having decided, "This is not going to be easy, Belle. You've survived attacks on your life during the course of this investigation and lost a dear one. Notwithstanding that he may have worked for the other side, I don't want to lose you, too. But you have satisfied my opinion in this matter. So, no, you have never failed me in anything I'd task you with and, being there when your mother died, was bittersweet."

He paused. Taking a deep breath, he set his eyes on her, sitting perfectly still, waiting for his decision with downcast eyes.

"Very well then," he continued, "I'm keeping you on the case. However, if I hear of any wrongdoing, I'll pull you right off. Are we in accord?"

Jacqueline Sinclair fell back on her seat and smiled, deep in thought for a few seconds, wondering what in blazes he meant by *wrongdoing*. But, if she met with Cory's killer, or anyone else associated with it, there would be no one to stop her from taking her revenge.

No one!

"Sure, Dad," she said, glancing at her father.

Agent Price stifled a quick, knowing smile at Belle.

Colonel Sinclair merely smiled. "Here, come forward and pick up a glass and let's toast to a satisfactory conclusion to your investigation."

Still standing, Price and Belle, with a glass each, downed the liquid in one gulp and remained standing, thinking that the meeting was drawing to a close.

Turning his gaze on Agent Price, Colonel Sinclair asked, "You've been silent throughout. Do you have anything to add to what was said here?"

Standing, Price looked at the colonel, then at Belle, then back again to the colonel, and said, smiling, "Yes, sir, I do. Can I date your daughter?"

Belle Sinclair immediately stood and skewered Price with her stare. She was totally taken aback by his comment. Then she turned and stared at her father, as if to say, "Help, Dad."

In response to her look, Colonel Sinclair leaned back in his chair and said, smiling, "Why are you looking at me?"

Turning back to Price, she fixed him with a level gaze. "We'll talk about this later."

"Now that that's been taken care of," Colonel Sinclair said, "why don't you two fill me in on your investigation so far?"

As they sat back down, Agent Sinclair reached behind her and pulled out the book she'd found in Cory's apartment. Opening it, she stood and placed it on her father's desk. As he reached for it, he said, "What's this?"

"That, sir, is Captain Cory's book. I found it when Tom and I went back to his apartment. It was pretty well hidden. It seems to detail transactions with dates and amounts and types of weapons and supplies, huge amounts of supplies. Tom and I were about to head back to my office and start seeing where all that equipment was shipped to or who had possession of it when it left Cory's unit warehouse."

"Yes, I see what you mean."

"There's more, Dad," she said, leafing through page after page. "There are phone numbers, names, and places identified throughout the book. Captain Cory kept a precise accounting of what he was doing. I would conclude that the FBI, with Cory's computer, comes up with a blank for information."

"You're going to share this with the FBI, correct?" asked the colonel.

Price stepped up to the PM's desk and said, "We were thinking of going through the book first, and then we would let the FBI in on it, too."

"I see. Make sure you do."

Belle said, "Yes, sir."

"Okay, here is the other reason I called you two," the PM said. "First, the OPLAN has a safe-mode set in. In other words, once started, it can't be stopped. And, roughly several hours ago, it was initiated. We're not sure if the targets are in North Korea. But it calls for it in the revised OPLAN. We have set in motion tactics to neutralize aspects of the OPLAN."

The PM paused and glanced at both of them. His gaze finally returning on Belle. He continued.

"Second, we know how the bombs will be launched. It's a B-2 Stealth bomber, and there are four US airbases where they could get their hands on one. All are being covered. Third, the US President and the North Korean President will host a summit sometime this week. When exactly it will take place is being kept a secret."

Another short pause.

"And last, I have instructed the MP's to place the four Generals whose children have been abducted and who planned the changes to the OPLAN under house arrest."

"Interesting," Belle said, glancing over at Price, "and frightening too. This could start World War Three."

"Yes, we're aware of that. That's why we need to get a better handle on this. And your main priority is finding General Scott's base of operation and those hostages. It is our belief, once the Generals conclude their part, they will eliminate the children."

"Yes, I'm thinking that too, Dad."

Price asked, "What's going to happen to the four Generals, Colonel?"

"They'll get their day in court, is all I can say."

* * *

The CAC – Missile Silo
In the communication room, things were not going as planned.

Corporal Raul Sanchez had taken over the communication duties in the past hour. The first thing they ordered him to do was get a bug placed in the Provost Marshal's Office. But in order to do that, the one person detailed for that assignment was Sergeant Richard Stevens.

The problem Corporal Sanchez encountered was that he was unable to reach Sergeant Stevens. Knowing that the Sergeant was detailed to breach Captain Cory's apartment for the purpose of retrieving his laptop computer and any other written notes or communications that could be of an incriminating nature, Stevens had been late in reporting in.

Corporal Sanchez had tried to raise him several times, but all he'd received was radio-band static every time. When that failed, he dialed his direct cell phone number, but it went straight to voicemail. He'd hung up, not leaving a message, as instructed to do when anyone was unable to contact any of the squads operating in the field.

He waited a whole hour before reporting it to Colonel Randall.

But now, after the hour had come and gone, he dialed his number and waited for it to be answered. "He's not going to like this setback," he muttered to himself.

"*Report, Corporal,*" came the reply.

"Sir, I've been unable to reach Sergeant Stevens either through his radio or his cell phone."

"*I see, and how often have you tried reaching him?*"

"I've tried several times within a span of an hour, sir."

"*I see. Corporal, contact the Delta squad leader and have him report to me.*"

"Will do, sir."

—Chapter Thirty-Four—

It was a fast-moving river. The currents were swift, and its great depths were all but void of underwater or surface rocks.

This alone may well have saved her life the instant her body struck the surface. The cold icy temperature and the murky river shocked her system awake. But the freezing waters also made it that much harder to breathe.

Opening her eyes, Helen Chapman couldn't see where she was going as she tumbled over and over, was dragged under, and resurfaced again.

Oh, my *God* . . . where was she? Why was she in the river? She only remembered waking up as if she'd been in a deep sleep, as the assault of the coldness of the frigid river stirred her to consciousness, of plunging deep down under the water then swimming upwards breaking the surface, her lungs aching for air as the furious currents swept her down river.

Other than that, Helen Chapman's mind had drawn a blank.

She was able to catch quick glimpses of high mountains on either side of the river. Is this how she fell into the river? However, she had no recollection of ever falling from any mountain. Or was she thrown in?

Dear Lord . . . why can't I remember?

Instinctively, Helen turned onto her back with her legs pointing downstream and her head positioned upstream, in that position she let the river move her along. Sometimes the reverse occurred, but she always tried to move with her legs downstream as she tried to keep watch on where the river was taking her and looking for any way out of this nightmare.

Still, she tried to remain as calm as she could, knowing that if panic were to set in, she wouldn't survive. "Breathe with the flow of the river," she heard herself say. "And keep an eye out for a protected spot where the water was moving more slowly."

Unfortunately, she saw none.

Her mind was working the problem, just not the *why* she was in the river, which was troubling enough.

The river meandered left and right, taking some sharp curves. She spied a large tree branch that jutted about three feet over the water, but it seemed so far away. Would she make it in time before she went under for the last time? *The tree could be my only way out of the river*, she told herself, desperate to stay alive.

Swimming in the branch's direction, Helen kept getting closer, fighting every inch of the way against the fast-moving river and the strong currents. Seconds later, she lost sight of the branch, as the rushing water rolled her onto her stomach, and then, rolling onto her back, she again caught sight.

Realizing she had only one chance of attempting to grasp the tree, the girl gathered herself for it. Almost upon the tree, and using her last ounce of strength, she leaped high out of the water as both of her hands grasped a wide branch about a foot above the water. As she dangled for a moment, Helen voiced her thanks to God.

Ever so slowly, she pulled herself out of the river's hold. How she found the strength, she didn't know. Finally, the girl lay on top of the wide tree. Straddling it painfully, she made herself move forward. And with the greatest fear she'd fall into the river once again, she hung on tightly.

Yet fear can work wonders.

Raising her head above the tree, she saw the river's bank and lush green grass and tall trees ahead. But, most of all, she saw safety and a chance to live.

Trying to stand, just reaching the root of the tree, the girl drew herself upright and almost fell back into the river. Then, while holding onto the few branches there were, she finally made the bank and lay on the thick moss of grass, panting with exhaustion and unable to rise.

For some time, she lay, and then, finally closing her eyes, she fell asleep.

Time passed, how much, she didn't know, and, with rain clouds overhead, there broke an unexpected sound of voices that startled her awake, which came from the thick of the forest. Too exhausted even to try standing, the voices kept coming closer and closer.

She hoped they were coming to her rescue.

Damn it, why can't I get up?

Her body had sustained several deep cuts and bruises from the tree, and she'd lost a fair amount of blood. Pain was radiating from her arm, and blood was seeping out. "When did that happen?" she asked herself. The side of her head was also painful.

"Come on, get up, get up," she muttered.

But it was useless. Try as she could, she just flopped back down on the grass and gave in, as she followed the voices that kept coming in her direction.

* * *

Gunter kept the pace fast, as his seven-year-old sister, Ursula, held the tackle box, and Gunter held their two rods and reels, their breath flaring in the cold, but not cold enough to keep them away from doing a little fishing. They both knew this side of the river was off-limits because of the rapid currents, but that didn't matter to ten-year-old Gunter.

"It's getting colder, Gunter," Ursula said to her older brother. "Don't you think it's colder?"

Slowing down almost to a stop, Gunter turned to face his sister. "Yeah but think of all the fish we will catch."

"I don't think I want to be out here in the cold," his sister lamented.

"Come on, it will be okay, promise," Gunter said, walking fast once again.

"How much further is it going to be?" Ursula asked.

"Not far, just around the corner."

Slowing down some, they rounded the corner and stopped when they saw a body lying on the grass by the river's bank. Gunter, his mind working overtime, thought it was a dead body. Should he go home and report it, or see if, whoever it was, was alive?

"Gunter, what are you thinking?" Ursula said, almost in a whisper while tugging at her brother's coat sleeves. "Come on, we need to go home now."

"We just can't leave," the boy insisted. "I need to see if the person is alive or dead."

"No, no, let's go home, please. I'm scared."

Not paying attention to his little sister, Gunter walked over to the body, then stopped just short of reaching it and saw it moved and raised her head to face him.

In German, Gunter asked, "Are you in pain? Do you need help?"

Helen Chapman roused herself just enough on her elbows and stared at the boy in front of her.

With her head cocked to one side and through a dry parched throat, Helen slowly said, "I don't understand what you're saying."

He bent his head in thought.

"English, yes. American, no?" Gunter asked staring at her.

"English, yes," Helen, said finally understanding what he'd asked.

Then in the limited English that Gunter possessed, he asked, "Do you need help? What is your name?"

"Yes, I need help, but I can't seem to remember who I am."

* * *

The CAC Missile Silo
There were 27 highly trained and capable men.

Seven of the 27 were General Scott's Staff Officers, all under age seventy.

Twelve were from America's elite military units—Special Operators from the Army Rangers, Delta Force, and Special Forces Green Berets, all under the age of forty. This force of men would provide airborne, light-infantry and direct-action operations. They handpicked six personnel that would provide infiltration and ex-filtration operations. Two were the designated B-2 Bomber pilots.

The rest of the combat personnel, eighteen of them, were the guards that secured the missile silo, along with existing personnel that manned the logistics side of the operation. These were the most highly motivated, well-equipped personnel that money could buy, along with three experienced medics.

The seven Staff Officers were the ones completely loyal, not because of payment, but due in part to having served with General Scott during wartime operations. They each owed their lives directly or indirectly to the General. Each had their own civilian jobs; jobs that included lawyers, successful stockbrokers, shipping, and a federal judge. These were all highly influential and wealthy individuals in their own right, and each had known and loved General Scott's wife and his son.

For the last twenty minutes, the CAC was a bevy of activity as the armed personnel slowly assembled around the conference table, waiting on General Scott, who was due shortly.

Sitting behind the huge conference desk in the Command and Control Center, with lights provided by forty, huge, well-placed, integrated LED floodlights, spaced around the cavern, sat Colonel Godfrey Randall in front of his laptop computer with a bulky folder set off to one side. Randall was the second in command behind General Scott. And, almost filling the seats with some personnel as he stood, standing and facing toward the front of the desk, were the 27 personnel responsible for carrying out the order of battle.

Already having the battle plan drawn up, Colonel Randall had assigned every person to specific missions. Although the exact time and date the operation would be activated was the responsibility of General Scott, Randall knew changes would be made to his plan.

But, for now, the OOB (Order of Battle) was completed. Staring at his laptop monitor, he went over the plan, checking and rechecking for any contingencies and or double assignments. Satisfied that he'd covered all his bases, he closed his computer and waited for his commander to arrive.

Back and forth, the conversation over the desk was heated and argumentative. The main parts of their conversation centered on timing and who were the personnel chosen for the specific assignment necessary to launch the attack. This was of paramount importance to them. It was why they were all summoned to the CAC.

The time had come to fulfill the OOB. This detailed order included the participation of all combat troops, the command structure, disposition of those troops, and equipment. And what to expect from the opposing force while deployed in the field.

Several moments later, from the main entrance to the CAC, emerged Brigadier General Thomas Randolph Scott in his battle dress uniform and his Colt .45 sidearm strapped low on his right leg, as he slowly made his way toward the assembled group.

As he finally arrived at his position behind the conference desk, all personnel rose and waited in deafening silence for General Scott to take his seat.

After taking his seat, General Scott glanced around those assembled, then at Colonel Randall, then back to the 27. "Gentlemen, please take your seats."

Waiting in anticipation, no one said a word as all eyes turned toward the General.

"You all know why you're here. The time has arrived to set our OOB in motion and assign missions. Once we've done that, there will be practice runs to ensure timing and coordination. Gentlemen, in the immortal words of the author Ian Fleming, of James Bond fame, and from his novel 'Casino Royal,' he wrote that—History is moving quickly these days, and the heroes and villains keep on changing parts—I'd like to think of us as the heroes in this endeavor."

All the assembled personnel just nodded, some smiled. But all were in full agreement with their Commander.

Then, turning to his second in command, he said, "Colonel Randall, please open with the mission parameters and assignments."

"Yes, sir," Colonel Randall said, opening his laptop and his folder. "As I call the Commander's name, please approach me, and I'll hand you your assignments."

Removing the first assignment sheet and holding it, he said:

"Call sign, Team-One, Commander Major Charles Mendez: assignment infiltration. Assigned transport for four Rangers, two Delta Operators and two B-2 Bomber pilots: Transportation from Special Operations Command area. The C-17 Globemaster has been allocated for transport to Whiteman Air Force Base, Knob, Missouri, cargo will include two B61-12 Nuclear Smart Bombs, there, a designated B-2 Spirit Stealth Bomber has been allocated. The aircraft's tail number is detailed in your order. The regularly assigned bomber pilots will need to be eliminated so our two pilots can take over."

"Four Rangers and Delta personnel are designated as follows:

"Two Rangers and one Delta personnel for Station A: Airborne assignment into North Korea territory from B-2 Bomber, 'light' target for the laser-guided system of the capital building for B-2 Bomber run, Bomber call sign–Eagle One. Delta Operatives will act as the covering force.

"Two Rangers and one Delta personnel for Station B: Target President of North Korea home grounds, located in Nampo province. Coordinates are listed. Light target for Eagle One run. Again, Delta Operative will act as the covering force.

"Rangers will secure the bomber forcibly, if necessary.

"Call sign, Team-Two, Commander Major Jack Webb: assignment ex-filtration of Station A and B personnel at the designated location, and an alternate extraction point is listed in your orders. Two Sikorsky UH-60, fully armed, and ready Blackhawk helicopters have been allocated for this mission, transportation into South Korea by waiting C-130 from Special Operations Command area. Standby ready is located in the outskirts of the South Korean city of Pocheon. Coordinates have been established."

The Colonel continued. "Base call sign will be changed; frequencies will also be changed. Check your orders for the correct call signs and frequencies, which will take effect once the operation is activated."

It had taken Colonel Randall two hours, but finally the last assignments were handed out. Now he had only one other assignment to hand out. Pulling his last sheet from his folder he said, "Captain Miller, you will appoint and supervise the disposition of the remaining captives."

Standing, Captain John Miller, at six-foot-two, with a fully shaven head and a full growth of beard, approached Colonel Randall and received his assignment. Eventually, he knew he would be the one to carry out their disposal or their killing. And besides this, they also charged him with the responsibilities for the entire exterior and interior security of the silo.

Once he gained his chair, he opened his orders, read through them, and noticed that the date and time for him to carry out his order was listed as TBD. *To be Determined—at a later date.* So, he had time. Still, it was a chore he'd rather not carry-out, having a daughter of his own.

Then, Colonel Randall faced the assembled personnel and said, "The meeting is terminated. Follow up with your men and keep me posted on your training. Please wait until our Commander has departed the area before leaving."

Facing General Scott, he waited for him to rise and leave. Once clear of the group, the Colonel was the last person to depart. Grabbing his computer and empty folder, Colonel Randall walked out of the CAC and back to his office. Unknown to General Scott, Colonel Randall had devised his own escape plan if everything went south.

—Chapter Thirty-Five—

Field Office of the DIA - American Consulate, Stuttgart, 4:30 PM, Monday

Throughout their drive to the American Consulate, the waning sun cast its shadows and the hazy gray of the fog made the dying light seem to come from all directions, as it turned the rest of daylight to dark yellow embers, and the fog was an unusual occurrence late in the afternoon hours.

Arriving, Tom Price presented his credentials to the security guard at the entrance to the consulate. Once cleared to proceed, he drove toward the rear of the prodigious and imposing structure. And it was vast. It had seven stories of office space, built in the middle of the nineteenth century and occupied by the Allied Expeditionary Force during World War Two.

Special Agent Jacqueline Sinclair reluctantly followed DIA Agent Tom Price down the stairs and into Agent Price's office. It was in a windowless basement and featured cinderblock walls painted over in white. They passed the office used by the FBI agents, Price showed her and, with the door closed, she couldn't tell if they were in or not.

If truth be told, Sinclair mused, she wasn't in any mood to share with the federal agents the information she'd gained from the book she'd found at Cory's place, nor the cell phone belonging to Sergeant Stevens.

No, not just yet. Not until I get what I was hoping to get, she thought.

Tom Price had sweet-talked her into using his office to follow up on the names and telephone numbers listed in the book, through a more secure means than her office phone.

His argument was valid, she thought. Valid to a point, which logic dictated was more workable than what she would want and agree to his request. According to Price, he wanted the use of his office instead of hers for the simple reason . . . *"I have a very secure means of transmitting and receiving information that you don't have in your office—an encrypted secured phone line to DIA center,"* was the line he fed her.

She followed Tom down the corridor. At last, the corridor ended, and his office was the last door on the left side bearing the single acronym, DIA. The door on the right bore the words DIA Communications Office. Without a key, Agent Price grasped the door handle, turned it, and pushed it open.

Tom Price stepped aside and gestured Sinclair to slip in past him. As Price closed the door behind him, Sinclair thanked him and stepped on through. Standing in the room's center, illuminated by six fluorescent wraparound ceiling lights, the first thing that caught her eye were the four bookshelves against the far wall.

A large double pedestal oaken desk in the room's center, with an open laptop computer, dominated the office. And behind the desk was another desk, but a smaller version, with phone, fax machine and an Apple desktop computer with two monitors hooked up to it.

On one side of a wall was a two-cushion sofa, a coffee table, and a table lamp. In front of the oaken desk were two leather armchairs and toward, the left side of the sofa against the wall, sat a small refrigerator. A door on the right side, she observed, led to a restroom.

His office was a far cry from her own plain Army-furnished office.

"All the comforts of home, I see."

"Perks of the job," Price replied. "Welcome to my office. Won't you have a seat?"

Pulling up an armchair, Sinclair removed her sports jacket, placed it on the headrest, sat, crossed one leg over the other, and waited on him.

The movement wasn't lost on Price, as he glanced over to her, admiring the symmetry of her body and her well-sculptured legs, and grinned.

She looked at him. "Why are you grinning?" He sat in his office chair behind his desk across from Sinclair.

"What?" he asked, feeling his face flush.

"Why are you grinning?"

Price swallowed, embarrassed by her question. "Oh that, nothing. Just thought of something funny, that's all."

"Want to share?"

"No, not really," Price said. "Later perhaps."

Sinclair shook her head. Although, she looked at him a little closer and marveled at how attractive he was. She thought maybe Tom Price was exhibiting feelings for her. What exactly those feelings entailed, she didn't know. And at present, she wasn't about to ask. Yet, she was becoming more comfortable having him around. She hadn't felt that way in a long time, not even with Cory. She felt ... secure in his presence.

The remark he'd made to her about dating her echoed in her mind. She'd have to address that, eventually.

Time wasn't on her side, and her biological clock was ticking. She needed to commit to the man that would ultimately win her heart. Thinking back to Jeffrey Cory, knowing he'd been the one.

Sinclair shook her head, closed her eyes a moment, and sighed.

"Hey, you okay?" he asked, glancing at her.

"Yeah, I'm okay."

Turning his back on her, Price fired up his fax machine, his printer, and, also his Apple computer.

"I got the printer running and my computer all set," Price said. "Now all we need to do is make copies of the pages and get them transmitted to my section chief, via secured encryption mode."

"I'll make the copies," she said, rising and coming around, stopping at the printer.

"And I'll jot down the phone numbers from Sergeant Stevens' cell," Price said, "and have it ready to fax along with the pages from Cory's book. I'll email my section chief and let her know they're coming and what we need from them."

"Okay."

Across the corridor, in the FBI office, agents Jesse Martinez and Dan Russell were waiting to hear from Langley. Twenty minutes later, Martinez's phone beeped. The text message stated the results of their inquiry, sent via encrypted email, would arrive shortly.

A moment later, his email program pinged new emails.

Martinez, opening Langley's email, ran it through his encryption program. After it cleared through the assigned protocols, the email subject label read: *Thomas R. Scott Investigative analysis and profile.*

They're getting slow these days, he thought. It had taken hours to compile the information.

Martinez clicked on the email and advised Dan of its arrival. "Listen to what they came up with, Dan. And it isn't much. I'd expected a lot more on the guy."

"It's about time they got back to us."

"Yeah."

Scrolling through the email, he read out the findings:

File: SUBJECT: Thomas R. Scott retired US Army. Current location: Unknown, believed to be somewhere in Germany.

Lieutenant General Thomas Randolph Scott is old money. His family dates back to the mid-1830s. The Scott family was best of friends with Andrew Carnegie and both became rich from steel. George Randolph Scott was, as was Carnegie, an industrialist and Philanthropist. But George Scott also purchased huge sums of land throughout the Massachusetts and New York areas. The family inheritance has passed on from father to son, down to Thomas Scott.

Thomas R. Scott's net worth tops twenty-five billion dollars in total assets.

He ranks up with the top twenty richest persons in the world, according to FORBES's annual rankings.

He has invested well over fifteen million dollars in INVESCO, an independent Investment Management Company. Scott is heavy into stocks and bonds and also into SPDR S&P, oil and gas and steel.

Holdings: Through several dummy corporations and some offshore accounts, it disclosed that Scott owns several large parcels of land and structures in the US and seven overseas, with four large land deals alone in Germany, although not in his name. One is a hotel. The others are abandoned properties. Plans are in the works for future development on those lands. One of those abandoned properties is an old German World War Two underground missile silo. Plans call for a museum to be erected on the site. Another site, a huge storage plant, also with underground tunnels used for storage of hazardous materials, has no future developmental plans, according to the German house of land management.

Complete land description and addresses to be provided in a separate email to follow.

Thomas R. Scott at nineteen, gained admission to West Point on the recommendations of his father.

No criminal or civil proceedings against Thomas R. Scott were found.

The analysis of the two videos submitted suggest underground filming. Nothing else useful could be gained from them.

The behavioral criminal investigative analysis concluded there were no abnormal characteristics that could attribute to any sort of disorder. More information would be necessary for a thorough analysis.

Nothing else follows.

"Interesting," Russell murmured. "Most interesting, especially, the land holdings. Specifically, the missile silo and the storage plant. Both underground."

Agent Martinez hemmed and hawed a moment then inclined his head. "Yes, those two seem to be viable candidates for a possible soft probe."

"Should we invite Agent Sinclair and Price?" Russell asked.

Martinez looked at him, thinking, and took a deep breath. "Good question. It's their investigation to begin with. We're just along for the ride. I say" . . . he paused for a second. . . . "Let them handle the legwork for us. We'll just sit back and see what they can come up with."

Russell hesitated. "And if they need our help?"

"We'll be there to give it."

Agent Russell curiously nodded as he peered at his boss.

Agent Martinez heaved himself to his feet. "Let's go see if Agent Price is in his office."

Within twenty-five minutes of transmitting his information to his section chief, Tom Price's phone rang. He perched on his desk, with Sinclair standing behind him, arms folded, as he lifted the receiver to his ear.

"Tom Price," he answered.

"Agent Price, my name is Clair Sullivan, analyst, DIA."

"You have news for me, Ms. Sullivan?"

"Yes, they have instructed me to provide you with our investigative findings," she said. "To begin with, the phone numbers you supplied have been crossed-matched and addresses listed. Second, identification of vehicles, weapons, and munitions shipped to Germany is listed, as those reported stolen."

A short pause.

In a detached attitude, Price was listening and jotting down the information being related to him. Sinclair picked up a bottle of beer from the desk that she'd gotten earlier from his small refrigerator. As she sipped the cool beer, she stood up and paced the office.

Then his fax machine beeped.

Clair Sullivan continued. "The findings so far suggest that the commander of the 113th Logistical Company did in fact circumvent the FPOP final point of delivery to an unknown location. The notes you furnished gave map coordinates, which we believe to be the FPOP. I've sent a fax to you detailing the information I've just described."

Agent Price said, "Yes, I've just received them."

A short pause as he took a sip of his beer. "Ah, anything else?" Tom Price asked.

"Yes, one more thing." Sullivan paused. "We tracked a number from the cell phone you furnished. It showed that it is assigned to the Communications Section of the Provost Marshal's office, somewhere in the second floor of the building."

Price realized the implication. And, incredible as it sounded, he quickly glanced over at Sinclair.

"What is it?" she asked.

Cupping the mouthpiece, Price replied, "Tell you soon."

"There is one last item, Agent Price," the voice said.

"By order of the section chief, if you have any further investigative leads for us to follow, fax them to me. Good hunting."

Cradling the receiver, Price turned and reached over to the fax machine and retrieved the two pages lying on the return tray. He glanced over his shoulder, turned, and saw Sinclair had the door open to the refrigerator, pulling out a second bottle of beer.

As she turned to face him, she asked, "Want one?"

"Please."

She reached in for another bottle and closed the door as she glided forward toward the desk and his outstretched hand. Taking the offered beer, Tom Price leaned back in his chair and studied her strong-featured beautiful face. Her deep-set violet eyes filled with warmth. Her short-cut brown hair offset the tan hue of her face. A remarkable woman, he thought.

Sinclair took a seat in front of his desk, and putting their beers aside, Price placed the two sheets of faxes sent by Clair Sullivan in between them both. Then, reaching over to his left side, he pulled open a drawer, rifled through it, and grabbed a map of Southern Germany. Once he opened the map, he read through the faxes and found the coordinates listed for the FPOP believed to be where the stolen property was diverted to.

After plotting it on the map, he looked over at Sinclair. "It's in the middle of nowhere."

"It could be just a drop-point," she said, "and the property trucked somewhere else."

"Hmm, but where? Damn, a dead end, if you ask me."

She shook her head. "No, no! I wouldn't call it a dead end."

"Oh, why's that?"

"Because it's more than what we had going in," she replied. "Consider it another step in our efforts of freeing those children and possibly putting an end to Scott's plans."

A pause. "Yeah, you're right," Price finally said, without making eye contact with Sinclair and feeling stupid for asking why, instead of remembering those innocent children that could die soon if they don't find where they're being kept. *But one thing at a time; children first, and I'll worry about Scott's plan after.* He had been more concerned with the terrorist side of the investigation than in their rescue. He won't forget again.

"What are the other coordinates?" Sinclair asked, breaking his chain of thought.

"Oh, right, let's see," he said. "Here it is."

Tom Price plotted the coordinates on his map. "Now, this one seems more promising than the last one. It's in a huge storage plant and, according to Clair Sullivan's notes, it has an underground storage facility as well."

Sitting forward on her chair, Sinclair took a moment to let that sink in. "I think . . . that's where the children are," she said in an unnaturally low, composed voice.

Price looked at her for a moment and nodded. "I agree."

"Let's plan to make a soft recon on those coordinates."

"Before we do," Price said evenly, "I have another piece of information supplied by DIA. They found that someone had traced a phone number from Sergeant Stevens' phone to a Communications Section. They placed it exactly on the second floor—of your father's building."

Sinclair nodded slowly as she stared at Price. Tom Price stared back.

A silence. "I'll send a patrol car to investigate and have 'em call me the moment they find anything."

"What do you think, Sinclair?"

"I think that . . .that's their central hub to the bugs we found."

"That's a damn good bet."

After placing the call to the MP Desk Sergeant and sitting back on her chair, Sinclair remained silent for a second or two. She picked up her beer and was about to toast and celebrate their find when a knock, then another knock, sounded from the closed office door.

Tom Price paused, frowning—who the hell could that be?

Then another rap sounded. He glanced at Sinclair, who shook her head.

Standing now, Price walked toward his office door. Once there, he slowly opened it and stood back.

Standing there was FBI Agent Martinez holding a file folder and Agent Russell standing behind him.

"Agents, what can I do for you?" Price asked surprised by their visit.

"It's what I can do for you," Martinez said.

"Oh, and what is that?" Sinclair asked, slightly surprised.

"We came to offer you and Agent Sinclair some assistance," Agent Martinez said, and, without asking, he stepped into the office followed by Agent Russell. "Or to put it bluntly, give you two our help."

Closing the door behind them, Price said, "What help can you give us, and what do you want in return? It's been my experience the FBI never gives up something without wanting something in return. So, what is it?"

Jacqueline Sinclair waited, arms crossed, for an answer to Tom's question.

A short silence. "We just want one thing in return," Agent Russell replied. "Just your word you keep us informed on any progress you two make."

Sinclair stood and approached Agent Martinez. "Depends on what information and help you can give, Agent."

"Fair enough," Martinez said, smiling, and then he gave her the folder he was holding.

Sinclair grasped the thin manila folder, opened it, and casually examined the two sheets of paper. "What's this?" she asked.

"Our help," Agent Martinez said. "Do we have a deal?"

"Let me check out this information," Sinclair said. "And if it's good, we'll have a deal. And if it's not, well—"

Agent Martinez, glancing at Sinclair and then at Price, said, "We'll be waiting for your answer in our office."

It seemed straightforward enough to Sinclair. But you never know. Hell, but the devil was in the details. They must know more than she did. That was quite evident. A moment later, the two FBI guys turned around and walked out of the office, closing the door behind them.

Once the agents departed, Sinclair turned to Tom Price and asked, "What do you make of that?'

"Don't know, but let's check out what they offered," Agent Price said. Walking around his desk, he sat down and waited for Sinclair.

Standing behind Price, Sinclair opened the folder and laid the two sheets of paper side by side on the desk.

"Let's see what they gave us," Sinclair said, "and if we can use it."

"Roger that."

Reading over his shoulder, she said, "I see two properties that have underground passages, one, a missile silo and the other is the storage plant, the one we think the children are being kept in."

"Yeah, something else, too," Price replied. "The coordinates for the missile silo are the same ones we thought was in the middle of nowhere. It's all underground."

Agent Sinclair couldn't hear what he'd said, she was lost in her thoughts.

"I have a feeling those two assholes already knew what we would do with this. They didn't want to dirty their hands, so they gave it to us as a favor. The rats!"

He turned and smiled at her. "Yeah, damn clear what those two wanted to begin with."

Sinclair had to stop herself from smiling. They had serious work ahead of them. She would have to check both areas; but they'd wait until nightfall to conduct a soft probe.

Oh, God, here we go again. Sinclair jotted down the two areas' coordinates in her investigative notebook she pulled from her hip pocket.

"Let's get ready to go," she said. "We'll meet at my office around eleven tonight. And bring something with a lot more firepower than your .45. I think we're going to need it, just in case."

"In case what?" murmured Price.

Sinclair nodded condescendingly. "In case the shooting starts."

She began walking to the door, opened it, and stopped. "I'm going to tell the FBI guys it's a deal. Be back in a moment."

—Chapter Thirty-Six—

The CAC, Missile Silo, 6:00 PM, Monday

It was a meeting he knew would come to pass, but not this soon.

The CAC, the biggest of all rooms in the silo, was brightly lit, packed with computers, desks, and too warm for comfort. He called the meeting, which he knew would not sit well with the General.

Sitting across from each other was Colonel Godfrey Randall and General Thomas R. Scott, the Commander.

Colonel Randall, glancing down at his notes, from a three ring-binder looked up, placed the palms of both hands on the desk, and met the General's eyes. "Sir, several things have come up that could bring this facility under police scrutiny. First, we could not locate Sergeant Stevens. Second, we have no confirmation that Helen Chapman, the prisoner that escaped, is dead, only the word of the two guards that chased her down. Third, with Captain Cory's demise, I feel discovery is imminent . . ." He paused. Colonel Randall felt the killing of Captain Cory was a fatal mistake by the Commander, a mistake that could spell doom for the cause. But knowing the General, he kept that bit of foresight to himself.

"I see. Thank you for the update, Colonel."

Ignoring General Scott's reply, Colonel Randall pressed on. "If, what I believe happened, sir, our communications room at the PM's headquarters, is in peril and soon CID, with the FBI, will identify it and conduct their search. If that happens, sir, all the communications logs that include our phone numbers could result in an attack here."

General Scott scoffed. But his reply was straightforward. "Do you have a recommendation you'd like to put forth?"

Colonel Randall thought for a moment. "Yes, sir," he said, clearing his throat. "Evacuate to our standby location as soon as possible."

"The storage complex, very well, I can understand your concern," Scott replied. "Get the staff and the men to load up mission-essential equipment, and, if what you say takes place, we don't want to be around when it does. Make sure all is concluded within a three-hour window and leave the surveillance cameras on active. If they come, I need to see who they are."

"Yes, sir. It will be done." The Colonel slumped in his chair. "I have one other thing, sir, the captives, do we take them with us?"

For a moment, the General did not reply. When he did, his voice was low. Maybe, Randall thought, there could be a change in Scott's outlook toward the captives. However, the next words Scott uttered sent a chill up his spine and confirmed the captives' fate.

"No, Colonel. Please advise Captain Miller to dispose of them. We don't need the excess baggage or the time for burials."

Colonel Randall felt a shiver. He said nothing and remained very still; he slowly nodded.

For a moment, they sat in silence.

As an afterthought, Scott said, "And, Colonel, once you have the equipment loaded and personnel evacuated from the silo, activate the OOB."

* * *

Two hundred miles south of Stuttgart

Helen woke, and the first thing that assailed her nose was alcohol.

Then, Helen Chapman realized where she was, a hospital—in bed. The room was large with three empty beds, with her the only occupant. The lights were off in the room, except for those above her head. Helen's gaze stopped at a window that had the curtains open and saw the darkness outside. When she tried to raise her right hand, she found it handcuffed to the bed.

Apparently, she thought, *so that I won't run away. Did they, whoever they were—she guessed the police—think I was a criminal? Hell, where would I go, I still can't remember what happened. I wonder if anyone misses me. I can't remember anyone or anything. The only things I do remember were trying to stay alive in the river and the two kids that found me.*

Helen Chapman sat up in bed. Attached to her left arm were various monitoring machines. A separate IV also was in her left arm. She was pale but feeling better. Her spirits were high, now that she was out of danger from the fast-moving river. Then she remembered a log sticking over the river and her pulling herself from the hold the rushing water had on her.

The second thing she saw was a man, wearing wrinkled scrubs, sitting in a chair, jotting down something in a steel medical chart. She thought he was a doctor or an orderly checking up on her.

The man looked up from his writing, closed the chart, stood, and walked over to her.

"Hello, Miss, I see you're awake. How do you feel?"

"You speak English," she said, relieved the man could understand her.

"Among other languages," he said. "I'm your doctor. My name is Anderson. We didn't think you would be up this soon."

"Where am I?"

"You're in the United States Air Force, 38th Tactical Missile base, in Sembach, Germany."

"How did I get here?"

"You don't remember?"

"All I remember are the two kids that found me by a river."

"They airlifted you to a German hospital, but, when they found out you only spoke English, they transferred you here to us."

Helen Chapman lay back on her pillow, blinked several times, as if to shake off some cobwebs.

"Young lady, your body has suffered several deep cuts and a deep gash on your forehead, and you suffered a considerable amount of blood loss," Doctor Anderson said. "I closed a bullet wound on your arm. You have a large bandage wrapped around your head for the gash. Can you remember how you came to having a bullet wound? And . . ."

"Doctor," she said interrupting him, "I can't even remember who I am or why I'm in Germany, let alone how I suffered a bullet wound."

"Apparently, you've suffered some form of amnesia, which would account for your loss of memory. We don't believe this is permanent, and, with the help of your parents—if we find them— we think it will gradually come back. You were found having no identification on your person. So, to see who you are, then, we have sent a photo of you to the MPs here and throughout Germany. Maybe they can get us some answers. But, in the meantime, you need plenty of rest, sleep, and food."

She lifted her left arm and felt for the bandage wrapped around her head. "What the hell happened to me?" she muttered. "Will I ever know?"

"What about these handcuffs?" she asked.

"We'll have someone remove them once we have an identification of you."

Then, she hung her head and tears welled up in her eyes as she thanked God she was still alive.

* * *

DIA office, the American Consulate

Just as they were preparing to get some much-needed rest and a bite to eat, not necessarily in that order, Agent Jacqueline Sinclair's cell phone vibrated against her right leg. Reaching into her pocket, she withdrew the phone, checked the number on the small screen, and raised it to her ear. When she did, she heard a male voice on the other end speaking. "Agent Sinclair, I'm one of the MPs guarding your prisoner at the German hospital. I was to report his condition to you. The prisoner is stable and wide awake."

Hanging up, she glanced over at Price. "Tom, we need to get to the German hospital, seems Sergeant Stevens is awake. Maybe we can get some answers from him."

Tom Price took this without replying and simply nodded.

Twenty minutes later, Sinclair parked her car in the hospital parking lot. Going through the self-opening sliding doors into the hospital, Sinclair asked the front desk receptionist for a prisoner guarded by MPs. Once she received the location, they walked down a hallway, past an x-ray room and other assorted clinics. Arriving at the room, she was met by two MPs, and, reaching for her credentials, she flashed her badge and was allowed to pass.

Entering the room, they found Sergeant Stevens lying in bed. His right leg was in a cast hanging by wires a foot above his bed, while his left arm was in a sling that lay across his chest. They cuffed his right hand to the bed rails. Whenever he needed pain medication, all he had to do was press a button on the pain pump. When they arrived, he had pressed that button once.

Walking up to Sergeant Stevens, Sinclair said, "I'm with the CID. My partner and I have a few questions for you. But, before we do, let me read you your rights. You have the right to remain silent. You have the right to have a lawyer present, anything you say or do, could be used against you in a court martial proceeding. Do you understand your rights?"

"Yeah, yeah," Stevens said. "Go ahead with your questions. But from the get-go, I ain't saying a fucking word to you until I see my lawyer."

"Now that's really smart," Sinclair said. "So, here's the way this will go down. If you don't answer my questions, we'll do things you're not going to like."

"Fuck you, bitch. You try to hurt me, and I'll sue your ass."

"Oh, I didn't say *I* was going to. Here, meet my partner; he's with DIA and a civilian. He's been around the block a time or two with interrogation techniques."

Taking his cue, Price walked past Sinclair, knowing they were playing good-cop-bad cop. Then, up against the bed, Price slowly lowered the leg. Taking a folded knife from his hip pocket, he opened it and placed the tip of the knife against Stevens' leg just above his knee, while, at the same time, he removed the pain-killing button Stevens was holding onto for dear life.

"Can't have you administer the painkiller," Price said, "just as I'm about to have some fun."

Stevens' eyes almost bulged out their sockets.

"That leg of yours sure looks nicely wrapped," Price said in a cold, menacing voice. "Wonder what would happen if I struck my blade through it a couple of times."

Acting out of false bravado, he yelled at Price, "Hey, asshole, you do, and I'll call for help."

"Not going to happen. So here I go."

Agent Price pushed the blade into the cast and Stevens yelled out some profanity laced with his cries, loud enough to be heard by the MPs guarding his room. One of them opened the door, saw what was going on, and closed it.

"Okay, okay, damn it, what do you want to know?"

"To begin with, who's your boss?"

"Shit, they'll kill me if I talk. They're a ruthless bunch."

Sinclair said, "Tom, press on."

Tom Price did as instructed and slowly pushed the blade a little deeper.

"Sonofabitch, alright, alright, shit! I work for a colonel named Randall."

Tom Price asked, "Randall what? What's his full name?"

"I wasn't that close. I don't know," the prisoner said.

"What about the children?" Sinclair asked. "Where are they being kept?"

Stevens nodded, swallowed, and, shaking his head, he said, "I know nothing about any children. My job was to place some listening devices into the Provost Marshal's office and other facilities and report by phone my observation to Randall." A slight pause. "Honest, that was the extent of my involvement."

"Where is your base of operations?" Sinclair asked.

"My base was the communications room, second floor next to the PM's Office."

"That's not what I asked," Sinclair said. "Where is your organization based?"

Silence.

Sinclair said, "Agent Price, please press on."

"With pleasure," Tom Price said, with a smile on his lips.

Down the blade went. It finally penetrated through the cast and struck the bone, as Stevens yelled out.

Agent Sinclair said, "Did you know that an arterial stab wound would likely result in continuous and profuse bleeding or maybe a hematoma?"

"She means a blood pocket," Agent Price said. "And those can be painful, could lose the leg too."

"Okay, shit," the prisoner, said. "They're in an old German missile silo. I don't know where, honest, you got to believe me."

"I think I do," Sinclair said. "Thank you for your help."

"Go fuck yourself, bitch!" Stevens shouted at her.

"You call her that again," Price said, "and I'll slide my blade all the way through. Apologize to the lady."

Looking straight at the DIA agent, Stevens saw a cold hard stare and the fire in his eyes and quickly said, "Sorry."

Agent Price removed the blade and wiped the blood on Stevens' bed sheets.

Sinclair felt her cell phone vibrate in her pocket. Pulling it out, she glanced at the screen and saw it was from her father.

"Hi, Dad," she said. "Whatever it is, it can wait. I'm terribly busy right now."

"Oh, too busy to hear what I have to say?"

"Okay, Dad, I'll bite."

"Good, the MPs in Sembach air base have a female aged about sixteen laying on a hospital bed with a bullet hole in her arm and several cuts about her body. I would hazard a guess that it could be one of our missing children. She seems not to remember a thing that happened to her. Her doctor thinks amnesia. They sent a photograph of her throughout military channels, hoping we could identify her. I'll text you the photo. Please take it and pass it around to the four generals and find out if she's one of those missing."

"Okay, sir," Sinclair said. "Also, we have identified Scott's base of operation and where the children are being kept. Price and I are doing a probe later on tonight."

"Fine work, Belle, be careful. If you need help, I'm a phone call away."

"Will do, sir." Then her phone beeped with an incoming text message. It was the picture of a young girl wearing a white bandage around her head.

She clicked off and looked over at Tom Price and said, "Tom, we have another assignment from the PM, before we conduct the recon. I have a photograph I need to show to the four generals; seems as if one of the kidnapped children escaped."

He smiled but said nothing.

She suspected this would not be easy for those officers. "We'll hit the Shaffer's first."

Several minutes later, Sinclair and Price stood outside the quarters of Lieutenant General James Earl Shaffer, the first of four they would call on. It was seven o'clock in the evening, on a clear and starry night, and it was dark as sin, the temperature just above freezing.

"You ready, Tom?" she asked.

"Lead the way, Sinclair. I'll be right behind you."

Approaching the front door, Sinclair knocked and waited. It wasn't long until General Schaffer answered. As the door fully opened, General Shaffer stepped outside and closed the door behind him.

General Shaffer thrust his hands into his pockets and stared at Sinclair. "My wife's asleep, don't want to wake her," he said. "Have you made progress in your investigation, Agent Sinclair? Have you found my daughter?"

This is going to be difficult, Sinclair thought; *if that was Shaffer's daughter, then this would be equally difficult. And if wasn't, well . . .* "I have a photograph I would like for you to look at and maybe make an identification."

Agent Sinclair pulled out her cell phone, scrolled over to her text messages, found the photo of Helen Chapman, and showed it to the General. Shaffer was taken aback by her appearance. Cuts, bruises, and a white bandage wrapped around her head. But she looked vaguely familiar.

"Is this your daughter, sir?" Sinclair asked.

"What, oh, no that's not my Lisa," Shaffer said. "But I believe that's General Chapman's daughter, Helen."

"Chapman you say?" Sinclair asked once again to confirm it wasn't his daughter.

"Yes, Helen. She's only sixteen years old you know," he said. "What happened to her, if I may ask?"

"Well, we believe she escaped her captors," Sinclair said.

"I see. Have you any word on my Lisa?"

"No, sir When we do, you'll be the first to know. Thank you for your time."

As they turned away from General Shaffer, Agent Price asked, "Chapman's quarters then?"

"Correct."

Ten minutes later, they knocked on his door. Getting no answer, Sinclair knocked again. A few seconds later, the front door opened, and there stood Chapman.

"Hello, Agent Sinclair," Chapman said. "Won't you come in from the cold? It's warmer in the house."

"Yes, thank you."

They were led to the living room. Chapman had been sitting by the fireplace, sipping wine.

"Hopefully you bring good news, Agent," he said. "Would you two care for something warm to drink?"

"No, thank you, we're fine." She hesitated. No reason to beat around the bush. Having the photograph tentatively identified as Helen Chapman, all Sinclair needed was a confirmed identification from her parents. The rest would be the responsibilities of higher authority within the command.

Sinclair then pulled out her cell phone and showed him the photograph. When she did, he tripped and almost fell. Shocked at seeing his daughter's face but also confused and excited too. The General took several deep breaths and fell into his chair. The room spun widely around him, and his hands trembled.

He waited until he had composed himself somewhat before he spoke. "What happened to her?" was his first question. "Where is she now? Can I go to her?"

"She was . . ." Agent Sinclair began.

"Oh, please, where are my manners," he interrupted her. "Please have a seat."

Once seated, Sinclair told General Chapman everything she knew about Helen's escape, the ride on the river, being found, and subsequently transported to an Air Force hospital in Sembach.

"Is she okay, Agent Sinclair?" Chapman asked.

"From my understanding, your daughter is suffering from amnesia. She can't remember anything at this point."

"Oh my God," Chapman said, "my poor little girl. Can I go see her?"

"That's out of my hands, sir," Sinclair replied. "I believe you must go through the Provost Marshal's office."

* * *

Missile Storage facilities - The Silo

Captain John Miller, late of the US Army Rangers and a Company Commander during the first Gulf War, was awarded the Bronze Star for bravery and the Purple Heart for wounds received in the face of extensive enemy weapons fire when his compound was seemingly on the verge of being overrun. Backed by six Rangers, they repelled the attack that lasted for six hours, but, in the process, he suffered heavy casualties. He was wounded twice, but that didn't stop him from his assault on the enemy. He and two other Rangers were the only ones left alive on the field of battle.

He was a killer made, not born. At six-foot-two with a full growth of beard, he was an imposing figure. Respected by his men and feared by others. He was responsible for the security of the silo and its prisoners held below. Five years ago, they accused him of a triple murder, when, in a drunken stupor, he killed his wife and seven-year-old son. And shot and killed a responding police officer.

He never served time. He, along with two other inmates being held for arraignment, staged an escape. Later, the two other inmates were captured, but John Miller fled overseas into Germany and hadn't been heard of since. He heard of recruitment for a wealthy organization and was hired on the spot by an ex-colonel named Randall.

When the word came that he was to dispose of the remaining prisoners, he was busy supervising the loading of vehicles for the move-out of the silo to its fallback area. Receiving the order, he placed someone else temporarily in charge until his return, *which shouldn't take that long*, he thought.

He, along with Corporal Brian Cooper, who had been tasked to guard the prisoners, arrived at the cell of seventeen-year-old Janet L. Rodgers. Standing back from the door, Cooper inserted the key into the lock, turned it, and opened the door for Captain Miller. Cooper, holding a flashlight, led the way in with Miller right behind him. They found Rodgers sitting in the darkness up against a wall.

Cooper, handing the flashlight to Miller, strolled over to her. "What do you want?"

"Get on your knees and turn around," Cooper said. "You're going somewhere nicer than this tonight."

"No, I'm not going anywhere with you," Janet Rodgers yelled out defiantly.

"Who said *I* was going with you," Cooper said. "Come now; let's not make this any more difficult than it is, young lady."

"The hell with you!" the seventeen-year-old yelled.

The plan was to blindfold her, then, coming from behind, Miller would put one bullet to the back of her head. A clean kill, she wouldn't see it coming. But now, that wasn't to be, he thought.

"Come on back," Miller told Cooper.

Cooper guessed what was coming. Slowly, he made his way beside his Captain.

Miller didn't let her see his right hand as he pulled out his weapon and held it by his side. While Rodgers remained sitting, watching him, Miller shined the flashlight on her face and watched with interest for a moment. Tilting his head side to side, he watched her drop her arms to her side. That was what he was looking for. She just didn't know this was her last day alive. Raising his weapon, he carefully took aim and fired off three shots into her body and one to her head. Holstering his weapon, he turned to leave the cell for the next prisoner.

"This could've been done so easy, but she had to play it the hard way," he muttered.

At the door, Cooper asked, "Should I close the cell door?"

"Na, leave it open."

A few minutes later, the door to eighteen-year-old Duane Hartman was opened. Death came quickly for the young man. Hartman didn't see nor did he hear the person who killed him. He'd been fast asleep when Miller pulled the trigger that ended his life.

With that part of his mission completed, he went back to supervising the loading of the vehicles and choppers, as if nothing had happened. Killing to him was always easy. Living with it was the hard part. And always he'd cope with it just fine. He didn't believe in all that PTSD crap. As long as he had a gun in hand, he had no worries.

Part Three

Shock and Awe

—Chapter Thirty-Seven—

The Silo – Above Ground Operations, 9:30 P.M. Monday, August 12

They were a half hour behind schedule.

The three-hour window imposed for a complete move out of the silo had ended. The only obstacles were the two bombs and the special operators. They were working under the cover of darkness, having killed all exterior power. The running lights of the choppers were also turned off, until the last possible moment when they lifted off, and a five-man security team was placed around the two Blackhawks.

Two UH-60 Blackhawk helicopters waited for their cargo and personnel to make it to the back of the silo's eastern grassy slope. The two cargo masters calmly waited just outside each chopper for the two crates and ten operators to arrive.

Then, less than ten minutes later, three Humvee vehicles finally made their slow appearance, followed by a forklift carrying two wooden crates.

Once the crates had been loaded onto the first chopper and personnel safely secured in the second chopper, the lead Blackhawk pilot plotted the coordinates onto his onboard computer, which would take them to their drop-off point; that being the Special Operations Command area where a C-17 Globemaster and a C-130 Hercules were waiting for group commanders, Major Charles Mendez and Major Jack Webb and their teams of special operators and cargo.

The three Humvee drivers and the forklift operator were secured in the second chopper and were being dropped off at the fallback location. The five-man security teams composed of US Army Rangers were the only ones temporarily left behind, with a pickup time of 12:30 that morning.

With their copilots, they ran through the pre-flight checks and started the rotors moving. Slow at first, then ever faster. The pilot taxied forward a few feet and lumbered into the air. Having gained sufficient altitude, the pilot changed directions and flew in almost a straight line toward their destination. The second chopper followed the exact path. With both helos airborne, it would take approximately two-and-a-half hours to reach their destination.

With a full moon at their backs, the two UH-60 helos slowly banked to the right, turning on their lights as the pilot set the cruise for 140 knots or 161 mph.

The flight lasted only two hours and, upon reaching Special Operations Command, the two Blackhawks landed beside the waiting C-17 Globemaster, known as the "Moose" for its bulky look, and the C-130 Hercules. Ground personnel were already preparing to unload their cargo from the Blackhawk and load onto the C-17. Once loading operations were completed, Team-One operators strapped into their seats, and the huge cargo-bird started to move.

The crew of the C-17 and its pilot, Major Steven Armstrong, were the unknowing pawns to the events being played out. Slowly, the C-17 taxied onto the designated runway, first turning left, then a right turn. Having been cleared for takeoff by the control tower, the plane moved steadily, then faster, until it gained the proper speed. With the war-bird hurtling down the airstrip, it took only seconds for it to lift into the air. Major Armstrong had already set his coordinates for Whiteman Air Force Base, Missouri, and placed the plane under autopilot for the long flight.

Once the C-17 was airborne, the C-130 Hercules with Team Two on board, comprised of Major Webb and two Blackhawk pilots, slowly taxied onto a runway. Having been cleared for take off, the huge rumbling war-bird streaked along and, seconds later, it went airborne. Banking left, it straightened its nose and headed for their destination at Kunsan Air Force Base, South Korea, for their waiting Blackhawk choppers.

* * *

It was a starless night, as a meandering fog shrouded the night ahead of and behind them, as Agent Sinclair drove along the unlit country road. With no vehicle traffic to speak of and with the thick density of the fog, she kept her speed down to about 30 mph.

They'd covered the distance straight from Kelly Barracks to about a mile of their target in a little over three hours, with only a gas stop along the way. Approaching a cut-off from the two-lane road, Sinclair saw that it veered off onto a wide dirt road.

With Tom Price navigating from his map, they knew the missile silo to be somewhere up ahead.

"Slow it down, Sinclair," Price said. "According to the coordinates on this map, there's supposed to be an unmarked road about a mile up ahead that will take us straight to our target."

Slowing to about fifteen mph, Sinclair turned on her Chevy's high beams. The effect the fog had on her senses made her feel as if she was flying through clouds. And every second that passed, the fog grew thicker, so she turned off her high beams.

"There, on your left side, that has to be it," Price said, as he pointed to its location.

"I don't see it, Tom."

"You should see it now," Price said.

"Yeah, I see it," Sinclair acknowledged as she drove on past the unmarked dirt road.

The road's entrance appeared to be an old dirt ranch road that disappeared into a thick dark forest, and, with the fog, she couldn't see past the forest line. According to the map, there were no ranches anywhere nearby.

Less than a quarter of a mile from the entrance, Sinclair drove the Chevy off the road into a thicket of tall grass and small trees. Pulling in as far as she could, she shut down the engine, pulled the lever releasing the trunk lid, and exited the car, with Agent Price right behind her.

Prior to leaving her office, she and Price loaded two M-4 rifles with plenty of ammunition, a set of Armasight PVS-7 (NVG) Night Vision Goggles, and two bulletproof vests. At the back of the Chevy, she opened the trunk. Sinclair pulled out an M-4 rifle and extra magazines; extra 9mm magazines for their side arms went into their pockets, along with a flashlight each. Slapping a magazine into the M-4, Sinclair pulled the charging handle and jacked a round into the chamber, and selected the semi-mode of fire. Then laying the rifle in the trunk, she grabbed a vest and, pulling it on, she said, "We'll walk the rest of the way from here, Tom." Grabbing her rifle, she slung the weapon over her left shoulder.

After donning his vest, Agent Price nodded, as he grabbed the second M-4 rifle and left his trustworthy shotgun in the car and pocketed several ammo magazines. Going through the same procedure as Sinclair on arming his M-4, Price was ready.

Grabbing the night vision goggles, Sinclair shut the trunk lid, and slowly stood to her full height. "Tom," she said. "We won't engage unless we have to."

Taking a slow breath, Agent Price let the air out and sighed. "I understand."

Moving through the darkness and the fog with Sinclair in the lead, they approached the entrance to the road that would eventually end at the silo. One thing Sinclair observed—as the beam of her flashlight played across the ground—the road had seen some heavy traffic recently. That made her think of the children: Did they abandon the silo and take the children with them or? . . . It was too horrible to contemplate the alternative.

The night air was cool, and all was silent except for the series of harsh scraping calls, which Sinclair guessed came from an owl close by, as they pressed on. With Sinclair's flashlight guiding the way up ahead, the road made a left turn. Slowly, moving almost soundlessly, the road once again continued straight.

Sinclair didn't know how long they'd walk, for ahead of them, they came upon a chain-link fence about two hundred yards down the road. Stopping, they kneeled down behind some tall bushes Sinclair strapped on her NVG goggles and turned them on. Through the eyepiece, she saw black and green images. She scanned toward the fence gate and didn't see a lock to suggest that they padlocked it. Adjusting the image enhancement control, Sinclair was able to see what she thought was a steel door. Scanning to the left and right of the door, she made out two infrared video cameras. She was able to make out a flashing red LED light on both cameras. Someone was monitoring and recording the entrance into the silo, she thought.

"Tom," she said, "I see two video cameras, one to each side of that steel entrance, which I think may lead straight down into the silo."

"Think someone is monitoring them?" Price asked.

"It could well be."

"You got a plan yet?"

"Give me a minute," she replied, taking off the NVG.

Tom Price was getting antsy, but he knew better than to pressure Sinclair. When she was ready, she'll deliver. He had gotten to know her well enough not to press the issue. And while he waited, he knew that the only way into the fence line was through the main gate, and if there wasn't any other entrance into the silo, then they would have to go through the steel door entrance. He saw no other alternative. "*Let's see what you decide, Sinclair,*" he told himself.

Sinclair said, "I've noticed that the cameras are stationary and pointing to the fence entrance. If someone is monitoring the cameras, then they know someone is coming. If that's the case then, let's show our hand and go through the fence gate."

Price asked, "What about going through the steel door—if it's open—once we get through the chain-link fence?"

"If they're waiting for us," she replied frowning, "the most reasonable place they would place themselves to repel an attack would be behind that steel door. I'm not going to approach it. It could well be a trap."

Price rubbed his chin, thinking. "Are you sure, Sinclair?"

"No, but it's a gamble," Sinclair replied. "I don't see any other way. Also, the top of the fence has barbed wire. No way can we get over that. And the fence looks fairly new. I don't think it has any broken links to it."

Price stared at her for a moment. "Okay, then what?"

"Once inside the fence line, we split and find some other way into the silo."

Sinclair rose and unslung the M-4 from her shoulder. "Time to go, Tom."

Agent Price rose and said, "Right behind you." And, as he unslung his rifle holding it across his chest, he added, "Let's go, partner."

Inside the silo, in the CAC area, the five-man team left behind waited for their turn to be picked up. With nothing else to occupy their time, they shared a 12 pack of cold beer, while Sergeant Alan Jasper, the leader of the team, a slim man in his early forties, kept his vigil on the security monitors in front of him.

Previously, they'd left the steel doors leading into the silo unlocked, just in case someone came investigating and to lure them inside, where his men could pick them off one by one. Sergeant Jasper was briefed on the possibilities of a possible military or police presence prior to their pickup time. Their orders were to repel any such excursion into the silo.

Finishing a bottle of beer, Jasper was about to open another, when, as he turned back to the monitors, he caught sight of two individuals slowly making their way to the gate entrance to the silo. It was a man and a woman, packing M-4 rifles.

Grabbing his own M-4 combat rifle, the Sergeant said, "Everybody, listen up, we have company. Standby your positions and look alive, it's ass kicking time."

As one, the four Rangers stared intently at their Sergeant, game faces on, as they locked and loaded their individual weapons and proceeded to their assigned positions.

Sergeant Jasper watched as his men dispersed to their positions. He was left to cover the steel doors. Finding a direct vantage point, he hid himself in the shadows and waited.

* * *

At that same moment, two hundred fifty miles west of the missile silo, in the new CAC, the two Agents, Sinclair and Price, were being closely watched by Colonel Godfrey Randall. As the colonel sat back in his chair, in the high-tech radio communications room, he knew the two agents would not make it out alive.

He'd given the order to allow the steel door entrance to be unsecured, for just this same purpose. If anyone came to investigate before the team was evacuated from the silo, they would be met with force.

* * *

The two agents slowly made their way unchallenged to the chain-link gate. With Sinclair leading the way, they stopped as she pushed open the gate and walked through with Price just to her rear. Then, Sinclair pointed to her left, the signal for Price to move in on that location, while she turned toward the right side.

It was pitch black as Sinclair slowly made her way toward the rear of the silo's entrance. With her flashlight guiding the way, she made slow progress. With her searching eyes ever moving, she came around the bend in the road and stopped. For, just ahead of her, her eyes settled on a large oval exhaust vent as smoke curled upwards into the dark sky. Just as she was ready to approach the vent, Price, seeing Sinclair's flashlight beam through the fog, made his way around and stood facing her.

"There is another one of these on the other side," Price said. "But I found a manhole that I think would get us down into the silo."

"Let's have a look," Sinclair said. "Lead the way."

Walking side by side through the darkness and the fog, Agent Price, guided by his flashlight, led her up to the manhole cover he'd found.

There, Sinclair did a quick assessment. It was approximately three feet in diameter, with a locking and unlocking turn wheel on its center.

"This is not a manhole, Tom," Sinclair said.

"Oh, what is it then?"

"It's a missile blast door," she said. "See if you can turn the wheel and get it open."

"Keep the light on me," Price said rubbing his hands together, "and let me see what I can do with this."

Planting his feet, Price struggled at first to turn the wheel. Grunting with the effort, he was elated when the wheel began to move, an inch at a time. Slowly at first, the wheel turned, when suddenly it opened up a small gap. Then, grabbing the wheel, Price opened it like a door and had it fully open enough so that they could get their bodies through. Using his flashlight, Price saw that there was a rung of steps leading straight down.

"I'll go first, Sinclair," Tom Price immediately said.

"I'll be right behind you," Sinclair responded with a smile on her lips.

Down they went, unknowing that a reception committee was waiting for them.

—Chapter Thirty-Eight—

SLowly, they descended.

Rung by rung, they worked their way down through the darkness, not wanting to turn on their flashlights in the event someone was at the bottom.

They would stop.

Listen.

No sound.

Then, they'd continue, ever mindful that each step could be their last. Tom Price, always catching a glimpse down the missile launch tube, prayed he'd see no one at the bottom looking up at them, pointing their weapons and sealing their doom. If he had to guess, Price figured, so far they'd traveled roughly 30-feet or more, and yet could not see down through the darkness.

Blinking away the strangeness of their downward entrance into the silo, Agent Jacqueline Sinclair kept glancing down at Price, as her mind processed the possibilities of ground fire shooting up at them and not being able to seek any form of shelter. And the question foremost in her mind was: will they reach the bottom safely? She caught herself, wishing that she'd gone through the steel door instead of this tube. At least then, she could return fire if fired upon but not here, oh no, not here. Sinclair wasn't afraid to die. But, if she was to die, she wanted to take a few of them with her.

Sinclair stopped and whispered, "Can you see the bottom?"

Price replied, whispering back, "No. Not yet. It's too dark."

The rungs were cold, their hands were freezing. *Damn, they couldn't keep this up much longer,* Sinclair thought.

At that very moment, Sergeant Alan Jasper, waiting behind his barrier for the two intruders to gain entrance, suspected something was wrong. He reasoned that the intruders should've made the front of the steel doors and, by all intentions, should have already been inside the silo.

No, something was not right.

"Team-Two!" he hissed into this throat-mic. "Get down into the tunnels right now! I suspect our intruders found some other way into the silo. Proceed with caution."

A voice exploded in his earpiece. *"Team-Two here. Roger that, on our way. Any idea where they may come through?"*

His mind raced. There was only one other possibility. "They could have found one of the silos," Jasper replied.

"Roger. Moving out now."

"Team-Three!" Sergeant Jasper said into his mic. "Separate and work your way through the front of the silos. If they made their way inside, we'll give them a welcoming salvo of lead."

In his earpiece, he heard, *"Team-Three here. Roger that."*

Now, they were playing a game of cat and mouse, Jasper thought. His men had the advantage. Hell, they knew the tunnels, and the intruders didn't.

"We'll see who'll be the last man standing," Jasper growled.

In what seemed an eternity of time, Agent Price felt solid footing under his left boot, and he breathed a long sigh of relief. Slowly he let down his right leg and felt the solid footing under his feet.

"Careful, Sinclair, two more rungs and you'll be on solid ground," Price whispered, gazing up at her and helping her set foot on the concrete under her feet.

Turning around and with her back up against the rungs, Sinclair tried to see past Price to a small slit of light coming from the opposite side of where they were standing. Agent Price saw it too and slowly they approached it.

Sinclair flicked on her flashlight and directed the beam past Price. They saw an opening to a high steel door, which once upon a time was used to conduct maintenance on the missiles housed in the silo. Slowly, Price pushed open the rusty door that squeaked loudly under the pressure as a small beam of light filtered through.

Sinclair shut down her flashlight.

"*Damn,*" Price exclaimed. "Hope no one heard that."

Stepping through the door, they were largely in a dark, cold, subterranean cavern, which ran left and right as far as the eye could see. The only light that crept through seemed to come from around a bend somewhere up ahead toward Sinclair's left side and it was very dim.

Sinclair, still peering down the length of the cavern, turned and glanced at Price. "Tom, move to the other side of the cavern, and I'll take this side," she said. "There may be bad guys waiting for us down this cavern."

"What do you want me to do, Sinclair?"

Sinclair replied, "We're going to move toward my left. There is a small amount of light coming from that direction. You keep behind me and cover my back. Don't want any surprises from that end. We move as one."

Price asked. "Where do you think this cavern will take us?"

"I don't know," Sinclair replied. "But I'm hoping eventually it'll maybe lead us to the top. In the meantime, we need to find the children, if they're anywhere down here."

With Sinclair's weapon leading the way, and Price pointing his weapon towards the back, the two moved through the cavern slowly, ever mindful of an attack.

A short while later, as they left the silo tube behind them, Sinclair came upon several high-ceilinged chambers. Some with open doors, some closed. As she passed these, she would flick on her flashlight and peer inside. So far, they all revealed a hollow emptiness inside. It would appear these chambers were once used to store missiles.

Minutes later, coming to a dark open chamber, Sinclair suddenly stopped and stood quite still as she faced the doorway.

"Hey, Sinclair . . ." Price said to her. "Sinclair. What's wrong?"

Tilting her head to one side, her mind slowly drifted to the day so long ago, when she was shot in the gut, as the dead and dying lay about her, and, sinking to her knees, she yelled out for the doc.

Then it hit her!

It was the unmistakable scent of human excrement and urine mingled with the smell of something else. Yeah, she knew *the* scent. Never would she forget it. She'd encountered it only on the field of battle. It was the smell of death! That pungent odor of death's distinctive smell as it curled around her senses.

"What . . .? Just a second," Sinclair said, shaking her head as she turned on her flashlight, playing the beam left and right inside the chamber. Suddenly, the beam caught what appeared to her to be a human body halfway toward the back of the chamber.

"Tom, cover me," Sinclair said in a hushed voice. "I think I found something."

Moving hurriedly into the chamber, she stopped and kneeled by the body. She held her breath as the foul stench wafted its way into her senses, causing a gagging nauseous sensation. Her flashlight in one hand, with the other she turned the body over onto its back.

Playing the beam over the corpse's face, she instantly knew the young girl was one of the kidnapped children. Which one? She didn't know. Reaching into her pocket, Sinclair pulled her cell phone and took a picture of the poor girl's death face. It was then she noticed strings tied around her neck. Either, Sinclair thought, the girl had been strangled to death or hung.

"Will I find the others in a similar fashion?" she muttered. *God, I hope not*, she thought.

Price, kneeling low on the ground, weapon resting on his knee, was glancing straight ahead, then toward his partner inside the chamber. He heard muffled shuffling sounds dead ahead, then a light beam coming from around a bend down through the cavern. Whoever it was, they weren't far, neither were they close.

With no time to lose, Price said, "Sinclair, get out of there now. We have company."

Leaving the side of the body, Sinclair joined Price by his side.

"What now?" Price asked.

"Now we fight for our lives," Sinclair coldly replied.

A short silence.

"Just like before, Tom," Sinclair said, breaking the silence. "Take that side, I'll take this side. Ready?"

"As ready as I'll ever be. Let's go."

Weapons leading straight ahead, knees slightly bent, they shuffled forward, step by step. She saw the beam of light as it played about at the other end of the cavern. Slowly, Sinclair moved the firing selector to full automatic.

She wasn't taking prisoners.

Then the light beams were all she and Price saw as they moved forward in their location. Suddenly, the beams were turned off, and the staccato of gunshots from two separate gunmen rang out from the other end.

They were deafening in the confines of the cavern.

The rounds came fast and furious, unrelenting, and deadly!

Feeling her blood rush, Sinclair, not wasting a second, returned in kind, firing in full auto, as the bad guys' rounds struck all around them. Sinclair felt a couple of rounds strike near her left foot as the ground dust swirled around her and kicked-up concrete chips cut into her ankle. Then she saw one guy fall to her bullets, as the other kept moving straight for them.

Sinclair glanced in for a split second on Price, who was kneeling on one leg, also firing in full-auto, as his rounds struck the second gunman, punching him backwards, but he soon recovered, firing his weapon once again.

"*Damn*, they're wearing vests." he muttered.

Suddenly, gunfire erupted to their rear, as two more weapons opened fire on their position. They were caught in a crossfire! No way were they going to make it out alive this time.

"Son of a bitch!" Sinclair yelled.

From the corner of her eye, Sinclair saw Price turn toward the new enemy, as she quickly returned her attention to the bad guy still alive ahead of them, who was almost on top of them.

Suddenly, she saw Price fall to the ground, unmoving. She had no time to think. She couldn't help him, without getting herself killed. Stepping quickly left and right, to keep from being an easy target and firing as she went, she mowed down the last bad guy to her front when her weapon clicked on an empty mag. Flattening herself against the cavern walls, she quickly loaded a fresh mag and charged her weapon.

Pushing off the wall, Sinclair started shuffling forward, firing her weapon as she went, when she caught a round to her left shoulder and another that grazed her right leg. She felt several rounds strike her bulletproof vest that saved her life, pushing her back an inch or two. That didn't stop her. Still firing, she saw one bad guy fall, but the other sought cover.

Click. Another dry mag!

Sinclair still didn't stop.

Ejecting the mag, she loaded another. And before she had time to charge her weapon, the remaining bad guy broke cover and drew his sidearm, and as he fired center-mass at her, he crept forward yelling like a madman.

The force of the bullets striking her vest at chest level pushed her back a few inches, stunning her for a brief moment. One of the attacker's bullets had damaged her M-4 rifle. In a matter of seconds, Sinclair, moving left and right, and in one smooth motion, dropped her rifle, drew her 9mm, dropped to her knees and fired almost point blank at the attacker, finding open areas around his vest, legs and one round that found his head, dropping him dead onto the ground.

Sinclair calmly walked and stood by her would-be attacker, and fired one last round into his head, as her weapon clicked on a dry mag, yelling out, "Die, you son of a bitch!"

She dashed over to Price, still holding onto her smoking 9mm. Her shortcut-hair was matted with sweat, despite the coldness of the cavern. She loaded a fresh mag to her 9mm and holstered it. Sinclair then dropped to her knees in front of Price and felt for a pulse. It was weak, but there.

"You hurt?" Sinclair asked, fearing the worst.

"*Christ. Damn* yeah, it hurts," Price replied through gritted teeth as he opened his eyes.

"Where does it hurt?"

"Got one in my right shoulder," Price said as his pain increased. "One in the right leg and one that found its way through my right side, and a few that my vest stopped."

"Can you get up?"

"Nope, not right now. Go on, finish this off. I'll be right behind you."

"Are you sure?"

"Go on, Sinclair, I'm no use to you right now."

Jacqueline Sinclair bent forward and kissed Tom Price on his lips.

"What's that for?"

"In case."

"In case of what?"

"In case we don't get out of this alive."

Staring at Sinclair, Price just smiled.

Standing, Sinclair pulled her 9mm, charged the weapon, turned and headed toward the bend in the cavern.

—Chapter Thirty-Nine—

In the CAC, Sergeant Jasper, sitting in front of his monitors kept watch hoping to catch sight of the intruders' location. The last contact he had from his teams was that they'd found the intruders and were positioning for the attack.

Muffled sounds of gunfire seconds later were heard all the way into the CAC. Jasper knew that a battle was brewing down in the caverns.

A few minutes later, complete silence.

Jasper waited for his teams to call in with a situation report.

Minutes passed, he didn't know how many and yet no call-in from his teams.

It wasn't like them not to check-in. They all knew the procedures.

"Team-One!" he demanded into his throat-mic, "SITREP!"

Placing a finger on his ear-bud, he heard nothing but static.

"*Damn!*" he muttered.

"Team-Two!" he hissed into the mic, "come in. What is your SITREP?"

Nothing.

He tried his comms again, but he still he got no reply. Even if they were dying, they would call-in—"so that means they're dead," he told himself.

"Shit," he growled, while taking in a deep breath and pulling off the mic from around his neck.

Sergeant Jasper checked his watch. If his pickup bird was on time, they should arrive in about forty-five minutes. He could wait it out and take care of whoever steps through the entranceway, he thought. If his men were all down, he reasoned, it was up to him to exact revenge. Or he could hop on a jeep and leave. He hoped the bird arrived before he had to fight it out with the two intruders.

Then his phone buzzed in his pocket. He dug it out and glanced at the caller ID; a call from Colonel Randall. "Shit," he muttered. "What now?"

"Yes, sir," he answered.

"What is your situation, Sergeant?" came the response.

"I have two intruders and . . ."

"We know, Sergeant," Randall cut in. *"We've monitored them through the relay feed here. They are CID Agent Sinclair and DIA Agent Tom Price."*

"Sorry, sir," Jasper swallowed. "Also, sir, my teams made contact with the two agents in the caverns. But, as of a few minutes ago . . . I lost contact with them. I presume they're dead, sir."

"I see," Colonel Randall spoke sharply. *"Your pickup helo has been turned around. Your orders are to engage the two agents, and once you're done, call for pickup."*

"Yes, sir."

Then, without another word, he put the phone away. The decision of leaving or staying was taken out of his hands.

Rising from his chair, he glanced down the entrance leading into the caverns. If anyone were still alive, they would be coming through that route. He decided to find a safe position to confront whoever came to meet their death.

He'll wait an hour he told himself, and if one showed he would start down into the cavern and see what needed to be seen.

With that thought in mind, he moved toward the further side of the CAC and directly in line and opposite to the entrance. He pressed himself against a concrete wall into a sniper's position. With his assault rifle in hand, he clicked the selector switch to burst-mode. Setting it aside, he pulled on his NVGs. Pressing the "on" button his eyes quickly became accustomed to the flickering green glow of the goggles as he concentrated on the entrance.

Glancing at the lights, Sergeant Jasper stood, strolled over to the electrical junction box and pulled the main control switch controlling all the halogen lighting. Bathing the CAC in darkness, Sergeant Jasper hoped it would give him an edge, as he returned to take up his watch of the entranceway.

Gradually, she moved.

It was pitch-dark. That was fine with Sinclair. The darkness kept her from being seen.

And it was cold.

Her hands were freezing, and her teeth chattered. She was bleeding from her gunshot wounds, but one thought foremost kept repeating itself—are there more of them up ahead? *No use worrying your pretty little head, Sinclair, you'll know soon enough,* she told herself. And what of Tom? *Can he stay alive long enough for me to help him?*

"Stop it, Sinclair. Concentrate on what you're doing," she muttered, moving forward to where she hoped was the top of the silo.

Minutes later, Sinclair stopped, holstering her weapon, as she remembered her NVGs.

Pulling the NVGs strapped from around her shoulder, she clutched them in both hands, pulled them over her eyes, and turned them on. However, nothing happened. Removing them, and praying no one saw her, she pulled her flashlight and clicked it on. Playing the beams on the NVGs, she turned it over in her hands and saw where a bullet hole had gone through into the optics, rendering them useless. The bullet striking the NVGs while strapped to her back, could very well have prevented a far more deadly injury or maybe even saved her life.

Turning off the flashlight and disgusted with the prospect of not being able to use the NVGs, she threw them on the ground, grasped her gun tightly in both hands, and continued in the darkness.

Several minutes later, she was past the bend in the cavern and still could not see any lighting when, spotting a dark open chamber on her left, she stopped at its entrance. Hoping not to have a repeat of another dead person inside, she turned on her flashlight and cast the beam it into the darkness.

She followed the beam left, right, up, and down and stopped, holding the beam on a corpse.

"Oh, *Jesus!*" she said, fetching a sigh.

It was sitting against a wall, head canted to one side, arms hanging down to its side resting on the ground, and blood pooled all around it.

Entering, she stopped and kneeled by the body of a young woman. It was another of the kidnapped children, shot to death. Shaking her head, she stood, turned, and walked out of the chamber. There was nothing she could do for her now.

That was two girls.

She'd known that another of the girls, Helen Chapman, had escaped and was being treated at an Air Force hospital.

So that leaves the boy, Duane Hartman.

She found him dead in another chamber a few minutes later, also shot to death.

Her mission of rescuing the children was a complete failure. It was no use thinking where she had gone wrong. She would worry about that later. Now, she was fighting for her life and that of Tom Price.

Then, remembering her cell phone, she pulled it out, tried dialing but was getting no service. Must be the cavern blocking the signal, she thought, pocketing the phone.

"That was useless," she muttered, annoyed.

Gun leading the way, Sinclair crept on through the cavern, when she noticed the cavern ground rising under her feet. Gaining confidence in her stride, she knew she was heading in the right direction. Straining to see through the darkness, she thought she saw a subdued light way up ahead but couldn't make out the source. She kept it as a point of reference and continued on straight for it.

Tom Price felt weak from loss of blood.

Several times, he tried getting on his knees to stand, but his wounded leg gave way each time, and he fell back on his side.

Out of the corner of his eyes, he had watched Sinclair disappearing around a bend in the cavern. His heart raced. *This was no good. She needs my help. Get up, asshole!* He heard his voice ringing in his brain.

"Shit happens," he muttered. "So, you're shot. So what? Now get the hell up and go help her."

Turning over onto his other side, Price slowly attempted to stand, and, using the wall behind him to support his weight, he finally managed to get on his knees. With pain stabbing through his leg, shoulder, and down his right side, Price pushed himself beyond the pain and stood using his right shoulder for support against the wall. Wobbly at first but with the wall as support, he pulled his gun with his left hand. Slow and painfully, he placed his left leg forward, then his right, walking after Sinclair.

"Yeah, shit happens alright," he muttered. "And I've been getting most of it since teaming up with Sinclair."

One way or another, he was going to be there for her yet again, even if it killed him.

She didn't know how long she'd walked.

The darkness had its own way of suppressing time and space. But so far so good. She hadn't made contact with the bad guys, which was a plus, because she wouldn't have seen them until they were right on top of her.

Glancing forward, the light far ahead suddenly shone brighter.

Running now, low and fast, she felt herself gaining higher ground. How long she could keep this up depended on her wounds and her loss of blood. But she'd continue on as long as she could.

With her eyes fully accustomed to the darkness, she made out a large opening ahead. Sinclair stopped running and cautiously, without a sound, approached it, flattening herself up against the wall on her right.

Then she stopped, kneeled, and listened for anyone or anything. This could very well be a trap, she thought. No use going in half-cocked and falling into it. She saw where the light originated from. Two sets of computer monitors were on a desk toward the far-left wall. She couldn't tell what was on the monitors. They were too far away to make out. Therefore, that told her, possibly, there were bad guys in waiting.

The low intensity radiance of the emitting monitors cast its glow through the opening, stopping about three feet from her position.

Try as she would, there was no way around the trap. There was no safe scenario she could think of. She had nothing to throw to see where the firing would come from—what angle, what height and how many fired. It was in these situations she wished she had a flash-bang grenade or two.

Well, she had to make the most out of a bad situation.

She had to be careful though, these were cold-blooded mercenaries who shot and killed innocent civilians. Anyone who kills children has a special place in hell, and she was going to help them get there.

But first, the trap!

She had to do something to flush out the shooters.

This is so surreal, she thought.

It took several minutes for Sinclair to figure out exactly what needed to be done. She wasn't too thrilled about it, but it seemed the only alternative.

Standing, Sinclair strapped her rifle across her back with the sling and pulled her handgun. Clenching her teeth and mustering all of her strength, Sinclair dropped her center of gravity, and, on bent knees, she ran as fast as she could, made the opening, and fired several rounds into the darkness. Then, jumping high, she propelled herself through the air. At that split second, as she was airborne, gunshots rang out from the far end of the entrance.

She saw the flashes of *one* gun. And felt two bullets striking the back of her vest, for she had turned in mid-air showing her back to the shooters. With a loud yell of pain, Sinclair fell out of the sky, landing on her back behind some wooden crates.

In her attempt to smoke out the shooters, Sinclair felt a bullet strike her right leg.

It could've been worse!

Without her vest, she would be dead right now. However, as it was, now she knew where the shooter was hiding, unless he'd moved. She was about to find out. Crawling to the far end of the crates, she pulled her flashlight and held on to her gun.

Still on the ground, Sinclair glanced for a second around the edge of the crate and jerked back. In that short period, she'd seen movement from a vague shadow and hoped that was the shooter. On her knees and holding the flashlight by the side of a crate, she was ready to take aim, as she held her gun on the side of the wooden crate, ready to fire at the shooter's muzzle flashes.

This was her plan, tricky and desperate, and it had a good chance of succeeding. However, she could only try it once.

With one hand on the flashlight and in the other hand, her gun, she was ready.

She reasoned, to be accurate in his shooting, he must have NVGs. So, the flashlight should be able to take care of it, she thought. Slowly, she raised the flashlight and aimed it in the general direction she thought was the shooter's position.

Sergeant Jasper knew his three-round burst struck the intruder. He could not make out which agent he'd hit, but, right now, that didn't matter. Killing did. He heard movements coming from the other side of the wooden crates, so he knew, whoever it was, was still alive.

With his NVG, he kept staring at the top of the wooden crates from where he saw the person last, when suddenly . . . *BAM!* the flash of bright light stabbed at his eyes causing a "bloom out," the effect of having a greenish-white flash strike his eyes, and, rubbing his blinded eyes, several rounds struck in and around his position.

Jasper, still on his knees behind the concrete wall, yanked off the NVG, dropped it on the ground and rolled, just as Sinclair stood and fired a three-round burst into the darkness where she thought he'd gone to ground. In the darkness, she just wasn't sure where she was firing.

He stood, raised his rifle almost blind from around the concrete wall, pulled the trigger, and cut loose one burst after another until the slide locked in the rear position and clicked on an empty magazine.

However, Sinclair, anticipating the shooter's response, had already moved far to her left, away from the wooden crates. Consequently, the rounds struck at where she'd been seconds before.

Taking aim, Sinclair fired a round at the shooter's gun flashes, while moving steadily forward. Then, only having fired that one shot, she heard her weapon click on the dry magazine. Kneeling, she reached into her pockets for a spare mag, but, search as she might, she had no more. The fight in the caverns must have exhausted her supply. She left it on the ground.

Sinclair brought her M-4 rifle from around her back, shouldering it. She aimed and pulled the trigger, but nothing happened. Pulling back the charging handle, she couldn't get it to fire—a miss-fire, she thought.

Then, hearing a weapon's hammer striking the back of the firing pin, Sinclair dropped her weapon to the side, stood as her instincts kicked in, and she ran straight toward the standing shooter she saw more clearly!

Another less trained person would have ran in the opposite direction—not Sinclair.

Sergeant Jasper was in the process of drawing his sidearm when he caught a glimpse of someone running straight at him, and, before he could draw, Sinclair's hurtling body collided with his own.

Down the two went.

Jasper's gun went flying out of his hand as Sinclair landed with her on top.

Half rising and straddling him, Sinclair delivered several punches to his face, but Jasper parried each blow. Twisting to his side, he managed to roll. And, rolling once, twice, they continued their struggle, trying to wrestle with each other.

But Sergeant Jasper was the stronger of the two.

With Jasper now on top of Sinclair, he delivered two massively strong punches. One struck Sinclair's on her left eye and the other on the side of her head so viciously that Sinclair lost consciousness, and her body went limp.

—Chapter Forty—

Jacqueline Sinclair woke, as consciousness slowly returned, startled and gasping for air.

As she slowly opened her eye, she seemed to be alone and could find no sign of the mercenary she'd fought with and lost. And the area in which she had battled in darkness was now bathed in light.

The air was cold and moist.

Her head was sore and hurting. She tried touching it and found she was sitting in a chair, arms and legs tied, and facing an array of computers situated on top of a wooden desk.

Damn! What a way to wake up.

She wasn't able to see out of one eye that hurt worse than she expected. Her right leg was also hurting. She stared down at her feet and noticed a small-congealed pool of blood, her blood, on the ground.

From the other end of the CAC, she heard noises. She was unable to turn her head to make out what or whom, but she was positive it was the mercenary.

A few minutes later, Sergeant Jasper walked around the other side of the desk facing Sinclair. He was holding onto several cable-wires and a video camera mounted on a tripod.

Stopping and placing the equipment on top of the desk, he turned to face her. "I see you're wide awake, Agent Sinclair. Glad to have you up and bushy-tailed this evening."

"Fuck you!"

She stiffened, possibly knowing what was coming.

Sergeant Jasper calmly walked around toward Sinclair, and, stopping in front of her, he drew back his right hand and backhanded her across the left side of her head. It was a hard strike as her head viciously snapped and blood seeped through from her open mouth. Clenching her teeth, she mustered herself with an effort. "Is that all you've got?"

"You're one tough little bitch," he replied. "If you don't behave, there's more where that came from."

"Promises, promises," she said, spitting out blood and feeling a false sense of bravado. She knew she didn't have long to live. With Tom Price—whom she believed dead—and no one coming to her rescue, it was all on her. She tried to think of avenues of escape, but she came up empty-handed.

Her captor busied himself with the equipment, when, a few minutes later, having finished with the cables, he positioned the tripod-mounted video camera and pointed the camera straight at her, then, he turned on a computer and a monitor that was positioned toward one side of the desk.

"Who the hell are you?" she demanded. "And why am I not dead?"

Smiling, Jasper replied, "All in good time."

Watching the monitor, Jasper adjusted the video settings and turned on the video camera. That done, he pulled out his cell phone and dialed the number of Colonel Randall's direct line. *"Report, Sergeant Jasper,"* came a voice from the other end.

Earlier, with Sinclair unconscious, Jasper called his boss and reported capturing Agent Sinclair. At that point, Jasper's orders were to have her ready for General Scott.

"Yes, sir, I have Agent Sinclair tied and ready for you."

"Fine work, Sergeant."

"Thank you, sir. The feed should go through as we speak."

"Yes, I see her now," Colonel Randall replied.

"Standby as I hold the microphone near her," Jasper said.

Then, coming around to Sinclair, he held the mic to her face and waited.

Several minutes later, Sinclair saw General Jason Scott on the monitor.

He said, "Well, *hello, Agent Sinclair, nice to see you again after all these years.*"

Agent Sinclair's gaze fell on the monitor. She wasn't surprised to see the general, but she didn't say a word.

"*Very well then, let's get on with this,*" Scott said.

Sinclair said nothing.

"*Who knows of my plans?*" General Scott demanded.

Just silence from her.

"*When will they attack my compound?*"

Still, silence. Sinclair just stared away from the monitor. She wasn't about to speak to the asshole in front of her.

"*Still quite stubborn and bull-headed too, I see,*" Scott said. "*You haven't changed at all, Belle. Sergeant, see if you can get anything out of her.*"

"Hey, only my friends and my father call me Belle, asshole," Sinclair said with a scowl on her face.

Sergeant Jasper then stood in front of Sinclair. Knowing what was to come, Sinclair gritted her teeth and waited for it.

Jasper, with one hand on her shoulder, bent low, and delivered a punch to her mid-section. It was a hard-felt blow, which literally drew all the air out of her. She felt dazed and pained. Then Jasper backhanded her once, then twice more, and, spitting more blood, she said in a low, strained voice, "You punch like a girl."

"*Agent Sinclair,*" General Scott, said, "*You have been a thorn in my side since the very beginning. Now, the tables have turned.*"

Jacqueline Sinclair drew in a sharp breath, gave a single brusque shake of her head, and turned her gaze away from the general.

Scott said, "*Well it's plain you will not answer my questions. Sergeant, you know what to do with her.*"

"Yes, sir, I do."

Turning off the video camera and monitor, Sergeant Jasper pulled out his Ka-bar fighting knife from his utility belt and held it in front of Sinclair.

Through her one good eye, she kept a steady stare on the knife as her heart sank.

Sinclair's mind raced, trying desperately to find some means with which she could extricate herself from this predicament. *It was bad enough the asshole beat me in the fight, but now he's aiming to plunge his knife into me. How humiliating*, she thought.

"Well then, let's get this over with," Jasper said as he smiled. "It's been awhile since I cut up a woman and a pretty one at that. Pity, we could've had some fun."

She didn't say a word, and, as if to spoil his fun, she just smiled.

"Yeah, you're one tough cookie alright, Agent Sinclair, I give you that," Jasper said, admiring her wit and courage. "You should've been on our side."

As Jasper drew closer, her eye opened wide, and closed as she waited for her time to die. She wasn't going to give him the satisfaction of screaming, that's for sure.

Opening her eye, she tightened her grip on the chair's armrest and waited.

As he placed a hand on her shoulder and held the blade's handle, Sinclair struggled with her bonds, but it was useless; they were too tight.

Jacqueline Sinclair watched as Jasper slowly drew the knife back, and, as she closed her eye, her only thought was that of her father. At the moment Jasper's thrust began, a loud gunshot rang out from behind them. Sergeant Jasper's head snapped up, then suddenly—

BAM! his head exploded!

It just literally popped, splashing several chunks of fleshy brain matter and blood onto her hair and shoulders, and, as she gazed at the gruesome sight, the body collapsed to the ground at her feet.

She was unable to see who the shooter was. About a minute later, Agent Tom Price came within her peripheral vision, and she smiled.

"What the hell took you so long, Tom?"

Tom Price replied in a serious tone, "Stopped off for a burger and Coke."

Smiling, Sinclair said, "Get me out of this chair, Tom."

"You're a bossy one, aren't you?"

"Okay, *please* get me out of this chair."

"That sounds better," Price said.

Watching Price bending to reach for the Ka-bar, Sinclair saw that he was bleeding from his gunshot wounds. How he was able to reach her, she'd never know. The man was tough and determined, she'd give him that. It was twice he'd come to her rescue. She knew she wouldn't ever live that down.

Standing in front of her, Price cut the bonds on her right hand, and then gave the knife to Sinclair, and, as if in a daze, Agent Price's eyes rolled up to his head, and, on wobbly legs, he slowly collapsed onto the ground. With closed eyes, he lay stretched out flat on the ground, dying.

"Hang on, Tom, I'm coming."

Once she was free of her bonds, she sprang to her feet, then, kneeling by the side of Tom Price, she felt for a pulse. It was faint and steady. Then, pulling out her cell phone—she finally had service—she first called the MP Desk Sergeant and had him call for a Medevac chopper to her location, and the German police.

Then she called her father, the Provost Marshal, and let him know what had transpired in the missile silo and of finding the bodies of the kidnapped children.

Colonel Sinclair, concerned with his daughter's health, gave up his chopper to her. After thanking him, she hung up. Waiting for the cavalry to arrive, she set about bandaging Tom Price's wounds and her own.

Two hours later, with the front entrance to the silo open, a bevy of German police and MP's and the FBI were busy searching the entire silo and the caverns below. After answering questions from FBI Agents Martinez and Russell, the two agents once again marveled at Sinclair's uncanny abilities to survive. They were in awe of the woman. She would be a great fit in the FBI, Agent Martinez thought.

Agent Tom Price was in critical condition when he was rushed by Medevac to the U.S. Army Health Care emergency room at Kelley Barracks.

With the military taking charge of the deceased children, the German police acted as back up for the military police, CID, and the FBI while they conducted their on-scene investigations. According to Sinclair's father, the FBI was now the lead agency in the investigation, which was now being treated as an act of terrorism.

It was one-thirty in the morning. Agent Sinclair, after being treated for her wounds, rode in her father's chopper to the Kelly Barracks emergency room for further treatment.

* * *

Airspace over the State of Missouri, USA
Sunday, August 11, 6:30PM (CST)

The Boeing C-17 Globemaster, a high-wing, four-engine, T-tailed aircraft soared through the nighttime sky at an altitude of 28,000 feet, with its cruising speed of 450 knots (.77 Mach). Having flown for nine straight hours and 4,700 miles without incident, it circled Whiteman Air Force Base, as the pilot waited for his landing instructions.

A few minutes later, the C-17, cleared for landing, started its slow descent.

Twenty minutes later, the sleek aircraft touched down, as Whiteman Air Force Base's Force maintenance crew was ready to inspect and pull maintenance on the aircraft.

Several minutes later, after customs cleared the personnel and cargo, Major Charles Mendez, Team-One Commander, made his way to the flight operations building. Once there, the major presented signed orders detailing his team and cargo to be cleared for the use of B-2 bomber number 21170, as specified in his operational orders. With prior authorization already approved and the pilots assigned, a cargo loading crew of two personnel were assigned to the major.

A short while later, an Air Force bus stopped beside the C-17. With Team-One personnel and their equipment, minus Major Mendez, they loaded the bus for their ride to the B-2 Bomber.

Then, two forklifts slowly made their way to the C-17, and within fifteen minutes, with Major Mendez riding a forklift, they pulled away from the aircraft carrying one crate each, as they made their way to a waiting B-2.

Arriving at a barracks like a one-story building, Team-One personnel made their way into the building where they were met by the assigned pilots of the B-2 bomber. As the two pilots were getting into their flight suits, a Delta operator drew his weapon, screwed on a suppressor and slowly made his way toward the two pilots. With their backs to the operator, he shot and killed the two.

Five minutes later, the two Delta operators and four Army Rangers set up a perimeter around the aircraft in the event that things did not go according to plan.

The two Team-One pilots found flight suits and dressed and, with flight helmets on their laps, sat to wait.

With the arrival of the crates and the loading team, along with the help of three operators, they unpacked the two B61-12 Nuclear Smart Bombs. Forty-five minutes later, the two bombs were loaded onto the bomb-bay's rotary launcher.

Once the loading crew, forklift operators, and the bus driver had departed the area the two pilots donned their helmets and made their way to the aircraft.

The B-2 Bomber, on a normal day, was designed to carry about 40,000 pounds of ordnance, but today it was only carrying two bombs, four Army Rangers, and two Delta operators.

In the cockpit, the pilots started their pre-check procedures of the aircraft. Shortly thereafter, the pilot slowly taxied and stopped, then, requesting take-off clearance, the pilots waited.

Minutes later, once take-off clearance was granted, the B-2 Spirit Stealth Bomber slowly pulled onto its runway. Gently lumbering ahead at first and then gaining speed, it thundered down the runway and, seconds later, lifted gracefully into the air as the landing gear retracted inside the plane.

An hour later, inside the Flight Operations building, Top Secret Communications were received to stop any unauthorized B-2 flights bearing operational OPLAN-8009 orders number 27729 from USEUCOM. However, the orders came too late.

All attempts at communicating with the pilots of the B-2 met with static. Ground radar had been unsuccessful in tracking the bomber's flight path.

Shortly after takeoff, the pilot had turned on its stealth mode package, and then it disappeared from the skies.

The sleek warplane with an altitude of 50,000 feet flew through the sky at subsonic speed, breaking the sound barrier. Its absorbent paint job and its flying-wing configuration and design, made it mostly impossible to see with the naked eye, let alone radar.

Rocketing through the sky at 628mph, the B-2 Bomber would travel 6,672 miles without refueling and make the outskirts of North Korea within less than eleven hours. Inside the plane the team of Major Mendez checked and double-checked their gear. They planned on a HALO jump from 45,000 feet. They would drop the equipment first, and the team would follow. The Landing Zone, a dense forest patch of lands in the central highlands and forty-two miles east of Pyongyang, the capital of North Korea, and their first target, had already been plotted.

Major Charles Mendez pulled his satellite phone handset from his equipment bag and turned it on. Then, dialing a pre-installed number, he heard it ring twice before it was picked up.

"Base, this is Major Mendez," he spoke into the phone.

"This is Colonel Randall," came the reply.

"Roger, sir. Team-One reports successful in acquiring the B-2, now on the flight path to target drop-off point."

"Major, once at your drop-off position, let us know before you execute."

"Yes, sir, I will."

"Good luck, Major."

"Thank you, sir," Mendez said as he turned off the phone.

* * *

Airspace over the Mediterranean Sea, Monday, August 12, 2:15AM (CEST)

The big C-130 Hercules four-engine turboprop aircraft with Team-Two aboard streaked though the sky at well over 369mph. They would land in Kunsan Air Force Base, South Korea, at 5:45 a.m., August 13.

Major Jack Webb sat to one side by himself as he rummaged through his equipment bag and pulled out his satellite phone. Turning it on, he dialed a pre-installed number.

"Base, Major Webb," he whispered into the handset.

"Go ahead, Major, this is Colonel Randall," the reply came.

"Yes, sir, airborne as we speak, should arrive in roughly eight hours' time."

"Excellent Major, do please let us know the moment you land."

"Yes, sir, will do," Major Webb, said turning off the phone.

—Chapter Forty-One—

Washington, D.C. Monday, August 12, 6:30 AM

At such an early hour, it was a cold, bright, sunny day with temperatures in the mid-forties. Lots of sunshine was forecasted for the DC area and high winds. However, the prevailing mood of those in the White House this morning was anything but sunny.

He was behind schedule. The FBI director, already at the White House, apparently was waiting on him and what he carried.

Charles Wright received the call from the director to have the portfolio and meet with him in the White House within the half hour. As the director's assistant, Wright, as he did each morning, was at the FBI building preparing documents for signature by the director when he received the call.

Twenty minutes later, the FBI Special Agent walked down the hallway and stopped behind those assembled personnel at the door that led into the Oval Office. Waiting just outside the door was Daryl White, the national-security advisor, along with Deputy Chief of Staff Matthew Goldman, and Walter Houseman, the director of the FBI, who had requested the counsel. In addition, there was General Allen Adams, the Chairman of the Joint Chiefs of Staff.

Seeing Director Houseman at the door, FBI agent Charles Wright waited for the right time to deliver what he was holding.

Phillip Anders, the President of the United States, serving his first term in office, was late for his appearance in the Oval Office. Still in the upper family floors of the White House, he kissed and hugged the First Lady. A moment later, she helped him slip into his suit jacket. It was the President's chief of staff, Julie Anderson, who advised her boss that all parties were waiting for his appearance. Anders, as a tall six-footer, slightly overweight, had thick wavy blond hair, cut short. A business owner who made his fortune in land speculation and construction, he was not a politician. However, he was learning fast. With deep-set pale eyes, his stare could truly unnerve most.

With the President's two-man Secret Service detail in the lead and the President right behind them, Julie Anderson opened the door to the Oval Office for those assembled. Once all were seated, they waited patiently for the leader of the free world. Moments later, Phillip Anders walked in and, as the Secret Service agents closed the door behind them, Anders walked toward the front of his oaken desk and casually leaned against its edge, crossing his arms over his chest.

The President, glancing around to those seated, said, "Good morning to you all."

Almost in unison, they all replied, "Good morning, Mr. President."

Although he suspected the meeting would revolve around his upcoming sit-down with the leader of North Korea, Pak-Un-Nam in Pyongyang, Phillip Anders had no intentions of delaying or canceling his meeting. However, he reflected, if it involved a life or death situation, he would decide based on the merits of the information presented to him.

Anders gazed at members of his cabinet, but, a moment later, his gaze settled on the director of the FBI.

"Well, Walter, we're all ears," Anders said addressing the director. "So, why don't you tell us why this meeting is so important it couldn't wait for later in the day?"

Walter Houseman, only on the job for less than two years, was in his late fifties, a tall, lean Texan with a ruddy tan and a runner's physique, known to have ran several marathons the past year. Houseman had been a trial lawyer most of his career before he was placed on the President's short list for the FBI director's position.

The Director turned and faced Agent Charles Wright seated behind him, nodding for him to approach.

The agent rose and walked over to the Director, and, once at arm's length, he handed him the portfolio and returned to his seat.

With the portfolio on his lap, Houseman pulled out several copies of his brief marked "Confidential" and again called Agent Wright and asked him to hand them out to the cabinet members and one to the President. As Wright walked to each member, Houseman pulled out his notes and, clearing his throat, he leveled his gaze on the President and, with a grim expression, said, "Mr. President, gentlemen, I . . . I have substantiated evidence that a nuclear attack on North Korea is imminent!"

Houseman let this grim prediction hang in the air, as it caused some tension among those gathered.

A hush fell over the Oval Office.

All eyes turned to the FBI director after the pronouncement, then to the President.

Daryl White, the national-security advisor, a heavyset, short— about five-foot-seven—man with steely gray eyes and thinning black hair, asked, rather incredulously with a hint of sarcasm in his tone, "A nuclear attack? Where are you getting this Intel from, Walter?"

The Director's eyes flitted between the President and the speaker, finally settling his gaze on White.

Houseman replied, "From credible sources in the DIA and the CID command and my field agents in Germany."

For a moment, silence reigned, as all the cabinet members waited to see what the President would say next.

Anders, glancing at the "Confidential sheet" in his hand, placed it on his desk, walked around it and, coming to a stop, pulled out his chair, sat, and leveled his gaze on his director. His thoughts on the possibility this meeting would revolve around the

Korean submit bore fruit. In a low-toned voice, Anders said, "Please explain, Walter."

You could hear a pin drop. Then Walter Houseman replied, "For the better part of two weeks, CID Agent Jacqueline Sinclair, a Warrant Officer, and DIA Agent Tom Price, working as a team and directed by the EUCOM Provost Marshal Colonel Richard Sinclair, were conducting a routine missing person's case involving the dependent daughter of General Earl Shaffer, the assistant deputy commander EUCOM. During the investigation, they discovered three other children were also kidnapped and held for ransom by retired General Thomas Scott and Colonel Godfrey Randall . . ."

"Wait, sorry to interrupt you, Walter," Phillip Anders said, cutting in. "You mentioned a General Scott. Didn't he have a son that was captured on espionage charges and died in the hands of the North Korean Government?"

"Yes, Mr. President," Houseman replied. "The same."

"Is that the same Scott whose wife committed suicide two or three years ago?" Matthew Goldman asked.

"Yes," replied Houseman.

"Please continue, Walter," President Anders said.

"Thank you, sir," Houseman said, leafing through his notes. "In the subsequent investigation, Agent Sinclair discovered the three other children kidnapped were the dependents of three Generals assigned to the EUCOM command." Houseman paused, letting that news sink in.

Then, continuing, Houseman said, "These four generals, sir, were—on death of their children—made to change OPLAN 8009, a first strike war plan. It also provides for the bypassing of Presidential authority for its initiation. Developed by the Army in conjunction with Air Force planning, it was and *is* a fail-safe first strike plan and . . ."

"A fail . . . safe plan, what exactly is that? And bypassing my authority?" the President asked, cutting in.

General Allen Adams cleared his throat and chimed in. "Mr. President, a fail-safe plan, once activated, cannot be reversed. In other words, sir, it cannot be stopped! Four years ago, a small group within the Joint Chiefs and the commander of USEUCOM had worked out this plan. It spelled out, in detail, what flight path

US bombers would take, which targets to hit, and how many nuclear bombs were to be used. All without the President of the United States' authority."

"Sweet *Jesus!*" President Anders exclaimed.

"Mr. President," Houseman said, lowering his gaze. "We believe that you and the North Korean president are General Scott's targets in retaliation for the death of his son. And, sir, the OPLAN, has already been initiated and is being implemented as we speak, sir."

"What is being done to stop this madman's plan, Walter?"

"Well, sir," Houseman began, "everything we can has already been implemented, and, so far, the agents have already uncovered one of Scott's bases of operations. However, when they arrived, it was empty. In addition, sir, they found three bodies that were identified as the kidnapped children."

As Houseman explained, Matthew Goldman paged through the brief prepared by the director of the FBI. Yes, he thought, in the brief and from Houseman, he mentioned four children kidnapped. Three found dead, but no mention of the fourth.

"What happened to the fourth child, Walter?" the Chief of Staff asked.

Houseman replied, "Miraculously, she escaped and has been reunited with her parents. The two agents, with the assistance of our field agents assigned to the embassy, are planning an attack on Scott's other possible bases of operations. Even if we can't stop the bombing, we'll arrest those responsible."

"So, what type of nuclear device," President Anders asked, "are we talking about?"

Once again, Houseman leafed through his notes. He said, "They're two B61-12 Nuclear Smart Bombs, and the delivery platform is a B-2 Stealth bomber, sir."

The President asked, "My God, how did they get their hands on a B-2 bomber?"

The FBI director once again cleared his throat and replied, "Through the OPLAN, sir."

There was a moment of silence. Shifting in his chair, the President shook his head. "So, is there any way we can intercept the bomber?"

"I'm afraid, sir, we don't even know its flight path," General Adams piped in. "And, even if we did, our radars are useless against the B-2."

There was another longer silence.

The President stood, and, with his hands clasped behind him, he came around his desk. "Then, gentlemen, I have no recourse than to cancel my trip to North Korea." He paused. "I will have to notify the Korean Government of the impending disaster on their capital." Again, he paused. "Walter, I will need you and the director of the DIA to keep me informed on the progress of your agents in Germany—what they are doing and not doing to catch this General Scott and his band of mercenaries. And, Walter, make sure those agents have all they need. The rest lies in the hands of my staff."

"Yes sir, Mr. President," Houseman said.

The Oval Office fell silent. After a moment, the President walked back around his desk, sat, and, lifting the receiver from his desk phone and staring at those seated, he said, "Thank you, gentlemen. That will be all."

—Chapter Forty-Two—

That same day and several hours later, CID Special Agent Jacqueline Sinclair woke straight up from her sleep and from her sense of unreality. With her eyes opened wide, she found herself in a semi-darkened room.

It was a restless sleep. A nightmare-filled sleep of death and dying. After a few seconds, as she recovered from her nightmare, she remembered the circumstances of her earlier encounter and of Tom Price. This just wasn't *her*—having nightmares—where did that come from, she asked herself. Not even when she sustained her wounds in combat, did she have such vivid nightmares.

She glanced around her, not yet fully aware of her surroundings. A table lamp shone dimly atop a nightstand to the left of the bed, *her bed, in her bedroom,* and, worse yet, as the bed sheet fell onto her lap, she noticed someone had dressed her in one of her nightgowns.

Glancing around the room, she noticed defused lighting coming from the crack of the bedroom door, the gurgle of running water, and of hushed voices. With the briefest of hesitations, Sinclair slowly unwrapped herself from the bedsheet, slipped out of bed, and, bare-footed, was about to set foot on the floor, when the door was opened. She took comfort in knowing the identity of the person who stood at the threshold.

For framed against the door, was the figure of her father, Richard Sinclair. Taking a step forward, he paused, and, with a hand on the doorknob, he said, in a sweet-sounding tone, "Belle, honey, I see you're awake. Good."

Standing by the edge of the bed, staring at her father, Sinclair blinked, tilted her head to the side, and asked, "Father . . . did you—?"

Her father, with downcast eyes, replied in a slightly hesitant voice, "Ah, no time for that now, honey. Get yourself dressed and come out into the living room. There are people that need to talk to you."

It was twenty minutes later, and, at the sound of the bedroom door opening, the sounds of conversations abruptly ceased. When Sinclair entered the living room, two men, including her father, rose.

She immediately identified the other two men as FBI Agents Russell and Martinez.

Agent Russell noticed she still had some puffiness around her eyes, but the swelling on her lips had gone down some since the last time they had seen her. Dressed in blue jeans, black blouse, and black short booties, she was irresistibly beautiful.

Smiling as she stepped forward, a little uncertain what the two agents were doing in her apartment, she stopped in front of them, and returned their smiles.

Belle Sinclair glanced toward her father and asked, "What's this all about, Dad?"

Agent Martinez answered her question. "Agent Sinclair, our embassy received a communiqué from the Director of the FBI and cosigned by the President of the United States to offer you all assistance in bringing down General Scott and his army of mercenaries."

Not saying a word, Agent Sinclair glanced at her father and back to Agent Martinez. Then, casually, she walked into the kitchen, preparing to brew some coffee. "I don't know about you gentlemen, but I could use some coffee. Does anyone care for a cup?"

Agents Russell and Martinez both chimed in with yes, while her father nodded. "Belle," he asked, "did you hear what the agent said?"

"Yes, sir," Belle replied, "I did. However, I think better with a cup of hot coffee in my hand, or a beer. Unfortunately, it's a little too early for the beer."

As the agents and her father sat on the sofa, Sinclair, without a word, busied herself preparing the coffee. After several minutes, and, with a tray of four steaming hot mugs of black coffee, she walked into the living room and placed the tray on the coffee table in front of them. Scooping up her mug, and as the three men picked up a mug each, Belle Sinclair walked around toward her rocking chair, sat, took a long drink of her coffee, and glanced from one man to the other.

They waited on her to respond.

Sinclair's father leaned back on his seat and, making himself comfortable, he sipped his coffee, all the while glancing at his daughter; the coffee was strong and black—just the way he liked it.

Agent Sinclair, in the meantime, sat quietly, rocking gently back and forth, for about twenty seconds.

Addressing the two agents, Jacqueline Sinclair's eyes lit up. "Wasn't the investigation classified as a terrorist act?"

Agent Martinez replied, "Yes, yes it was."

Sinclair shrugged and said, "So, why do you still need me?"

Agent Martinez regarded her for a few seconds, bowed his head slightly, and rising, leveled his gaze on her. "If it was up to me," he replied, "you and your department would be off the case. However, according to the FBI Director, you and Agent Price have shown exemplary performance in your investigation, and the POTUS was impressed with both of you. It was his recommendation that you two stay on the case, that is, with FBI assets."

Sinclair blinked once, and then twice, trying to hide her excitement and allowed herself the faintest hint of a smile, as she said, "I'm flattered."

Leaning forward on his seat, Agent Martinez took a sip of his coffee and, turning back to Agent Sinclair, asked, "So what do you need from us?"

Their meeting went on for two hours. In that span of time, Sinclair came up with a plan that the two FBI agents tentatively approved. It would necessitate going to the director of the FBI for final approval. How long that would take, she had no idea, but she strongly emphasized the element of time as being crucial at this point. It was a bold plan and one that, if everyone played their part right, had a very high chance of succeeding.

Who better than her to know that no plan was perfect.

Knowing she had no control of the events that would ultimately unfold in North Korea, Sinclair had concentrated on her target—General Scott and his mercenaries. To that end, her plan hinged on the element of surprise. If that even was a sound concept now. A sudden thought flashed through her head: *Probably, General Scott was already waiting on them.* Nevertheless, Sinclair understood the risk and was ready for any eventuality.

So, her plan was simple. She laid it out in two parts.

The first part would involve both physical and drone surveillance. She needed to know the makeup of Scott's base, the number of guards, and where they were placed, before she could set up an attack plan. She also needed to know the layout of their base's perimeter.

The second part was the actual attack itself. Her strategy called for a lot of planning, manpower, and armaments. She left the coordination of the German police up to the FBI. They had very little time to plan and coordinate the force going in before Scott and his men disappeared. She was hedging her bet that Scott and those around him would not leave until he was positive his plan was going to succeed.

According to Agent Martinez, the Department of Defense and the Chairman of the Joint Chiefs of Staff, in conjunction with the U.S. Air Force, had their own plans on stopping the B-2 bomber before it entered North Korean airspace and launching the two bombs.

No sooner had the two agents left when Belle, alone with her father, turned to face him. She tried to relax, and immediately she posed the one question to him foremost in her mind.

"Any word on Tom's condition, Dad?" she asked.

"Honey," her father replied, "Tom is suffering shock from his gunshot wounds. He also suffered several bruised ribs. When I left his side, he was still in the operating room."

"But he'll be alright?"

"He's a tough one, honey, but, yeah, he'll pull through okay."

"Dad," she said in a mellow voice, "did you . . .? you know, change my clothing?"

"I did, but it's much ado about nothing. Besides, I had my eyes closed all the time. And I've changed you many times before."

"Yes, Dad, you did, but I was a little girl then."

"You've always been my little girl, honey, and always will be."

"Thanks, Dad. I love you."

"Yeah, I know."

It was four-thirty that afternoon when Agent Sinclair arrived at his hospital room. Tom Price was awake and sitting up in bed, with an IV attached to one arm, and sipping through a straw from a plastic apple juice container.

She remembered the last time she had seen the agent; he had been very pale from loss of blood. Now, there was color to his skin, a clear sign that he was recovering from his wounds.

"Hey, you're a sight for sore eyes, Sinclair," Price said, as he threw the empty juice container toward the wastebasket across the room, missing.

"You're looking a lot better, Tom," she said, approaching his bed. "So, what have they been feeding you?"

Tom Price shrugged and tried to change his position on the bed when, with a wince, he replied, "One unit of blood, water, and apple juice, and I'm just about ready for a three-course meal."

Jacqueline Sinclair shook her head, smiling.

"So, you didn't come all the way here, just to take a gander at my handsome face. What's the plan?" Price asked, as he slowly started to slip from his bed, dangling his feet over the edge.

She said, "Whoa, there, Tom, where do you think you're going?"

"No time for this," Price replied. "Would you get my clothes?"

"Hell, no," Sinclair said. "You're not getting out of here anytime soon."

In reply, Tom Price stood, swaying a little almost imperceptibly for a second or two as he placed his feet on the cold hospital floor. Then, pulling out his IV from his arm, he steadied himself by the edge of the bed.

She realized then that it was useless to argue with him. Sinclair grabbed his clothes lying on the chair by the bed and handed them to him. Although, deep down inside, Sinclair wanted Price to be by her side for at least the planning stages. He had saved her life twice, and she owed him for that. She just could not leave him out now, after all they had gone through together.

Sinclair turned and walked to the side of the bed and drew the curtain. "Hurry then, we have a lot of work to do," she said.

Smiling Tom Price replied, "Damn! Pushy, pushy, aren't we?"

* * *

Halfway around the world, a C-130 Hercules was making its final approach into Kunsan K-8 Air Base located at Gunsan Airport at the Southern Korean peninsula, bordering the Yellow Sea. The air base is approximately 150 miles south of Seoul, the Capital of South Korea.

On board the aircraft were Major Jack Webb and his team.

After receiving permission to land, the C-130 touched down, taxied, and finally aligned on the west side of the landing strip.

Their part of the plan was just beginning.

—Chapter Forty-Three—

Airspace North Pacific Ocean, 13 August 0945 hrs, Local Time

The B-2 Stealth Bomber flying wing aircraft soared through the bright, clear, day sky at subsonic speed.

Fifteen minutes earlier, the aircraft dropped its air speed and made an approved scheduled rendezvous with a KC-135 Air Refueling Tanker out of Japan. Once refueled and more than halfway through its flight, the two pilots, looking through the aircraft's bowed cockpit windows, turned on its stealth properties, while switching off their GPS, and continued with their mission.

Unknown to those aboard the bomber, their current location was tracked using the refueling tanker's GPS coordinates as the pilots radioed their confirmation to their base. Ten minutes later, two F-15 Eagle fighter jets out of Japan, ordered to intercept the bomber, were inbound to their location and would be able to eyeball the bomber within minutes. Ground command at Yokota Air Force Base, Japan, were under orders from the Pentagon to allow the bomber to refuel as a way of holding the bomber until the F-15s reached them. However, no sooner had refueling been complete, than the bomber was once again on its way.

For the two pilots, this was their first mission outside United States airspace. This would make it their first time having humans drop from the belly of the aircraft rather than bombs. It was a challenge of sorts for both pilots and for the soldiers strapped in their seats in the plane's bay.

Another first for the pilots was flying to the west coast of the US to reach their target, Korea. Both pilots had received half of their pay deposited into their accounts, with the other half payable once the mission was complete. They were hoping to have a successful mission and return home to their families.

With blue skies above and the blue ocean beneath them, they would make their drop-off target within twelve minutes. Once in North Korean airspace, the pilots knew North Korea's obsolete IADS (Integrated Air Defense Systems) could not detect them. The North Korean radar was ubiquitous and not mobile. The pilots both knew where the radars were, and they would fly between them as much as possible.

They would also fly high enough that, in the off-chance they were detected, any salvos of the deadly S-125 Neva surface-to-air missiles or better known by NATO as the SA-3 Goa could not reach them. They had a tiny window in which to operate before they encountered any counterattack.

The two F-15s arrived ten minutes later but could not make eye contact or radar verification of the bomber and were ordered to return to base.

Twenty minutes later, the B-2 bomber flew through North Korean airspace undetected by ground radar.

Team-One Commander Major Charles Mendez, breathing through his high-altitude facemask attached to a small oxygen tank strapped on his chest, stood behind the two pilots, unaware that two F-15's tried to intercept them.

Then, the aircraft commander, Major Craig Thornton, spoke through his mask, addressing the Major, and said, "We are at 50,000 feet, Major, and five minutes out. So far, ground radar has not detected us. Your men are in the clear for the drop."

Major Mendez, with his throat-mic wrapped around his neck and through his earbuds, picked up the pilot's words and replied, "Roger that."

Mendez then strode into the stealth bomber's bomb bay. Reaching his men, he said through his throat mic, "Five minutes out. Gear up, men."

His men were all professionals, all had several HALO jumps under their belts, and this was nothing new to them. Then, the aircraft commander's voice came through Major Mendez's earbuds once again: "Two minutes."

Showing two fingers to his men, they knew they had only two minutes before drop time.

With that, a minute later, the belly of the aircraft slowly opened. A Delta operator stood and pushed a large, orange-colored container to the open bay doors and dropped the container through the sky.

Charles Mendez and his men, dressed in white winter combat uniforms, all wore personal equipment backpacks, body armor, standard LBE kit, MC-5 parachute, O2 oxygen tanks—without the oxygen they would asphyxiate—and helmet. They'd had their oxygen masks on since they reached 45,000 feet and, as they stood and shuffled to the open bay door, they waited. Then, when the signal came from the B-2 commander, one by one, they fell through the bomber's bay doors into the clear blue skies.

Free-falling through to 45,000 feet, Major Charles Mendez kept an eye on his ticking altimeter wrapped around his right hand and watched as the ground came up fast. Adjusting his location in the air, he guided down, observing the area of the LZ.

At 5,000 feet, they all engaged their chutes. Mendez looked down and saw their container and, pressing a button on a remote pad he clutched in his hand, he immediately saw the chutes opening, as it slowly descended.

Suddenly, they floated as the ground came up to meet them; then, with pinpoint accuracy, they landed within a few feet of each other and right next to their equipment container.

They were on a snow-covered trail not over twelve-feet wide and bounded by tall trees and snow-capped black rocks that stabbed upward from the ground. There was a thick blanket of snow all around them. They saw no human prints anywhere, except for their own and only small animal tracks leading down the hill. That, in itself, said the area was unpopulated, which was good. They would have killed those who showed themselves on the hill.

And it was cold!

Not wasting any time, and, once Major Mendez confirmed all of his men were unhurt, he quickly opened the container, as two Army Rangers reached behind them, pulled their M-4 rifles and, jacking rounds into their rifles, secured the landing zone, as the other men helped pull out the equipment. Major Mendez designated two Delta operatives to carry the precious equipment.

The landing zone they had chosen was between the villages of Yangdog and Koksan. These two villages were deemed less populated than those around any area nearer to their target. It was a perfect LZ. The two villages were separated by a distance of ten miles, and this was the tallest point in the area.

Kneeling, Major Mendez pulled out a map from his side pocket and his lensatic compass and, shooting an azimuth, he plotted his route to their target objective.

That done, the rest of the operatives grabbed their M-4 rifles, attached suppressors, inserted a magazine, pulled back the charging handle, and armed their weapons. Then, they stood, turned, and, keeping a distance of a few feet between each man, and without a word, they started their forty-five-mile trek, heading due west to the target area with Major Mendez in the lead. As they would near their objective, a team of two Rangers and two Delta operatives would break away from the squad and proceed to their second objective.

In the meantime, the B-2 bomber headed to a pre-arranged landing zone located in an abandoned Russian airstrip about one hundred miles east of the team's LZ and waited for the teams to *light-up* their targets.

* * *

It was 10:15 a.m. on that cold sunny morning, when Major Jack Webb and his two pilots, immediately having arrived at Kunsan Air Force Base, South Korea, were transported to their waiting Blackhawk helicopters on the other side of the tarmac.

In route, Major Webb reached into his equipment bag for his satellite phone and dialed the number for the communications room at the CAC to make his report.

In the commo room, Corporal Raul Sanchez's Sat-phone rang. He grabbed it and glanced at the screen. It was the number for Team-One, Major Jack Webb. He pressed the answer-button.

"Corporal Sanchez here," came the voice on the other end of the line.

"Corporal, Team-One here," Major Webb said. "We have landed and on our way to the Blackhawks as we speak. Any further orders?"

"Negative, Major."

"Right then," Major Webb said, "I will call again once we're airborne."

"Yes, sir, and how long will that be?"

"Twenty minutes, give or take," Major Webb responded.

Sanchez said, *"Thank you, Major, I'll relay your report to Colonel Randall."*

Major Webb pressed the end-button, ending the call, and returned the phone to his bag.

Several minutes later, arriving at the hangar, the first thing they noticed was that the overhead gate to the hangar was halfway open. As they approached the inside, they were struck with how huge it was. It was enough to store a 747 Jumbo jet and have room for a B-2 bomber, but no helicopters.

The hangar was empty.

"Empty!" Webb muttered.

Webb shook his head, as his eyes opened wide, but said nothing else.

Instinctively, Major Webb knew they'd been discovered. How was unimportant—although several scenarios raced through his head.

Webb hesitated, then they exchanged looks, surprise and worry written on their faces; worried that someone had finally put two-and-two together and that they may not leave this place alive.

The trio immediately drew their sidearms and slowly backed out of the hangar. From the rear, six armed special security force police came up behind them, and Webb heard someone yell out,

"Drop your weapons, or you won't give us any choice but to open fire!"

Webb shrugged, as if to say come and take them.

As the trio slowly turned toward the voice, six more special security force police officers appeared from the front of the hangar pointing assault weapons at the three men.

They were trapped. Caught in a possible crossfire from which the inevitable would surely happen, death!

For him and his two pilots.

Major Webb knew that their mission ended here, today.

They had but one choice and one choice alone. Either they gave themselves up, or they shot their way out of the hangar. All three knew what to expect if they surrendered, possible life in prison or death. They knew the outcome the moment they signed up to do the mission. At least their families would be taken care of.

Major Webb frowned, already deciding, and, removing his sunglasses, he suddenly raised his weapon and the sixty-two-year-old major ran to his left as he opened fire at those in front of him. The two pilots, not wasting a second, followed suit, and, with drawn weapons, they ran to the right, while at the same time, opening a salvo of rounds at the police.

The gunfire was loud in the hangar, but it grew louder when the police sprayed the three mercenaries with suppressed gunfire while in full automatic mode from their M-4 assault rifles.

The two pilots went down first even before they took three steps, and then, almost at once, as Major Jack Webb's knees went weak, he buckled, when round after round struck his upper torso and, screaming, Webb's body fell forward onto the concrete floor of the hangar as his screaming stopped.

Slowly, the police approached the three bodies.

* * *

The Storage Complex Control Center, CAC, Somewhere in Central, Germany

In the communications room, Corporal Raul Sanchez waited for further confirmation of the mission's ongoing operations, that of Team-Two.

Already receiving situational reports from Team-One to the effect that the first part of their mission was completed without mishap, and that the B-2 was on its way to its pre-determined airstrip, Sanchez had not received word from Team-One, Major Webb, for half an hour.

Corporal Sanchez got a strong gut feeling that something or someone may have prevented Team-One from completing their mission. What or whom was the burning question.

Grabbing his cell phone, he called Colonel Randall, his commander.

Waiting for the colonel, Sanchez grabbed his Sat-phone and dialed the number for Team-One, but the phone kept ringing without being answered.

He hoped that nothing could have prevented them from acquiring the helicopters. He knew how vital they were in the plan—that of successfully extracting fellow operatives from North Korea alive.

* * *

It was 6:45 p.m., at the very moment Corporal Sanchez waited for Colonel Randall, in the American Consulate offices of the DIA in downtown Stuttgart, Agent Sinclair, Price, and FBI Agents Martinez and Russell, sat around Tom Price's office desk.

With beer and pizza, they went through Sinclair's plan. Back and forth went the conversation as they tried to fine-tune it, when Sinclair raised the question as to the number of properties owned by Scott and their locations in Germany.

Martinez provided that information. "Our investigation into General Scott," the agent began, "turned up three huge land purchases in the US and four here in central Germany—"

"Yeah, okay," Sinclair cut in, slightly impatient. "So how are we going to watch four properties here? We just don't have the man-power."

Agent Tom Price chimed in, "I may have just the solution for that."

"Oh, pray, tell," Agent Russell asked in a slightly sarcastic tone.

"I have a UAV controlled US Army RG-11B Raven that's capable of traveling six miles and sustained flying time between 60-90 minutes. It's the one being used in Iraq and elsewhere, which should do the trick. I can operate it from the safety of my vehicle. They won't even know it's there."

Price turned to Agent Russell and said, "Think that'll do it?"

'Yeah, yeah, smartass," he replied, smiling.

Staring at Agent Martinez, Sinclair said, "When we find out where their base is, we will need your men at the embassy for backup and to help plan our attack."

"No problem," Agent Russell said, "I've already called them. They should be here in three hours."

"In the meantime," Sinclair said, "let's get those addresses and get the UAV ready, I feel this will be a long night."

As Agent Martinez pulled out his notebook from his briefcase, Agent Russell pulled a map of Southern Germany from his briefcase, opened it, and laid it flat on the desk.

Then, as Agent Martinez sounded out the address to Agent Russell, Russell read out the map coordinates to Martinez, who jotted them down next to the physical address in his notebook.

Ten minutes later, after doing the same for the remaining three, they were set. The only thing left was to get the UAV ready.

That job belonged to Agent Price.

Twenty minutes later, with Sinclair driving, Price navigating, and with the UAV in the back, they set out to their first address.

—Chapter Forty-Four—

Hill country, North Korea

E arlier, Major Charles Mendez oriented his map with the outlying countryside. The land they would travel through was a series of medium to large-sized mountain ranges and several hills, separated by deep, narrow valleys, of which he hoped to stay clear.

They were moving through some rough terrain. The weather was cold and dry and heavy snow kept falling, which made their progress slow. Tall alpine forest and farmland were visible in the distance.

Major Mendez kept his team off any dirt tracks and away from rivers or streams, and, in this manner, he hoped to avoid contact with anyone or any large towns along the way.

Having studied various satellite images of the terrain they'd be moving through and the tight security the North Korean military had established in a forty-mile radius of their capital, not to mention the radar positions inside the city of Pyongyang, they all were in for the HALO jump and the long walk through hostile territory.

His plan did not call for walking the full forty-five-miles, which would have taken them part of the day and maybe into late evening, so he was gambling on making contact with a small farm and hoping they could steal a car or truck for the rest of their journey.

Five miles into the heavy snow, the team rested by the side of some tall pine trees. After enjoying a meal of beef-jerky and washing it down with their canteens of water, they started once again.

After an uneventful eight miles, they stopped at a small rise, gazed down into a valley, and saw a farmhouse about half a mile away. Pulling out a pair of binoculars from his equipment bag, Major Mendez peered out and saw an old beat-up truck with a canvas cover. Scanning the area, he saw no signs of movement or smoke from the chimney.

Major Mendez, staring over at his men, said, "Need two volunteers to get me that truck."

Two Rangers, Sergeant Edward Phelps and Corporal Lee Evans volunteered. "What if they . . . don't want to part with their truck, Major?" Corporal Evans asked.

"Do whatever it takes but get me that truck."

"Yes, sir," replied Sergeant Phelps.

Leaving their packs and equipment with the team and carrying only their sidearms, Sergeant Phelps and Corporal Evans slowly made their trek through the high-packed snow down to the farm.

Fifteen minutes later, as the major peered through his binoculars, he saw a Ranger head to the truck and slip in. A few seconds went by when they heard the engine crank up three times. Then with white smoke pluming out of the rear muffler, it started up and stayed on. Minutes later, running through the deep snow, the team came up to the shack.

Sergeant Phelps said, "Sir, we saw only one person in the house, and he was asleep. Sorry to say it's going to be a permanent sleep for him. And there's plenty of clothing; could use some to cover up our uniforms."

After another ten minutes, the team was ready as they climbed into the truck with Mendez navigating and Sergeant Phelps driving. With the vehicle in gear, they pulled away from the farmhouse.

The road they traveled on was deep in snow, so they drove slowly, but it was better than walking.

Driving for two hours and not encountering anyone on the road, Major Mendez instructed Phelps to stop. Then, turning in his seat, he spoke through the gap separating the cab from the bed of the truck. "Team-Three operatives, this is your drop-off. Your target is ten miles southwest of here."

Two Rangers and a Delta operative dismounted the truck as their equipment was passed down to them.

Major Mendez said, "Good luck, men."

The Delta operative replied, "Same to you, Major."

According to his map, Major Charles Mendez and his team had only fifteen miles left before reaching their target. Then, in the distance, he saw what appeared to be their first encounter with the North Korean soldiers or police. For, just ahead, were two guards, one inside a gate shack and the other outside by the door, enjoying a cigarette, as a white pole that stretched across the road blocked any further progress.

Once again, he turned and addressed his team in the back of the truck. "Look sharp, men, we have a roadblock up head. One of you dismount and work your way behind the two guards and take them out."

Thirty-six-year-old, heavy-set Ranger Luke Sheppard jumped down onto the snow-covered road, and, with his M-4 with suppressor attached, he ran to the left of the truck and made his way around and behind the shack and the guards.

With the snow increasing in its intensity, it made visibility difficult as the truck slowly approached the gate shack, and, as it came to a stop several feet from the gate bar, the second guard walked out of the shack. Just as the guard started toward the truck, two low muffled sounds erupted almost as one, and both guards dropped onto the snow, dead before they ever knew anything was amiss.

As Sheppard lifted the bar, the truck drove through it, and, without the truck stopping, the Ranger ran, jumped, and hopped onto the bed of the truck.

* * *

Ottenbach, Southern Germany, Approximately 30 miles East of Stuttgart, 7:15 P.M.

Two hours passed as if it was only minutes.

The first three properties Jacqueline Sinclair and Tom Price checked turned up nothing. All deserted, and it appeared as if no one had visited in years.

A total blank!

With a light snowfall, moderate cold breeze, and broken clouds, they drove on for another half hour, mostly in silence, each in their own thoughts, occasionally glancing over at one another and keeping those thoughts to themselves.

They had one other property to check, the last on their list. It was located on the outskirts of Ottenbach, in the thick of a large forest just outside of the town. The town itself was bounded by flat lowland terrain with numerous bogs, rivers, streams, and mostly used as farmland. It was a perfect place to hide a small army. It took a whole thirty minutes to drive to and another ten minutes to find. They had a hard time finding the place; there just weren't any street signs or any indications that the property ever existed.

As they drove, Tom Price rolled down his window, turned on his flashlight, and set its beam onto the side of the road. Then, at one point, he noticed a small sign in German turned sideways showing that the property was off-limits.

"Sinclair, stop the car," Price said. "Backup slowly. I may have found the entrance."

Coming to a complete stop, Sinclair shifted into reverse and slowly backed up.

"There, stop," Price said. "See the sign?"

"Yes, I do."

It didn't look abandoned.

Fresh vehicle tracks led in and out of a wide dirt track. Pulling the Chevy to the side of the road, Sinclair opened her door and was about to step out when Price gently pulled her back inside. "Hey, it's my turn to check the area out, remember."

"Okay," she said, smiling.

"I wouldn't stay parked here," Price said once he was out of the car and leaning on the door staring at Sinclair through the open car window, smiling at her. "Never know if this is the place. You know, stay on the safe side."

"I was just going to do that, Tom."

"Yeah, of course you were," Price said, smiling.

Turning up the collar of his trench coat and steadying himself, the pain in his leg acted up again. The same one where a bullet just missed the bone. Reaching into a coat pocket, he pulled out a small plastic medicine vial of ibuprofen and swallowed four tablets.

Going slow and keeping to the side of the road, Price slowly entered the dirt track. He didn't dare use the flashlight that could tip someone to his presence; he followed the dim light of the moon.

The dirt track turned twice and, as he came off the last turn, suddenly a six-foot-tall double wrought-iron gate appeared twenty feet ahead of him. Dropping to his knees, he crept low, keeping to the dark shadows, and stopped as he heard movements and talking but couldn't see where it was coming from. Crawling up to the gate, he saw several military Humvees, the military's all-purpose, modern-day jeep, parked along the side of a large metal building. There was subdued lighting coming from two overhead gooseneck lights hanging from the side of the building.

This had to be the place, he said to himself.

Slowly and quietly, he crawled back the way he'd come. Once again standing, he limped back to Sinclair. Slowly, he reached the road, glancing left and right, saw the Chevy on his right and walked to it.

Agent Sinclair, kneeling far to the left of the car, heard someone approach and pulled her sidearm. As the figure slowly appeared, she took a deep breath, and holstered her weapon, as she confirmed it was Tom Price.

Price saw Sinclair standing by the car and, limping to meet her, stopped in front of her.

"You're limping, Tom," she said, with a sense of concern in her voice. "You should've said something."

"You sound concerned, Sinclair," Price said.

Jacqueline Sinclair felt something building deep down inside her heart for Price. They had worked closely together, been shot together, and helped each other. Whatever those feelings were, it just wasn't the time to reflect on them. Will there ever come a time she would? she asked herself. She just didn't know.

She cleared her throat and smiled. "Hey, I'm your partner. Why shouldn't I be?"

"Your partner, eh?" he replied, and, in the darkness, he couldn't see her smile.

Glancing over her shoulder, she asked, "Well—what'd you find?"

"My God, we got em', Sinclair," Price replied in a low excited voice.

"*What?* You're sure?" she said, as excited as he was in finally getting lucky.

Agent Price nodded and replied, "I heard talking and saw military vehicles. Let me get the UAV ready."

One thought kept running through Sinclair's mind, *got you, Scott, you son of a bitch!*

Opening the back door to the Chevy, Price pulled out the UAV that resembled a miniature plane and handed the remote-controlled module to Sinclair. The UAV was equipped with a CCD color video camera and an infrared night vision camera too.

"Sinclair," Price said. "Turn on the module. I already turned on the plane."

The module, a black box about the size of shoebox, resembling a model airplane control box with a seven-inch screen, lit up the moment Sinclair turned on its power.

"It's on, Tom," Sinclair said.

"Okay, here it goes," he replied.

Agent Tom Price, holding the UAV in his right hand, extended it behind him, threw and launched the Raven UAV into the air out in front of him, and watched as Sinclair piloted the UAV. Banking and gaining altitude, she used the joystick and flew the Raven. Through the monitor, Price, standing beside Sinclair, watched the UAV fly around toward the back of the property, recording it all on the console's digital recorder.

Seen through the eyes of the Raven were three metal buildings, built recently, and three Blackhawk helicopters, fully armed. There were several walking armed guards and four stationary guards positioned at each corner of the grounds.

Sinclair flew the UAV toward the back of the structures, recording the layout of the grounds, and noticed the lack of forest for about a quarter mile back from the fence line. They fortified the grounds with concertina wire or dannert wire, a type of barbed wire or razor wire expanding the width and length of the compound, and, in conjunction with plain barbed wire and steel pickets, it resembled a military-style wire wall.

Sinclair said, "I think we've seen enough, Tom."

"Yeah, this is it, alright."

"I'm bringing in the UAV for a landing," she said, as she moved the joystick, and, with the UAV overhead, she maneuvered a two-point landing and brought the Raven in for a stop next to her Chevy.

Sitting in the driver's seat once again and storing the UAV in the back seat, Sinclair glanced over to Tom Price and said, "We're going to pay hell getting inside that compound."

Agent Price replied, "Was thinking the same thing, partner."

"We need a good solid plan," she said.

In the compound in what had been referred to by its members as the new CAC, a large open room, laden with state-of-the-art communications and monitoring devices, were General Scott, Colonel Randall, and his operations chief. They all sat around a monitor, satellite linked to the B-2 bomber pilots, and waited for the bombing to start, which should be within two hours if it all went according to plan.

General Scott, puffing on a cigar, would soon have his ultimate revenge. The President of the United States, that spineless politician, and his cabinet didn't do a thing to bring his son home alive. Instead, he and his cabinet just sat back and let his only son rot and die at the hands of the North Koreans.

Soon, very soon, they will know what he had done, and, in some circles, he would be called a hero to his country for standing up for what he thought of as his God-given right to seek the death of those responsible. What kind of man and father would he be if he just sat and did nothing in seeking his revenge? No, no man at all, nor a good father. However, his plans did not stop there. His plans also called for the death of those in the CIA who knew where his son was being held and still did nothing. Yes, they will experience his wrath as well.

Leaning back in his chair, he flicked the ashes of his cigar onto the floor, lifted a glass of bourbon from the desk next to him, drained what remained in the glass, and waited.

Unknown to the general, behind the scenes, the President of the United States had called the North Korean regime and alerted them to the possible attack on their nation by rogue American mercenaries. They canceled their summit meeting. In addition, they agreed they would not inform the media. The Korean dictator removed his immediate family and himself to an unknown location and waited.

The President of the United States had, by alerting the North Koreans, prevented a third World War from happening. Worse, they knew that the Chinese government could have responded in kind.

—Chapter Forty-Five—

Major Mendez and his three operatives were exhausted but operationally alert.

Having left their truck behind them—once it had broken down—they'd trekked for about seven miles through heavy snow, high winds, and total darkness, when Major Mendez called for a brief rest. Finally halting, all puffing slightly, they sat on the hard-packed snow under a forest of tall Loblolly pine trees.

Pulling out a penlight and his map, Mendez noted they were about four miles south of the outskirts of Pyongyang, the capital of North Korea. Snapping off his light, he returned the penlight and map to his right side arctic trouser pocket. He hoped to find a vehicle they could use to gain entrance into the city.

Glancing over at his men, Major Mendez was proud of the team. Although burdened with wearing the Army's Manchu Version of Land Warrior equipment and pack, a collection of highly sophisticated command-and-control systems that included an intra-team radio, giving them the ability for rapid communications between individual soldiers and command; a helmet with a head-mounted display positioned over the soldier's dominant eye; his individual weapon, the M-4 Carbine, with .223 caliber with a thirty-round magazine, they showed strength and fortitude in completing the mission.

Wearing the Korean heavy winter coats over their equipment, and as his men chewed on strips of beef jerky, Mendez took in a couple of strong cold breaths and, slowly exhaling, watched the cold vapors as it left his mouth and listened for any out-of-place sounds as the winds blew through the pine trees.

He felt as if they were all alone, in a vast jungle of white.

. . .Or were they?

Seconds later, an all-too-familiar sound caught his attention—he thought he'd heard the faint thumping of a helicopter—but couldn't be sure; the sound was too far away.

The major glanced at his Army luminescent watch. Four a.m. They'd made good time, considering the weather. Standing and straightening up, he glanced over to his men.

"Time to go," Mendez said.

"Major," the Delta operative, Sergeant First Class Terry Webster, a tall African American, said. "I thought I heard chopper sounds in the distance."

"Yes, I heard it too," Mendez replied.

"Think it could be trouble?" one of the Rangers asked.

For a moment, Major Mendez remained motionless. Then he shook his head.

"I don't know."

A brief silence fell upon the men.

Mendez wasn't sure if it was trouble for his team. He couldn't make out anything from the sounds. Either it was flying in their direction or away; it was too hard to tell. *Or, had they already been detected, and soldiers were now on their way to stop them?* The thought crossed the major's mind.

"Everyone ready? Good, let's push on," Major Mendez ordered. "We have a little over four miles to the city's outskirts and six miles to our target."

Adjusting his goggles over his eyes, Mendez started walking north to their destination as his team followed.

They walked in silence, knowing they were nearing their final position in which to *light- up* their target for the bomb run. His thoughts also swayed toward his second team, that of Lieutenant Jacob Reynolds. Mendez wondered if they had already positioned themselves enough to their target. He wouldn't know until he established a SITREP once he'd setup his own men.

Unknown to the Team-Two Commander Mendez, a Russian Mi-24 Hind gunship chopper full of North Korean soldiers were on their way to the security checkpoint through which the team had passed earlier.

The remaining three operatives, call sign Team-Three, led by Lieutenant Reynolds, the Delta Operative, watched Major Mendez' truck pull away, and ordered his team to affix noise suppressors to their weapons. As one of the Rangers picked up the equipment, Reynolds dropped to a knee, pulled out his map, compass, and penlight and determined their location in relation to their target.

Standing, Reynolds pulled down and adjusted his night-vision goggles mounted on his helmet, as his men followed suit.

The snow hadn't stopped since they'd left Major Mendez, and it was thick snowflakes that fell. They had ten miles to go through the snow and high winds that whispered through the trees. The ground snow was high and soft, and, with each step they took, their boots would sink up to their knees, making it difficult going.

No sooner had Reynolds figured they'd made roughly six miles without meeting a single soul, when, up ahead, the lieutenant heard noises. Giving the hand signals to stop and go to ground, Reynolds made out three men, through his night-vision goggles, walking toward them about a half a klick or 500 meters away.

If the three individuals maintained their route, they would come face to face with his team. Reynolds knew they could not afford to be seen, nor to have one of those men somehow survive to tell of the encounter.

Keeping a close eye, the lieutenant estimated the three woodsmen, as he suspected them to be, would intersect their location within a few minutes' time. Two of the men were pulling a makeshift sled with several cut logs strapped onto it, and one was walking ahead with a flashlight leading the way.

"Bill, Jeff," Reynolds said through his mic, "come forward and form a line and get ready to take out our visitors. They can't see us, yet. On my word, shoot to kill."

"Copy that," came the two responses.

Seconds later, the two operatives kneeled and took up positions by the side of their commander. All three operatives had a clear line of sight, each aimed at one of the visitors.

"Bill, which one do you have?" Reynolds asked.

"Left one holding the sled," Bill responded.

Jeff said, "I got the one holding the flashlight."

"Okay, I have the last one," Reynolds said.

Slowly the three woodsmen approached, conversing and laughing, unknowing that death awaited them with each step they took.

At 100 meters, Reynolds said, "On three, ready. . ."

. . . "One," each operative slowly caressed their weapon's trigger and set a bullseye on their target's center of mass.

The three woodsmen were talking loudly now and, mingled with their talking, was laughter from one of them, as if one had cracked a joke.

. . . . "Two," Reynolds counted out, yet unseen by the woodsmen.

Wincing slightly inward, Reynolds, taking a deep breath, exhaled slowly, regulating his breathing, which allowed his heart to slow somewhat, and said. . .

. . . "Three."

Three triggers were pulled simultaneously. As the bullets left the barrels of the three M-4 rifles, they made a cracking sound as they exploded out of the silenced weapons. Three soft cracks and three men jerked away slightly as they were knocked to the ground, making deep impressions in the snow.

All three operatives stood and walked forward.

Reynolds heard a soft cough from one of the fallen.

The lieutenant turned in the cough's direction. And, when he heard it again, he identified the woodsmen that was coughing. Walking up to the body, he aimed the muzzle of his rifle between the man's eyes and calmly pulled the trigger.

Turning to his men, Reynolds said, "Let's go, we have just a few miles to our target."

Single file they moved, each with their own thoughts, but all wanting to get home safe and sound.

A half hour later, they approached their target and halted on a steep mountain cliff, for they were overlooking a small valley with two large mountain ranges on either side. Tall pine trees surrounded it. A wide river cut through the back of a three-story house—their target. In the back was an Olympic-style swimming pool, empty except for the snow.

To get a better perspective, reaching for his binoculars, Lieutenant Reynolds pulled them from his side pocket, brought them to his eyes, adjusted the focus knob, and scanned the grounds down below, a quarter mile from their location.

The house and a separate structure he believed to be a barracks of sorts, surrounded by six-foot tall stonewalls. In the center was an iron gate standing about seven-feet-tall, the only way into the grounds. A long, wide winding paved road, cleared of any snow, led up to the front doors of the house. The house itself was bathed by seven large florescent spotlights. There wasn't a dark spot anywhere around it.

Two armed guards guarded the gate and the outside of the property was protected by two roving mobile patrols. But what caught their eyes were the two Mi-24 Hind gunships. One flew the circumference of the grounds while the other kept a watchful eye on the two surrounding mountain ranges.

It was going to be tough getting closer to the house. It wasn't impossible, however, and Reynolds had the experience in penetrating much more difficult structures. Not a piece of cake, but not impossible, he thought.

Scanning over to his right and about forty feet below him was an outcropping of rocks that could afford some cover, and the distance to the target should be just right for the laser-aiming equipment.

Getting his men together, Reynolds gave the order to climb down, reach the ledge of rocks and the ground below, move to a distance of about 500 meters, and set up.

Fifteen minutes later, after working their way through the darkness, all three operatives were kneeling in front of some outcroppings of rocks, the CGLTD-111 hand-held laser designator equipment, nicknamed 'The eye of God,' was in the lieutenant's hands, and, as he turned it on, the blue-beam of light illuminated his target. The beam could travel a distance of about one mile. With the test completed, Reynolds set his map coordinates, jotted them down, and waited for Major Mendez for the SETREP.

What the team didn't know was a sensor had been triggered the moment they walked up to the cliff ledge. Down below and south of the team's location, two armed squads, unseen by the team, each comprised of eight men, were slowly making their way up to the ledge.

* * *

CID Special Agent Jacqueline Sinclair pulled out her laptop from her backpack, laid it on the desk, opened it, and powered it up. Then, pulling out a Micro SD memory card from her pocket, she inserted it into the reader port of her computer and waited. The SD Card contained surveillance of the property owned by General Scott. As she waited for the videos to pop-up, she stared at the people standing around the desk. People she knew and people she didn't. People she'd be working with very shortly.

It was 8:45 p.m. when she and Agent Price made it back to his office, after determining the location of General Scott's base of operations. Tired and hungry, they forestalled dinner to show the videos to those gathered around her tonight.

To her right were FBI Agents, Martinez and Russell. On her left were seven hard looking men, FBI Agents assigned to the Terrorist Task Force from the American Embassy in Frankfurt. They were all dressed in Army combat camo uniforms. They were lean and mean, six feet or taller men. But their eyes told Sinclair all she needed to know. They all had that far-away look about them. Here were men that had seen combat, had killed, or had friends that died in combat.

Next to these men stood DIA Agent Tom Price, who was staring at Sinclair, smiling.

And, to one side, stood six Feldgendarmerie, German Military Police officers, dressed in their black combat uniforms. They had a role to fulfill. It was their country where they would all see combat alongside the American police officers and *her*, the only female in the group.

Having all seen the videos, it was Agent Russell, the lead in the assault on General Scott's base, given command of the assault team. All had their ideas on how to storm the place, but the one thing they all agreed on was that lives would be lost tonight on both sides. Therefore, no matter how they approached it—it was going to be bloody.

It was forty minutes later, when a sound three-prong attack was agreed upon, with the German MPs in the lead. They would provide the frontal attack; the seven FBI agents would branch out in two groups to provide cover fire and attack from both flanks. FBI Agent Martinez, Agent Price, and Sinclair would come from the rear of the property.

Once Russell gave the go-ahead signal, a M1126 Stryker Armored Troop Carrier, APC, parked outside the consulate would provide covering fire. The APC would provide fifty-caliber machine gun support along with three 40mm grenade launchers and would transport nine soldiers along with its two-crew operators and would leave the consulate grounds right behind the rest of the strike personnel.

Local German police cruisers were to block all traffic coming into the combat area.

Agent Price and Sinclair would ride along with FBI Agents Martinez and Russell.

Without another word, all personnel slowly walked out of Tom Price's office. All except Price and Sinclair.

As Jacqueline Sinclair stored her laptop in her backpack, Tom Price walked to a steel-gray wall locker. Inserting a key Price took from his key chain, he unlocked it, and opened its two doors. There standing side-by-side were twelve M-4 assault rifles. Pulling two down, he opened a drawer and reached for twelve magazines full of .223 ammo and placed them in the bag.

With her backpack on, she stared at Price's back, curious what he was doing. Her curiosity was rewarded when Tom turned holding two rifles and a bag of magazines.

As he handed her an M-4 rifle, with a shrug, he said, "Didn't think you'd head to your office for some firepower. . . So, what do you think?"

"What do I think?" Sinclair said with a little hesitation and the trace of a smile. "That you sure know how to treat a lady. Just what I wanted too."

"I have some grenades," Price said, smiling, scratching his head, "if you want them too. You know, get a big bang out of all this."

Sinclair stared at Tom and said with a straight face, "Maybe we'll have our own big bang after all this."

Tom Price didn't know what to say to that. Because there simply wasn't anything to say, except to smile.

* * *

At that very moment, Major Charles Mendez and his team were in a sedan they'd appropriated, as slowly they approached the city limits of Pyongyang without headlights. The city was quiet and in total darkness; they saw no streetlights for miles, not a soul in sight. In the city proper and edging closer to their target, the major instructed the driver to pull into an alley, when, far to their left, he saw the subdued headlights of an approaching vehicle. It could be nothing, but he wasn't taking any chances, not at this late stage of the game.

Once in the alley and in full darkness, he ordered the driver to shut down and keep his foot off the brakes. Ahead of them was a large plaza where parades and other state-run festivals were conducted. And, centered around the plaza, was their target, the North Korean Government Building. Several lights were on throughout the large imposing structure.

A weak winter moon struggled as thin clouds covered most of the moon rays trying to filter through. It was cold, freezing. The snowfall was unyielding.

The Major allowed himself a brief grin. While his team had set up facing their target, he alone would *light up* the building. He couldn't contain his sense of euphoria as he looked over at his target. They had arrived without incident and not seen any other human being for miles. It would seem as if providence smiled down at them.

Headlights suddenly shone through the darkness from around the edge of the Government building. Slowly, the light penetrated the darkness as they heard a vehicle's engine. Then, a military canvas covered truck—the size of a US Army half-ton truck—rolled into the plaza. Slowly, it turned, following the snow-covered streets, as it veered off into the night and around the other side of the building—a patrol vehicle, the Major surmised.

Panic never entered the Major's mind, nor fear. The two qualities unknown to an American fighting man.

From the back of the sedan, the Ranger designated as the team's radioman, listened as he received confirmation that Lieutenant Reynolds and his team were at their target location and ready.

"Major," the radioman said, "Lieutenant Reynolds and his team are all set, sir. They have radioed in their coordinates to Eagle-One."

"Good," Major Mendez replied.

Reaching into his trouser pocket, Major Mendez pulled out his Sat-phone and called the CAC. After two rings, it was picked up.

"Sir," Major Mendez said without preamble, "all in place. Will start the run in twelve minutes."

Then, immediately, he hung up.

Turning slightly around, the Major spoke to his radioman. "Contact Eagle-One, give them our coordinates, and have them start their run."

"Yes, sir," the radioman, a tall stocky Latino, an Army Ranger for the last ten years whose operational code-name was Curly, for his thick black curly hair, said into his mic. . .

"—Eagle-One, Team-Two, standby for secured transmission, over—"

"—Team-Two, Eagle-One, go—"

"—Eagle-One, coordinates are twenty-three degrees, forty-two minutes north. Fourteen degrees, forty-two degrees east, be advised danger close, repeat danger close—"

"—Team-Two, Eagle-One, copy danger close, ETA to target ten minutes, over—"

"—Eagle-One, Team-Two, roger that, start your run, over—"

"—Team-Two, Eagle-One, affirmative, out—"

—Chapter Forty-Six—

The City of Offenbach, Approximately 30 miles East of Stuttgart,
10:30 P.M.

On the outskirts of the city of Offenbach, and half-a-mile south from the entrance to the suspected storage complex of General Scott's base of operations, three black sedans and a US Army APC, (Armored Personnel Carrier), the Stryker, colloquially nicknamed the 'battle bus,' parked back to back on the left side of the gravel road. And on the right side were four German police cruisers, each with two officers, also parked back to back.

With snow falling lightly for the better part of an hour and the winds settling down some, the weather, it seemed, would help in the forthcoming engagement. They all knew a battle would ultimately play out here tonight; there was no mistaking that fact. From the intelligence reports of the American agents, received by the German authorities, there were close to fifteen highly-trained, heavily-armed, American mercenary soldiers ready to fight to the death to protect the facility.

Standing by the APC were Agents Sinclair, Price, Russell, Martinez, and the leader of the German Military Police officers, a trim, tall, and erect man, a lieutenant, Sinclair surmised from his

German rank, with short-cut blond hair, parted in the middle, his face expressionless under the night's darkness.

Agent Russell, appointed the lead in the assault by Agent Martinez, was the more experienced and tactically qualified person to lead the group. He gathered all the men by the APC and instructed the German Police to start the barricade of the road. Russell then stared at Agent Sinclair.

"Get your people together, Agent Sinclair," he said, "and start your way around the back of the property. You know what needs to be done. Don't start until the assault begins."

Agent Sinclair nodded and turned toward Tom Price and Agent Martinez. She said, "Tom, take the lead, Martinez, take the rear, you're our radioman, I'll be in the middle. Ready, guys?"

Martinez nodded.

Price said, "Let's get this show on the road."

The trio was going in blind, with no night-vision equipment. Sinclair knew they had to take it slow to adjust to the darkness rather quickly.

Making sure their weapons were hot, they slowly started walking down the road. After half a mile, they came upon the entrance. Keeping a steady, slow walk, the trio entered the entrance road, weapons pointing to the sides, as they maintained a three-foot interval between each other. It was pitch black, and the going was slow. The dirt track, covered in thick snow, twice turned, and, ahead of them, Agent Price halted and crouched to one knee, while motioning them forward.

Cautiously, Sinclair and Martinez joined Price as they kneeled next to him.

A brief silence fell between them as Sinclair and Martinez waited to hear what Price had to say.

Tom Price exhaled. "There's a six-foot-tall double wrought-iron gate about fifteen to twenty feet just ahead. Stay low in the woods, we'll turn left and follow the track around toward the back. Make sure you keep the interval. There are guards posted everywhere, so maintain silence until we reach the back of the building. Let's go."

They knew from the aerial footage that four walking guards, positioned to each building, patrolled the roof of all three metal structures, and four additional guards were posted on each corner of the large building they suspected housed the command-and-control offices. The trio knew this and adjusted by staying well back in the forest line for cover.

After, once again, taking the lead, Tom Price, just inside the cover of the thick forest and hidden from the possible view of the guard on the corner roof and any of the roving motorized guards they'd yet seen, was about twelve feet from the gate when his foot triggered an infrared silent intruder alarm system that broadcasted their presence onto a computer screen inside the large complex.

The new base of operations for General Scott had been under construction for the last year and a half. Built over an old underground mine, it was well suited for what Scott had envisioned, that of a secondary fallback location in case they would discover the silo.

The new CAC was located in the rear right section of the complex. A set of stairs led down to the second floor into a huge well-constructed complex, with enough room to house two F17 Cobra fighter aircraft side-by-side. It had large areas of living quarters for all personnel. Two kitchens and shower stalls were off to the left of the stairs. And the personal living arrangements for the seven members in Scott's cadre were to the right.

A long, wide tunnel that started from the personnel living quarters ran under the complex, which led to a parking lot of sorts that housed several sedans, jeeps, and Humvees with a well-hidden ramp leading to the outside grounds beyond the fence line, over to the right side of the structure. A second set of stairs led to the outside of the complex to the three waiting Blackhawk attack helicopters

Inside the CAC and sitting around the communications array, were General Scott, Colonel Randall, and Corporal Raul Sanchez, the radio operator, monitoring the communications between Eagle-One and the ground teams in North Korea.

Suddenly, they heard a shrill beeping sound from an apparatus behind Sanchez. He instinctively knew what it was—the intruder alarm system! Sanchez immediately rose, went to the equipment, and switched off the clamorous beeping. Returning to his desk, he turned a video monitor around so they could see the intruders. In the shadows of the forest line, he saw three distinct individuals, two men and a woman slowly making their way through the left side of the building back in the forest line before disappearing from the view of the cameras.

Glancing at the two officers, Corporal Sanchez said, "Sir, we seem to have company."

Colonel Randall immediately stood and approached his radioman, while General Scott kept a watchful eye on his second in command and a careful ear to the activities in North Korea.

"Corporal," Colonel Randall said, "rewind to the beginning. Let's see who our visitors are."

"Yes sir," Sanchez replied. Standing, he moved to the control station and fiddled with the controls. Then, pressing the rewind button on the digital recorder, Sanchez came to the beginning of the footage, and he pressed play.

In gray tones, Colonel Randall made out the figures of Agent Jacqueline Sinclair, Tom Price, and another agent he couldn't identify. Randall tensed, knowing the general will probably be disappointed at this turn of events.

Exhaling deeply, Colonel Randall relaxed slightly, then turned and faced General Scott. "Sir, it would appear that CID Agent Sinclair and a couple of her friends just made the complex. They are just entering the area outside of the gate."

"Son of a bitch!" Scott exploded as he faced the colonel. "That woman is dangerous. She's a detriment to our plans. Alert the sentries, I want her and whoever she's with stopped and killed. That bitch and Price have been a thorn in my side for far too long."

"Sir, with all due respect," Colonel Randall said, shaking his head and shifting from one foot to the other. "I don't think it's just them. I would suspect she didn't come empty-handed. And I think there's more of them out there waiting on her."

General Scott raised his eyebrows and calmly said, "You may be right. Get a chopper in the air and find out once and for all."

Colonel Randall glanced at his radioman and gave orders to have the chopper up and have the guards shoot to kill into the forest line at the three intruders.

Corporal Raul Sanchez did as ordered. Alerting the perimeter commander of a breach in their defense, his orders were to shoot to kill. The sentry commander relayed the message to his guard on the left corner of the building and ordered him to shoot into the forest line, and then he ordered the motorized roving patrol to the left side of the building by way of the rear of the structure. If the guard didn't kill the three intruders, then they would be met at the rear of the structure with a hail of bullets from the second roof guard toward the rear of the roof and that of the roving patrol.

Corporal Sanchez, still monitoring the commo between Eagle-One and the ground troops, heard that the bombing run was under way and relayed the information to Colonel Randall and General Scott.

"Now, nothing can stop my revenge!" General Scott said.

Then, two things happened almost simultaneously.

The guard, positioned on the roof toward the left corner, acknowledged the order and grabbed an M406 40mm high explosive grenade from his supply box at his feet. He opened the M203 port of the weapon's launcher, inserted the grenade round, closed the launcher, aimed the M4 with the over-and-under M203 grenade launcher into the forest line where he believed the intruders were, and fired the weapon.

With a velocity of 250-feet per-second as it leaves the muzzle of the weapon, the grenade flew through the darkness and, seconds later, the impacted explosion was so loud and deadly that anyone within a radius of about 15 feet was sure to be killed instantly.

At the moment of impact, only one person was caught in the grenade's killing radius, Agent Martinez, who was in the process of reporting their progress to Agent Russell and had fallen back from the other two. As the thick red-hot metal shrapnel flew, it struck the agent in the back, as it literally pushed through him and attempted to exit through his chest.

He was unable to even scream.

Sinclair glanced over her shoulder and, to her horror, she saw Agent Martinez fall headfirst onto the ground. Then, she heard Price yelling at her to run, as both agents dashed away at top speed.

With both agents running through the forest line, from atop the roof of the structure, a guard cut loose with a barrage of automatic weapon fire into the area, missing his targets by several feet.

Reaching the edge of the forest line, Sinclair and Price momentarily stopped. They both knew there was another guard on the end of the roofline to the structure and a roving patrol that could appear any second. Price didn't feel like being cut down, so they waited to catch sight of the guard. Scant seconds later, the guard leaned over the edge of the roof and was killed instantly as Price and Sinclair both let off with a stutter of automatic weapon fire from their M-4 rifles.

However, at that very moment, a Humvee with two guards stopped just at the edge of the structure. One guard was preparing to fire his M60 machine gun from atop the Humvee when Sinclair and Price, once again, cut loose with automatic weapon fire.

Agent Sinclair loaded a fresh mag and immediately charged her weapon. Aiming at the Humvee driver, she kept a steady fire as the windshield shattered into pieces, but that didn't stop the Humvee.

Both agents, running on the fly now, reloaded fresh magazines.

With the M60 gunner being cut down before he could place his finger on the weapon's trigger, the Humvee's driver suddenly stomped down on the gas pedal and, with a surge of power, drove it straight toward the two agents. Unknown to Sinclair and Price, the driver was already dead, and, as the Humvee barreled down on them, it crashed through the concertina wire fence and came to a full stop with a loud resounding *Bang*! as the tall thick trees on the forest line halted its forward momentum.

Coming to a stop, the agents had watched the Humvee hurtle through the fence line. Then, Sinclair turned and walked to the fence, stopped, turned again, and faced Price, who hadn't taken a step forward. "Well, aren't you coming?" she asked.

"I'm right behind you," Price replied.

Yeah, right, she told herself. *He's just jealous 'cause I thought of this first.*

"Come on, now," she said, "let's go through the fence and continue the assault."

Damn! Tom Price glanced at Sinclair and said to himself, *Should've thought of that first. Probably won't hear the end of it.*

From the entrance onto the dirt track, FBI Agent Daniel Russell, once he heard the explosion and automatic weapons firing, was pissed off. He specifically told Sinclair not to start until he made his move. "Screw this shit!" he said aloud, while shaking his head. "It had to be done *her* way."

Suddenly, from the sky, he heard the familiar sounds of chopper rotors as it circled overhead, and he saw it fly into the complex.

Son of a bitch, Russell thought, as he watched the helicopter fly away.

Immediately, he had the German Military Police strike team personnel loaded into the APC, and, with one soldier operating the automatic 40mm grenade launcher, the APC started up and slowly moved forward, gradually picking up speed as it lumbered ahead, until it reached speeds of over 30mph, and, with the remaining seven FBI terrorist strike team members running, they brought up the rear.

The Stryker plunged through the darkness, and, with a loud rumbling noise, it came crashing into the solid gate and stopped twenty feet into the complex. The gunner opened fire with the automatic 40mm grenade launcher firing off not one, not two, but three grenades, as each made a loud deep *thump!* sound successively upon the roof of the large building in front of them. Sailing through the night air, the grenades, once reaching the top of the roof, exploded in a hail of red-hot shrapnel, as a fire quickly engulfed the roof, killing the guards.

From the control module, the APC operator flicked a switch and the rear-power operated ramp rumbled open and, with a resounding *clang,* it struck the ground. And, as it did so, with Agent Russell leading the way, they poured out of the belly of the APC running, with the rest of the FBI assault team right behind them. Right above them, the chopper, a Blackhawk gunship, appeared explosively on the battle scene.

* * *

City of Cherskiy, Russia, abandoned Russian airstrip, 600 miles north of the City of Pyongyang

After receiving their go-ahead, Major Craig Thornton glanced at his copilot, Captain Jack King, and, before they started their cockpit pre-check sequences, Thornton asked, "You ready, Jack?"

"You think we're still doing the right thing here, Craig?" King asked, instead of replying, as, once again, he was having his doubts and fully realizing this could be his last hurrah.

"Well, the money is great," Thornton replied, "greater than military pay. The mission, not so much. But we both signed up for this, and I'll get us home safe and sound. Have I ever steered you wrong?"

"No, can't say that you have. And, yes, the money is great. Paid off my house as it was, and my wife and kids are doing better for it."

"So, what's the problem? We had this conversation before."

"Nervous, I guess. Thinking, this could be my last ride," King replied, his voice tightening.

Glancing over at King, Thornton came to that same conclusion, but didn't voice his concern. Instead, he said, "I won't let that happen, my friend."

Jack King shook his head. "But you do know this is crazy, right?"

"Yeah, yeah, I know," Thornton said to himself.

A few seconds later, once King gave the go-ahead to Thornton, he pushed the small engine hydraulic accumulator or starter button and seconds later heard and felt the engines start up.

No sooner had the engines reached a certain level, the Major released the brakes and slowly taxied the B-2 Bomber onto the runway. Slowly, the bomber sped up, and, while speeding down and reaching its top speed, the bomber's front nose wheels gradually lifted off the ground.

When the front nose wheels lifted, the bomber's speed increased, and slowly it lifted into the air, then its main wheels also left the ground. As it soared into the sky, with the wheels locking in place and gaining an altitude of 30,000 feet, Major Thornton turned the aircraft to the left toward his two targets, turned on its stealth properties, and with a flying time of about ten minutes, should have no difficulties reaching their targets.

Flying at subsonic speed, the aircraft arrived briefly over the Pacific Ocean. Then, a quick bank right and it entered North Korean airspace, undetected by Russian or North Korean radar. Captain King said into his mic . . .

"—Team-Two, Eagle-One, ETA one minute, light up the target, over—"

"—Eagle-One, Team-Two, target is lit, repeat, target is lit, danger close, over—"

"—Team-Two, Eagle-One, roger, danger close—"

At a press of a button on his computer console, Captain King released the first of the two B61-12 nuclear smart bombs from its cradle.

"Bombs away," King said through his mic. "And may God forgive me," he told himself.

Dropping straight down, the bomb's rocket engine ignited as it started its flight to its designated target. It flew like a cruise missile and was guided by the GPS ground laser target designator or 'Eye of God' operated by the Delta operator of Team-Two.

The B61-12 Nuclear Smart Bomb hit its target dead-on!

It penetrated the concrete surface in between the four-sided, four-stories of the huge building as the shock wave blew out all its glass windows. Then, after penetrating through the earth efficiently, the bomb, with a total yield of 7.5 kilotons warhead and its death dealing accuracy of 30 meters circumference, detonated, as it transmitted its explosive energy through the ground killing all one hundred and seventy-five men and women personnel in the underground offices and two hundred workers in the four-story government building and everything else in its destructive path.

The explosion of thunder that came out of the huge gaping hole ignited several gas lines, as they too exploded, and a black and red fireball streaked a line to two other buildings to the left and right of the main government building, igniting those buildings as the fire blew through the offices. Seventy-five men and women were burned to death in both buildings.

All the government buildings were lit by the angry explosion that crackled in the air.

A moment later, the B-2 Bomber screeched across the sky, on its way to its second target.

—Chapter Forty-Seven—

The City of Offenbach, Southern Germany, 30 miles East of Stuttgart

The Sikorsky MH-60M Blackhawk, a four-bladed twin-engine medium attack helicopter, armed with 2 x M134 miniguns, two M230 30mm chain guns, and 2 FFA 2.75 inch 19-rocket pods, with its pilot, copilot, and two crew chiefs or door gunners, thundered over the Stryker. Making a half circle around the APC, the copilot ,having seen soldiers pouring out of the back of the iron beast, triggered the two miniguns, opening fire with its 7.62mm ammo, as it blazed a trail of death down on Agent Russell and his men.

The Stryker's gunner didn't know what hit him!

Before the gunner could take aim at the chopper, he was cut down in a hail of bullets that riddled his body and *thumped onto the* APC like hard rain striking a windowpane. That left the outside forces of the Terrorist Task Force behind the APC, having spread out into a defensive cover to deal with the enemy's attacking Blackhawk.

Three German police officers were cut in half by the miniguns. The rest remained inside the APC, while one, the German lieutenant, crept up to the door's opening and, aiming his assault rifle, cut loose a steady barrage of fire on the chopper.

Running behind the 'Battle Bus' and away from the chopper's direct line of fire, Agent Daniel Russell took aim at the Blackhawk's underbelly as it flew over the APC. Firing in full auto mode, Russell cut loose with a full magazine from his M-4 rifle at the fleeing chopper. Watching the aircraft fly away, Russell released the spent magazine and quickly jammed in another and charged his weapon.

The Blackhawk, having taken ground fire, scooped to its left and circled back around toward the APC. Once in firing position, the pilot hovered the aircraft—which would be his undoing—and fired an armor piercing FFAR 2.75-inch rocket at the side of the APC. A second later, the rocket struck the side of the 'Battle Bus' penetrating into the heart of the cargo area, exploding from within and killing the rest of the German military policemen inside.

The blast struck the lieutenant who was still standing by the door of the APC in the back. As shrapnel flew into him, his dead body was thrown forward, landing half in half out of the ramp; his corpse erupting into flames.

Before the rocket struck the Stryker, Agent Russell ran to the side of the building on his left, as several heavily armed mercenaries streamed out of the CAC and onto the battleground. Then multiple firefights erupted all around him. Taking aim, Russell shot and killed two Mercs, while two members of the US Embassy's Terrorist Task Force were killed as they made their way around toward the right side of the building.

Suddenly, from another pair of task force members, came *swooshing* sounds of two M72 LAWs (Light Anti-Tank Weapon) rockets being fired almost simultaneously, and, as the rockets' six fins sprang from the firing tubes, they stabilized the warheads' flight as both jolted a beeline toward the Blackhawk.

One of the side door gunners saw the flash of the rockets streaking toward the helo, and his eyes lit up. "Evade, evade!" he yelled into his mic. "We got incoming rockets!"

However, before the pilot could take any necessary evasive measures, the LAWs rockets penetrated the Blackhawk. One flew through the pilot's side door and the other through the cargo bay, as two thunderous explosions resonated. The chopper exploded from the inside out in a white and yellow ball of fire, lighting up the battlefield. The MH-60 Blackhawk, or what was left of it, tumbled to the ground bursting into flames, killing all aboard.

Toward the back of the CAC's main building, Sinclair and Price observed an almost hidden ramp leading down into the complex and steel metal double-doors in the center of the building. Then, abruptly, they came to a halt, immediately dropped, and laid-out flat on the ground, as they saw the steel double doors slowly start to open. And, through the crack of the doors, light flooded out, illuminating the night's darkness. In an instant, from behind the doors, there came four black-clad Mercs aiming assault rifles ahead of them, walking toward the Humvee.

"Did you hear that, Tom?" Sinclair whispered.

"Yeah, sounded like a huge explosion," Price replied. "Someone's having fun."

"Yeah, aha," Sinclair said half smiling, half-serious.

Not taking his eyes away from the four Mercs, Price asked almost in a whisper, "What now, Sinclair?"

"Let's take the fight to them," she replied.

"Eh, what do you . . .?"

Before Price could finish his sentence, Agent Sinclair rose, cradled her assault weapon, bent her knees, and slowly started walking forward, aiming her weapon at the closest of the two Mercs. Before she could pull the trigger, Tom Price was at her side, weapon up and aiming at the two Mercs to his left. Then, almost as one, they fired in full auto-mode, and, seconds later, all four of the enemy were cut down by the barrage of 5.56mm bullets.

Lowering their weapons, they kept walking up to the doors, Sinclair on the left and Price on the right side. Once there, they leaned up against the doors, and, walking sidewise, they came to the opening. Taking a quick glance inside, Sinclair came around the opening and dashed inside. Tom Price executed the same movements as Sinclair. Then, coming to a stop, they kneeled on one knee with weapons up and ready.

Inside the CAC, Colonel Randall and General Scott both heard the explosion and the gunfire coming from the front and rear of the building. But that did not deter Scott from continuing to monitor the bombing run of the B-2 Stealth bomber.

Then Corporal Sanchez perked up and, removing his earphones, said, "Sir, you have to hear this." Placing the audio on speakers, Sanchez spoke into his mic and said . . .

"—Base, Eagle-One, repeat your last, over—"

"—Eagle-One, Base, roger that, first target destroyed, preparing run to second target, over—"

"—Base, Eagle-One, roger, copy that—"

Colonel Randall stared at Scott, wondering if he would give the order to evacuate the building. "Sir, the order to evacuate?"

Turning to glance over at his second in command, Scott said, "No, not until the second target is confirmed destroyed as well."

Sanchez and Randall both stared at each other. They both knew there wasn't going to be a way out before too long. They both had their escape plans ready to execute in the event things went south. Which they were beginning to. . .

* * *

North Korean Airspace

"—Team-Three, Eagle-One, ETA one minute, light up target, over—"

On the ground, Team-Three Delta operator Lieutenant Reynolds heard Eagle-One through his comm's radio but he also heard one of his team members, Sergeant Jeff Stein, warning him of an inbound chopper.

"How far, Jeff, and is it coming our way?" Reynolds asked through his mic, as his eyes narrowed.

Sergeant Jeff Stains, who was positioned about a third of a mile to the right of Reynolds, kept hearing the chopper getting closer.

"Still too far to tell, sir," Stains replied. "But it's getting nearer to our position."

Reynolds frowned as a sense of alarm ran through his mind, but it only lasted a split second. He knew the risks going in and, now, the reality of it was starting to sink in.

Reynolds nodded. "Copy that," he acknowledged. "Keep me informed."

Reynolds' hands tightened on the 'Eye of God' and concentrated on the B-2 Bomber. Then, aiming the laser at the mansion just below him, he turned on the unit, and its blue beam traveled a little under a mile and aimed at the mansion just below him. Through his mic, he said:

"—Eagle-One, Team-Three, roger, target is lit, danger close, over—"

"—Team-Three, Eagle-One, roger, target lit, danger close, out—"

Unknown to Team-Three, a platoon of forty NKA (North Korean Army) infantrymen, who'd been following the team's snow prints from the beginning, were just a half a mile from the team's location and moving fast. And, as the helicopter drew even closer, the NKA infantry were in constant contact with the inbound chopper with an arrival time of about three minutes to their position.

Seconds later, Sergeant Bill Johnson, positioned about a hundred yards to the left of his LT, spied through his night-vision goggles shining lights heading up to their location, and, behind the lights he made out what he surmised were armed North Korean soldiers.

Sergeant Johnson calmly squelched his mic and said, "LT, we have armed NKA coming up the hill, ETA about five minutes, and an inbound chopper coming our way. Don't think they're bringing us breakfast and coffee, sir."

"I need less than a minute," Reynolds said. "There it is, coming in hot."

Scant seconds later, they heard, through the darkness, a muffled jet engine sound. Johnson saw the bomb speeding through the sky, honed in on the laser; he saw it strike the center of its target, heard the violent explosions following it, and saw a ball of fire erupting high into the sky resembling a mushroom-shaped top.

Once again, the LT squelched his mic and said, "Group up on me, men."

Less than a minute later, they were together, once again kneeling in the snow.

Then, a few seconds after that, they saw the B-2 Bomber streak across the night sky barely visible across the wide expanse of the heavens, as the snow started falling once again.

Standing, Reynolds said, "Time to get out of Dodge, men."

Then, turning toward Bill Johnson, Reynolds said, "Bill, take point. Jeff second; I'll bring up the rear. Bill, get us down this hill."

Glancing quickly behind him, Reynolds caught sight of a dust cloud plume rising from ground zero, then a huge bright red-blue ball of fire shooting into the night's cold sky. He couldn't make out any structures through the dust, snow, and fire.

One of the two Mi-24 Hind Armed Assault Helicopters patrolling the outside grounds was caught in the blast. As it caught fire, it spiraled down from the sky and crashed into the ground in a huge ball of fire.

Inside the home of North Korea's dictator, four maids were burned alive, while all the perimeter guards were instantly killed.

Reynolds's job was complete. What he didn't know was that none of the North Korean dictator's family were home. Did it matter that much to him? He wouldn't think so. Now the LT had to get his men and himself to safety and onto his designated pickup point.

What the LT also didn't know was there were no extraction choppers to pick them up. They would be on their own.

With the lieutenant bringing up the rear, they heard the ominous sounds of the inbound chopper growing louder by the second.

Suddenly, the LT stopped, turned his head around, and, as his eyes opened wide, he saw, lit by its running lights, a gunship low in the sky and just a half a klick behind them. Then, he caught sight of the blast trail from two rockets pods. A split second later, two rockets came streaking down, bearing fast on their location.

"Oh, shit!" he said and turned back and yelled into his mic, "Run, run fast, guys! Rockets inbound!"

Meanwhile, the NKA soldiers had now topped the ridge they'd just vacated. Weapons up and aiming at the three men, they cut loose a barrage of small arms fire from AK-47 Kalashnikov's as they ran forward after the fleeing figures.

Bullets flew like angry bees all around them.

Running in an evasive pattern, the three operators ran a left right-right left sequence when Jeff Stein caught a bullet in his left arm, and Bill Johnson took one in his right leg, almost toppling him forward when his LT caught him and helped him on.

Seconds later, the two rockets impacted to their right, missing them completely, just as the helicopter turned left, coming around for another pass.

In the meantime, the NKA soldiers swiftly ran after the trio of American Mercs, as their weapons unleashed an unending barrage of automatic weapons fire.

The Hind pilot positioned the aircraft about 1,000 yards out in front of the fleeing Mercs. The pilot smiled as he hovered the aircraft. Framed in his front windshield were the three enemy soldiers. Then, cutting loose with its two 12.7mm four-barrel machine guns, he laid out a stream of deadly fire. Instantly, the three Mercs turned as one to the noise of the chopper, but were cut down, dead before they could raise, aim, and fire their weapons.

* * *

37, 000 feet, 14 miles southeast of Pyongyang, North Korea Airspace

The night sky had a gently silver tinge to its otherwise black emptiness, as the pilot of the Russian-made MiG-29, Major Ri-Jung-Hye, banked the plane left, just away from Pyongyang. Information relayed to the Major from ground control provided details of a possible United States Air Force B-2 stealth bomber being responsible for the attacks on his capital and that of his commander-in-chief.

Major Hye, equipped with night vision goggles and a fully armed aircraft, suspected the bomber would take a direct route out of Korean airspace and head into safe waters off Japan, which is where Major Hye would also steer his MiG-29.

His orders were to shoot the bomber down at all cost.

Major Hye knew that the American stealth bomber was defenseless. It was just a matter of seeing one. He knew the tactics involved in shooting one down. His fourteen years behind the controls of the Mig-29 would test his mantel.

That is *if* he could set his eyes on it.

Just out, after pulling two massive precision strikes on the North Korean capital and that of the North Korean dictator's mansion, the B-2 Commander, Major Craig Thornton, and his copilot, Captain Jack King, had their aircraft flying at medium altitude and subsonic speed with emissions restricted. Now all Major Thornton and Captain King had to do was get themselves out of Korean airspace in their nearly invisible aircraft, and the closest land would be Japan. Then, ditch the aircraft and leave before anyone became the wiser.

Thornton knew that his aircraft was quiet and, with its painted black color, could blend with the night sky. The chances of an enemy fighter pilot visually acquiring them were almost zero. Thornton and King knew that the North Korean air defense network would be up looking for them. So, they stayed alert for any possible lock on their plane.

Twelve minutes later, and, having flown halfway through North Korea, the MiG-29, flying at just under 1,490 miles per hour, thought he spotted what appeared to be a small slit in the night sky. *Is that the American bomber?* he asked himself. But he couldn't see it. He wasn't sure it was an aircraft.

Checking with ground control, he asked if there were any other aircraft in his vicinity. Getting a negative reply, he assumed what he was seeing through his night vision goggles was the bomber. Then the Major turned his aircraft and aligned himself with what he thought was his target. Major Hye gently moved the stick forward and his MiG-29 closed the distance to the sliver of silver as he increased his airspeed and set his aircraft high and behind.

Suddenly, a warning light appeared just to the right side of Thornton's controls, the light that showed an approaching aircraft was behind them. There wasn't anything they could do but add on more speed and attempt to out-fly whoever was behind them. It could be nothing, but Major Thornton wasn't taking any chances.

But it was already too late for the bomber.

Closer now, Major Hye could make out through his night-vision goggles a dark ghosted image ahead of him. Now he knew he was facing the stealth bomber! He switched on his GSh-30-1 cannon. Clamping down on the trigger, the 30mm rounds tore through the night and disappeared into the darkness. Not knowing if he scored a hit, he pulled back and tilted his stick to the left, trying to avoid the possibility of a collision.

Far in the distance, Major Hye could see a small speck of fire in the sky.

Alarms went off in the cockpit, Major Thornton gently pulled back the stick but couldn't feel any control response, and, with the aircraft's nose down, it began to topple head over heel. The altimeter registered 15,000, then 10,000 feet. At that altitude, both pilots gripped their ejection levers and pulled, but nothing happened. The aircraft continued its death spiral to earth and plunged into the North Korean landscape as a large ball of orange fire sailed into the sky.

—Chapter Forty-Eight—

The CAC, City of Offenbach

With firefights raging outside, and an explosion that occurred several minutes ago toward the building's left side just above the ceiling and catching on fire, Corporal Sanchez, the radio operator, pulled off his earphones after hearing the chatter between the B-2 bomber commander and Team-Three on its successful bomb drop on the residence of the North Korean dictator.

"Sir," Sanchez said, as he glanced at Colonel Randall and General Scott, "Just received confirmation from Team-Three. The second bomb run was successful in destroying its target."

"Excellent news, Corporal!" General Scott said. And, as an afterthought he said, in a subdued voice, "And what about the team? Can they make it out of there before they are confronted by the Koreans?"

"Don't know, sir," Sanchez replied. "I've lost commo with the team just after their last transmission."

"With no extraction possible," Colonel Randall explained. "We're not sure if Team-One could complete an extraction going forward."

But they all knew that Team-One had not given a SITREP for hours, leading them to think that Team-One were arrested and or killed in getting the two helicopters as arranged.

General Scott said, "So, what you're saying, Colonel, is that Team-Three personnel are on their own?"

Randall swallowed. "Yes, sir. There is nothing we can do for them."

A pause.

General Scott fixed his glittering eyes on Randall. "Colonel, give the evacuation order. We have work to do at home."

Randall took a long deep breath. "Roger that, sir," he replied, excited now that the order had been given.

"Corporal Sanchez," Randall said glancing at his radio operator. "Contact all personnel and give the evacuation order."

"Yes, sir, copy that," Corporal Sanchez acknowledged.

Without wasting time, and, abandoning his own plan of escape, Colonel Randall followed General Scott down into the underground bowels; a driver was waiting to take them through the tunnels where a path led approximately a mile before coming up into open country. And, with the general's trusted staff already gone from the complex, they would soon be together once again back in the US for the general's further plans.

Once Corporal Sanchez had given the evacuation order for all non-combat personnel, the CAC became a beehive of activity as personnel ran to their evacuation sectors. Sanchez quickly stood from his communications equipment, grabbed a canvas bag from the back of his chair, pulled out his 9mm handgun, and dashed to the stairwell.

At that moment, Agents Sinclair and Price were taking up firing positions inside the CAC and watched as personnel ran and some walked out of the CAC. Sinclair immediately identified General Scott with another uniformed man by his side and saw them casually walking toward a stairwell, as an unknown soldier with a canvas bag slung over his shoulder followed a few feet behind them.

Then, two things happened almost in unison.

Rising, Agent Sinclair, yelled out, "Scott, stop or I'll shoot!"

Reaching the stairwell, Scott and Randall, without a backward glance, dashed down the stairs and out of sight of the agents, just as Corporal Sanchez, weapon in hand, raised it and took a bead on Sinclair.

As Sanchez squeezed off two quick rounds in her direction, Sinclair ducked for cover behind a desk on her left, and Agent Price, weapon raised, aimed and shot Sanchez in the head and chest. Sanchez's body was thrown backward, dead before coming to rest on a wooden desk behind him.

Four Mercs appeared as if from nowhere and joined in the shooting, laying down a salvo of small arms fire at the two agents from behind some barricaded defenses. Agent Price took cover beside Sinclair, as both raised their weapons and returned fire until their weapons locked on empty magazines. The Mercs, sensing that their targets were out of ammo, stood up and walked away from their positions firing at the agents' position. Slowly, they walked forward, changing magazines on the fly.

As Sinclair and Price jammed fresh magazines into their weapons, suddenly . . .

. . . from the front of the CAC, they heard an explosion. Seconds later, they watched as, through the front entrance into the CAC proper, the rest of the Embassy Forces with Agent Daniel Russell in the lead came pouring in through the blown outer doors.

Taking cover, two of the four Mercs immediately opened fire on Russell's force, and the other two Mercs kept firing toward Sinclair and Price. Bullets flew as if several beehives had been cut loose in the complex.

One of those bullets found the left shoulder of Agent Russell just as he attempted to seek cover, and one of the Embassy operators directly behind him was struck dead. Russell, gaining a semblance of cover behind a wall, tore a strip from his shirt and tied it around his shoulder, but blood still oozed down his arm.

Another of Russell's operators jammed a HE (High Explosive) round into the breach of his M203 over-and-under grenade launcher on his M4 rifle and fired into the four Mercs position. All four were killed instantly. A deadly quiet reigned in the CAC, but sporadic fire was heard from the killing grounds outside the complex.

"Come on, Tom!" Jacqueline Sinclair yelled, her eyes blazing. "We can't let them get away."

Agents Sinclair and Price stood and dashed toward the stairwell, hoping to catch up to Scott and his people.

Agent Russell watched as Sinclair and Price ran toward the stairwell. Shaking his head, he yelled out, "Go on, go after them; I'll take care of things here. Um, no need to worry about me." If they heard his yelling, Sinclair and Price paid no attention to it.

Russell and what were left of the Embassy Forces spread out through the complex of buildings, meeting little resistance along the way, as they cleaned out the area of Mercs and arrested those that gave up without a fight.

Down the stairwell ran Sinclair and Price into a labyrinth of tunnels. But there was one large tunnel big enough to drive a Mack truck through that caught her eye. Not thinking, she ran through it and saw dim lighting just ahead of them.

Halfway through, they heard a car start up and saw it slowly backing out. From its back window, she was able to see the shadow of General Scott glancing at her. Before the driver was able to straighten out the vehicle, Sinclair burst into the huge tunnel, stopped, and, taking careful aim, fired round after round into the vehicle, shattering the rear window into thousands of pieces, and blowing a tire off its rim, as Price, coming up behind Sinclair, joined in the shooting.

With General Scott riding in the back and Colonel Randall riding shotgun, they were crouched down in their seats, as Randall, peering up at the driver, saw the man's head explode as blood and brain matter were sprayed onto the windshield.

General Scott, sensing the car was out of control, lifted his head momentarily, and was instantly struck by two bullets that entered the back of his head and came out through the front. Colonel Randall suffered a bullet wound to his left shoulder. The dead driver's foot stomped down on the gas pedal, sending the car careening into the path of two iron posts headfirst. With the shattering of metal and a loud *Clunk!* the car came to an abrupt stop.

Sinclair and Price slowly walked toward the vehicle, weapons up and ready, just as Colonel Randall opened his door, staggered out and, drawing his weapon, took aim at the two figures. Sinclair and Price reacted as one, and they shot the colonel before he could trigger his weapon. Down went the colonel, thrown back by the impact of the bullets that flew, thwacked, and pounded into his chest. Barely alive, landing on his back, he was coughing up blood as a pool of blood spread underneath him.

Agents Sinclair and Price approached the dying colonel, and Sinclair kneeled down next to him. Eyes merely slits, Colonel Randall said in a low whisper, "Thank . . . you," and, as his head canted to the side, his eyes closed for the last time.

Standing back up, Sinclair walked over to the sedan and looked in. She pulled a black briefcase from the backseat, as she saw General Scott slumped over, his head almost on his lap, dead from what appeared to her was a head shot. *Hers, or Tom's?* she asked herself. *No matter,* she thought. It was done, and Scott and his cohorts were dead. But she had no idea of the horrible bombing that was just being reported in South and North Korea and the US through the media.

Not yet.

The mop-up operation was in full force, and, with the help of the German police and Military Police and the FBI, a score of personnel had been detained and or arrested and turned over to military authorities. Several German nationals were also rounded up, and those were released to the German police for charges and prosecution. Boxes full of evidence were gathered and sent to the FBI lab.

The whole operation took less than two hours.

The bodies of General Scott and the other individuals in the car with Scott, identified as retired Colonel Godfrey Randall and the driver were in body bags laid out on the floor of Scott's CAC center and would be released to US authorities. Twenty-one bodies, those of General Scott's forces, were also laid out covered in body bags as well. Several bodies, presumed Mercs, could not be identified. Five Embassy Forces personnel were killed. FBI Agent Martinez's body was bagged, waiting transportation to the Embassy. Of the six German Police personnel, only two were left alive and unscratched.

The German chief coroner and his staff of three personnel, along with four ambulances, two from the city of Offenbach and two from the US Army in Stuttgart Kaserne, administered aid to the wounded. Blankets for those that needed them were given out, and hot coffee was brought in by the German police staff along with donuts.

In the CAC, trying to stay warm and sitting in chairs wrapped in warm blankets, were Agent Jacqueline Bell Sinclair and Agent Tom Price, with coffee mugs in hand, surrounded by a pair of CID Agents. Off to the side was FBI Special Agent Daniel Russell—in one hand a hot cup of coffee and, in the other, an unlit stogie.

Sitting beside Agent Sinclair was the Provost Marshal, Colonel Richard Longstreet Sinclair, father of Belle Sinclair, sipping on his coffee, as from time to time he'd glance over to his daughter, thrilled that she'd made it through in one piece.

They were all staring at a TV set tuned into a German news station.

They watched in silence as photographs, probably taken by amateur photographers, videos with an iPhone, and news crew videos showed on the screen the total destruction in North Korea of a state-owned building and surrounding structures by some form of blast.

They were calling it a gas main explosion.

But those involved in the past few weeks knew different.

The newscaster reported that the current death toll was at 127, but authorities were expecting it to rise. There was little hope of rescuing anyone alive, the newscaster mentioned, but crews were sifting through the rubble, hoping to find survivors.

Suddenly, the newscaster shifted to the scene at the home of the Supreme Commander of North Korea, where, according to a reliable source on the ground, it was reported that a gas main explosion utterly destroyed the mansion. No signs of any standing structure could be seen in the live broadcast. How or why is only speculation, the newscaster said. The investigation is only just beginning. They didn't know if anyone was home. The Supreme Commander and his family were not home when the house exploded, the newscaster finally announced.

A pause.

"Our part of the job is done," Agent Daniel Russell stated the obvious as he addressed those gathered. "Now the President has to forestall a third world war from happening, if that is even possible."

Price sighed. "That's assuming the North Koreans even want to talk."

They all fell silent.

Agent Sinclair sat quite still for several minutes. Slowly, she glanced at her father, offering him her smile and gave thanks that he was still alive after the attempt on his life. Her thoughts turned to Captain Jeffery Cory. She felt sorry for him. She had fallen in love for the second time in her life. Sinclair thought back to the children that were killed and of the one that escaped; she only wished she had been in time to complete a rescue. She'd failed in that respect, and she believed the children were the greatest tragedy in her investigation. The bombing of North Korea was another failure. She'd just been a little too late in stopping General Scott's plans.

Agent Price glanced over at Sinclair and watched a change come over her.

He'd worked with her long enough to recognize the moodiness he saw in her face. He pulled his chair closer to her, and, in a low tone only she could hear, he said, "I know what you're thinking, Sinclair. Don't. This whole thing wasn't your fault. We both tried to rescue those kids and stop the lunatic with his plans. We did our best."

She sighed. His words were true, but she couldn't help feeling slightly responsible.

Glancing at Price, Sinclair smiled, and thanked him for his kind words. "Let's find my car, Tom. We still have a lot of work to do before we close this investigation."

"I'm right behind you, partner."

—Epilogue—

Three days later, Patch Barracks, Stuttgart, Germany

It was a cool, breezy, Sunday morning. The sun was shining, and it held the promise of a warmer day ahead. He checked his watch: 10:15. And he was late.

"So, what else is new?" he muttered.

Wearing a two-piece gray business suit and white shirt, sporting a light stubble beard and sunglasses, he stepped out of his vehicle, closed, and locked it. Standing there, he stared at the building with a sign posted by the sidewalk that led to the field offices of the US Army Criminal Investigation Division.

Rubbing his chin, Agent Tom Price shook his head, thinking about the first time he'd entered these offices; he had been late then too. Price had been working with Agent Sinclair for the better part of three days, finalizing their reports, and furnishing evidence on the late Brigadier General Thomas Randolph Scott and his mercenary army. She, forwarding her reports to the CID headquarters in Quantico, Virginia, he to Defense Intelligence Agency (DIA) located along the Potomac River at Joint Base Anacostia-Bolling, in Washington, D.C.

Sinclair and Price had been instructed to write their reports and label them 'Top Secret,' before sending them forward.

Both agents had already briefed the command structure in Stuttgart and the Staff Judge Advocate (JAG) on the evidence she would present in case JAG would initiate an Article 32 hearing or a preliminary hearing in civilian law, if and when it came to that. As well as the area Provost Marshal, Colonel Sinclair, whom earlier was being considered for his first star.

The agents had taken turns meeting at their offices, Price at her office and Sinclair to the DIA offices at the consulate in Stuttgart. The briefcase Agent Sinclair pulled from the backseat of Scott's sedan contained invaluable information that named all of Scott's seven staff officers and all the mercenaries and non-combatants who pledged their support, offering their knowledge and expertise, for a price. That price was shown by the name of each staff member. The list had been forwarded to the offices of the Federal Bureau of Investigation at Pennsylvania Ave, Washington, D.C, with a CC to Special Agent Daniel Russell at the US Embassy in Frankfurt, Germany.

The file read like a Who's Who in the Delta, Rangers, and Special Forces operations.

The two agents, working side by side since the very beginning when Sinclair had been called to investigate a possible kidnapping, had been too busy to socialize with each other, only meeting to provide information and coordinate the writing that was intrinsic to any investigation: The who, what, where, how, and why of police writing.

Turning away from his car, Agent Price walked up the sidewalk, entered the CID building, and showed himself in. Walking toward the back of the building, he came to a set of stairs and climbed up to the second floor and to the office of the Officer in Charge (OIC) and Chief Investigator Special Agent Jacqueline Sinclair.

Since it was a Sunday, the Chief's secretary wasn't at her desk, so he stepped up to the door that was slightly ajar and gently pushed it open.

"Hey, Sinclair, are you in there?" he asked, without stepping in.

"Come on in, Tom, and pull up a chair," Sinclair said.

Tom Price had only been in her office once, and, as he entered and stopped in front of her desk, Sinclair glanced up from working on her laptop and smiled at him. "Hang tight for a few minutes, Tom, as I finish writing this report."

"No problem, partner," he said, as he took a seat in a leather armchair.

Price glanced around the office and noticed that it had a very decisive feminine touch. And, although it was a military office, there wasn't anything written in the regulations that prohibited pink curtains. It was the complete opposite of the office on the ground floor she once used, bare walls, dark and lonely. Photographs of her and her father sat atop a credenza behind her, with a vase of roses. Several awards hung from the walls along with photographs of her graduation from CID academy and her time in Afghanistan with friends. The office smelled of her sweet perfume, and, watching her, he felt a deep warmth creep up his spine.

Tom was there to finalize their reports, but he was also there to ask her out to dinner and drinks. Would she say yes? he thought. Hopefully, she'll accept, if not, well . . .

Sinclair, once she'd finished, glanced over at Price. "Hey, just got an email from Agent Russell at the FBI. They've been rounding up what was left of Scott's staff since they were all back in the US; they have been arrested and held without bond."

"That's good news," Price said.

"So, what are you doing for the rest of the day, Tom?" Sinclair asked with a smile on her lips.

"Don't know, yet. Why are you asking?" he replied, ready to ask her to dinner later tonight.

"Oh, just wondering," Sinclair, said. She too wanted to ask him out but thought better of it. *Let him ask first,* she thought. She wasn't sure if he wanted to go out on a date.

"Well," he said clearing his throat. "Thought maybe you would like to go out to dinner."

"You asking me out on a date, Tom?"

There was a silence for a moment.

Something almost like a smile crossed Price's lips. "Indeed!" he replied.

Lowering her gaze, Sinclair smiled. "Damn, I didn't think you would ever ask."

Woah! he thought. And sitting forward on his chair, he leaned back and inhaled. Then, exhaling, he said, "Pick you up at eight, then?"

"Sure."

It was 6:45 p.m. when the car stopped at the apartment in downtown Stuttgart. She slipped out of her car, picked up a paper-bag from the front seat, locked her car, and walked toward the apartment complex. She knew where to go, having been there once before.

Once inside the building, she turned left and found the apartment she was looking for. Standing in front of the door, she knocked twice and waited. After the third knock, Tom Price opened his door and was utterly surprised to see Jacqueline Sinclair standing there. He froze for a second, as he took her all in. She was stunning in a sheer, off-the-shoulder, sequined, sleeveless, dark dress that cascaded to the floor.

"I just couldn't wait for eight, so here I am," Sinclair said smiling. "Are you going to let me in? See, I brought a bottle of champagne to celebrate."

Price hadn't moved or offered her to come inside. He just stood there.

Sinclair, placing the bottle on the floor, strolled up to him and wrapped her arms gently around him. Price was stunned. But not too stunned as she leaned in and, tilting his head slightly, kissed him, and he kissed her back. Their kiss lingered, his passion blossomed, and, pulling her inside, she closed the door behind them.

THE END

Hope you enjoyed Victor M. Alvarez's

REQUIEM
FOR THE
DEAD

Turn the page and read on for his thrilling preview of

The
Theseus
Conspiracy

A CID Agent Jacqueline Sinclair Novel

—Coming Soon—

—Chapter One—

Major Jessica Alice Wayne—better known to her friends and subordinates at the 64th Military Intelligence Brigade subordinate to the US Army Intelligence and Security Command (INSCOM) Joint Military Base at Wiesbaden Army Airfield, Germany, as Jessie—stumbled and crawled her way through the darkened and empty streets of Stuttgart, Germany. It was one-forty-five in the early morning; the skies were dark, the ground wet as the rain kept falling all around her. With her hair matted and dirty, she only wore a white short-sleeve dress and no shoes. It was cold; the temperatures reached forty-eight degrees and holding.

Clutched in her right hand, she held on for dear life, was a small computer thumb-drive. She barely remained standing let alone walk. However, she had to keep going. Those that chased her would not give up. She was already bleeding from two gunshot wounds, one to her chest that lodged close to her heart and the other to her left shoulder. Her white dress now soaked blood red. Her legs were bleeding and aching. Major Jessie Wayne felt herself losing consciousness. Jessie had to make it to her only friend. She would help. They didn't know about her friend, or so she kept telling herself.

She tried earlier on reaching Colonel Alex Simmons, her commander. However, as she entered his quarters, they were waiting for her. She found Alex dead on the living room floor. The two gunmen laid in wait for her. Yet, she escaped. In the chase that ensued, she'd lost her high-heel shoes—which may have saved her life—and made it to her car. Earlier, she called another friend, but they seemed to have second guessed her whereabouts and shot and killed the friend, wounding Jessie in the process as she once again fled for her life.

After a grueling long drive, and, arriving at the outskirts to the City of Stuttgart, she spied their car behind her. They chased and twice shot at her. she'd lost control of her car and careened into a tree, but before they reached her car, she was nowhere to be found. On foot she began her long and dangerous trek.

Thunder and lightning scrawled across the sky illuminating the otherwise darkened streets. She stumbled and fell to her hands and knees, crying, trying to stay alive long enough to reach her. Jessie hoped and prayed they didn't know about this friendship. She slowly regained her feet, and taking one step at a time, she kept on going.

Jessie couldn't go to the police, they would have surely found her, then it would be all over. No, the police were out of the question. She was unable to call for help, having lost her purse which held her cell phone, and her identification.

Throughout her ordeal, she had met no bystanders on the cold and rainy street she could've asked for help.

She wasn't certain if she was at or near her apartment, and for a minute everything went black. Was she lost? Then she read the street sign and guessed she may have just a block or two further to go. With hope blossoming in her heart, Jessie willed herself to go on.

Somehow, she had lost those that chased her, as she had earlier crawled into a trash can in an unlit alleyway. And earlier while in her car from which she escaped from when they peppered it with bullets; and when they chased her on foot through the alleyways. Her military training was all that saved her from a sure death.

Jessie tried controlling her limbs. At one point she thought, she'd just sit and die somewhere, but what she held in her hand was much more important that her own life. She had to get the information into safe hands.

A half hour later, as the rain settled to a drizzle, to her delight, she saw her apartment from around the corner. Just then, a black two-door sedan came speeding around the corner and with tires screeching came to a stop in front of her apartment. Ducking out of sight, she saw two men exit the car and pull out what she believed were handguns. My God, she thought, how could they have known about her friend. What now?

As she stood in the dark, waiting, deciding what to do next, Jessie realized that there were no further options opened to her. Her friend was her only hope.

Major Jessica Wayne leaned her back against the side of the building, crying, trying to stay in control, otherwise there would be no hope for her. Slowly, she felt her knees buckle under her as she began sliding down her back, coming to rest sitting with her legs stretched out in front of her, watching the two killers enter the apartment complex and disappear inside.

As Jessie's eyes began to close, she heard from inside the apartment loud gunshots. Then silence. After a few minutes she heard more gunshots, this time muffled. Slowly she stopped breathing for about twenty seconds as she finally closed her eyes. Jessie startled herself and taking a deep breath she glanced to the front of the apartment and saw her silhouette backlit against a streetlight, standing on the sidewalk with a gun in her hand.

Forcing the last ounce of strength in her body, Jessie began to crawl on all fours straight to her friend. Bathed in the soft glow of the streetlights, and as she reached the end of the sidewalk, she heard running footsteps.

Reaching Jessie, the friend kneeled beside her, and gently cradled her head in her arms. "Jessie, it's me, Sinclair. Say nothing, I'll have an ambulance here in a few minutes, hang on to me."

Jessie tried to get up and failed. With CID Agent Jacqueline Sinclair's face close to hers, Jesse pulled Sinclair's face down to her and whispered in her ear. As blood seeped through her open mouth, Jessie said, with tears streaming down her eyes, "Not . . . going . . . to make it. Take this . . . it will explain everything." Opening her hand, the thumb-drive slid to the ground beside them, as Major Jessica Alice Wayne's head lolled off to the side and with one last breath, Jessie closed her eyes for the last time.

Numbed at the possibility that Jessie had died, Sinclair placed two fingers on her neck and wrist, but couldn't find a pulse.

Reaching over and pocketing the thumb-drive, Jacqueline Sinclair reached into her pocket and pulled out her cell phone and dialed the Military Police Desk Sergeant, ordering an ambulance, and German police to her apartment, along with the duty CID Agent.

Fifteen minutes later, with two ambulances, the coroner's vehicle with several German police and Military Police vehicles, there was a bevy of activity in and out of the Sinclair's apartment. Sinclair watched as they placed Jessie's body in an ambulance.

The military police along with the German Police and the duty CID Agent Ricardo Stubbs, moved through Sinclair's apartment, that according to Agent Stubbs, it resembled a battlefield. Two dead bodies both shot center mass, were found. One in the living room, the other in the kitchen, and her apartment was in shambles.

A few minutes later, as the rain came to a complete stop, a red 1969 Chevy Camaro, came to a stop alongside the yellow tape markings. From the driver's side, emerged a tall straight man, with a six-foot-three frame, and broad shouldered, who appeared to be in his mid-fifties. As he stood by his closed car's door, and, wearing a windbreaker over a black T-shirt and blue jeans, he turned his head here and there, as if he was looking for someone.

Through the crowd of police officers, his gaze finally settled on her. She was standing in front of a German police patrol car, speaking with a German police officer and MP. Her face was flush with anger and concern, her hair plastered to the sides of her face from the rain and wind, as she wore a gray, long-sleeve sleeping nightdress, and bedroom slippers. Waving his arm he called out to his daughter, Jacqueline Belle Sinclair, as he stepped under the yellow police tape.

Meeting her father halfway, she fell into his arms exhausted. After a moment Colonel Richard Longstreet Sinclair, the Provost Marshal, slowly grasped her face, and stared at her eyes. They appeared haunted, dark, as if she'd lost someone dear to her.

Colonel Sinclair removed his jacket, placed it around his daughter's shoulders and gently nudged her toward his car. He held his hand out and she took it. "It was Jessie, Dad," she said in a low measured tone, "she's dead."

Turning his gaze on his daughter, the PM, stunned by her revelation said, "My God, Belle, she was over for dinner just last week." And as he lowered his gaze, he asked, "Do you know how it happened?"

"No, but two goons kicked in my door," Agent Sinclair replied, "and tried to kill me. After that I went outside thinking there could be more of them and found Jessie. She died in my arms, Dad, but not until she gave me a thumb-drive and said it would explain everything."

He nodded in reply.

She caught her breath. "She was my best friend, Dad."

"I know, Belle," her father said, using her nickname. "Let's get you in the car and drive you home to my place, where we can figure this out and have a look in that drive."

NOTE FROM THE AUTHOR

Word-of-mouth is crucial for any author to succeed. If you enjoyed the book, please leave a review online—anywhere you are able. Even if it's just a sentence or two. It would make all the difference and would be very much appreciated.

Thanks!
Victor

—About the Author—

Victor M. Alvarez was born in Puerto Rico, and, at age nine, his family moved to New York City, and he was later drafted into the US Army. He received airborne training, ranger, military police school, and, later, jungle warfare training. His military awards range from Jump Wings, Vietnam Cross of Gallantry, awards of the Purple Heart, Air Medal, and Army Commendation Medal, among many other awards. He makes his home in New Smyrna Beach, Florida.

Thank you so much for reading one of our **Crime Fiction** novels.
If you enjoyed the experience, please check out our recommended
title for your next great read!

Caught in a Web by Joseph Lewis

"This important, nail-biting crime thriller about MS-13 sets the
bar very high. One of the year's best thrillers."
–BEST THRILLERS